VALENTINE'S DAY

KISS OF DEATH

Cambridge Murder Mysteries

by Charlot King

Copyright

DEDICATION AND THANKS

I dedicate this novel to my father. I have lost both parents over the past five years, which has been terribly hard. I miss their conversations and laughter, everything. They are still voices in my head, and will never fade. While my mother would always read to me at night as a young child, my father cast me in my first ever play, aged nine, in a troupe he had which performed in schools. He was an inspiration. A great actor, director and raconteur. He'd recite poems, took me countless times to the theatre, discussed writers, poets. Without him guiding me in my formative years, I probably would never have picked up a pencil. I am and always will be in his debt.

I would also like to thank John, Robin D and Penny, for reading the final draft before publication. I am truly grateful. Thanks to Robin H for his super illustration. I had the idea for this book and planned it out before the pandemic, but wrote it up during 2020. My family are so wonderful and I am so lucky to have had their love throughout the year, and would like to thank them too.

Finally, a big thank you to all my readers. I am so very grateful for your encouragement and support. You are my new friends, and I really hope you enjoy this story.

CHARLOT KING

PROLOGUE

The average heart beats somewhere in between sixty to a hundred times a minute. But no one has an average heart. Don't be too keen to give away your heart on Valentine's Day.

1
VALENTINE'S BANQUET

It is a February night in Cambridge, and the streets are stone-cold quiet. A solitary Porter guards the centuries-old Christina College Lodge. Just outside the window, in Christina's Front Court, ancient walls are floodlit in rosy red, as fairy lights twinkle in the avenue of leafless cherry trees, flanked either side by lawns manicured within a millimetre of their life. The only feet to cross the threshold of this hallowed ground tonight are students and Fellows. Some with hearts aflutter as they wear red bow ties or silky red dresses under their formal black gowns for the grand Valentine's Banquet. Others entirely used to this nonsense, having been Dons at Christina's for decades – some would say too many.

Inside the College, in Bramble Court, an old oak door to the Banqueting Hall creaks as it is pulled back by white velvet gloves attached to a doorman wearing a flowing cerise coloured cape, allowing stragglers to take their places. The hall is filling up with undergraduates laughing and kissing. As the last guests enter, they are immediately welcomed by a harpist plucking her strings, surrounded by dozens of red and cream roses in vases balanced on columns of gold. Down the other end of the hall, beside the Master's table, a large cherub sculpture holds up cupid's bow which points at guests as they take their glittery heart covered chairs under low hanging cream lanterns and more flowers adorning each corner.

Under a mural with the words 'Christina's Valentine's Banquet,' an a capella group quietly sings to the Master 'I've Got You Under My Skin', as the Master wears – somewhat ironically – a red mortarboard and gown. As she waits for everyone to settle, she converses over an aperitif about gruyere she ate while in Switzerland skiing last week. Her pleasant company responding with little ripples of laughter and guffaws broken by sips and clinks. Meanwhile, sitting farthest away from the Master as possible, near the serving hatch, a raucous group of undergraduates raise their voices over one another. Set apart from the other students not only by location but in both their confidence as well the thread on their backs. A rather tall young man, with tousled mousey hair to his shoulders and a long straight nose, sweepingly raises his glass, spilling some on the table. "I'm in love!" Lance Fernard shouts across the table, opening his arms out wide.

"Who's the unlucky victim? And, are you even capable?" Darcy Nighy scoffs. Her classic beauty with straight brown hair and brown eyes all in proportion, her voice low and resonant resembling a Dame before her time, and wearing plimsols under her gown which is hiding an old cardigan.

"I'm in love with life. Isn't it wonderful? And, you meanie, plenty have fallen for this love machine." Lance Fernard smiles, then carries on, "Love is to breathe deeply in the bosom of this world and be enveloped by its caress and comforting familiarity. Yet, excited by all the opportunities that await."

"Stop being a bore, there's a darling," Darcy Nighy curls some of Lance's mousey hair around her finger, and in return, he kisses her cheek. Then she pulls the curl a little too forcefully.

"Ow! Put your paws away," Lance grips Darcy's hand then softly places it on his own heart. "I make no apology for being an incurable romantic, especially on this enchanting evening. A Valentine's Banquet no less. Come now, unlock your heart." Lance rubs his scalp with one hand and puts Darcy's hand now on her own heart.

"It's days early. We aren't even there yet, darling. Still, lots of time for mischief," Darcy replies, winking at him. Lance Fernard then leans across to his right to give a kiss to Nisha Acharya-Gorpade, a painfully thin girl with large brown eyes and long black hair tied tightly with flower patterned grips, and wearing a dark green silk blouse under her gown. She coyly retreats from Lance's kiss, so Lance turns back to Darcy and grabs her for a kiss instead. Nisha Acharya-Gorpade watches and smiles a little embarrassed.

"Hey! Leave my girlfriend alone!" protests a svelte young man, Miles Bonneville, his face mostly hidden by his curly brown fringe.

"She's all yours. Bros before–" Lance replies.

"Charming," Darcy interrupts, then punches Lance's arm. Lance winces and looks at Darcy confused.

"I thought you were all eating at Snobs tonight?" Godric Cartwright-Green arrives, his scratchy voice piercing eardrums. "You don't want to turn yourselves into foie gras, the most horrific thing! Need to stay hungry if you are ever going to put on the performance of a lifetime. You little darlings need to behave." Godric Cartwright-Green smiles at the three of them, taking his seat, and making a late entrance as he always does. In spite of his voice, women and men up and down the hall turn their heads to ogle at his beauty. A tall young man with blonde hair which smells of summer flowers. His grey eyes flecked with diamonds so sharp they can pierce your heart. His black suit fitting so tightly under his gown that it leaves very little to the imagination. Godric smiles, flashing his pearly whites at Nisha, handing her a gift in a rather trendy looking grey and silver bag.

"We did, we did. The most wonderful truffles, not even in season. Perfect magicians. We gave Darcy a real treat!" Hugo Grader's red flame hair and cut-glass accent scream upper-class roots. He continues, "Though we're still waiting for her to sing for her supper!"

"Stop trying to expose me, darling," Darcy replies, trying to cover for her lack of funds. "I have more class in my little finger," she hides her embarrassment.

"I ask my question again. Then why are you all here for the 'peasant's' food?" Godric asks, digging into the wine.

"Why are *you* here, Godders?" Miles Bonneville feigns fake affronted, looking at Nisha open her present, which is an orchid corsage. Miles watches as Godric ties the corsage around Nisha's wrist and she kisses him on the cheek. "Just because you're our director, it doesn't mean you can cling on to our coat tails. This isn't even your College dear boy."

"Aww, don't be jealous. I got you a present too, Miles," Godric beams, enjoying Miles's grumpy look. "I didn't bring it because I thought you were spending the night poshing it up? It's also too big to carry."

"Presents?" Miles changes his tone, now interested.

"For the play. You are all working so hard at it. As a little thank you."

"I thought you said mine was big."

"It is," Godric laughs. "Gosh, Miles. Who knew you liked presents like a small child?"

"Tell me about it." Miles leans in.

"Let the poor man eat supper," Lance says, pulling out a cigarette tin unclipping it then sniffing the tobacco before putting it back, "I hear the food at Bene't's is inedible. And, what did you get me, you rascal? I have no gift for any of you. Let me be clear," Lance smirks.

"Thank you for being my guest tonight," Nisha replies, smiling at Godric. "This is beautiful, thank you." Nisha

Acharya-Gorpade kisses Godric's cheek again and then looks at her flower.

"Careful. People will talk," Godric beams cheekily, looking to see who is watching. He notices a bevvy of young women along the long trestle table are looking disappointed that Nisha has been given the gift and not them. And, a couple of men.

"Sorry, Darce. I didn't know you were going to be here?" Godric looks at Darcy Nighy, pulling a face.

"Oh, I don't care much for corsages myself," Darcy replies, raising her eyebrows.

"Two meals conundrum?" Godric continues to press.

"In answer to your perfectly reasonable question, Goddy, pertinent question." Hugo Grader shuts his eyes and wobbles his head. "I rather like your interest in my life and all the rest of it. Better to be the object of someone's attention, eh what?" Hugo Grader opens his eyes and looks around his friends for acknowledgement.

"The object of someone's affection maybe, attention it depends," Darcy replies.

"You're always quick to the point, for sure," Godric can't help but think that Hugo already looks plastered.

"We're here, old bean," Hugo starts up again, stroking Darcy Nighy's back, "as this is where we shall all satisfy our carnal needs!" Hugo beams, "For, it is the bewitching hour for love. And you are more than welcome, as our guest and esteemed director, to feast tonight on love if you can find it. For it is a poor man who is alone on Valentine's." Hugo lifts his glass and clinks Godric's. "Let's call it preliminary research," Hugo cheers, swaying. Godric nods and smiles back, then gulps back his wine.

"To love, and all who sail," Godric finishes his glass of wine in one, and lifts the bottle to pour another.

"Oh, why don't you button it," Miles Bonneville stares at Hugo.

"He's being gooey," Lance Fernard replies, "You know you can't stop him when he's on one."

"I'd like to propose a toast." Hugo Grader kicks back his chair and jumps up on the table, swaying a little while holding a bottle in his hand.

"Get down," Darcy insists, tugging at his trousers. But she can't tame Hugo, as he begins to recount a poem. From his chair, Godric starts to mouth along with Hugo, holding his glass high in salute.

"Up! Up! my Friend, and quit your books;
O surely you'll grow double:
Up! up! my Friend, and clear you looks;
Why all this toil and trouble?"

Hugo pauses, having forgotten the next line and grins at a woman on the table further down, then winks at Nisha. His legs wobbling a little.

"Come down, you pillock," Miles jibes frustrated at Hugo, pulling at his trousers, causing Hugo to stumble back a little into a dish of stuffed mushrooms that only seconds ago had been placed there by a catering waitress.

"Whoop! Whoop!" Shouts Godric, using this as an excuse to finish his next glass of wine he only just poured.

"Hugo!" Darcy shouts, as a mushroom squirts off the plate and into her lap.

"It's okay, it's okay, shh," Hugo flails his arms then puts his fingers to his lips. "Shh, now. I have an announcement. Shh, listen."

By this point, other students further up the long banqueting table, are becoming distracted, are tutting and rolling their eyes, disturbed by this 'noisy inebriate'.

"Speech! Speech!" Godric shouts then laughs at Hugo's inability to behave. Nisha shakes her head and flinches as a few more mushrooms fall off the table.

"Get down. No more Wordsworth, please. I don't want to get kicked out before the Mille-feuille!" Miles hits Hugo's leg, causing his knee to buckle. Hugo decides to sit on the table, right on top of a flat dish of sliced tomatoes and cucumber. Hugo looks down and sees tomato juice has squirted on his trousers. He takes a swig of champagne from the bottle in his hand. The table falls silent.

"Shh. I want to say something."

"You've already got a captive audience now, dear boy," Lance raises his eyebrows and his glass. Hugo picks a cherry tomato and throws it at Miles, hitting him in the face.

"I just want to say, the three amigos, compadres, besties. I couldn't think of two nicer guys to be making sweet music with," Hugo shuts his eyes and smiles. Lance grabs Hugo's hand and attempts a high five.

"Is that why you've put your shoe in my plate?" Miles aggressively swaps plates with Hugo, giving him the dirty one. Hugo Grader leans across the table and grabs Miles's shoulders, then pulls Lance in for a three-man bear hug.

"Mr Grader, I hope you're going to be okay for tomorrow. I need you up, bright as a button. We have so much to do in this next rehearsal, bromance aside," Godric says, then leans across the table to get some roast potatoes as a catering waitress brings him a nut roast.

"Seriously, why are you here?" Miles asks Godric, pulling himself away from Hugo's clutches, "stop banging on."

"While I can hold my booze, I'm making sure you don't overindulge, Mercutio, so you're fresh for tomorrow's rehearsals."

"Right, just what we need, a pissed enforcement officer." Miles pulls a face.

"Look, shh, shh. We have sweet music to celebrate!" Hugo takes another swig of champagne from the bottle he'd put between his legs.

"Good job they didn't use this image of the three of you for the band's promotional pictures," Darcy says, picking a mushroom off her lap.

"It's such great news," Nisha lifts her glass to cheers. Hugo clinks his bottle of champagne with her. Then grips

Lances head in his arm, messing up his hair.

"You're a mad maestro genius!" Hugo says as he kisses Lance's head. "Cut our whole album together in the studio. Wrote the lyrics. Edited the lot. We don't even need a record deal really, do we? Just for show! Are you looking at this mad genius, Godric?" Hugo shouts as Godric nods in acknowledgement.

"Yes. Yes, mad genius. Cut the whole album," Godric replies, looking at Lance.

"Alright, save some of my brain cells for writing the next album," Lance protests at Hugo fussing over his head.

"Are you excited for us, Nish?" Hugo then turns to Nisha only half-listening to everyone else.

"You're all such talented musicians," Nisha replies, "I think the world needs the 'Three Charming Men' she breaks into a large smile and laughs as Hugo throws a tomato in the air, catches it in his mouth then smiles at Nisha.

"To a creative bunch of arseholes! I love you all. Here's to a bun fight of a night, and remembering lines tomorrow!" Godric bangs the table and then clinks his drink with the rest of them. There is much laughter.

*

Up the other end of the room, at the top table, Fellows continue to quaff wine and converse about important things, far too immersed to notice a student sitting on a table in the far corner. Dr Guinevere Trotsham, her fringe cut high across her forehead making her look a lot younger than her years, wears a slightly revealing dress under her gown. She raises her glass in a communal toast to the Royal Family. A man sitting beside her, Professor Barclay, with salt and pepper hair and a gap in his front teeth like Terry Thomas, sucks in air as he looks at a small red stain where Dr Trotsham's glass has been placed on the white linen tablecloth.

"Messy Missy," then smiles a gappy grin as he looks around the hall. "There's enough testosterone in this place to turn a nun into a prostitute."

"I hadn't noticed," Dr Guinevere Trotsham replies.

"Pish. Your eyes haven't stopped mechanically scanning all night. No fresh rapscallions caught your eye this time?" Professor Barclay hisses through the gap in his teeth.

"Barclay, sometimes you go too far. Too far."

"You've got a couple more days to get a date before Valentine's Day, Gwynnie." Barclay leans back in his chair considering his stomach, having taken a lot more than his share of the food from the dishes on the table, his plate now piled high.

"What d'you know?" Dr Trotsham is irked by Professor Barclay's teasing.

They both watch, as the Master gets up and wafts through the hall with her crimson mortarboard, disappearing for a moment before re-entering alongside a butler wheeling a trolley carrying a large tiered cake. The Master indicates for the lights to dim, and they turn red as they fade to a warm glow. There is much 'oohing', and 'aahing before the a capella group reassembles again, this time to sing 'I've Got A Feeling I'm Falling.'

"If the Master can have a capella and cake, then I can have my theatre. At the very least, to take us out of Bene't's and All Saint's shadows," Barclay says.

"I thought the Master said she wouldn't fund it?" Dr Guinevere Trotsham asks.

"When has the lack of the Master's generosity ever stopped me before? Cartwright-Green needs to pull it out of the bag at the Swan. My high donors will be watching. They'll want to know we have the best actors. Miles Bonneville is in that troupe, he'll be part of my new Christina Theatre. We need them to pull out a perfect performance."

In the centre of the room, Barclay watches as the catering staff, having now cut many slices of Valentine's cake, are starting to distribute it to diners. The Master passes slices along the top table, before resuming her seat after mingling with the undergraduates and chatting to them briefly at their tables.

"You think you'll get your theatre past her?" Dr Guinevere Trotsham asks, glancing at the Master.

"It's not her I'm worried about," Barclay replies, as he stares into the distance at the students, Hugo now up on his feet having pulled a rose out of the display in the corner and is bringing it back for Miles.

*

Back at Hugo Grader's table, Hugo has sat back down, this time on Lance Fernard's lap, as Miles picks up a dish of peas and pours them all over Hugo in retaliation for tomatoes being pelted at his face.

"A pea shower. Superb." Hugo laughs as Lance laughs behind him. Hugo starts to hum a tune.

"Nish, would you pass the carrots?" Godric asks Nisha, treating these antics as completely normal, as many who have been to public school will know. Nisha passes the carrots and takes some for herself, then tucks into the food on her plate, admiring the flower on her wrist.

"Have you told Barclay yet?" Darcy asks Hugo and Lance. It's clear from her friends' faces that they haven't. Miles scowls.

"That man is the bane of my life. I hope he chokes on his carrots!" Miles takes the carrots from Nisha and chucks some at Hugo.

2
FOXES' HAVEN

Through open French windows, two rather regal Afghan Hounds, Hector and Monty, and a shaggily clipped Old English Sheepdog, Clive, can be seen chasing about in a game on the lawn, then sniffing borders and generally expending energy as dusk turns to dark. That is if anyone is looking. The house is silent. The only light coming from the last flicker of an earlier lit fire, the drawing-room now bitter cold.

Inside in the gloom and perched on the edge of the settee, Professor Elizabeth Green sits hunched over with glassy expression, rolling a ribbon around her finger one way, then unravelling it only to rewind in the opposite direction. As the dogs continue to play outside, a biting air whips through the doors and circulates around her. Elizabeth's arms are covered in goosebumps, but she ignores the cardigan resting on the arm of the settee and continues to stare at the wall. Her green eyes fixed ten feet across from where she is sitting. She has been staring at the wallpaper for over an hour. At the pale pink peonies. Unable to move and in a state of malaise, not having spoken to anyone for a good many hours, her jaw feels locked tight. She doesn't notice her most loving of cats, Bertie, who rubs himself against her legs, only to give up and walk off a little disappointed. The telephone trills from the telephone table in the hallway behind her. But Elizabeth isn't listening.

She knew there would be days like this. Days when clouds would loom in her mind. When she would lose hold of the wheel. A few hours ago, she tried to reason, tried to remind herself it was just a 'mood'. But she lost the battle. It's taken grip. She cannot see clouds passing as everything is dark, apart from the pink peonies. She counts them again.

3
HUGO GRADER'S ROOMS

Some of the older Cambridge Colleges have larger sumptuous rooms for the most privileged of students. Often, these rooms are given in reward for excellent exam performance, or for having made it to the final year of studies. Sometimes the reason is a pure mystery, as is the case with Hugo Grader. For Hugo meets no criteria at all. To say that he is an errant young reprobate is the world's most immense understatement. He is as wayward as they come, and so rarely seen in the library or at lectures that some of his tutors often mistake him as an imposter. Many envy his rooms, which have their own internal corridor leading to a second ensuite bedroom, boutique bathroom, pantry and kitchen. Despite all this, Hugo feels no gratitude at all for his College privilege. Having practically his own castle in Yorkshire his father gifted him for his eighteenth birthday, Hugo Grader looks upon his College 'digs' with disdain for being a little too 'pokey' for his liking. This accounts for the random custard spillage on the rug, and how every surface has used wine glasses, overfull ashtrays – despite the College operating a strict no smoking policy.

In the mess of lecture notes, music books and vinyl records which are spilt out everywhere stands a huge four-poster king-sized bed, covered with rose petals, and cross-legged in the middle, playing the guitar is Hugo. Miles Bonneville, who accompanied Hugo from supper earlier, is also now strumming along on another guitar while leaning against an open window and peering out at the most romantic bridge in Cambridge along The Backs. The water sparkling in the moonlight.

"Got any whisky?" Godric asks, following Nisha Acharya-Gorpade into the room, not sure how he ended up here with this bunch of kindred reprobates, and heading straight for what looks like a cocktail cabinet.

"In the corner," Hugo nods towards the cupboard "Pour one for me, old chap."

"And me, if you're going to help yourself to my friend's liquor the moment you arrive," Miles adds, then nods hello to Nisha. "Where's my present?" Miles asks Godric again, looking at Nisha's corsage.

"That tune sounds really good," Nisha offers, listening to Miles and Hugo playing, "Is it off the new album? I don't think I've heard it?"

"New one of Lance's. What did I say?" Hugo momentarily stops strumming and singing so he can point at Lance Fernard, who all this time has been sitting in a deep red velvet reading chair flicking through an art book. Almost as still as a statue. "He's a genius!" Hugo shouts.

"Next time you hear it, you might have to pay to listen," Miles announces to Nisha.

"What's with all the petals?" Darcy Nighy asks, entering Hugo's rooms. She walks over to the bed, picks up some in her hand and throws them at Miles, before draping herself around his neck and giving him a big hug and a kiss.

"I was hoping to get lucky, before you lot descended," Hugo says through a plectrum between gritted teeth.

"Don't you mean luckier, dear boy?" Godric replies, looking around at the wealth in the room before pouring whisky into half a dozen crystal glasses for everyone. "Who's for a game of poker?"

"Hugo couldn't get any luckier. He's the luckiest man alive," Lance laughs, taking a whisky from a tray of glasses Godric has just poured, "And, I'm in."

"Bravo!" Godric replies to Lance. Then to Hugo, "Stardom awaits! I hope you remember us mere mortals when you're up in the clouds."

"I hope you're all going to ruddy well miss us," Miles adds, as he strums a complicated bar. "And we're rehearsing. No time for winning all your money off you again, God."

"Maybe I'll miss Nish when we're on tour," Hugo winks at Nisha. Miles spots this and starts to strum more loudly on his guitar, nodding for Godric to put his whisky down on the window seat, then noticing Hugo fall back on the bed and shut his eyes, letting go of his guitar.

"Just concentrate on the chords for chrissake, Hugs. You said if I came up here, you'd take it seriously," Miles stops playing himself, to try to get Hugo to focus.

"Alright, easy," Hugo says, pausing before opening his eyes. "Just resting. Rest easy."

"When are we going to tell them we're outta here?" Miles gives up on Hugo and walks over to the window and leans out, shouting at the top of his lungs "I quit! D'you hear?! I'm leaving this godforsaken tight arsed, repressed, stuffy, pompous pit of tedious, tiresome, tame, stale, monotonous foramen!"

"Hey!" Hugo opens his eyes wide and finds some energy from somewhere and springs off the bed. He grabs his gown off the back of a chair on the way, and shoves it out and shouts at the top of his lungs, "Me too!"

"Yeah, well, I'm coming back for my exams, so don't lump me into your schoolboy antics," Lance says, pulling out his cigarette case and lighting up.

"You're in your last year. We've got another year and a half in this hell hole if we stay," Miles replies. Hugo searches for more things to chuck out the window. He finds his College tie and throws that out. "This is fun!" The moonlight illuminates Hugo's hair, and he laughs maniacally, then grabs his whisky and tips his head back to empty his glass. Miles grabs his own gown and College scarf and goes back to the window and throws them as far as he can. He sees the gown land on the gravel pavement and smirks to himself.

"Freedom!" Miles shouts out the window, then looks at Lance smoking in the chair. "Come on, Lance. Give me your tie." Miles laughs.

"Not on your nelly. I fully intend to use it as a chain flush in my downstairs bog when its uses around my neck come to an end. This is good silk." Lance strokes his tie, "Anyway, you know full well I would've stayed longer if Barclay hadn't turned me down for a PhD. I'm more attached to this place than you. If he complains about our absence, he only has himself to blame."

"Yeah, he kept setting me essays and expecting me to write them?" Hugo says, outraged. Then Hugo walks over to Nisha who is now sitting on a sofa by a coffee table, picking up dropped cocktail sticks but looking rather hot and flustered. "You can come with us, you know, Nish. Be the band's groupie," he says, hugging her.

"I've already asked her. Our lucky charm," Miles winks and for the first time lets out a wide smile at Nisha.

"Hey! I'm your girlfriend. Don't forget it," Darcy says, walking over to the window and throwing out her glass which smashes on the gravel.

"My Nanna bought me those crystals," Hugo stops hugging Nisha and looks at Darcy, upset his glass has gone. Darcy realises she doesn't know how to play the game. "Give me your gown." Hugo starts to pull Darcy's gown from her back. Darcy knows she doesn't have the money for another.

"I'm cold." She says, hanging on to it, "and, unlike Nish, have not been asked to be a groupie, so shall need it next week for another of these wretched suppers, when you'll all be off swanning about god knows where." Darcy manages to persuade Hugo to let go of her gown.

"Can I throw out the scripts yet? You know your lines?" Godric spots 'Hugo Grader's' script of Romeo and Juliet next to his bed.

"Toss it," Hugo replies, swaying.

Godric leans over to get the script from the bedside table, with no intention of throwing it out the window, rather to test Hugo on his lines. But as he leans over, all of a sudden, he feels wretched. He looks around the room. He notices all the others joking and laughing, but spots Nisha also looking a little peaky too.

"I have physics coursework over Easter, so I can't travel with the band then unfortunately and–" Nisha takes a shallow breath, shutting her eyes for a while, "Sorry, I, er–"

"Maybe I should walk you back to your room," Godric seizes the opportunity to extricate both of them from this night without making a fuss about his rapid turn for the worse. "And I hope to see you all in the morning. You promised to finish the play before you leave."

"Okay, Herr Direktor, keep your hat on. We'll be there." Miles looks at Godric, still with a glass in his hand, "and leave the whisky."

"I'm not going to pass up playing Romeo now, am I?" Hugo bounces enthusiastically to Godric to shake his hand. "Good night, good night! Parting is such sweet sorrow. That I shall say good night till it be morrow." Hugo flutters his eyelashes at Godric as he sways, then steadies himself.

"Stop showing off!" Miles shouts at Hugo. "We need to rehearse the music. Never mind Shakespeare."

"You don't have to be so jealous of everything I do all the time. I'm a man of many talents." Hugo wobbles his head at Miles, shutting his eyes again.

"You have the biggest head," Miles replies.

"They're fighting already, and it's only the first world tour." Lance inhales his cigarette.

"Well, he's always bigging himself up," Miles pushes Hugo.

"Cut it out. Did you not hear Goddy?" Darcy Nighy scowls at the men, "You'd better turn up for rehearsals tomorrow, or I'll have all your balls on a plate. I've got a London agent coming up to watch us on opening night," Darcy then turns to Nisha "And you. You'd better get the lights right. I don't want to be in the shadows again."

"Lay off. Nisha's an excellent tech director. Just focus on finding your mark, luvvy." Godric defends his friend, taking a deep breath to try to feel better.

"I beg your pardon?!" Darcy shouts affronted by the lecture.

"And try to shout less," Lance interrupts, for his own amusement.

"Who made you director?" Darcy says to Lance, then turns to Godric "Are you sure you know what you're doing?"

"I'm the Student President of the Swan Theatre. This is my third play at Cambridge. And I am your director, Darcy. Whether you like it or not. And, I'm inclined to agree with Lance, the multi-talented genius that he is," Godric looks at Hugo, then back at Lance, then at Darcy, "You are a shouter."

Hugo drags Darcy to the window and puts his arm around her, then forces her to look out onto The Backs and the willows floodlit by red lights for Valentine's Day. Hugo spots Professor Barclay.

"Hey!! Hey, Badger! Go back to the woods!" Hugo laughs. Darcy is mortified and tries to wriggle free from Hugo's grip, but it is no use. Hugo pulls her back. Barclay sees them both.

"Badger? Is that the best you can do? Is he not a pitiful

excuse for a man, whose only achievement is plagiarism?" Lance says, then, "Plagiarist!" he shouts from the comfort of his chair towards the window.

"I'm sorry, I don't think I feel..." Nisha rushes to Hugo's bathroom, and they all hear her throw up. Lance gets up to see if she's okay, and Godric follows. Meanwhile, Hugo and Miles start throwing empty bottles out of the window. Then they accidentally throw a full bottle of gin down.

"So that's alright to throw, but not one glass?" Darcy is still annoyed by Hugo's earlier reaction to the crystal glass.

"I hate waste." Hugo ties towels together and drops them out the window and attaches the other end to the bedpost then climbs out the window to retrieve the bottle of gin, stuck in a hedge midway between the window and the ground below. But, as Hugo descends, the towels prove slippery, and Lance comes back just in time to grab Hugo's foot as he starts to lose his grip. Lance only just catching him to be able to pull Hugo back into the room. Miles, meanwhile, stands by, wholly frozen to the spot. Godric walks back in from the bathroom and sees the commotion.

"Good job you're a cricket man," Godric says to Lance as cool as a cucumber, "nicely played." But, Godric's eyes are in shock that Hugo Grader very nearly fell out of the window.

4
NEW BEGINNINGS

A line of pretty blonde stone cottages raised five or six feet above the pavement, curl along Broadway. They line this road which heads into or departs from Grantchester, depending on your journey. Eight or nine steps take you up through their petite front gardens, crammed with winter flowering jasmine, hellebores, daffodils and white roses. Box and beech hedges offer shelter to buds on irises waiting to burst out at the first sign of spring. The homes are picture postcard, nostalgia oozing from the brickwork to the old fashioned windows. Each individual. All much loved. All, that is, apart from one. A shabby looking house smack in the middle of the long row, visibly bringing the neighbourhood down.

Ivy and an overgrown hawthorn have taken hold outside this house's front door. A curtain inside hangs crooked precariously from a thread, while sun-bleached cardboard covers upstairs windows in place of curtains. It is the steps of this house which Inspector Bob Abley climbs, pulls out a key and sighs. He looks behind him, his shaggy beard illuminated by a bright moon, before disappearing inside.

As Inspector Bob Abley shuts the front door he stumbles over a sea of post, which he scoops up and carefully places on an old hallway table, the top letter addressed to a 'Mr Robert Abley', from Bocklett and Sprackle. Bob Abley catches a glimpse of his chest in a hall mirror. He ducks down a little to look at his own face. He has lost weight. He can see the dark circles under his kind eyes. He's aged, even if tanned beyond recognition. At least his full blonde beard hides his gaunt cheeks, he thinks. He rubs his chin, raises his caterpillar eyebrows and sighs deeply. He peeps through a door and looks around a living room. There is not much to take in, just a few old box-crates resting on the floorboards in the gloom, a saggy sofa, and a TV on the floor, its wires trailing like a snake to a far plug. All delivered earlier by Constable Petticoat in his father's van from Abley's rented flat, as a favour for that thing neither of them will mention out loud ever again, but has put them both off high bar stools and gherkins for the foreseeable.

From Bob Abley's vantage point, he can see right through the house and out to the back garden. In the dusk he can just about make out that it continues for over a hundred feet before coming to an abrupt end at the end of a farmer's field currently growing – he thinks – what looks like kale. But it is difficult to see in the dark. Bob Abley walks fifteen feet, turns slightly to the right into a galley kitchen, which itself leads into a bathroom, and flicks on the light. He steps in and sits on the toilet – its lid closed – stretches out his arm and can almost reach a fridge that has been left behind by the previous homeowners. He notices several magnets stuck to it, including one which says 'Sunny Torquay' and has an image of a beach and a yellow sun above it, with deck chairs. "Handy", Bob Abley says to himself, as he shivers in the cold. He gets up and walks over to the end of the kitchen and to the back door, wrestles with a stiff lock, then steps out into the rear garden. The first thing that hits him is the quiet, the second that it is as cold inside his new home as out. He doesn't bother shutting the back door behind him.

Two low wooden picket fences mark the boundary of his property; small enough to step into adjacent gardens either side. He notices on one side there is a severe bout of mildew in need of a wire brush to rectify, and deduces that must be his fence as the other side, even in the gloom, glows a glossy white. He looks around his garden full of weeds, comparing his neighbours well attended, even pretty plots. He envies two gardens over, which has a lawn – despite it being February – like a putting green. Inspector Bob Abley bends over and almost involuntarily starts practising a putt. It is when he is lining up his imaginary ball with an imaginary hole that he notices a rather large hole in his back door, approximately one inch thick. He frowns, then walks over and puts his finger in it. Then, he sees similar holes in some old wooden patio furniture left by the previous owner. Bob Abley sighs.

After a few practice swings, now aiming his imaginary golf ball into the farmer's field, Bob Abley strolls to the end of his garden and looks back at this tiny house. His tiny house. His new home. It feels alien. Unfamiliar. Not having had any share of the proceeds from the sale of the old place he had on Park Parade with Maureen – she has better lawyers, a barrister in fact – that they bought decades ago for pennies and sold for a pretty one. No, he is left having to start again with a new mortgage. Despite being an Inspector, this is in fact at the very top of his range. Granted, Grantchester doesn't come cheap. And, despite the estate agents saying it had "promise" and was modest but "a great little opportunity", he can see, anyone can see in fact that it is one big – or rather little – dump! He stares at the warm glow of his next-door neighbour's lights. It looks inviting and cosy, then back at his. Cold and dark and empty.

Bob Abley doesn't miss his old house overlooking

Jesus Green. It is an increasingly busy spot outside for tourists and the ever-swelling population of Cambridge. But he longs for the home inside. The home they both created, bought up their children in. It isn't the house. It is Maureen. Park Parade still had Maureen in it right up to the day he gave back the keys, even though she had moved out many months before. The marks on the carpet in the bedroom where she would spill her wine she drank in bed while watching films. The scuffs on the bannister at the bottom of the stairs where she would throw her bag strap over when she came home and the strap would wear off the varnish. The discoloured wood on the kitchen surface, where she made countless cups of tea and left the spoon on the side. The marks that the little bits of tape she put on the windows to stop the birds flying into the glass, which had become part of the view into the garden. The wisteria – which Elizabeth bought Maureen – which Maureen loved so much and would repeatedly tell him to take photographs of her standing underneath. He still had those on his phone. But everything else, he could not take those things with him. He had lost them forever.

Worse yet, the memories are fading, like how Maureen would call up to him when he was in the bedroom to tell him the golf had started on the television, or how she would buy him golf magazines to read in the bath. It is all gone. And, there is nothing he can do to bring it back. All the ways she'd tease him, reprimand him, listen to him, hold him, even shout at him. It all made him feel alive. Now, it is all quiet. He knows he has to sign the papers but can't bring himself to, not yet. Not this month, not ever. He will ignore the letter he just picked up from the doormat, the one that looks official, the one that is from her solicitor.

Bob Abley looks up and sees a security light go on in the garden of the house next door, and an elderly gentleman stepping out of his backdoor. Abley watches as the man slowly shuffles down the garden in his slippers towards him, until finally in earshot.

"Are you the new tenant?" He asks, frowning.

"Just bought the place."

"Ah, good." The man replies. Bob Abley watches a cautious smile shoot across the neighbour's face, who then says, "That's good news. They're always so noisy. I'm Sid."

"Bob. Who's noisy?"

"Renters. Wait. You're not going to rent it, are you?" Sid realises hell might return. Bob Abley shakes his head. "Where's the wife. Indoors?" Sid asks.

"I'd love that cuppa, Sid," Bob says. Sid looks at Bob Abley, trying to remember if he had just offered him a cup of tea.

"Bit late for tea, isn't it? I can do one better than that. Come over here. I don't bite."

Bob Abley steps over the low fence and follows Sid to a shed. He watches Sid open the door, flick on a light, then open a fridge and pull out two real ale bottles. Then Sid shuts the shed door and turns on a heater and pulls up a bar stool for Abley to perch on next to a window table.

"She says I clutter up the fridge, so I keep them out here. My man cave."

Both men take sips of their beer, and Sid turns off the light so they can just about still look out the shed window at the farmer's field, though not see very far in the dark. "Welcome to the neighbourhood, Bob." Sid watches Bob Abley stare a little vacantly out at the crops. "Kale, that is. New-fangled food. An old food comes back in fashion. You're going to sort out your garden, aren't you? I can lend you a spade."

Bob Abley has the feeling Sid isn't so much asking as telling, looking at all of Sid's garden equipment hung up tidily around his shed. Yet, he feels like he's just made a friend. He takes a sip of his beer, smiles then nods. Sid clinks his bottle on Bob's.

"To new beginnings," says Sid.

"New beginnings," Bob Abley replies, thinking how

much he is looking forward to new beginnings. Suddenly, Inspector Bob Abley has a pain in the pit of his stomach. How is he going to cope without Maureen?

5
GODRIC FEELS ILL

"She wants to be alone," Lance Fernard walks back from the bathroom, where he has left Nisha Acharya-Gorpade throwing up.

"I'm feeling quite queer," Godric falls back into Hugo's bed of petals.

"As a director, you're not big into do as I do, are you," Miles replies.

"I'm a big believer in owning one's feelings. And I kid you not, I'm close to evacuating both orifices." Godric frowns and holds his stomach.

"Try not to do it over Hugo's petals. We can't shatter his hope for a conquest," Darcy smirks.

"I'm going to ride a bus, and there are two buses. Are you coming? No, shut up, leave the lemons," Hugo says to an empty chair as if he's seen an imaginary person, but nothing is there, "Waffles, the machine needs waffles." Hugo downs Godric's whisky.

"You are talking gibberish now, Darling. Lance just had to stop you dropping to your death. Did you leave your mind out on the tiles?" Darcy blows a kiss to Hugo, then shakes her head and looks at him like he's an idiot.

"Are you feeling any better?" Lance asks a rather pale looking Nisha, who walks out of the bathroom and starts to gather her things.

"I am sorry, Hugo. I'll come back and clean your bathroom in the morning," Nisha says quietly, putting on her coat. Godric starts to move off the bed.

"I'll see you back to your room," Godric walks over to Nisha and holds her arm.

"Is it more serious? Do you need a doctor, Nisha?" Lance asks.

"We have rehearsal tomorrow. You'd better be okay for that," Darcy says coldly to Nisha. "I need to run through my lines with you, Goddy. You need to stay, actually. It is a perfect time to do it here. I fear this play needs saving."

"Nonsense. And, I'm afraid, I feel really too dreadful." Godric picks up his scarf.

"Too much free whisky?" Miles barks.

"Well, I need someone to help me. Waify, you'll have to do it." Darcy watches Nisha pick up her bag and then starts to say some of her lines from the play.

"I think I'm going to be sick again. And can you stop calling me that?" Nisha drops her bag and runs to the bathroom. "Wait out here." She tells Lance and Godric, who have started to follow.

"People will do anything to avoid watching your performance," Hugo says to Darcy of Nisha's quick exit. "But I'm here. I will watch with my learned colleague here." Hugo stares at the empty chair some more as if someone is sitting in it, then back at Darcy.

"Stop being mean about my girlfriend," Miles ticks off Hugo talking to Darcy about it.

"Hope that's not a sign for opening night," Godric quips at Hugo's inadvertent put down of Darcy, as Hugo lays down on the rug again and starts to sing and strum on his now imaginary guitar.

"Like I said, I have an agent coming. This play is about me. No one spoil it," Darcy says to the room and anyone who will listen.

"And there I was, thinking it was all about the Capulets and Montagues," Lance quips pacing near the bathroom.

"No, Darling, it isn't," Darcy corrects him, "It's my one lucky chance, and none of you are going to ruin it for me."

"I'm feeling decidedly queasy," Godric gathers his gown and bag, having wrapped his scarf around his neck so many times it almost covers his mouth. Then they all hear sirens outside.

"Taxi?" Hugo whimpers, his eyes now shut, stretched out across a mess of vinyl albums already on the floor.

"I should be lead vocals. You'll murder our songs!" Miles shouts at Hugo's lazy demeanour.

"He's already on all the marketing material standing in the middle," Lance chips in.

"I'm a better singer, better actor too," Miles replies, looking at Hugo lying on the floor, dribbling. "You really are pathetic sometimes."

"I'm not acting, I'm authentic," Hugo grabs his imaginary guitar and starts to play again.

"Talking of acting, just try to practice to be off script soon, eh Hugo?" Godric asks Hugo. Hugo deliberately ignores Godric. Godric puts his rucksack over his shoulders. Miles begins to pace. He stops at the window and sees Professor Barclay, still outside.

"What is Barclay doing? He's waving. Didn't he hear us?" Miles waves back half-heartedly.

"Teacher's pet," Lance replies.

"What's he doing?" Darcy peeps out the window to look. They watch as a Porter bangs a post into the ground. Miles picks up a pair of binoculars.

"The Christina Theatre!"

"Oh, that's his baby," Lance says, walking over to the

window.

"You'd better tell him soon," Darcy replies.

"I'm worried about Nisha," Godric says quietly, walking towards the bathroom, disappearing around the corner.

"How can he build a monstrosity on such a beautiful garden. What a Neanderthal," Lance says while rolling a joint and walking over to lean against the wall of Hugo's hallway. At this moment, Godric emerges from the bathroom carrying Nisha.

"Can someone stop that racket, I'm trying to play," Hugo says, hearing more sirens closer than before.

"There do seem to be rather a lot," Darcy says, listening to the now multiple sirens.

"We need to get Nisha in one," Godric replies, making his way to the door. Lance grabs the door and follows Godric out, his lit joint now in his mouth.

"Yeah, well, I'm off too. This is pointless in your state," Miles gently kicks Hugo round the head then steps over him, "I'm a better singer, better actor, no returns." Darcy grabs a chocolate from a box on the side, kisses Hugo and follows Miles out, but not before looking back and saying, "If you don't want to be Romeo, then let Miles do it? He knows his lines and yours backwards. Don't balls this up as well."

*

Outside, three ambulances are parked by the front railings. Godric and Lance look at the pandemonium going on. Lance offers to take turns carrying Nisha Acharya-Gorpade as they walk quickly towards an ambulance, Godric relieved, having already carried her down the stairs and feeling more than ropey himself. Students are collapsed on the lawn around them. Some bending over shrubs to be sick, some in what looks like a queue to see a paramedic.

"Like rats to pied-piper," Lance says, weaving his way through ill people, with Nisha in his arms.

"What the heck?" Godric says as he stops to help a poorly student who seems to have fainted right in front of them. Lance cuts the queue and lifts Nisha into the back of an ambulance. He places her gently on a bed only to be told he himself has to leave. The paramedics take in three more sick students who sit on another bed, and then before Lance or Godric can say goodbye, they shut the doors in preparation to leave. Lance looks around at the chaos and sees Godric struggling. He makes his way back to him.

"Have they got her?" Godric asks, leaning over.

"She's going to hospital. You go home. I'll make sure she's okay."

"I feel like that might be a good idea," Godric replies, walking off into the night. Lance stands rooted to the spot, his shoes treading on Nisha's corsage which has fallen to the ground.

6

THE CHRISTINA THEATRE

In the grounds of the College on the other side of The Backs and away from the chaos of students being bundled into ambulances outside Christina College Porters' Lodge, Professor Barclay is still pacing around the space for his new theatre in the dark. A gardener has taken over as his aide, as the Porter has been called away to help clean up sick in the Lodge. The gardener follows Professor Barclay with small wooden pegs and a hammer, beating them into the ground, while Barclay points at the precise spot each time.

"This will be magnificent. The great and the good will flock to see the very best of English performance at 'The Christina Theatre'," Professor Barclay says with a flourish, having imbibed more than his fair share of brandy at the Valentine's Banquet earlier.

"I don't doubt it, Sir. We have the trees we can plant around its border. I can come and find you in the morning if you like? When we can see better?"

"No willows. Deep roots only." Professor Barclay ignores the gardener's subtle plea to down tools which he should have done hours ago before he was nabbed by the Porter to babysit this neediest of Dons.

"I know my trees, Professor. Don't you worry." Then the gardener looks up at a window in the building across the river. It still has a strong light beaming out. "Ruddy student is always tipping things out of there. Landed right on my hellebores and crocus buds tonight."

"Yes, well, the abuse of privilege is rife with that lout." They both look at the flashing red light coming from Hugo's rooms, and the towels dangling out of the window with a pile of bottles smashed in the flower beds below.

"It wouldn't surprise me if he's behind all these ambulances," the gardener tuts.

"Yes, well, I suppose I'd better retire. I just thought, given you were here, you could do this while it was quiet," Barclay instructs the gardener to stay.

"Right you are, Sir. Would you like me to finish pegging this out, or leave it until the morning?" Professor Barclay nods a yes, then walks off.

The gardener stares up at Hugo's bedroom again, then back down at the lawn in the darkness. Who other than Professor Barclay would keep him working in the night? He was only going to get a midnight snack when the Porter grabbed him. The gardener pulls up a stake and places it carefully on the ground beside some string. Through the railings, down the side of the building, he catches a glimpse of the mayhem going on beside the ambulances. Something terrible is surely afoot, and he's sure as hell not going to do any more of this tonight while sick kids need his help. What kind of Professor takes himself off to bed in a crisis like this, he thinks, as he heads over the bridge to lend a hand?

Already now in Bramble Court, Professor Barclay gives the front of the College a wide berth and thinks how he can avoid all these needy people. He sneaks up a stair case away from all the young people in need. He has something else on his mind. Something altogether more dramatic.

7
ZOMBIE APOCALYPSE

The gardener walks across Front Court and under the arch of the Porters' Lodge until he sees what Lance Fernard and Godric saw just a short while ago. Dozens of students lying on the grass, throwing up, or doubled up in agony. He walks to the closest and picks them up to carry them to an ambulance. Two ambulances are now parked up on the street, with paramedics taking blood pressure of students and starting to cram a dozen in to rush them to hospital.

An ambulance whisks like the wind down Hill's Road. In its backdraft is a taxi with Lance inside. Still wearing his gown, his expensive suit and white starched shirt underneath a contrast to the tatty backseat.

"It's all kicking off," the taxi driver tries to make conversation.

"The zombie apocalypse," Lance replies, wanting the driver to shut up, "don't lose that ambulance."

*

For some time, the emergency department is swamped with Christina College undergraduates, the most seriously ill wheeled into a ward and many placed on temporary beds. The sheer number crushed in like farm animals in a holding pen on the way to slaughter. Lance peeks through the doors, and looks everywhere for Nisha, but cannot find her. "What's happened?" Lance asks a nurse. "What's wrong with them?" A student lurches forward from his chair and throws up on Lance's shoe. "Oh, Christ!" Lance hops towards the bathrooms, holding his shoe, he spots Nisha. She is lying down on the floor in the corridor in her own sick, a nurse rushing towards her.

8
BUNNY

Feeling guilty for having left Nisha Acharya-Gorpade in an ambulance, Godric promises himself that as soon as he has had a few hours with his head down, he will go and visit. He walks in the dark of the night along Trinity Street. Everything is quiet. He often likes to walk the city centre at night, especially when it is empty in the winter. But not in these circumstances, not tonight. Not when he feels so ill. He can still hear ambulance sirens in the background. How many are sick? He thinks back to how much alcohol he drank and whether that is behind his feeling so queasy.

Godric turns into Bridge Street and notices a street cleaner and nods as he walks past. A couple of upper-end restaurants still have people inside, finishing their coffees, long after official closing. Food smells still emanating out onto the pavement from past eaten dinners. It makes Godric feel even more queasy. What is this feeling he has all over his body? He feels sick and aches. Can he just sit down here? Just for a minute? On the pavement? Inching towards Magdalene Street, he finally stops and leans on the brow of the bridge to catch his breath. He stares at Castlebridge College and down onto the water at Sandymee's punts, all chained up together for the night. A man glides past behind him on a bicycle. Godric wants to get home but feels so weak. Glancing back at the River Cam, he notices a dozen or so swans floating up towards All Saint's College. Their white plumes shining back in the blackness. He must move forward. One step after the other. He can feel the pull of Foxes' Haven.

With heavy steps, he tries to think happy thoughts. Godric loves living with his nanna – his Bunny. Initially, it was for the sole reason of tormenting his mother. For he knew all too well the level of animosity between the two women, and how his choice of Foxes' Haven as a residence would cause a flare-up. His sympathy always falling on the side of Bunny on these occasions. But soon he felt guilty for causing this tension, for putting Bunny through it. He knew how mean his mother can be, and when she offered to pay for large rooms in Bene't's College, it slipped off his tongue so quickly that it took both his mother and nanna quite by surprise. "No. I'm living with Bunny!" He was quite adamant.

Now that Godric is feeling particularly poorly, he is looking forward to the fuss he will receive when he gets in. No matter how late, there is always a hot chocolate in a flask and biscuits left out for him, and a lit fire in the knowledge that he'll like to lay with the animals before crashing to bed. And what a bed. His favourite lady in the world purchased the softest pillows and fluffiest duvet. No wonder it is hard to get out in the morning. At least, that's his excuse for missing umpteen morning lectures. Being spoiled rotten by someone you know loves the bones of you is the best feeling in the world. And, he likes to think he spoils his Bunny back - though knows he doesn't do it enough. Although Godric is now finding every step hard, he knows he will be soon in the warm and Bunny's love is pulling him home.

By the time Godric reaches the front door, his fingertips are numb, and he feels like he has the first stages of hyperthermia. So, when he turns the key and cold air blows through, he can't stop himself from frowning. Immediately, it is clear something is amiss. The dogs thunder up to him, their feet muddy.

"Bunny?" He calls as he steps into the hallway. He walks through to the drawing-room and shuts the French windows which are wide open and letting in the freezing February air. From a hall cupboard, he flicks on the central heating. Then he turns on the lights. Godric stumbles up the stairs, past Bertie and Soot – who are both feeling sorry for themselves in this chilly home, their fur plumped out like fluffy armour. "Bunny?" Godric knocks on his nanna's bedroom door. He can see a line of light underneath by the carpet. "Bunny?" But nothing. He tries the door, but it is locked. Godric frowns. He feels very ill. He walks into his bedroom and through to his ensuite and immediately throws up in the toilet. He reaches for a glass and pours himself a water. He wants to sleep right where he is. He can feel the bathroom radiator kicking in. Here will do. Please take this misery away. But something isn't right. He drapes his duvet over his shoulders, spots a beanie hat on the back of his door and shoves it on, then walks back to his nanna's room.

"Bunny, I can see you're up. Your light is on? Is everything alright?"

"I'm fine," Professor Elizabeth Green replies.

"The French doors were open. I've put the heat on. It's like an igloo in here." But no reply comes back. "I'm not feeling very well. Perhaps you have what I have?" Godric asks. Still nothing. "It was a weird night. Supposed to be all love and hearts, but poor Nish has gone off to hospital. There were quite a number ill. Could be poisoning? Don't know if you wanted to maybe call Inspector Abley? See if he needs you to look at it?" But Godric's suggestion is met with silence. "You are his best

Consultant. You know they all call you Professor of Poisons." Godric smiles. But, still nothing. "You could sort me out. I feel poisoned. I'm going to go and visit Nish once I've had a few hours sleep. Too ill myself at the mo." Godric waits to hear a reply to this news. But nothing comes back. "I've just thrown up." Godric listens again, but nothing. He frowns.

He starts to feel his legs give way, feeling faint, so he lies down on the landing floor outside his nanna's bedroom. "There were at least three ambulances. I've never seen anything like it. I'm okay. I just feel like I need sugar," Godric, now flat on his back, feels in his pockets and finds some mints and pops one in "S'ok, I've got mints. They were taking some students out on stretchers." Godric is quiet, hoping to hear his nanna get up, open the door and hug him and send him to bed with a hot water bottle. But there is nothing. "You okay?" Godric asks, but hears nothing back. "You know, I think you'll like the play. This set of actors, they're all such characters. They're larger than life. Bunny?"

Monty, Hector and Clive run up the stairs. Not usually allowed up on the first floor, as Elizabeth says it is the cats' privilege for some peace and quiet. But, perhaps knowing these are unusual circumstances, they now bound all over Godric before plonking themselves down inches from his head. "Have the dogs been out?" Godric asks his nanna but more silence. He thinks that it might fall to him, for once, to take them out. But remembers the doors were open, so they are probably alright. He puts his hand in the soft shaggy hair of Clive and rolls into him for a hug. Realising Clive is hot, Godric snuggles in, hoping this will make him feel less nauseous. "The play," Godric continues. "It means a lot to me." He pauses, hoping his nanna will speak, but then talks to her anyway.

"You were always telling me to follow my passions. Well, it is my passion — the theatre. I mean, I think it's what I care about. More than anything. I don't know what

I'd do without it. And yeah, this troupe are a bit nuts but there's some talent in there. Real actors. Even if they seem to care more about other things. It falls naturally from their lips, acting. You know." Godric yawns and shuts his eyes. "It's all I want to do. This play, it's everything." Godric slowly falls to sleep, curled up in a ball feeling poorly but tucked in among all the dogs now lying down around him. He dreams of Montagues and Capulets fighting over honour and name. The dream is violent.

*

In her room, Elizabeth sits in the middle of her bed, her head resting on her knees. She stares at the art deco pattern on her duvet, one finger follows the triangles on the fabric, moving across each as if checking them off in some sort of duvet pattern standard checking procedure. But Elizabeth's mind is elsewhere. In fact, she can't hear anything outside the voices in her own head.

9
CORRIDOR DONS

It is very late, and Professor Barclay and Dr Guinevere Trotsham are huddled outside the Senior Common Room at Christina College. Professor Barclay, having come inside from pegging out the boundaries for his new theatre, is surprised to find Dr Trotsham still up. But less so when he notices so many students are still milling and filling up all the Common Rooms and shared spaces, some being checked over by university doctors woken up by the Master.

"How the hell did I get roped into this?" Dr Trotsham says, offering Professor Barclay a cup of tea from an urn she is currently administering for the students still awake, after seeing their friends taken off to hospital. "Kitchen staff have gone home. The Dean thought it would be a good idea if we all muck in to help calm the nerves of the little darlings. Where've you been? You escaped."

"They're all such snowflakes," Barclay replies. "I tried to get to my rooms, but people kept knocking on the door. I had to escape."

"I think it's serious by all accounts," Dr Guinevere Trotsham says, showing some signs of concern.

"Yes, but this remaining rabble would do well to stop making a fuss and go to bed. Not be drinking tea. They're not ill. Especially when you look at how many digestive biscuits they're consuming." Professor Barclay watches a student snuggled into a high-backed chair pop a whole biscuit into his mouth, with half a dozen chocolate digestives balanced on the arm still for consumption.

"They're in shock? I wonder if their peers have been poisoned? That would explain why some are worse than others, surely?" Dr Trotsham wonders almost to herself.

"I've never in all my years seen an act on such a large scale. I expect the Master is reeling."

"The Master was taken to hospital with the first group," Trotsham replies, pouring a tea for a student who has come up to the stand. "That's why we got our instructions. She gave them before the ambulance doors closed. 'Take care of our students'".

"Well, while the cats are away, I suggest we take all these down," Professor Barclay looks at a poster for the Swan Theatre play that Godric is directing. "I can't look at Mr Grader's face." Barclay frowns at Hugo Grader's happy face staring out as Romeo from the poster.

"But I thought you needed it to be a success and that your high donors are going to see it?"

"They are. I do. But, I don't need the Master thinking there is an alternative theatre which works just as well as my precious creation. Let this show happen in secret. Then Christina's Theatre can rise up and outshine it very soon. It's a tight line, but I can do without seeing his face too. Bleugh."

"Did you know they're leaving soon, to go on tour?" Trotsham asks, biting into a rich tea biscuit.

"I heard. I blame this ego-maniacal menace," Barclay now rips up the poster and Hugo Grader's face on it. "If he's as bad at music as he is at acting, they'll sink without a trace in a matter of weeks."

"They're not too bad actually," Trotsham replies,

"although Miles Bonneville is the better actor, but the band is good."

"Well, Mr Grader is most definitely not lead material. If he were not in the play, I'd stand a better chance of convincing donors that we have a good acting pool."

"I suppose I should get this urn refilled. Though why I should be doing everything. Surely some staff can be called back?" Dr Trotsham says, not knowing what to say about Barclay's obvious dislike for Hugo Grader.

"Do what you like, I'm retiring before I get dragged into whatever this is," Barclay replies.

"I've always hated Valentine's Day. This lead up has made it even worse, and the day's not even here yet," Dr Trotsham finds a large empty jug under the urn ready to fill with more water.

"Yes, all those hormonal bodies are probably just wilting from having imbibed too many love potions." Professor Barclay looks at some of the students, then recites Shakespeare.

Love is not love
Which alters when it alteration finds
Or bends with the remover to remove
O no! it is an ever-fixed mark
That looks on tempests and is never shaken;
It is the star to every wand'ring bark"

"Thought you were the cynic? Sonnet 116, eh?" Dr Trotsham raises an eyebrow.

"Hate and cynicism are two quite different emotions, Gwynnie. Very different."

10
NEEDY NISHA

It is the middle of the night, and the ward is packed full of the ill from Christina College. Lance helped a nurse carry Nisha Acharya-Gorpade up off the floor, and the hospital finally found her a bed. She is wearing a hospital gown and is hooked up to a drip, her trainers down on the floor, her socks pulled up to her knees.

"When will you know what's wrong with her?" Lance Fernard sits in a chair by her bed, looking up at the nurse who is cleaning sick out of Nisha's hair.

"You should really wait outside, in case it's contagious." The nurse pulls the curtain around Nisha's bed.

"You'll have to call in your brutes to prise me away," Lance replies.

"There's a waiting room along the corridor. No one is calling security."

"What a shame, I feel like punching someone. Preferably the person who's done this," Lance purses his lips.

"You think someone did this?" The nurse is surprised.

"Someone always does this."

"You need to tell the police if you think that," the nurse replies.

"I hope they're already speaking to people?" Lance says, leaning back into his chair. "Aren't they here yet? Huh." The nurse leaves, and Lance pulls his chair closer to Nisha's bed. He sits for some time and watches as Nisha's eyes open. "Back in the land of the living?"

"Hello," Nisha looks around.

"Hospital, yes. Very fashionable."

"I feel terrible." Nisha takes a while to get her bearings. "Thank you for sitting with me."

"Someone had to be here when you woke up to remind you that Darcy needs you to go back straight away hear her read lines," Lance teases, then takes her hand. "How are you feeling?"

"I have a thumping headache."

"I'll get someone," Lance gets up and peeks through the curtain to look around for a nurse, to try to attract attention.

"No, don't fuss. I'm sure they'll be back."

"I can't believe half of the dining hall is here? You've obviously all been poisoned in the same way. They look much worse than you, Nish, if that makes you feel any better?" He walks back to sit down on the chair.

"No, not really." Nisha moves her neck and winces. "I don't think I congratulated you properly on your music deal?"

"I think you have. And, er, stop thinking about

anything other than getting better."

"It will be amazing." Nisha tries a smile. "When are you leaving?"

"Next week? After the play by all accounts. Only if Hugo and Miles stop fighting. But as for the details. No idea. Miles has the itinerary, which seems to be a lot of photoshoots with Miles and visiting Miles's favourite towns."

"You write some beautiful songs?"

"Some?"

"I meant all," Nisha looks tired.

"I'm going to speak to someone about you getting your own room." Lance looks at the other patients through a gap in the curtains.

"Oh, no, please." Nisha grabs Lance's arm. "Does Darcy hate me?"

"Why d'you say that?" Lance looks at Nisha, a little confused at why she is asking.

"I always seem to annoy her. She's your friend."

"Everyone annoys her. That's Miss Nighy."

"I'm serious."

"Hopefully, the drip will cure that," Lance smiles.

"You should go," Nisha smiles.

"Hurry up and get better then."

11
A BED OF PETALS

Despite it being the early hours of the morning, music blares from one of the student suites situated on the rather exclusive staircase 'C' in Christina College. The Porters know it well, and tonight this Porter drew the short straw with his colleague back at the Lodge when it was decided who should climb the steps and have a word with a certain occupant. For it is not uncommon to be halfway up only to be met by objects being thrown down, or buckets of water hurled. How this one resident has not yet been suspended, despite umpteen complaints is anyone's wonder. Though some insist otherwise, money and title still hold sway in certain Cambridge Colleges. And this Porter arrived at the conclusion himself many years ago. Blind eyes are indeed turned where entitled undergraduates are concerned.

Perhaps it is the considerable generosity of the particular noise-making resident, combined with profuse apologies he always showers on all concerned after the event, that make his errant acts forgivable. The Porter can indeed remember one time being sent home himself with a three-tiered celebration cake. The young man had told him that he'd "ordered one with pink frosting by mistake and he wasn't eating that!" So, "take it away. Give it to your wife or lover", was the throwaway remark before the young man threatened to throw the thing down the stairs. The cake, resembling one which might find its way onto an upmarket wedding table, did indeed feed the Porter's wife and all her friends for over a week. Said wife often still asks if she can get another, but having retrospectively investigated the value of the edible delight, the Porter had to manage her expectations when instead he brought home a supermarket's own brand one tiered Victoria sponge to show his love. There was also that time the gentleman concerned gave this Porter two tickets for a hot air balloon trip that the young man had won in a card game but "wasn't fussed about. Take 'em", as he held the keys to a car that he'd also acquired at the same time. The Porter enjoyed that very much, as the balloon almost clipped the top of Ely Cathedral and made his wife squeal. Then there was the bottle of port he and all the other Porters got at Christmas since this young man had joined College. When his wife looked up the price she made him sell it online, and it paid for Christmas dinner and all the grandchildren's presents. So, the perks were, well, considerable and to say this room was filled with an ordinary student would not quite be the truth of the matter.

As the Porter draws closer to the top step, the music begins to drown out his thoughts. He doesn't recognise the tune but thinks the voice sounds remarkably like the actual man he is going to have a quiet word with about the levels. As he tries to distinguish the different sounds, the Porter wonders whether he will be met with a full band, as he can hear drums, guitars and what sounds like a backing orchestra.

Pushing back the door, which is already ajar, it doesn't

take many seconds before his eyes are drawn to the bed. A large four-poster with rose petals scattered across it and all over the floor. Holding a guitar, the amp of which is feeding back a track from an album, is Master Hugo Grader. His head upside down and off the edge of the bed. When the Porter catches a glimpse of Hugo's face, he is shocked that his eyes have daffodil heads taped over them. It is clear the young man is dead.

The Porter falters a little and leans against the door frame, but then wanting to stop the deafening noise, looks for the power supply and pulls out the plug from the socket. He then walks over to Master Hugo Grader and shakes him.

"Come on, lad, don't be silly," he says, in a panic, knowing his shakes are futile. He can feel that Hugo Grader is cold. The Porter covers his mouth in shock and then tries to find a pulse, but nothing. He runs out of the room, locking the door behind him, hot-footing it back to the Lodge to call for an ambulance.

Back inside Hugo Grader's room, Hugo's phone trills. The caller ID showing up on the mobile, which is now on the floor in the middle of the room, is 'Nish The Dish'. Around the room is evidence of a night of partying, a red wine bottle spilt on the floorboards, its contents sticky and spread wide. Snacks dropped into the rug, the window sill wide open with a towel hanging half in, half out. Nisha Acharya-Gorpade's bag on a chair, and umpteen vinyl albums out of their sleeves, scattered on the floor.

Through the window, the sun still isn't up. A swan glides past along The Backs, its beauty framed by the black river. Everyone is now asleep. A groundsman turns off the red Valentine's Day celebratory lights which have been floodlighting the lawn in Bramble Court below. The same groundsman, unaware of what has happened above through the open window, starts to pick up all the empty bottles which were earlier thrown down into the flowerbeds.

12
MOST DETACHED

Professor Elizabeth Green sits on her bed in the gloom, having hardly moved from earlier. Her feet and hands are cold, but she's too far away in her own thoughts to do anything about them. She cannot seem to close her eyes to sleep.

Instead, she remains paralysed by circumstance. She is well aware of the human condition. That it is possible to be strong and weak at the same time. How other humans seek to confide, some on everything, some on that one secret that is eating them up. While others, her included, say nothing. Bury everything until it is so deep they cannot remember where they put it. She knows that tears are meant to relieve tension, rest helps to recover from pain. She knows all this and more. Professor Elizabeth Green is unquestionably the best-read person she knows. But there are some things that cannot be explained about the human condition. Some things that seem to exist in the air around us, which cannot be denied. The moments when we feel most detached. When the point ceases to matter, or fails to be found at all. When all sense has flown out of the window with reason. When one step cannot be put in front of the other. When there are no words. Elizabeth has been having one of these moments since yesterday afternoon. She has disappeared from the world. Checked out. Put a sign on the door saying 'closed'. She hears Godric's voice, but from very far away, as if he were a moth fluttering in the light.

*

Godric is finding it hard to rest on the floor outside Elizabeth's room. She clearly isn't going to open the door to him anytime soon. As the hours go by, he begins to think that he must have done something unforgivable that his Bunny just can't move past. That she has barricaded herself into her room until he starts behaving or maybe she is waiting for an apology.

He knows he broke a couple of pots last week when he came home drunk and fell over outside the front door, exposing one of her favourite plants to frost, causing it to die. He's sure he cracked a rib that night and although she kept telling him to go to hospital, he ignored her. Then, a few days ago, he accidentally shut Soot in the airing cupboard. That time she was very cross, as it was quite a while before she found him and the cupboard was hot and Soot rushed out to drink water.

Then there was that time two weeks ago when Godric fell asleep with a cigarette on his chest in bed. She went apoplectic over that. Fell rather silent for a full day. That was the worst. But things have been back to normal in between that and this? Godric felt she had moved past it. In fact, one thing Godric loves about his nanna is that she does not hold a grudge.

As Godric racks his brains, he decides to feed the cats, who are rubbing themselves against his legs and have been doing so for some time. He walks downstairs and starts to open the cupboards in the kitchen, moving two huge boxes of flowers to the side as the cats jump up on the kitchen surfaces and rub against his hands.

"She can buy flowers but not feed you, eh?" He says to Bertie. "What's wrong with Bunny?" Godric then walks back out into the hallway. "Where d'you keep the cat food again?" He shouts up the stairs to his nanna, mildly ashamed he doesn't remember, rarely actually doing jobs about the house. He waits for a reply, but nothing. Godric feels unnerved. To ignore him is one thing, but not to respond when the animals are in need, that is altogether another, and nothing like the nanna he knows. "They're telling me they're hungry!" He shouts up again. But, still nothing. He tells himself that perhaps his Bunny has fallen asleep, and then regrets having called her at all. But he doesn't really believe it.

Bertie and Soot have followed him out into the hall and are now following him back into the kitchen. He's flummoxed, having opened all the cupboards. He looks again and can't find cat food, but spots a couple of tins of sardines. He shuts the kitchen door, as he knows full well the dogs will be in like a shot once the cans are open. Godric lifts Bertie back up onto one counter and Soot onto another and opens the cans. Both cats purr, their tails hitting the flowers as they flick them with delight. Godric holds his nose, the smell of the fish making him physically sick. After he has fed the cats, he runs into the downstairs toilet and throws up.

*

Back in her room, Elizabeth is in the same position. She takes a deep sigh and pulls a pillow from behind her. She places it by her side and finally lies down, still outside the duvet, and still her eyes refusing to close.

13
SERGEANT LEMON

Inspector Bob Abley pulls up in his new Tesla Model 3 outside Christina College in the dark. His headlights, though dipped, illuminate the back of Bene't's College Chapel across the street, which looms over this more modest-sized neighbouring College. Despite being the smaller cousin, Christina is no less splendid, situated as it is along The Backs and out of the way from the usual hubbub on King's Parade. Indeed, one might say it is a hidden jewel. It's courts pretty and symmetrical, many of its buildings much older than one might suppose, some dating as far back as the fourteenth century. Beacons of sheer classicism. But all this is wasted on a very tired and unappreciative Inspector. Who having only just moved into his new Grantchester terrace is already more than mildly irritated by the firm who sold him a bed, promised it would be delivered before he moved in, and are now not picking up the phone. He had only just managed to find a comfortable position on his sofa before his phone rang!

So, as Inspector Abley turns off the car and the radio

falls silent, he pulls a face as he rubs the crick in his neck. Knowing he is about to see the body of a dead young man, who had so much ahead of him no doubt, Abley doesn't feel like this is the morale booster he was hoping for today, of all days, what with it being the first day of a new chapter for him. And, he knows that sounds selfish, so tries to reset his priorities.

Inspector Abley looks along the road where he is parked. It is a double yellow, so it is quite remarkable just how many cars are lined up. An ambulance, two police cars, a couple of taxis and one or two unidentified. Bob Abley understands he is going to walk into quite a commotion, no doubt with many questions from some of his least favourite people – Fellows. So it is a relief when he spots Sergeant Lemon walking towards his car. Sergeant Lemon!

"Inspector." Sergeant Lemon peers down into the window that Abley has hurriedly opened, giving Abley one of his lanky crooked smiles.

"Lemon," Abley beams at Lemon, noticing how much his Sergeant's tall frame has to bend to get down this low. "Thanks for coming out. Let me get out." Abley shuts the window just as Lemon speaks.

"I was on duty, Sir. Nights. Nice wheels. You making up for all those pesticides on the golf course?"

"Just a minute," Inspector Abley mouths behind the closed window, understanding but choosing the ignore his Sergeant's gripe about his hobby. He locks the car and follows Lemon through the Porters' Lodge and Front Court to Bramble and heads for staircase 'C'. They are joined by the Porter who found Master Hugo Grader's dead body.

"He has already given a statement, but stayed after shift, just in case," Lemon explains about the Porter's presence.

"Thank you. Much appreciated. You must be tired. We won't keep you much longer."

"I saw him larking about this evening. I mean yesterday evening," the Porter corrects himself and checks his watch, "He was a loud one."

"Loud?" Abley asks.

"Always playing music, parties. You're supposed to get permission if you have more than six in a room. Health and Safety. He was one of those young lads always flouting the rules. But, such a nice young man. We all liked him, at the Lodge I mean. A very generous, warm young gentleman."

"Second year. Studying English." Lemon continues to fill in Abley.

"I don't care what he was studying," Abley replies, then hearing how ungrateful he sounded, checks himself, "But very helpful to know, thank you, Sergeant Lemon." As Inspector Abley walks up the staircase to Hugo Grader's suite, he notices all the posh wallpaper and lights.

"Is this the new thing? More like a boutique hotel," he comments.

"Oh, no. He paid someone to decorate the it," the Porter explains, "And there was an agreed bill to remove it once he left."

"More money than sense," Lemon observes quietly. The black flock wallpaper lining the staircase, the art deco light and the towering palm like potted plants, looking like no other College staircase he has ever ascended. The Porter turns to leave.

"Where are you going?" Abley asks, surprised.

"I can't spend another minute in that room. I'm at the Lodge if needed," the Porter says, apologetic.

"One thing. Did he have any enemies?"

"I don't know, Sir. Perhaps best ask his friends."

"And who might they be and where might I find them?" Abley replies.

"Was the kind who had a lot. I can't imagine he had any enemies. He liked a drink, was always around and about."

"Where do you suggest we start? The bar?"

The Porter scratches his head.

"Oh, he was in that play. Posters up around College. Maybe some friends from that? He was popular. Terrible shame, a tragedy," the Porter explains before turning to leave.

Lemon picks up paper shoes and a SOCO overall from Constable Petticoat waiting at the top of the stairs and hands some to Abley. Abley nods and smiles at Petticoat, a short rather rotund man, probably a few years younger than Lemon, Abley thinks. Still with rosy cheeks beaming from the sides of his proportionately over-large head. They both walk into the room, SOCO suited.

The body of Hugo Grader is still being photographed, along with his guitar. Abley picks a record sleeve from the floor. It says, 'Three Charming Men'.

"Never heard of them?" And looks to Lemon, who shrugs, so continues "Thought you were supposed to be young and hip?"

"Working here?" Lemon raises his eyebrows and notices a woman's bag on the chair.

"Let's find her," Abley says. Lemon nods to Constable Petticoat and hands over the bag to a SOCO.

"Sir, they're a local band. He is, was the lead singer, Sir," Constable Petticoat offers, picking up a different record sleeve, showing the deceased on the front cover.

"Well, we'll need to speak to these two chappies," Abley replies, looking at the Constable.

"I believe they're all students here, Sir," Petticoat adds.

"It won't be hard finding them. Good job, Petticoat, thank you. Can I leave that in your capable hands?" The Constable nods, and Lemon winks at the Constable then looks back at the body.

Abley notices Leedham, a skinny bald man, the Cambridge Police Chief Pathologist, who has come out without his toupee and is still wearing his pyjama top under his coat. Abley watches Leedham examine the body.

"Another young one bites the dust. What is it about students? Supposed to be the time of their life," Leedham says, staring up at Sergeant Lemon, light bouncing off Leedham's bright orange spectacles.

"Time of death?" Abley asks.

"I'll need to look in more detail. I can't be making guesses. You know that," Leedham replies, frustrating Abley. Leedham spots something in Hugo Grader's mouth and pulls out a pair of tweezers from his pathology bag. He delicately extricates the object and – to Abley and Lemon's amazement – removes a wet piece of paper. Lemon pulls out an evidence bag, and Leedham carefully places the paper on the bag, not wanting to pull it apart, the paper still wet. Abley takes the tweezers from Leedham and starts to tease at the paper.

"It's from a book?" Abley says in surprise. Abley carefully pulls open the page a little until he sees the word 'Wordsworth' at the top and 'daffodil' on the page. "Wordsworth?"

"Ah, a host of golden daffodils," Leedham replies.

Abley hands the tweezers to Lemon, who points to a SOCO to deal with the wet paper.

"Can I have my tweezers back?" Leedham says, leaning across Abley and snatching them out of Lemon's hands.

"It was a Valentine's Banquet tonight in College, apparently. Which might explain the petals," Lemon walks with Abley over to the other side of the bed.

"Already? That's not for a couple of nights." Abley picks up a petal and sniffs it. "They never usually smell, do they? The mass produced ones. But these smell wonderful. Of course they do." Abley looks around the room, wealth oozing from every corner.

"It's all getting stretched out a bit more these days. So people can get in their romantic bookings, I think? Restaurants need to keep afloat," Lemon suggests.

"Terrible mark-up. A time to avoid at all costs."

Abley looks at Leedham, and wonders if he too is alone this Valentine's. Abley shuts his eyes and puts the thought of Maureen out of his mind.

"Can we speak to those he sat next to at this Banquet? I'm assuming he went?" Abley asks Lemon, opening his eyes again.

"Apparently, and some saw him stand on the table. Throwing food," Lemon shares, looking at his notepad.

"Course he was," Abley isn't surprised anymore by the distinct lack of respect for food some of the wealthiest observe. "Can we speak to these witnesses?"

"According to the Porter, most are in hospital," Lemon replies.

"Proving to be an eventful evening, isn't it?" Abley raises his eyebrows at Lemon, then smiles. "It's good to have you back."

"Hmm, I know when someone compliments me like that it means they need me to forgo my beauty sleep and pay a visit to a hospital, perhaps?" Lemon asks.

"You know me so well. Lunch later?" Inspector Abley asks Lemon.

"You're not going to suggest at the golf club, are you? In your new wheels?" Lemon replies.

"They're just on a month's trial. And, what do you take me for? Much better than that. Can we also talk to the Fellows who were at the dinner? Especially in the English department. The poetry experts. Looking forward to that," Abley says, lifting a textbook on English literature from the side, then sighing.

Lemon leaves and Abley has one last look around. He picks up the album cover, now in an evidence bag on the side and looks at Hugo, centre stage in the photograph. His eyes then wander to the two other young men either side. He thinks they look so young, but also cocky and a little too confident in the photograph. Abley wonders if they were with Hugo Grader last night.

14
LANDING CARPET

Godric has fallen asleep on the landing carpet outside his nanna's bedroom. As he closed his eyes earlier, he decided he had wanted to be there when Bunny came out, to apologise for whatever it was he had done before. Surrounded by dogs, stretched out asleep by his side, they long since stole the duvet from his legs. Had it not been for Godric's phone persistently beeping, there he would have remained until at least midday. He finally stirs to find ten missed calls from Nisha. He messages her and says he cannot speak right now. Truth is, he is too tired. Godric sits up against the hall wall and doesn't know what to do when she messages back. Reading her message, he cannot believe his eyes.

"Bunny, are you awake?" he whispers to her bedroom door. "Someone is dead? From the Valentine's Banquet last night. You don't know him. I'm going to find out what's happened. Call if you need me. I'll be at Christina's." Godric expects his nanna to open her door. Surely, this is serious enough to shake her into action. He stands up and waits, listening. Nothing. He tries to convince himself that she is asleep, but only half believes it, "If you're awake, I'll be back soon. I have to go and see for myself." He listens but still nothing. "I'll leave a cup of tea on the landing."

Godric reads more messages from Nisha. One says, 'I need you more than ever now.' What does she mean? And, 'Darcy is sending me messages saying she's watching me'. Godric doesn't know what Nisha is talking about, so replies 'What?' Then another message pops up from Nisha saying, 'We got into a spat about the play. She's really mean. I don't think I can work on the play anymore. I want to go home.' He tries to call Nisha, but her phone goes to voicemail, so writes 'Pick up!', but nothing when he tries again.

Godric can feel the stress building in his body and feels sick. He runs down the stairs, shoves the kettle on, plops water in a cup with a peppermint tea bag, then leaves it on the landing by his nanna's door. He knocks. Nothing. So, he heads back downstairs, grabs a coat and shuts the front door behind him.

*

In Professor Elizabeth Green's bedroom, tears well up in her eyes in the dark. One runs down her face and drips onto the duvet. She finally shuts her eyes.

15
COLLEGE LIBRARY

It is very late at night or very early the next morning now in Christina College, depending upon your persuasion. Some are tucked up in their rooms, either blissfully unaware of the dark events that have happened around them, or trying to get some shut-eye still a little poorly themselves. The corridors, however, are slowly coming back to life as police begin to knock on student doors. Lights start to flicker on from windows in Bramble and Whisper Court.

One Don is wide awake. Standing waiting among the book stacks in the College library on the first floor of the Mitre Building, checking his watch every few minutes. Finally, the College library door creaks open, and Professor Barclay hears the footsteps he is expecting and hoping for.

"Stop phoning me," Miles Bonneville storms in, raising his voice to Professor Barclay.

"We had to speak."

"It's late. What can't wait? I've just lost my best friend.

Didn't you hear the police cars? They knocked down my door," Miles says, still glaring at Professor Barclay.

"You're not ill?" Barclay asks.

"Hugo is dead!"

Barclay tries not to react.

"No, I'm glad, that's all. That you are well. Me too, peculiarly. I tend to suffer most common ailments."

"What do you want?" Miles asks.

"With so many going down. I had to talk to you, before anyone else. About the theatre."

"You don't seem bothered that your precious College has lost an undergraduate. Your pupil," Miles waves his hands about at Barclay.

"You should play the lead now, you must. I had to talk to you before everyone assembles." Barclay ignores the news.

"What are you on? Who's going to think about a play? My friend is dead! He was Romeo. He was the play! He was alive! I was with him." Miles swipes some books on the floor from a trolley, angry at even being here.

"Shh, it's a library," Barclay says, stepping back a little. "I'm just saying, now there's no Hugo, there's a gap. It would look good for the College. Now you're not leaving I presume?"

"How d'you know what I'm doing?" Miles is surprised that Professor Barclay seems to know his business, adding, "What's it to you? Yes, I am definitely leaving. Straight after Godric's play. Can't wait."

"But, this band of yours. It can't continue now, surely?" Barclay is taken aback.

"You seem completely unphased by the news? Hugo is dead. What are you on?" Miles looks at Professor Barclay with anger and confusion. He starts to walk away.

"Wait!" Professor Barclay shouts. "D'you know the stakes I'm talking about? We need a strong lead to woo high donors."

"You need to think about something other than your

new theatre. It's just a few sticks in the ground. Get over it. And Shh," Miles replies.

"It's never going to happen, your music. You'll be sticking around. You need to help me. I made you."

"Is that a threat?" Miles glares. "Just watch us."

"You have to play Romeo if you know what's good for you."

"So, you are threatening me."

"You didn't act, didn't perform. You owe me. This play has to go ahead. And now, with you as the lead. We stand a better chance of convincing them."

"I owe you nothing!" Miles spits at Professor Barclay before storming out.

16
TIME FOR QUESTIONS

Sergeant Lemon has got his Constables knocking on student rooms and walking up staircases of sleeping young things. At first, just a few trickle into the dining hall, feeling a sense of déjà vu, some having been interviewed only hours ago. But it isn't long before the place looks like one big pyjama party, with dressing gowns and slippers everywhere.

Godric arrives back at College, still wearing the same beanie hat, guessing that if Nisha was correct, he would find out more here. Then he spots Inspector Bob Abley and Sergeant Lemon. Godric's heart sinks when he sees them standing outside the Banquet Hall, about to go in. The news must be true. But more, why are they here? Didn't Hugo Grader just die from whatever is making Godric feel so ill? And what are the Inspector and Sergeant doing here? He doesn't have the stomach for this. Wants to make a hasty retreat. Now he's seen the truth for himself. Godric wants to take to his bed for a couple of days. But Sergeant Lemon spots him and points, causing

Inspector Abley to glance across. Godric nods and with heavy heart and feet, starts to walk over. He is pleased to see them, but also still feeling poorly and sick to his stomach for Hugo. He hopes they are not going to make him speak.

"Did you have a good New Year?" Inspector Bob Abley asks, smiling and patting Godric on the back.

"Yes, Happy New Year, Inspector. Too late?"

"Just a tad," Lemon replies.

"You're back then," Godric asks, "for good?"

"Can't keep me away," Sergeant Lemon nods.

"Shame it is under these circumstances we meet," Godric tries to raise a smile, but it doesn't make it up to his eyes.

"Did you tell your, did you tell Elizabeth?" Inspector Abley asks, noticing Godric looks like he is still in formal clothes. "You don't look so good yourself. Have you been checked out yet?"

"I can't believe it. I whispered it through the door, but she didn't stir. I thought I'd come to see if it was really true first. Is it?" Godric looks at the door where a Constable is standing talking to a SOCO. "I was just with him. And why are the police here? We've all just been so ill?"

"With Mr Hugo Grader?" Abley asks.

"Yes, Hugo. But I left. I mean he was very much alive when I left. He was bonkers drunk, but just having fun. Celebratory, in fact."

"Celebratory?" Lemon questions.

"Just a state of his life, I think? Blessed people are always celebrating, aren't they? Outwardly, at least," Godric replies.

"What time did you leave?" Abley asks.

"I'm not sure. Didn't check my phone. Had to leave in a hurry, why?" Godric begins to feel very queasy.

"Who told you?" Inspector Abley nods.

"Oh, Nisha. Friend of mine. I think you might have

met her at hospital already? That was my hurry. Getting her to one of the ambulances. A rather crazy night, might I say. People dropping like flies. What happened?"

"Thought you were a Bene't's man?" Lemon says, knowing it to be the case.

"Valentine's Banquet. Invited. Hugo's in my play." Godric, feeling rather weak, leans against the Banquet Hall wall outside, his coat now in the ivy growing up around the windows, his face almost disappearing into the greenery.

"Play?" Lemon asks "I thought your forte, and the Inspector's, was pantomime?" Lemon smirks quietly about the Christmas panto from Oxford last year.

"Ah, yes. Inspector Abley looked very good in that get up," Godric smiles, adding, "No, this is at the Swan Theatre here. Romeo and Juliet. Opening night's Valentine's Day–" Godric pauses. "Or, least it's supposed to be." He rubs his hair, then his forehead trying to think, "I'm directing. Though I don't know what I'll do now. Hugo was Romeo. Not that it matters. It's just a play, I mean, isn't it? When someone's–" Godric opens his eyes wide and sighs, leaning down to put his hands on his knees for a moment.

"Right. What else can you tell us about last night and seeing Mr Hugo Grader?" Lemon asks. Abley leans into Godric, concerned about the state of him, and props him up a little.

"A bunch of us went back to Hugo's room. Rooms. Had an after-party. Soirée. Just a few of us in involved with the play I suppose. It was billed as 'more booze at mine'."

"What time was this?" Abley asks. "Why don't you sit?" Abley points to a bench just behind. "It's a shock."

"Like I said, I don't know. Not that late. After dinner. We didn't stay for the Banquet music, some fresher band. Hugo said they were dire," Godric sits, taking out a cigarette from his coat pocket. "I've no idea."

"Was he taking any illegal substances?" Sergeant

Lemon asks.

"No idea on that either. They move in different circles. I mean, there's money, and there's that kind of money. Presume he could get anything he wanted. He was pretty sloshed anyway," Godric begins to feel uncomfortable with the line of questioning.

"Were you taking any illegal substances?" Lemon spots cigarette papers in Godric's cigarette tin.

"What?" Godric lights a cigarette.

"Were you taking any illegal substances, Godric?" Abley adds, raising his eyebrows.

"Whisky. Very expensive as it happens from the label on the decanter. So that can't be the thing making me feel so wretched." Godric pauses. "D'you think I'm ill with the same thing that killed Hugo? I mean, it's likely, isn't it? Why not the others? Why just Hugo, Nisha and me?" Godric doesn't like the Inspector probing him like this when he feels so ropey.

"Well, we're investigating any possible links, with the high number of undergraduates needing medical attention. But we cannot talk about that with you. You know that." Inspector Abley smiles at Godric, not able to share with him what they already know, and sits down next to him on the bench.

"Have you been in touch with my Nanna recently?" Godric takes a long drag from his cigarette and scuffs his shoes in the gravel below the bench, looking out in front across the College lawns and back towards the Lodge.

"No, why?" Abley asks.

"Just wondered," Godric exhales dramatically.

"Why?" Abley senses Godric's concern.

"Just wondered if she'd been working for you at all since Christmas? She's not said anything to me. But then the play's kept me pretty busy," Godric explains, trying not to show how worried he is about his nanna.

"We did ask her to double-check a case that went to court over some warehouses leaking poison, but she declined. Said not her area," Lemon replies.

"When was that?" Godric asks.

"Oh, couple of weeks ago. Maybe three?" Lemon says.

"Oh, I didn't see her for that?" Abley replies unconcerned, adding, "but she did buy me a bathroom mirror, one of those magnifying ones. Popped it into reception. No idea what that was about. I guess she knows I've moved. House warming?" Abley suggests. Lemon and Godric look at each other, then glance slyly at Abley's new shaggy beard. Lemon stifles a laugh. Godric takes another drag of his cigarette, to avoid a momentary chuckle.

"How do you think Hugo died?" Godric asks, exhaling smoke.

"It's an open investigation. We can't talk to you or anyone about the case. Could be natural causes. Ruling nothing out. If you know him, saw him, you're in the mix," Abley shrugs.

"In the mix?" Godric coughs. "You mean this wasn't natural death?" Godric feels sick again. Sick to the bone. He puts his head between his knees and inhales on his cigarette.

"There are so many possibilities, Godric." Abley rubs his hands together, now feeling the cold sitting here with Godric. "If you're feeling poorly, you should stub that out."

"He was very healthy. I mean, he was a gym bunny and had a powerful voice. Bit too in your face sometimes. Never took my note to modulate and moderate. Bit late now," Godric says, rubbing his forehead again then taking another drag on his cigarette. "In the mix? What does that mean?"

"You may have been one of the last people to see Hugo Grader. That makes you, well, in the mix," Inspector Bob Abley sighs.

"What are you saying?" Godric looks up at Sergeant Lemon to see if what he is hearing from Inspector Abley can be true, then back at Bob Abley.

"I just work with facts, Godric. You must know that by now," Abley looks at Godric right in the eye, which unnerves Godric somewhat.

"Could it have been suicide?" Godric asks, "Pressure and whatnot."

Abley and Lemon glance at each other, knowing they can't tell Godric what they already saw in Hugo's room earlier.

"With all that money?" Abley replies.

"It's all relative," Godric suggests. "He had a lot going on. His band, he was leaving Cambridge to go on tour. Pressure?" Godric says.

"Your friend, Nisha Acharya-Gorpade. Does she go to this College?" Sergeant Lemon shifts the conversation.

"Yes." Godric exhales.

"Can you find her? We'd like to speak with her." Sergent Lemon walks closer to Godric and pulls out his phone. "If you have her number?"

"She's probably still at hospital. I'm sure you will have already if the police have been there. She said they were."

"I'd like to speak with her. You didn't go with her?"

"Her friend took her, Lance Fernard." Godric pulls out his phone, obliging Lemon with their phone numbers, as he can see they are not going to give up.

"We need to find him too," Abley emphasises.

"What if she's asleep. She was very ill," Godric says.

"Wake her up," Abley replies.

Godric gets up from the bench, nods, then starts to walk off.

"Oh, and Godric? Don't go anywhere," Abley adds.

"What?"

"Until we know what type of investigation this is, I have to ask you not to leave Cambridge," Abley says.

"You're joking," Godric pulls a face to show his shock.

"Do I look like I'm joking?" Inspector Abley opens out

his arms in an effort to make it feel more friendly. But as Godric walks off, thrown by Inspector Abley and Sergeant Lemon, he feels worse than he did when he arrived. Surely, his friendship should put him above any suspicion, if there is suspicion, which it feels like there is. Even though they didn't say. Don't they know yet? The cause of death?

Sergeant Lemon pulls back the heavy oak door to the Banquet Hall.

"You don't suspect him, do you?" Lemon asks Inspector Abley as they start to enter.

"Friend or not, he has to be a person of interest, like all the others who were with this Hugo Grader before he died. Glad you came back?" Abley looks at Lemon. Lemon sighs then smiles at Abley. Strangely, despite the circumstances, Lemon is pleased to see and be working with his favourite Inspector again.

Godric looks back as they disappear into the Hall. His heart turns over. Hugo. The crazy, mad, loud, often drunk bag of noise of a man. Godric couldn't say that Hugo Grader was his friend. Different College, different social group. But through the play, he had gotten to know him. Seen that he was a good egg. And talented to boot. His music, his performances. A live wire. Funny. Fun. Godric can't believe it. Feels like he's been too wrapped up himself in feeling unwell. Now he knows what it must be like for his Bunny. Turning up to these things to help the police. But she only comes when there has been foul play. So, why did they ask if she knew about this?

17
PRETTY LITTLE DAISIES

Professor Elizabeth Green sits up and swings her legs over the bed, the room still in semi-darkness, just a small table light on across the other side of the room near the door. She slowly stands up and walks into the ensuite bathroom, her legs stiff, her hands and feet cold. But she cannot feel a thing. Instead, she turns on the bathroom light, which now also spills out into the bedroom and onto her wardrobe.

Elizabeth opens the wardrobe door and separates some of the hangers until she spots an item covered in a dry-cleaning cover. She lifts the hook and lays the garment on the bed. Gently, she starts to slide a cream chiffon dress with pretty little daisies out of the protective sheath. Once she has laid the dress out on the bed, she then turns back to the wardrobe and searches the bottom for a box. She lifts out a shoebox and perches again on the side of the bed before opening the box on her lap. Inside are a pair of tiny heeled cream shoes, with a strap and button across the top. They look like they are made of silk, but Elizabeth knows Gerald would have known better than to buy her something which exploits any animal. Next to them is a handwritten note, which reads: 'You are all the flowers in the meadow'. A tear escapes onto Elizabeth's cheek. She takes the shoes out of the box and holds them tight to her chest, before collapsing back onto the bed, the shoe box falling to the floor.

18
FOUNTAINS AND DRAINS

Inside the walls of Christina College, in Whisper Court, Miles Bonneville sits on the edge of the fountain, his feet – still in shoes – immersed in the cold water. The Court is quiet, just a few lights on from student windows, those who are still awake after the events of the evening or police questioning in the small hours. Miles pulls at his hair, his eyes closed, his jacket open to the night air. He doesn't hear Dr Guinevere Trotsham approach, so flinches when he feels her hand on his shoulder and leans away as she crouches down next to him on the fountain wall.

"I'm so sorry," she says, then leaves a long pause before adding, "I can't believe it. So many have been taken to hospital."

"He seemed fine. Drunk but fine. Everyone was worried about Nisha, not Hugo. I know Lance went with her to the ambulance. Have you seen her? She's not answering her phone." Miles asks, but Dr Trotsham shakes her head. Miles gets out his phone and texts Nisha again.

"Maybe everyone was poisoned. I mean accidentally.

The water? The police are here. Have they spoken to you yet?" Dr Guinevere Trotsham asks.

"Hugo doesn't drink water. Have you seen his wine bill?" Miles nods about the police.

"But you're alright?" Guinevere leans in.

"Of course, I'm alright. Why? Why am I alright?"

"I don't know, nor what to say," she replies. "But you won't be if you keep your feet in ice-cold water."

"I should have stopped him drinking. He'd had way too much. We argued. But he was happy. We were all happy. Why has this happened?" Miles asks, still pulling at his hair.

"Sometimes life makes no sense, and those with the brightest lights burn out the fastest."

"I can't stay here. Not now," he says.

"Sleep on it."

"I can't be alone. Will you walk me to my room?" Miles puts his hand on Guinevere's thigh.

"I don't think that's a good idea in the circumstances. D'you?" she replies.

Miles splashes her with water as he lifts his feet out of the fountain. Guinevere watches him disappear around the corner. She cannot understand why he blows so hot and cold like this.

19
A GRANDSON'S LOVE

Godric opens the front door now in the small hours of the morning, exhausted. He has come home with more questions than answers and is so tired that he feels ill again. The death of Hugo Grader has sobered him up without a doubt. But whatever poisoned him last night is still in his system. He looked everywhere for Nisha while at Christina's earlier – as she had apparently been discharged from hospital – but couldn't find her. Nisha has been ignoring her phone for a while, so Godric decided home was the best place for now.

Godric is greeted by three happy dogs, who have clearly been sleeping in the downstairs hallway, perhaps waiting for him to return, probably aware that things are not right. As he opens the door, they can see that it is still dark outside, and cold, so make no attempt to rush out. Godric walks into the kitchen and gets out a pint glass and fills it with water. He opens the cupboard doors, looking for sugar to settle his shakes and finds some bourbon biscuits. He picks up the packet, turns up the heating, then walks to the back garden to let the dogs out. They are very quick to do their business as it is so cold, and he shuts the French windows again, walks back into the kitchen to get them all dog treats, then wanders upstairs to go to bed.

He thinks he will leave his nanna until the morning. But, when he gets to the top of the stairs, he spots the cup of tea he made her earlier still there, and the light under her bedroom door again still on. It is making him anxious, and he can feel beads of sweat on his forehead.

"Bunny?" Godric watches as a shadow moves across the light spilling from under the door, "Are you okay?" He waits for a reply and tries the door, but it is still locked. "Can you open the door, please? This is really freaking me out. What if you're being held at knifepoint?" Godric waits, but gets no reply. He stands still for some minutes but then decides that if his nanna is in trouble, any intruder would have to be keeping impossibly quiet. He realises she is alone and choosing to remain silent.

Godric cannot seem to drag himself away from his nanna's door. The dogs jumping and bumping around him, he slides down the hall wall, finding the duvet where he left it. He pulls it up around him. Well, if she isn't going to speak, then she can't stop him from doing so. He needs to talk her. He doesn't know what to do and he needs his nanna.

"You'll not believe the night I've had." Godric takes a small sip of water. "I told you, someone's died at Christina's. Hugo. One minute he was okay, then. I've just got back. No one knows what he died of. It's just terrible. I was just with him, Bunny. He was so alive. He was talking about finding love, or action at least. Had petals on his bed. Bit of a romantic at heart, I think. He quoted Wordsworth at supper. He was as mad as a box of frogs." Godric pauses, utterly sad about the silence back. "Now he's gone. I can't believe it. And the police were funny with me. Bob. Told me not to go anywhere. Lemon asked if I was on drugs. Just because I was with Hugo before he died." Godric pauses. "Bunny, he's dead. My Romeo. What can I do? What would you do? How can I help to make this all better?"

Godric pauses again while cuddling the dogs. If only his nanna would say something. He wonders if she cannot hear, so starts to speak more loudly. "Apparently, about a hundred people have gone down with something too, likely the same thing. I've been sick a few times. About thirty or so were taken to hospital. Some are talking about something in the water?" Godric looks at his water glass. "Who'd put something in the water? It could have been in the pipes maybe. You know, lead poisoning, some were saying. A lot of plumbing is ancient in Christina's." Godric looks at his nanna's door and listens again. But everything is quiet behind. "They could do with you to find out what they've all taken. Get them better. I couldn't find any of the drama bods when I looked for them. No Nisha, Darcy, Miles, Lance. They've all disappeared into thin air. No one's answering their phones."

Godric pulls out his phone to see if Nisha has called since he last checked. He sees that she has messaged him just now and mentions that Lance has 'taken me to his private doctor in London to get checked over'. That she's back tomorrow and that she'll 'see you at rehearsals hopefully'. Rehearsals? Really? He thinks. Godric replies by message, saying 'That's a long way?', but Nisha just responds, 'I was too weak to fight him off. He insisted. Kind.'

Godric drops his phone on the landing carpet. He can't keep his eyes open and lays down with the dogs. His eyes shut, just as the sun is coming up. He hopes Nisha is going to be okay.

*

A few hours later, Hector, Monty and Clive can't wait any longer and start to paw at Godric until he wakes, wanting both food and garden comfort breaks. Godric peels open his eyes. His nanna's bedroom door is still shut. His strong, determined and reliably always there for him nanna, is acting very strangely. Very strangely indeed.

20
SWAN THEATRE

The next morning and Godric opens the double doors to the Swan Theatre on Park Street. He climbs the stairs, his head throbbing from whatever poisons still lurk in his body from the night before, his heart uneasy about what happened to Hugo.

Godric's keen to come into this 'so called' dress rehearsal to catch up with Nisha, but also the others, and call time on the play. Walking over to the theatre this morning, he has decided that no matter how much he wants to put on Romeo and Juliet at Valentine's, this is not the right moment anymore. His heart is breaking, but, more important, he just needs to see the cast and crew to check that they are all alive and well. That Nisha is okay. It is all too close to home. Godric wants to look into their eyes and experience any shared understanding of the past twenty four hours and this insanely terrible event. Surely, there will be some comfort they can take from each other?

As Godric walks through the bar to get to the dressing room, he sees Alex standing behind it, wiping up glasses.

"Watcha," Alex beams. Probably unaware of the news, Godric thinks.

"Hello, you good?" Godric stops, allowing Alex time to speak, in case he needs to share anything about the bar or production.

"Yeah, really bad about Hugo," Alex replies, far too chirpily for Godric to comprehend.

"Oh, it's just that you smiled, like you're happy. Thought you might not know," Godric replies, a little confused.

"I was smiling at you. You know, a ray of sunshine on a dark day." Alex does his signature trick with two glasses. He throws two full drinks in the air and, juggling, swaps them around in each hand in mid-air without spilling a drop.

"Yep." Godric tries not to look too impressed as he glances back at Alex, whose grin is now spread wide across his face. Even in the midst of all this, someone somewhere is always thinking about hanky panky, Godric thinks. Godric looks at Alex's dimples and even on this awful day, cannot help but smile back. A moment of sanity, he thinks, in all this.

Then a thought passes across Godric's mind, bringing him back to earth. He remembers how he finished with Ben before Christmas, for saying that little four-letter word. How could Ben spoil it like that, and try to get all sentimental and gushy? He liked him for cripes sake. He still feels bad. Has seen Ben since, once or twice, walking to the Grads Café.

Godric then thinks about the hunk he met immediately afterwards. That strong, tall chap in the Panto, back over Christmas in Oxford. Quite the surprise. Witty and handsome. Such a rare find. But no. Too far away. He's not old enough to do long distance. Not yet. No, perhaps Alex is just what he needs. This doe eyed, beardy – and quite frankly rough looking – young man with his dimples and beaming smile. Alex, who is clearly giving him the eye. Where did this come from? Godric can't help himself. He looks back at Alex and holds his gaze just that little bit longer than is usual. After turning on his heels, Godric then tries to straighten his hair as he leaves the bar and heads backstage, to prepare himself for what he is about to walk into. The seriousness of the day comes crashing back.

*

When Godric opens the dressing room door, the first thing that hits him is the quiet. It's most unusual. The other day he had been greeted by a cacophony of argument and sniping, so much that he had a sore throat after he left, having to bark notes at them all.

Darcy is sitting on Miles's lap in the corner, looking at her hair in the mirror and fiddling with her fringe. Lance is looking in the mirror and has started to put on make-up. This is a dress rehearsal.

"Are you okay?" Godric spots Nisha and walks over, hugging his friend. "I was so worried about you. Why d'you want to go home?" Then teasing, "I hope you weren't allergic to the corsage."

"It's such a shock. Hard to stay with everything coming crashing down." Nisha tries to smile, and, "Oh, no! I lost your flower. I don't know when?" Godric notices how pale she looks. She adds, "I was lucky–" Nisha can't finish her sentence, but she is thinking how lucky compared to Hugo.

'I'm just glad you're okay. I thought if Lance was with you, you wouldn't need us both. But I'm sorry I wasn't there. I was throwing up." Godric strokes Nisha's arm. He spots an unopened bottle of water and reaches for it to give Nisha.

"He's been a dear. Took me to Harley Street. I slept on the back seat all the way there and back. I'm so tired." Nisha looks at Lance further along the dressing room, then back at Godric. "How are you feeling now?"

"Much better," Godric lies, nodding frantically, "thank you for coming." Nisha shakes her head and takes a sip of water. They hug again for the longest time, glad they have both survived whatever just happened, and sad for Hugo.

Godric looks at Hugo's chair in the dressing room and feels a somersault in the pit of his stomach. "I just can't believe it. Hugo. He was just here. To be honest, I don't know why we're all here?" Godric looks into Nisha's eyes. "I thought I'd better turn up in case others did. I can see some of the troupe and crew are only just finding out now. I suppose now we have everyone here we can see how people feel. In the circumstances, it feels like cancelling is the right thing to do."

"What? No! The show must go on!" Darcy overhears Godric and jumps off Miles's lap to come over.

"Well, I thought I'd ask everyone first, honey. How are you?" Godric replies to Darcy, a little surprised that, like Alex, she appears unphased by the gravity of the situation.

"They're here, aren't they? Shows everyone wants to do it. We're all ready. Don't put a spanner in the works. This isn't your play, you know," Darcy replies. "You're just a director."

"Darcy." Godric is irked by her pushy nature and surprised by her lack of compassion for Hugo.

"Well, just get it over with then. Say what you've got to say. But I bet most want to continue," Darcy shrugs.

"If I can have your attention for a moment." Godric feels corralled into speaking but is also interested in what everyone feels. He looks at the packed dressing room, actors still chatting.

"Oi! Shut up you rabble!" Darcy shouts.

"Right," Godric is not happy with Darcy's abrupt order and pauses for a moment and then leans back and sits on the dressing room makeup counter. "We're all completely devastated by the news this morning of Hugo's death. It's beyond tragic. I know a lot of us are still only just finding out. I completely understand if people need to go." Godric pauses, allowing any to leave the room if they choose, if him speaking is too much for them. After a moment, when he can see no one is leaving, he continues. "For those of us here this morning," Godric pauses again, then adds, "Perhaps it might be appropriate to have a couple of minutes silence for Hugo. Together. To mark this moment as one." Godric shuts his eyes and notices the room has fallen silent. The peace is enough to make him feel a little calmer. He takes a breath and embraces the moment, trying to come to terms with the past twenty four hours.

As Godric remains in silence, he tries to think about Hugo. Who was he, really? A live wire, irreverent, verging on the illegal. A large, strong man. Gone. Godric cannot fathom it. His mind wanders to the room and the people around him. He can hear them breathing. Godric begins to panic. How can he direct a play with the leading man taken? With this hanging over it. He has to close the production. The room remains silent. He worries about his nanna. Why won't she speak to him? His day could not be worse. Then he feels guilty. He could be Hugo. It could be worse.

After what must have been more like two and a half minutes, Godric finally opens his eyes and can see most have done the same. Nisha nods at him. Godric decides to say a few more words.

"Some who knew Hugo very well and were close friends are in the room today. I'm grateful people have turned up this morning, but would have completely understood if you hadn't." He pauses some more, then adds, "But here we are. If anyone needs to talk about what's happened, I'm here." There are murmurs of 'big shock', 'too young' and 'so sad'. "At least we have each other," he adds. Godric then continues, "I'm in two minds whether to cancel the performance in the light of the terrible news, out of respect. It somehow feels inappropriate to be having fun." There are some sighs, and Darcy bellows an "ugh", very loudly.

So Godric says, "On the other hand, I wondered if by carrying on with the play, it might bring some sense of routine for us all. Give us a purpose? Do people think we should do it in honour of Hugo?" Godric isn't convinced of his own words, but feels the room support the idea, and sees some quiet nods. "Although I didn't know Hugo as well as some of you here, I was beginning to get to know him," Godric says, looking around the room, then continuing, "He would have said he probably didn't care what we did, as he has gone. But then would have wanted us to do what made us happy. Happy, in these circumstances isn't the right emotion. But the play might bring us and those watching it something positive, at least. So, I can't make the decision alone. I want to turn it over to you. By a simple show of hands, who thinks the play should be cancelled?" A couple of hands go up, including Miles's.

"Are we really doing this?" Darcy shakes her head.

"And who thinks we should carry on?" Godric asks. The majority of the hands in the dressing room go up.

"Thank you," Darcy nods.

"Okay, it looks like we're doing this. Right." Godric pauses, unable to believe what has just happened. "In that case, let's be ready in ten minutes to rehearse. The show must go on." Godric says a little louder, but not feeling it. Godric looks at Nisha, who smiles a little then he watches her leave for the gallery, shaky on her legs.

Godric then walks over to Lance, who is rubbing his head in surprise and bewilderment – having abstained from the vote.

"I'm sorry about Hugo. Like I said. I didn't know him well, but he did seem to be the life and soul," Godric says.

"Thanks. I can't believe it either. You look terrible." Lance looks at Godric's clothes, as it is clear he hasn't changed since last night.

"Right. Slept on the floor," Godric says.

"Don't do that," Lance replies, finishing his stage make-up in the mirror.

"Thank you for Nisha. For looking after her. What did the doctor say? She shouldn't be here. Let alone be about to do lights."

"No problemo. Food poisoning, he thought. She'll be okay. Plenty of water. Yes, she should be in bed. She just wanted me to bring her here. Wouldn't let up until I agreed. Said she didn't want to abandon you," Lance scoffs, looking at Godric in the eye. "Why on earth anyone cares about this wretched play now."

"Quite." Godric says. "That's good news about Nisha. Do you think Hugo died of the same thing that made myself and Nisha ill?"

"No idea, Old Boy," Lance replies.

"It didn't affect us all the same, did it?" Godric wonders again.

"I just have a hangover. If I could have swapped places." Lance looks again at Godric in the mirror.

"The police asked me if we took any illegal substances."

"Ha! What was Hugo not taking?" Lance leans across and opens Hugo's drawer in the dressing room, and they find some of Hugo's drugs.

"You're kidding," Godric's eyes pop open.

"Calm down. Purely recreational. He knew what not to take. He wouldn't have overdosed."

Godric looks in the drawer at what looks like at least six different types of drugs. He shuts the drawer dramatically. "Does this thing have a lock?" Godric looks around to see if anyone else saw inside. Then moving away, he wanders along the dressing room until he gets to Miles.

"Ten minutes, everyone!" Godric shouts back up the length of the dressing room. Then Godric turns to Miles. "Can I have a word?" Godric moves closer to the chair where Miles is still sitting. Miles pushes Darcy away. She huffs then, using the mirror, starts to put on some thick red costume lipstick.

"What is it, Director?"

"I need you to play Romeo." Godric looks Miles directly in the eye.

"I did wonder. I'm not keen. Thought maybe you'd step into the breach?" Miles ripostes. What about Lance? He can do it?"

"You know the part. You read lines with Hugo all the time. Don't think I didn't notice how you helped him."

"He's my mate. Please don't make me do it," Miles tilts his head to one side and then lets it fall onto his chest dramatically.

"Of course not. We'll find someone else." The last thing Godric wants to do is pressure Hugo's friend right now. But he has no idea who could do this.

"Hugo would want you to do it," Darcy urges Miles, "do it for him."

"The pressure is just too much," Miles replies.

"Dear boy, what are you pillocking on about? Do the ruddy show. Then we can get out of here with heads held high," Lance interjects across his shoulder, hearing the conversation from his seat across the dressing room.

"Looks like I'm bloody Romeo then," Miles sighs, "but it doesn't feel right."

"Okay, well, thank you. I know you'll do your best," Godric suggests.

"He'll do better than that. He'll pull it out and wave it about," Lance says.

"Do you feel ill?" Godric asks Miles.

"I'm okay. Are we really honestly doing this? Shouldn't we cancel anyway?" Miles says quietly.

"I know, but we'd have to give all those tickets back I suppose. This place does need it," Godric suggests, not convinced by his own words.

"Hey! We're doing this. The show must go on."

Darcy waves her brush in their faces.

"And your agent is coming," Lance replies, snatching her brush off her. "You're beautiful enough."

"I just can't see why we're arsing about with a play when our friend is dead?!" Miles flounces off the chair, then storms out.

"Don't worry. He's just getting into character. Want me to have a word?" Godric nods at Lance's offer to help. Lance sighs and follows Miles out onto the stage.

"He'd better bloody do it. We've been rehearsing this for two weeks," Darcy replies, slamming her way out of the dressing room.

Godric is left alone, staring at himself in the mirror. He notices his eyes are bloodshot from a night sleeping on the landing. He takes out his mobile and phones home. He hears the ringing and imagines the dogs going berserk around the telephone table in the hallway. He hopes his nanna will pick up, but it clicks onto answerphone. He listens to his nanna's recorded voice. Reassuring. Comforting. How she lets people know the number they have just called, including the dialling code. Who does that in the twenty first century anymore? Who else, but his Bunny? Godric cuts the call, sighs and leaves the dressing room.

*

Nisha Acharya-Gorpade is at her tech station, behind a glass window elevated above the back row of seats in the stalls. She places a spotlight on Darcy who is now dressed in full Juliet costume and make up. Darcy is standing beside a photographer, who has come in - prearranged – to get shots of her in full costume for her would be agent.

"Nisha! I'm in shadow!" Darcy shouts. Nisha turns up the lights to dazzle. She spots Dr Guinevere Trotsham walking down the aisle towards the stage. No one is pleased to see her, least of all Miles.

"What are you doing here?" he hisses.

"I've come to lend a hand in the circumstances," Dr Trotsham replies.

"Interfere more like. Bugger off," Miles says quietly as she approaches the stage.

"You only have a few days before opening. You can use all the help."

"Stop patronising," Miles replies.

"Hello, Dr Trotsham?" Godric walks over, surprised to see her.

"Just came to lend a hand," Dr Trotsham shrugs.

"We really have it covered," Godric suggests.

"Let me watch a rehearsal before I go then. It's the least I can do. Most unusually, I have a free morning. They've cancelled lessons and lectures today, because of the College sickness."

"Let's just get on with it then, shall we?" Godric says, returning to his seat in the stalls.

"I'm not doing anything with her here." Miles stamps his foot.

"I'm Deputy Head of your faculty. You can't speak about me like that." Dr Trotsham replies, going to sit a row or two behind Godric.

"I'll speak how the hell I like. I'm off after this."

"Please! Everyone. From the top!" Godric cuts across the argument aware but choosing to ignore the frisson between them. There is enough to deal with today. He gets up to wander back up the aisle, deciding to watch from the tech booth.

"How do they look?" He asks Nisha as he reaches her.

"Are you okay?" Nisha asks, still looking pale herself.

"Is anyone or anything okay now?"

21
COLLEGE GARDENS

It's a cold, crisp morning along The Backs. The trees, their spines exposed, hang still against a clear pale blue sky. Ducks deftly dodge the occasional brave souls who have elected to take out a punt. Laden with blankets, the silhouettes of lovers drift quietly by.

Professor Barclay has called Dr Guinevere Trotsham to the site of the new theatre in Christina College's back gardens. He wants to talk to her out of earshot of other snooping Fellows. He saved the heart shaped bunting from last night's Banquet and is currently stretching it along the line of stakes to make the spot more noticeable, moving a few stakes out wider to make the foundation space bigger on the lawn.

"Just making it stand out," Barclay suggests.

"What am I looking at that was so urgent that I had to leave rehearsals? Rehearsals you asked me to attend in the first place," Dr Trotsham says, still a little out of breath from rushing over from the Swan Theatre.

"It's the foundations. Oh, my theatre will rival The Globe. Even more splendid for these surroundings. At one with nature," Barclay replies, pleased with himself.

"Yes, I saw you had the gardener to stake it out last night." Trotsham looks around the dormant garden. Just a few early daffodils out. "A theatre is hardly going to save the birds or bees is it. Has the College actually given final approval for you to take this land?"

"It's happening," Barclay replies without a shred of doubt in his voice.

"They said they wouldn't put in a penny. They haven't, have they?" Dr Trotsham asks.

"They will. When I get the funding from the high donors, they're bound to match it. It's a cert now that Miles Bonneville will be Romeo. He will be Romeo, won't he? Tell me the director saw sense."

"Yes." Trotsham wonders how Barclay could have been so sure. "You really didn't like that Hugo boy. Poor boy."

"We will get it, once we have the final donations coming in," Barclay says, ignoring her words, and then looking at Dr Trotsham suspiciously, adding, "You're on board with this, aren't you?"

"If you think it is needed, then yes. But, don't you still need a lot of donations or investment?"

"Why do you sound so unconvinced?"

"It's nothing, it's–"

"Spit it out."

"Well, won't it undermine the funds the College currently provide to the Swan Theatre?" Dr Trotsham asks.

"And?"

"Will this theatre of yours do as much for the local community?"

"Dr Trotsham." Professor Barclay scowls, "I hope it will feed the souls of the great."

Guinevere Trotsham looks at Professor Barclay disapprovingly, but says nothing. She is interrupted by Inspector Abley's approach across the Bridge, waving at them both.

"Mapping out another croquet lawn are we, Sir?" Inspector Bob Abley asks Professor Barclay.

"And whom might be inquiring? This is not a public space. You might like to exit the College to walk along Queen's Road." Barclay makes the assumption he has run into a 'townie' judging from the clothing the Inspector is wearing, and points up an avenue of trees which would take the Inspector back to the public footpath. Inspector Abley has clocked this Fellow before he'd even opened his mouth and really cannot be bothered to play alpha males with him this morning, so opens up his badge.

"Inspector Abley. Cambridge Police. Professor Barclay?"

"Yes," Barclay looks at the badge and then back down at his bunting.

"Dr Trotsham, Inspector," Guinevere introduces herself.

"Ah, yes, I need to speak to you both, actually. What's the saying, 'feed two birds with one scone?' A friend of mine is always correcting me on that. Yes well, anyway–"

"Inspector, to what do we owe the great honour?" Barclay interrupts, turning his back on the Inspector, already irritated.

"Ah yes, I was coming to that. It appears neither of you came to the hall last night, as requested, to give statements. I was told you were out here," Abley looks at both the Fellows, who don't reply, so he adds more forcefully, "We're going to have to ask you to come over now. A Constable is waiting in the breakfast hall, if that's what you call it."

"What is this, the Spanish inquisition? I didn't get ill. I saw nothing. That is the end of my statement. I'm far too busy," Barclay scoffs, "apart from the Master wearing that ridiculous red mortarboard. I'll add that in. What was she thinking?"

"Busy doing what, exactly?" Inspector Abley asks.

"Things you wouldn't understand," Barclay replies.

"Well, I'd like you to document those things with one of my Constables in the hall, and we can see if we understand them, can't we. You can choose to speak to our Constable with a degree if you prefer. Oh, hang on. They both have degrees – oh, but in science, not English. In the meantime, I understand the young man who lost his life, Mr Hugo Grader, was a pupil of yours in the Faculty of English?"

"We have a number of students, Inspector. It's called a university. We can't be expected to remember every one of the twenty seven thousand undergraduates attending." Barclay ignores the dig over the arts.

"But only thirty nine study English from your College. This College," Inspector Abley looks at his notebook. "My Constable checked. That is right, isn't it, Sir?"

"There is only one talent among the lot of them, and it certainly wasn't the deceased," Barclay replies.

"You have no contact with your undergraduates in College?" Inspector Abley persists.

"I teach a lot of Professor Barclay's tutorials these days," Dr Trotsham explains.

"She knows more about young men than I do," Barclay adds. Dr Trotsham glowers at Professor Barclay's barbed comment.

"Please excuse Professor Barclay. He does like to exaggerate. As I say, I end up taking most of his classes as he apparently doesn't have time. I knew Mr Grader," Guinevere replies.

"What can you tell me about him?" Abley asks.

"He was unusual in that he was wasting his talent. I don't want to speak ill of the dead, but few who make it to Cambridge choose to throw it all away. They work hard, often too hard. But he was surviving the course only by the seat of his pants, heading for a third. Capable of much more. He didn't seem to care."

"Oh? And, why was that?"

"Because he was a lazy, impertinent, over-privileged wastrel, who made an awful racket in College to boot!" Barclay replies.

"Poor boy. There have been quite a lot of ill students, haven't there," Dr Trotsham adds.

"Yet you are both well?" Inspector Abley observes, watching Professor Barclay continue to stretch bunting around some pegs in the ground.

"Iron constitution," Professor Barclay replies.

"In fact, none of the Fellows were found to have suffered. Apart from the Master," Abley adds. "Strange that?"

"Hmm, that is a turn up. We're all very stressed. I'm surprised," Dr Trotsham replies.

"Well, thank you. What are you doing here?"

"Marking the grounds of a new theatre, Inspector," Dr Trotsham explains.

"Hugo Grader was an actor, I understand? You say not the one you think has any talent?" Abley asks.

"He liked to think so. Few were convinced," Barclay replies.

"He was making his way in the pop industry as well, I hear?" Inspector Abley bends down and pulls at the bunting.

"Don't touch that!" Professor Barclay glares at the Inspector.

"I think the band is more rock-indie," Dr Guinevere Trotsham adds helpfully, "But yes, they would often hold closed College concerts."

"More my bag, music, or film. Not the theatre," Abley replies to Dr Guinevere Trotsham. "Always plays about nineteenth century Russian women, or men stuck on stage unable to move talking about waiting for stuff? I don't get it?"

"And, that is why we need this theatre here," Barclay says, looking at Dr Trotsham.

"I used to go with my wife. She was the theatre buff," Abley continues, missing Barclay's elitist comment to Trotsham. "Drag me to the panto. Or give me Bruce Willis and a box of popcorn any day. You know where you are. Funny plus action, a winning combo. Will you have much of that here?" Abley looks at the pegs and the bunting flapping in the wintery morning and doubts it.

"Thankfully, no," Barclay replies.

"I suppose your College is coughing up for all this?"

"Actually, no," Dr Trotsham answers.

"Ah. I know you Profs like a good scrap over money. Is this anything to do with your theatre?" Abley looks back at the College, intimating all the poorly students.

"I beg your pardon? Do I have to make a call?"

"Excuse me?" Inspector Abley is thrown.

"To your superior? You come in here and start insinuating all sorts of utter drivel."

"Do come to the hall now please." Inspector Bob Abley's tone changes from chatty to firm. "And you can tell my Constable exactly where you were between the hours of eleven last night and one thirty this morning," Abley turns, not waiting for either of them to follow.

*

Inspector Bob Abley walks across Whisper Court in Christina College, the fountain gushing, and onto Bramble Court. He climbs the staircase to Hugo Grader's rooms. Constable Petticoat guards the room, and one SOCO is still inside, gathering more evidence. Inspector Abley points at the albums on the floor.

"Can you pass me some of those?"

"Sir?" The SOCO picks up the vinyl and heads over to the Inspector by the door.

"You mentioned you'd heard of this band, the 'Three Charming Men'. Do they have CDs?"

"No, Sir. But they're online," Constable Petticoat

offers.

"Oh."

"Yes, I went to see them, Sir. Just the once. This, he, well, the lead singer was great. Quite a character. You know, threw himself around in the crowd, kicking amps until they set on fire. Quite the punk. He's got red hair here, but last year it was blue," Petticoat looks at the photograph on the sleeve of the album.

"And that is the way we decide if someone can sing these days? What a hoot. I was told they were rock-indie?"

"I guess, bit of punk too."

"Edgy?"

"Nah, safe really. Most bands are safe these days, aren't they, compared to when you were young," Constable Petticoat replies and chuckles a little. His rosy cheeks glowing.

"I'm not going to argue with that," Abley replies, all of a sudden feeling old.

Inspector Bob Abley spots a flyer for the play Hugo Grader was also in. He indicates to the SOCO to take out an evidence bag and pop it inside. The SOCO then hands it back to the Inspector. Abley looks at Hugo Grader all dressed up as Romeo. He wonders what young man would be a lead singer and a lead actor and now be dead. One who has enemies. But, why is Professor Barclay so scathing of his talents? That is when Inspector Bob Abley notices Godric Cartwright-Green's name as director. Godric did mention that he knows them through the play. He wonders what Professor Elizabeth Green's grandson, his very own police consultant's grandson, may not have told him about last night?

22
BEST FRIEND

In life, everyone needs someone to have their back. Sometimes, it might be the spouse, sometimes it comes down to the dog or cat. That living, breathing creature, human or otherwise, that knows you so well and loves you more than most. Other times it is your best friend. Emily Masters, dressed immaculately in a tight primrose yellow twin set and holding a basket full of food, rings the doorbell at Foxes' Haven. She has had a call from Godric, and so dropped everything. Emily isn't the kind of person to barge into another's castle. After a time knocking, however, and hearing the dogs agitated on the other side, she pulls out a key attached to a diamante Scotty dog keyring and turns the lock.

The first thing Emily notices is the heat. She walks through the house, spots a thermostat on the wall and turns it down, the dogs bounding up to her. Hector stuffs his head into her food basket, and she strokes him and guides him away.

"Where is your Lizzie?" She asks the dogs. "Lizzie?

Elizabeth?" Emily says quietly, from the bottom of the stairs. Nothing. "Professor Elizabeth Green!" She shouts again, louder this time while holding the bannister. Still nothing. Emily walks along the hallway, then pokes her head into what Elizabeth calls 'Godric's den', with all his computers. Nothing. Then she peeps into Gerald's office. Empty. Emily walks through the drawing room and opens the French doors to let in some air into the stuffy home. She walks into the garden to see if Elizabeth is sitting in the greenhouse or her new spinning pod room – which is highly unlikely in the cold this time of year. No Elizabeth. Emily returns to the house, bringing the dogs back in, shuts the French doors then slowly starts to climb the stairs. She knocks quietly on Elizabeth's bedroom door, the dogs having followed her up, still happy to be breaking all the rules today. Emily gets no response, so knocks again quietly.

"Elizabeth, it's me. Open the door, or I shall break it down." Emily waits, "Right, I'm dialling the fire brigade. You could be dying in there." Emily gets out her phone and pretends to dial. "Yes, hello. Please may I have the fire brigade?" Emily pretends to wait to be connected. "Hello. Fire brigade? Thank you. Yes, a friend of mine is trapped in her room. Yes, I'll hold. Yes, the address is—" Emily watches the door open, "Never mind, we've managed to open the door. Thank you, sorry to trouble you. Thank you." Emily pretends to cut the imaginary call.

As Emily enters the room, Elizabeth has already gone back to laying down on the bed. She is dressed in the cream dress with tiny daisies all over and is wearing the shoes from the box. The dogs run in and jump on the bed, so pleased to see Elizabeth, but Emily can sense immediately that it is worse than she thought when Elizabeth doesn't react to the mess they are creating.

"Off! Off! Emily shoos the dogs out of the room, though doesn't notice Bertie and Soot sneak in under her feet before she can shut the bedroom door.

"It is running out," Elizabeth Green tells her friend.

"What is? What's running out?" Emily sits down beside her friend and rubs Elizabeth's back, not happy with her friend's unusually quiet demeanour. Emily sees Elizabeth is holding something and prises open Elizabeth's hand to reveal a small green glass perfume bottle. Elizabeth clings to it like it is about to be snatched from her fingers. Emily doesn't know what to say. For the first time since entering the room, her friend makes eye contact. Emily can see right into Elizabeth's broken heart. Emily moves closer and puts an arm around her shoulder.

Bertie and Soot jump up on the bed and Bertie tries very hard to jump onto Elizabeth's lap, but Emily remembers that the dress Elizabeth is wearing was a present from Gerald, as she helped Gerald shop for it at the time. Emily grabs a blanket from the end of the bed and tries not to pull a face when she feels the man-made fibres between her fingers, and quickly drapes it over Elizabeth's lap. Bertie takes his cue and jumps on Elizabeth's legs and turns around until he flops down. Emily notices Elizabeth's tears. Emily can tell that Elizabeth has no words, so she just sits with her and strokes Bertie on Elizabeth's legs.

After a while, Emily speaks.

"What we'll do is go to the perfumier and buy a new bottle of the same perfume. You can wear that. That way, you can keep this bottle he gave you forever? Yes, I think he would like that." Emily hugs Elizabeth harder, and Elizabeth leans her head on her friend's shoulder. The two sit again for a while in silence, until Emily decides to try to make Elizabeth laugh, or at least lift her out of what seems to be a dark place. "Let me tell you what I have in store for Valentine's Day. Sub-zero temperatures! Cuthbert is in Russia and expects me to join. Bought me an ushanka and overlarge coat. I look ridiculous. If he were in the Caribbean then yes, I'd be there in a flash. But I'm dreading it." There is a silence, then.

"Keep talking," Elizabeth says. Emily squeezes her friend's hand, not sure what to say next.

"I brought some food. Popped into Café San Marco's. Had to buy some olives. Thought I might as well drop some stuff off for you as a thank you for those lemon puffs you made me last week. This stuff isn't as nice as those, Emily looks at the big bag of delicatessen food inside. I'm rationing myself and still have some puffs left, so I can eke out the pleasure." Emily lies through her teeth about Elizabeth's inedible lemony present. I do love the San Marco's vegan apple frittelle di meles. They melt in your mouth. So, I bought a couple of those and some of the chilli peanuts you like. Want one?"

"You talk." Elizabeth shakes her head. Emily struggles with what to say that won't make Elizabeth feel worse than she already does.

"Oh, there's an exhibition on at Kettle's Yard. Lupercalia and Valentine," Emily remembers and suggests, but gets no reaction. "No, I don't really fancy it either. Let's go to the house again soon though, eh?"

The two friends sit looking out the window at the morning sunshine. One unable to move due to heartbreak, the other overcome by deep compassion.

"I know you didn't really call the fire brigade," Elizabeth says, squeezing her friend's hand, while still holding the perfume in the other.

*

A while later, and Elizabeth is drinking peppermint tea Emily has made. She sits on her bed stroking her cats, Bertie still on her lap, Soot now by her side. Emily's phone goes. She sees it is Godric.

"I won't be a minute. I'll get a fresh brew." Emily walks out, shutting the door. Elizabeth doesn't react. "Hello, yes?" Emily replies to Godric as she walks downstairs. "Well, I'm not bothering her with that," Emily listens again, then replies, "I know, but that's the last thing she needs to be worrying about right now. He'll just have to work it out for himself. You already said earlier that he's got his Sergeant back." Emily listens, shaking her head. "He should have thought of that. He's got to stop playing so much golf and drinking so much beer then he could do his job properly!" Emily pauses to listen to Godric, then adds, "She's in no state. Listen, I'll speak to you later. I'm glad you're feeling a little bit better. Thank you for letting me know about Lizzie. Look after yourself today, and don't worry about your Nanna. Try to focus on the play. I've bought myself a ticket for the evening performance. If I'm not in Russia that is, I'll be there. Yes, bye, Darling."

Emily hangs up and walks into the kitchen. She is followed in by the dogs, who are hopeful for treats. She reaches into the jar on the side, which has 'dog treats' written on it. Then she fills the kettle. Emily glances at the side and can't believe she missed them before. Two large bunches of flowers, white and red roses. Each bunch must have over two dozen in its display, and still all wrapped up in their cardboard delivery vases. The small note cards accompanying the displays have been opened and are still on the kitchen side. Emily feels terrible for snooping but picks up one of the cards and reads, 'To my darling wife. Happy Valentine's Day. I'll always love you, your devoted Gerald xxx'. Emily is shocked, and a little confused so picks up the other card which reads, 'Elizabeth, you are an amazing woman, thank you for being my best friend for all the years. Be happy on this Valentine's Day. Love, your Gerald xxx'. Emily rubs her nose and looks at the flowers. She's not entirely sure what she is seeing. It makes no sense.

*

Elizabeth can hear Emily downstairs. She feels less alone when she knows her friend is here. Just like last night, when Godric was outside. Comforting. Under the blanket on her bed, with her feet up, she has a hand on each cat as she leans against the headboard. The perfume now beside her on the bed. She glances across to the side. She hasn't moved anything over on Gerald's side of the bed since his passing. His bedside cabinet still has his reading glasses on the Bill Bryson book about some forest in America, together with the last newspaper he read. Elizabeth lives with these items, giving them room in her life, to give him his space – as if he's just popped out and will be home at teatime. She closes her eyes. Sometimes, when she's not thinking properly, Elizabeth wonders if Gerald has come back to her in the form of Bertie. All these animals she now shares her home with, who Gerald never met, that give her so much love. Sometimes, they give her so much love it feels heaven sent.

When she opens her eyes, she sees Bertie staring up at her. She wonders if she will ever feel happy again. She knows the answer. Having Gerald taken from her feels like a wicked trick. Something so utterly unthinkable that most days she deliberately doesn't dwell, or it becomes too consuming, too unbearable. Soot climbs further up the bed to be closer to Elizabeth. Not recognisable as the Soot she rescued from All Saints' Porters' Lodge, who was a scruffy, dusty ball, and a little bony in places with sores on his leg. Now resembling the cat who got the cream, all four kilos of him thumps his way into her lap, trying to nudge out Bertie. Elizabeth struggles to breathe under the weight of them both. Her breathing becomes so shallow. She wonders what it would be like if she stopped breathing.

She closes her eyes again and can see Gerald. He's lying on the bed next to her. She keeps her eyes closed but turns her head to see him. He is reading the paper and eating toast. He smiles as he drops crumbs. He offers her a piece of toast already in his fingers. But tricks her and takes a bite himself then passes his plate so she can take a piece. Elizabeth can almost smell the marmalade and his coffee on his bedside table. He smiles again at her, and Elizabeth smiles back. Then he disappears. Tears spike in her eyes she keeps closed. As she opens them, she looks for Gerald, but he's not there, only the book, the newspaper and his glasses. They are so precious. Irreplaceable. Emily comes back with a fresh teapot and goes to move them.

"Stop!" Elizabeth shouts, causing the cats to jump from her lap.

Emily looks at what she was going to move and thinks of the flowers downstairs.

"Why didn't you say anything?" Emily asks.

But Elizabeth doesn't reply. She cannot find the words. Her husband is gone. Everything is gone. Today, she can see no point. No point at all.

23
CARROTS

Inspector Bob Abley and Sergeant Lemon have paid the Cambridge Policy Pathology department a visit, hoping to find that Leedham has been working hard. They find him with the radio blaring

"It really is good to see you back, Lemon. Oxford isn't a place to live, just somewhere to visit for tea and crumpets. Why did you ever leave last year?" Leedham asks Lemon, then looks at Inspector Abley knowing it is a sore point between the two of them. Neither respond, so Leedham adds, "Didn't I hear that you were in a pantomime as the camel, Bob?"

"No. No. No," Abley replies firmly.

"Actually, I saw a photograph. Took a copy. My screensaver." Leedham gets out his phone and shows Inspector Abley a photograph of a pantomime horse. "From something Professor Green's grandson was in? Backstage? You tried it on? I think you are good as the back end." Leedham laughs then looks at Sergeant Lemon, who himself tries to stifle a smirk.

"It was Cinderella. How the hell did you get that picture? And that's clearly a horse, to pull the carriage thingy. We weren't in the pantomime. Just well. Look, we were off the clock. It was an aftershow party." Abley says, adding, "Don't you go to parties?"

"Yes, but I don't horse around as much as you," Leedham chuckles.

"Groan," Abley replies.

"Well, I'm certainly pleased Sergeant Lemon has decided to return to our stable, as it

were," Leedham looks at Lemon to see if he is going to give away just what happened to make him leave in the first place. But Lemon is tight lipped.

"The case at hand?" Lemon changes the subject, glaring at the police pathologist. Not wanting to revisit the prior rift between himself and the Inspector, which is all water under the bridge.

"Quite." Leedham fiddles with his pen in the top pocket of his white lab coat. "Carrots." Leedham looks at some data on a screen in front of him as Inspector Abley leans over his shoulder, not understanding how carrots and a computer full of code both add up together.

"Carrots poisoned the students at Christina College," Leedham reiterates.

"Really?" Abley continues to look at the data, not understanding.

"Oh, I can't take credit. I have confirmed it through with my own tests now. No, when one hundred and fifty members fall ill in a Cambridge College, d'you think they are going to wait for the police to work out why? With all their money? And, the Master ill too? No, they have a Head of Toxicology from the School of Biological Sciences. Their lab looked at everything straight away. All food types consumed, the water, even sent air reports. It would have taken me ages to do all that. They must have had a sizeable team."

"So, all the students and staff who went to hospital

were poisoned by carrots?"

"Only the Master from the staff, Sir," Lemon corrects Abley.

"Something to do with the wrong dose of pesticide spread on the crop. Systemic intake of organophosphate poisoning. Same stuff they use in nerve gas. Also used in dodgy insecticides. Can't quite believe it."

"We put that in our carrots still?"

"I didn't think we did, but something went wrong, maybe. Anyway. They isolated the carrots. It was useful to have the Master's statement. That's what sped up their diagnosis. You see, the top table had none of the carrots the pupils ate, had a different type. Those posh little ones, with their greenery all still intact. Came from a different farmer."

"But what about the Master?"

"Apparently, she liked to mingle with her students, and had sat and spoken to a table of PhD students and picked at the dish of carrots as she conversed. Or, so the science report they shared with me stated."

'And the Hugo Grader boy? Did he die of carrot poisoning?"

"No," Leedham is firm.

"What?" Abley says in disappointment.

"No organophosphate in his body."

"So what did he die of?" Sergeant Lemon leans in to look at the screen as well.

"I'm running tests," Leedham replies, then looks round to see Lemon and Abley peering at his screen. "Not on this computer. I don't know why you're huddled over my shoulder. This is my vegetable planning for the allotment this year." Lemon looks at them like they're idiots.

"Oh, for god's sake!" Abley turns on his heel and walks to the window, his head now in his hand.

"Why are the tests not back on Mr Hugo Grader?" Lemon asks Leedham, also walking away from Leedham's computer.

"Because he's dead, so it is harder to interview him. Even their own scientists couldn't do that. They are leaving this one to us at least."

"Were there illegal substances in his body? Can you check?"

"It's next on my list. Blood tests over there." Leedham points to a contraption with pipettes and liquids.

"And?" Abley's ears prick up.

"I'm getting to it."

"Can you hurry it along?" Abley is disappointed to hear that all he has is Leedham on the murder and the College has pulled back.

"I go at the speed I go. Any faster and I would not be able to conduct proper tests."

"You could stop doing your allotment planning for a start!" Abley replies, frustrated.

"It might be time to call in Professor Green?" Lemon looks at Abley and whispers quietly.

"Ugh. I heard that," Leedham says. "How is the pernickety creature? Oh, how I miss being cajoled by the green-eyed pixie woman. Bit odd she's not knocked down your door already, isn't it? Doesn't she have a grandchild in the system?"

"You must have scared her off," Abley replies, heading for the door with Lemon. "Just do what you can to get us something as fast as possible."

"And perhaps you should be nicer to Lemon. Don't want to lose him again now, do we?" Leedham replies bravely as he watches them leave. Abley pops his head back in the room.

"Really?" Abley asks.

Leedham squirms and hangs his head.

"I shouldn't–" Leedham starts to apologise.

"Just get us some results, soon eh?" Abley smiles, forgiving Leedham for his caustic remark and stopping him from feeling bad. "Just find out what killed his young man."

24
THE HEART OF DOGS

Emily has tried but failed to persuade Elizabeth to get changed out of her beautiful dress. Though Elizabeth has remained quiet, she has not resisted the suggestion of a walk, perhaps hopeful that a change of scene can't make matters worse. So, wearing her duffel coat, and holding onto three leads, they wander over Jesus Green Lock Bridge and into the park. Emily having popped home to pick up Pepper.

Emily has not reminded Elizabeth that today is the 'Hearts of Dogs' event on Midsummer Common, where dogs dress up for Valentine's Day to raise money for local canine charities. Emily has also not told Elizabeth that she has fashioned some red coats for Hector, Monty and Clive, with small white hearts glued all over them, as Emily fears Elizabeth might not wholeheartedly approve. Emily decides to whip them out before the dogs are let off the leads, and then stands back and enjoys watching the dogs turn peoples' eyes. Just to see if it brings a smile to Elizabeth's face.

"It's cruelty," Elizabeth whispers, "animals are not for amusement."

"It's for charity. They don't mind. Come on." Emily is disappointed but not surprised. Elizabeth grudgingly walks with Emily towards Midsummer Common. Her best friend has now linked arms just to be sure Elizabeth doesn't turn around and escape back home. It is another chilly day, with little breeze and a bright blue sky. The red coats make Hector, Monty and Clive look like circus dogs. They start to play tumble, and it isn't long before they lose their heart patterned jackets in the mud.

"See, my clan won't be told," Elizabeth whispers quietly. Ordinarily, Emily would be slightly annoyed at the lack of Elizabeth's gratitude for her handicraft. But now, she is just relieved that a change of scene has helped her friend find her voice.

"Isn't this nice?" Emily tries to lighten the mood.

The two women walk under Victoria Avenue Bridge and start to notice a number of dogs wearing fancy dress. Emily bursts into laughter with joy. Elizabeth, however, scrunches up her face in disapproval. In the distance, near a marquee, what looks like Valentine's Day doggie games are already taking place. Emily clings onto Elizabeth, refusing to let go, despite Elizabeth's attempts to wriggle free.

"Five minutes. Let's just see, shall we?" Emily urges Elizabeth not to just turn around and go back home, "It's for charity."

"You've said that." The dogs have already smelt treats and go bounding off towards doggie food stalls. Elizabeth sees a Dachshund dressed in a pink ballerina costume, a Weimaraner dressed as cupid with a pair of wings and a fake arrow on his back, a Dalmatian wearing heart shaped deeley-boppers, and a crossbreed fashioning a bow tie and boots. Elizabeth thinks the whole thing is ghastly and she cannot stand it. She calls her dogs and puts them on the lead, then hands the leads to Emily.

"That's it? You're just going to leave me here?" Emily looks surprised.

"I'm sorry. Can you take the dogs back when you go past?"

Emily can't believe what she's hearing.

"You're not even going to talk to me?" Emily raises her eyebrows in frustration.

Elizabeth just looks away, to the river. "I'm right here, you know," Emily continues. "All ears. Talk to me!" Emily cannot believe she has just raised her voice at her friend but is so frustrated with the situation.

"I'm sorry. I can't do this," Elizabeth says as she starts to walk off. "Nothing feels worth it anymore." Elizabeth's voice is so quiet. It drifts away into nothing.

But before Emily can say anything else, Elizabeth has turned and is walking towards the top exit from the Common.

25
TAKE FIVE

"Have you had a break this morning yet? You okay?" Abley asks Lemon, as Abley's car approaches the Swan Theatre on Park Street, with the Sergeant in the passenger seat.

"Breakfast? What's that?" Lemon jokes.

"I just wondered if you were okay?" Abley asks again.

"Stop asking me if I'm okay, and I'll be okay. Okay?" Lemon raises his eyebrows at his Inspector.

"Okay, gotcha," Abley nods. "Shall we go in and see if we can close this case down, so we can get elevenses?"

"Sounds good to me," Lemon straightens his scarf.

Now they know the College illnesses were caused by carrot poisoning, the Inspector is relieved, to say the least. There is no mass murder attempt, or anything as dark as that. However, they need to work out how Hugo Grader died. And inside this theatre, they are hoping to find something that could lead them to the answer.

The tactic this morning is to quiz his friends as many times as possible until one gives them something. Waiting for Leedham is not an option. They both enter the theatre and pop their heads backstage. It is immediately apparent to both that a full dress rehearsal is taking place. Inspector Abley hasn't got time for too many niceties and walks straight out onto stage, putting an abrupt halt to rehearsals.

"Can you put the lights back up!" He shouts out to the stalls and up at the technical booth, hoping someone can hear him. Miles and Darcy, playing Romeo and Juliet, break out of character and Godric, sitting in the middle of the stalls, takes one look at Inspector Abley and calls five. Darcy and Miles walk off stage and Sergeant Lemon, noticing other actors also begin to follow, shouts.

"Nobody go anywhere!"

Darcy, Miles, Lance and the other actors, quite surprised by the tone of this Sergeant, shuffle back on stage. Inspector Abley waves to Nisha Acharya-Gorpade to come and join them. Once silence has descended, Inspector Abley leans on some steps which are part of the set.

"It has come to our attention, and some of you may already know, that students ill at Christina College were poisoned by carrots," Abley explains, waiting for some element of surprise from those assembled. Indeed he hears some gasps and 'that makes sense' from some, then continues, "In the light of this information, we want to talk to you about your friend, Hugo Grader." Inspector Abley can still hear all the 'omgs' and 'so that's what it was?', 'wow's, about the news of carrot poisoning, and 'I didn't know, did you?', or 'I thought it was carrots', and 'carrots? I could have died', but Abley ploughs on with his questions regardless. "Was Mr Grader allergic to any food groups? Did he have any intolerances? Was he gluten free, dairy free? We're trying to make any possible connections with food groups and Hugo's death." Inspector Abley stops talking and waits for someone to speak. Standing in front of Row A of the stalls, Lemon gets out his notebook.

"Hugo had the constitution of an ox, Inspector," Miles jumps in, sitting down on the edge of the stage.

"Though he did have unusual tastes."

"His hatred of marshmallows," Lance walks over to sit next to Miles.

"Oh yeah, how could I forget. He wasn't fond of squidgy food. It wasn't an allergy, more a phobia. They made him want to gag," Miles adds.

"Were marshmallows served at dinner?" Inspector Abley asks?

"Not as far as I know. But, Inspector. Hugo didn't eat at Christina College," Lance offers.

"What? We have statements that he was there, at the Valentine's Banquet?" Sergeant Lemon looks back a few pages in his notes.

"He was, but we ate at Snobs," Lance replies.

"Why eat twice?" Inspector Abley asks.

"I asked them that," Godric chips in from the stalls.

"We didn't eat twice. We drank in College." Lance replies.

"He went for booze and women. Two of his favourite hobbies," Miles adds, a little sheepishly, "and we followed." Miles adds, knowing Darcy is nearby. "He was mainly just larking about. We were demob happy if that's what you call it. We're leaving."

"Who's we?"

"The band. Hugo, Miles, myself and the groupie, Plummy here," Lance says.

"Hey!" Darcy objects to the nickname. "You never asked me. Only Nisha. Don't drag me into this."

"Snobs," Inspector Abley says, thinking to himself. "Get someone on it." Abley looks to Lemon, who nods then makes a call for Constable Petticoat to pay a visit.

"The food is ten times better," Miles tries to explain. "Caviar and whatnot."

"So, none of you ate?" Inspector Abley asks.

"Hugo seemed to spend most of the time throwing Banquet food," Lance offers.

"I ate, and Nisha," Godric replies, correcting the

others. "We ate a normal meal."

"And the carrots?" Abley asks. Nisha nods and looks at Godric.

"And the carrots," Godric replies. "So it all makes sense," Godric thinks about his own poisoning, and Nishas.

"Hugo doesn't do vegetables. I doubt he touched a carrot. A carnivore, if ever there was," Darcy says.

"So you ate in College?" Abley turns to Nisha. "Your bag was found in Mr Grader's rooms. It was stuffed with science books and a fancy looking bag. Present?"

"I must have left it there after the Banquet," Nisha looks at Godric, wondering if he remembers, then shrugs at the Inspector.

"What's this?" Inspector Abley puts the empty silver and grey bag on the police table.

"That had a corsage in it. From Godric. An orchid. I lost it when I fell ill."

"We all went back to Hugo's, I mentioned earlier," Godric answers Abley's question, still processing the fact that he was poisoned by carrots. "Carrots? How can carrots make us all so ill, so quickly?"

"Apparently, it can be as rapid as a few hours. And, it is pretty serious poisoning. Relative of nerve gas apparently," Lemon chips in.

"What were you all doing at Mr Grader's?" Inspector Abley asks again.

"Carrots." Godric is stunned and wipes his forehead with his handkerchief.

"We were celebrating the news about our band," Miles replies, "Supposed to be rehearsing. If only Hugo had an early night. He might still be alive."

"I've heard some of your music," Abley replies, raising his eyebrows.

"What d'you think?" Lance asks.

"Oh, I don't think it's for my demographic," Abley replies, turning to Miles. "I hear you were a little jealous of

Hugo Grader's leading man role, Mr Bonneville?"

"Eh? What's that got to do with carrots?" Lance defends his friend.

"Were you?" Inspector Abley asks Miles again.

"I was a bit jealous that he was lead singer of the band," Miles's cheeks flush and he stumbles over his next words. "We, we often fell out about it, I guess? I mean. But, if I was really jealous of anyone, it would be Lance. He writes the songs," Miles frowns at Lance, then sighs a heavy sigh.

"Don't be jealous. They're nothing special." Lance grins.

"You're the reason we got the deal." Miles states matter of factly.

"D'you think there is something suspicious about Hugo's death?" Nisha asks the Inspector.

"He was built like a rugby player, constitution of an ox, seemingly everything to live for and didn't eat carrots," Lance replies, "It looks suspicious to me."

Miles is quiet and starts to play with his shoelaces.

"That's terrible," Nisha replies. "Could it have been an underlying health issue?"

"We're checking." Inspector Abley replies.

"Inspector, d'you need anything else? As we need this rehearsal time," Darcy tells more than asks, then turns to Miles, "As much as I love you, Darling, you haven't nailed this yet, and we open in two days."

"I haven't nailed it because this is my first proper dress rehearsal. And, with all apologies to the director," Miles looks at Godric then back down at his feet, "I can't wait for this to be over, so we can all get out of here." Miles fidgets with his hands.

"I'd like to ask that no one leaves Cambridge for now. Not until we get a diagnosis on cause of death of your friend," Abley says firmly, getting off the stage prop stairs.

"All of us?" Godric asks Inspector Abley.

"All of you," he replies knowing full well he has already asked his consultant Professor Elizabeth Green's grandson not to leave town when he saw him earlier.

"Bang goes our first gig then," Miles replies glancing at Lance.

"Well, she's bad news," Darcy says to Abley while looking at Nisha. "Always hangs around here. Hung around Hugo."

"Er, I'm doing the lights here, and Hugo is my friend?" Nisha says, defending herself.

"I mean after the lights. No one wants you." Darcy says.

"Why do you hate me so much?" Nisha looks upset. "I've done nothing to you."

"Oh, you know," Darcy replies.

"Stop!" Miles shouts at Darcy. Nisha runs off stage and climbs up into the rafters.

"What was that about?" Inspector Abley walks closer to edge of the stage to be closer to Godric in the stalls.

"I really have to remain in Cambridge?" Godric asks Inspector Abley quietly, leaning forward.

"Why, are you planning a trip abroad?" Inspector Abley asks, knowing full well it is highly unlikely and that Godric is just challenging the principle. "You're directing a play. Tell me. What was that?" Abley looks at Darcy now on the far side of the stage talking to Miles.

"I'll cooperate I suppose," Godric replies, his neck cricked up to look at the Inspector, slightly unnerved by the whole situation, and realising Abley has no idea yet why Hugo died. "To be frank, I think Darcy is jealous of Nisha. Female rivalry."

"We'd like to interview you all again please," Inspector Abley turns back and shouts to everyone on stage, in the stalls and lurking by curtains backstage. "Tell the others not here. All in this production. Don't leave until you have given your name to Sergeant Lemon, and he will make a time in the diary for you to come to the station. We need to get to the bottom of Hugo's death. Thank you!" Inspector Abley jumps down off stage and sits in the stalls next to Godric. Abley looks back at Sergeant and the students who start to walk towards Lemon, poised with his notebook.

"What do you make of all this?" Abley asks Godric.

"Thankfully, it's not my job to think about it," Godric sighs.

"Quite, but if you did think."

"I'd think you need my Bunny," Godric gives Inspector Abley his toughest Paddington Bear stare. "She is the best police consultant on poisons you've ever had."

*

The smell of burning dust on the spotlights is pungent. Nisha sits with her legs dangling, as she watches the others mingling below, whispering to one another about Hugo.

"Back in ten!" Godric shouts to all from his seat, as Lance climbs up to sit next to Nisha.

"I always find the performance better from this angle. Much less spit." Lance says.

"I told you. She has a thing against me."

"Life is a cruel journey, and then you're dead, it would appear."

"I should have been nicer to Hugo," Nisha says thoughtfully.

"Hugo could have been nicer to a whole lot more people. Comparisons are useful."

Nisha half-heartedly smiles at Lance. While below them, Darcy walks back on stage and looks up.

"Are you coming down, Waify? Don't keep us in the dark."

"You just told me to leave?" Nisha replies.

"I wish you would. I fear I am stuck with you."

"Want me to say something?" Lance says quietly to Nisha.

"No. I have to start fighting my own battles. And one in particular."

26
FLORISTS

Elizabeth walks to the top of Midsummer Common and turns back to look at the dogs. She doesn't want them to see her. She knows they will follow. She can see that Emily has kept them on their leads. That could have gone better, but feeling both raw and numb she simply doesn't know what to say to her friend.

Elizabeth's eyes wander across Midsummer Common, noticing all the changes made over the past decade. Most but not all of the trees are still standing tall. But there are new boathouse buildings, larger homes and expensive flats squeezed in between. The Cambridge Regional College has long since moved sites, and the space turned into yet more 'executive' hubs. More cyclists cross the paths on the Common. The city is inevitably getting busier, with new faces all too unrecognisable. A landscape without Gerald.

She pictures him, sitting on the grass, under the largest willow tree on the Common. It must have been four or five years ago. Hanging branches swaying between them.

He sat her on a blanket and made her wear a daisy chain he had linked together for her. Back then, it felt like such a waste of time. She can remember being a little short with him for making it. She didn't need a daisy chain as she had some lecture to go to, so couldn't wear it. Where did it all that go? She longed to be back. All those precious moments. The memory has faded at the edges. Elizabeth looks at the tree. It is just a stump now. She never did find out why it was felled. She knows if she were to be cut open like that tree, the word Cambridge would run through her veins like a stick of rock. But right now, without Gerald, she feels a stranger in this place.

Elizabeth turns and heads up onto Auckland Road. She crosses over Maids Causeway and walks towards the Grafton Centre. On the corner of Eden Street, she comes to a florist, 'Thorn and Thistle'. When she enters, a bell tinkles. A couple of customers are browsing the shop, which is packed tight with little objet d'art, bars of soap and pottery cats. Her eyes are drawn to a pink porcelain elephant, whose trunk appears to be a lamp. Elizabeth finds the courage to walk up to an assistant behind a counter. The assistant is very young and chewing gum while checking her phone.

"Hello."

"How can I help?" the assistant replies, uninterested.

"I received some flowers yesterday."

"Great."

"From here. Two bouquets actually."

"You must be popular. Was it your birthday?"

"From my husband."

"There you go. Love's not dead, even when you're older."

"He's dead," Elizabeth replies, ignoring the young girl's ageist remark.

"Excuse me?"

"For Valentine's Day," Elizabeth explains.

"But, Valentine's Day is in two days. Are you sure

they were from us?"

"Yes."

"Do you have a receipt?" The assistant asks, confused.

"How would I have that? He might have had that, before."

"I don't know. I was just thinking it might help trace. Could he come—"

"No, he can't come in, because he's dead," Elizabeth says flatly.

"Right, er. Can you give me your name?"

"Don't you need his name? He sent the flowers," Elizabeth stares at this girl, who is clearly out of her depth. She wonders whether just to leave. This is going nowhere.

"If we have your name and address, then I can check if we sent the flowers yesterday. They might have come from elsewhere?"

"Are you calling me a liar?" Elizabeth's prickles are now up.

"There is no need for that tone. I am just trying to help."

"Oh, but I think there is," Elizabeth stares at this young girl, wondering if she spent less time on her phone and more reading if they would be having the same conversation.

"Please wait a moment." The assistant pockets her phone and disappears behind a curtain. Elizabeth can hear her talking to a colleague out the back, but not exactly what they are saying. It is taking every ounce of Elizabeth's willpower not to walk out of the shop right now, but she wants to know, wants to feel the connection it brings to Gerald. To think he must have come in here at some point? She looks around again. After a while, a different woman steps out from the back, the younger woman now absent.

"I'm so very sorry. Professor Green?" The shop manager makes a stab of a guess. Elizabeth nods. "There must have been a mix up. We are having training challenges here at the moment," the woman shakes her head about the young woman behind the curtain, "I do believe I remember your husband. He came in a number of years ago and left a sum. He said he had asked the funeral directors to inform us when he died, should he ever be the one to go–" The more sensitive shop manager says, trying to avoid saying if he were to go first. She continues, "He had the nicest smile. A kindly man. I remember him. You were supposed to get some last year, actually. Perhaps because of probate, we were only informed recently? I'm not quite sure. So, we thought you'd like to receive last year's as well. But they arrived too early. I am so very sorry for the distress this has caused you."

"Okay, thank you." Elizabeth spots the woman she spoke to first now lurking in view. The kindness in the shop manager's voice, a stranger, makes Elizabeth feel wobbly. She cannot stay in the shop a moment longer. She heads to the door for some air. The bell tinkles on the door as she steps out onto the pavement. Fitzroy Street is busier than she remembers. Everyone rushing to and from somewhere. But for what? Elizabeth thinks, frozen to the spot.

27
DRAMA IS EVERYTHING

Professor Barclay and Dr Guinevere Trotsham are in the Faculty of English building on West Road. The rooms and Faculty library are bursting with young romantics, composing Valentine's Day poems for loved ones, or writing word slams for open mic nights about love and hearts and red roses. For the English Faculty is where you come to study if you believe in love, unrequited or otherwise.

Professor Barclay, on the other hand, has an altogether more practical concern on his mind. He sits in his rooms at his grand office desk which overlooks The Backs. Dr Guinevere Trotsham, perched on a chair at the table usually used for discussions and tutorials, is helping herself to a biscuit from his elevenses tea tray.

"We should do something to pay our respects to poor Hugo Grader, as a Faculty. He was one of us," she munches.

"Nonsense. Let the Master of College take up this ceremony. Flowers are already being placed at the bottom of his staircase. Completely over the top."

"Students are struggling with the news," Dr Trotsham

replies, popping in the rest of the biscuit she has just dunked in her tea.

"You're too soppy. Death is part of life. It is sad, but he wasn't your friend. At least I don't think he was one of your special friends." Professor Barclay gives her a knowing look, before sipping a black coffee.

"Leave it," Guinevere glares at him, shaking her head, "And, isn't your heart full of love the day before Valentine's?"

"Will people stop going on about Valentine's Day? We've had the Valentine's Banquet, Valentine's breakfast. Did you get the heart shaped potato croquettes this morning? Ridiculous. Look at the biscuits," Barclay protests. Guinevere picks up another red coloured shortbread in the shape of cupid with his bow and arrow piped in icing, resting on little heart shaped doilies.

"You're lucky you get such attention from kitchen," Guinevere replies.

"Huh. We need to advertise the auditions for this year's Edinburgh production. Have the posters gone up yet in all the Colleges?" Barclay asks.

"I've been a little busy," Dr Guinevere Trotsham says, picking up another biscuit.

"Today, please. If you will."

"Miles Bonneville told me you've already asked him anyway. He seems to be the only one you're obsessed about," Dr Trotsham raises her eyebrows.

"Of course. He is the only actor. But we need a supporting cast around him."

"What is it about him?" Guinevere looks at Barclay in the eye.

"You tell me," Barclay grins at her, the gap in his teeth showing.

"Why is he such a favourite?" Dr Trotsham gets up and looks out the window at the winter lawns and borders of the Faculty gardens.

"Because he delivers. Do I have to spell it out?

Drama is everything. It's my food, my life, my soul. If you don't feel the same way, what are you doing here?" Barclay frowns.

"He's leaving. You know that. He won't be available." Dr Trotsham says, matter of factly, irritated by Barclay's lecture and assumptions about her own passions.

"I've told him he owes me. He'd better step up, or else. He'll just have to come back, or better still stick around. He's doing this or he'll have me to answer to."

"I don't think you can stop him from leaving?" Guinevere is confused by Professor Barclay's words.

"Watch me."

28
LOCAL RADIO

Inside a tatty yellow building on Mill Road, sit Darcy Nighy and Miles Bonneville sharing a microphone and looking straight ahead at a thirty something presenter, who is still wearing his sunglasses indoors. They have been invited onto 'Beat', a Cambridge local radio station which boasts how it broadcasts to the entire county, 'keeping it local'. They have been asked to talk about their play. The presenter, Jared, has decided that 'Romeo and Juliet' is topical, what with all that talk about love and romance the week of Valentine's Day. It might be far too highbrow for his audience (for him), but it fits the bill. After all, he has got three hours to fill. Darcy and Miles have committed to the interview and come dressed up in costume. Wearing cans over their ears, they lean in.

"Hello," Darcy says.

"Good morning," Miles adds.

"So formal. We are on Beat radio, the radio station that brings news about what matters to you, right now. Keeping it local. We have two good looking young things in the station with me. If you don't mind me saying for the listeners at home, check out the webcam. You're hot!"

"Thankfully, I'm thirty-six point seven degrees Celsius. Not a degree hotter," Miles replies.

"I concur. Though, judging by the lack of heating in the studio, we might become quite cool as this interview progresses." Darcy adds.

"I'm guessing you're expecting snow in here? Surely, that can be the only justifiable reason for wearing sunglasses, indoors, in February?" Miles asks.

"No, Miles. Jared's a trendsetter." Darcy glares at Miles, as she speaks into the microphone.

"So why Romeo and Juliet?" Jared asks, ignoring the slight about his shades.

"February the fourteenth might have something to do with it. We open on Valentine's Day, to a matinee and then evening performance. We still have some tickets, but they're selling fast. It's a Shakespeare for everyone. Love, romance, fighting," Darcy explains.

"Is all the cast from Christina College?"

"No, it is a mixed collegiate affair," Darcy replies.

"So, it's completely university, for the university?"

"Shakespeare wrote for everyman, Jared. This is a play for all. Our Director is a Bene't's man. He's studying science," Miles says.

"Oh, is there science in this version of the play? Is it a mash up? Does Romeo have a cell phone? Are you going for a modern twist?" Jared runs away with his own idea, waving his arms about.

"What? No. We have stayed true to the original script," Miles replies, growing frustrated by this idiot.

"Oh, it's just some Shakespeare plays these days are set in the sixties, or have the cast all wearing docker outfits. To keep it real. I'm just saying." Jared looks at the webcam and pulls shapes with his hands.

"It is set in Shakespeare's time." Darcy corrects Jared.

"Okay, so no science. What twists have you given it?

I can see you're not in modern dress. I'll post a photograph of your costumes on social. They look old. Are they actually from the olden days, you know, from Shakespeare's day?"

"That would make them over four hundred or more years old," Darcy frowns. "They're costumes." She opens her eyes wide at Jared in bewilderment at the stupidity of his questions.

"Did you do all your own stitching?"

"What? No." Miles looks at Darcy, then back at Jared. "Look, the play is about a vendetta between two powerful families. There's love, bloodshed. It's got everything. It's still relevant today. Tickets are available at the Swan Theatre. Come and watch. It's very romantic."

"Alright, thanks for that. I think I watched it with my Gran once," Jared says, pulling another face at the webcam. Then continues, "So, you're all amateur actors? Who steals the show, the one to watch? You know, who's gonna be the celebrity? The uni is always turning them out."

"Miles is a fantastic Romeo, he gives such an honest and truthful performance," Darcy explains.

"Aww, thank you," Miles replies.

"Hang on. I recognise you. Aren't you from the 'Three Charming Men'?" Jared pulls a face as the penny drops.

"I've come to talk about the play," Miles replies, trying to dodge the question. "Like I say, we do still have a few more tickets for the weekend performances."

"Oh yes, I heard the terrible tragedy. Was that your lead singer?" Jared presses more questions on Miles.

"I'd rather not talk about that." Miles leans back in his seat and takes off his headphones.

"What happened? How did he die?" Jared asks.

"Did you hear him? It's off bounds. Stop asking," Darcy replies.

"Yes, of course. It's just that people hear about these

things and want to know the facts. It was in the paper this morning. Common knowledge. On peoples' minds. My listeners."

"Is it? I mean, how many people listening actually knew our friend?" Darcy is cross, "We came to talk about Shakespeare!"

"Yes, do tell us more about that. Spoiler alert, they die in the end, don't they? We'll be back soon, after this break." Jared slaps on an advertising bed, the first one being for the latest blockbuster film with shooting and gangsters. Darcy shuts her eyes.

*

Shortly afterwards, outside the radio station, Darcy and Miles start to wander back up Mill Road towards Parker's Piece.

"I said you were the best actor in there," Darcy says.

"I know, thanks, Babe."

"Don't thanks Babe me. You were supposed to say how wonderful I am."

"You are good," Miles replies.

"It's no use now. We're not on the radio."

"Ah, I see. So, you were only saying it to get a compliment in return?" Miles is mildly affronted.

"It's called promotion." Darcy raises her arms and drops them back by her sides.

"Well, it's bullshit. I'm a good actor. I know I am. You saying I am won't make me more successful. I'm not going to argue about it."

"You're such a dork. I need this. You're leaving to start a music career. I want to make it in the movies. You have a trust fund. It's not the same for me." Darcy chokes. "You know, you're always paying for me. For my food. It's embarrassing."

"Am I leaving? I want to. But I don't know what Lance wants now," Miles replies. He looks at the cars doing five miles an hour down the centre of the road.

"You'll go and forget all about me."

"You'll just have to learn how to turn tricks." Miles laughs and hugs Darcy. From over his shoulder, Darcy grimaces.

29
HOME IS WHERE THE HEART IS

Sergeant Lemon opens the gate, climbs up the steps to the front door and knocks. He kicks at some weeds as he waits for an answer. Broadway in Grantchester is quiet this lunchtime, with just a car or two passing every ten minutes. It was easy to find a space for his police car. Something the neighbours will have to get used to – as he sees curtains twitch two doors down. The front door opens, and Inspector Bob Abley stands in the entrance. Lemon can see an empty house behind him. Lemon smiles as Inspector Abley nods.

"Glad you could make it. I've got a microwave. Ready meals, but they don't look half bad. Not got the oven working yet."

"Oh, need a hand?"

"Ah, your electrician days. Thank you, but I fear they may go to waste again. It's not hooked up to the gas yet." Abley puffs out his chest and lets out a long sigh. "Come on in." Lemon follows Inspector Abley into his galley kitchen. Local radio is blaring with the same presenter on 'Beats' – this time talking about music and love ballads. Abley turns him down.

"I brought you this. Thought you might not have had a chance to nip to the shops yet. Well, Rosie organised it actually," Lemon hands his Inspector a bag of food he has brought with him.

"Bread? Olives? Tomatoes? Humous? Pine nuts? Pesto? Pasta? What, no wine?" Abley looks at Lemon, touched but also aware of the reasoning.

"Bit early for drinking at lunchtime?" Lemon tries to brush over the fact that he didn't bring wine as his Inspector already drinks far too much.

"This looks better than those. Oh–" Inspector Abley trails off his conversation, bored that he was going to talk about food, looking at his pitiful microwave meals. What was he thinking?

Sergeant Lemon looks around the house. A TV blares golf in the corner, beside an old sofa. In fact, there is little else, save a few boxes and of course his Inspector's golf clubs and putting contraption. Lemon wonders where Inspector Abley will be able to relax.

"Looks like a nice place," Lemon says, telling a small white lie.

"It's warm and dry. Once I've sorted out how to work the heating, that is. Let me put these on. We don't have long." Inspector Abley puts the food into a microwave after piercing the lids.

"Grantchester eh? You gone all posh on us?"

"Ha! I'm on the right side for the Goggs," Abley shouts back, as Lemon wanders off into the living room having a look around.

"Ha!" Lemon shouts back. He can't help himself. If he cut his Inspector open down the middle, he'd expect golf balls to tumble out.

"Plus, Maureen never liked the village, so well, there are no memories. Clean slate."

"Good idea." Lemon looks out the window at the messy back garden.

"She took the cat. Maybe I'll get chooks."

"Can't see you as a country bumpkin. You going to leave the golf course early to shut them up safe for the night from the foxes?" Lemon wanders back into the tiny kitchen, aware there is nothing else to see.

"Ugh. Maybe I'll get another mouser then."

"What are those weird holes in everything?" Lemon looks out the kitchen window and sees the round holes in the furniture and fence posts.

"Large woodlice? I don't know."

"Bit empty in here? Gives you a chance to choose what you want." Lemon looks around some more.

"Maureen took it all."

"Everything? What about the stuff you had in your flat?" Lemon asks.

"Rented mostly. At least she's not asking for maintenance. She's with a wealthy chap, thankfully."

Lemon can see that his Inspector desperately misses his wife.

"Fresh start. Man pad. No pink."

"I have a pink–"

"Golf shirt." Lemon finishes his Inspector's sentence, pointing at Abley and acknowledging that he has seen it before letting out a chuckle.

"There's nothing to keep us linked." Bob Abley tries to raise a smile, but it is false.

"Yes, there is. Your children."

"I can't find the cutlery." Abley fights back his emotions as he scrabbles about in a box. The microwave pings. He takes the ready meals out and thinks how awful they look, so throws them into the sink. "C'mon. Pub. Oh, wait, look at this first." Abley reaches into another box and pulls out a small wooden sign.

"'The Putt'?" Lemon asks, being ushered out of the house.

"Great, isn't it?" Abley puts on his jacket and shuts the front door behind them both, then balances the new house sign on an outside shelf. "The Putt, haha. Let's go to the Blue Ball. Such a long trek."

Lemon is mildly concerned that Inspector Abley's local pub appears to only be five doors down.

"Don't spend much time here–" Lemon starts to lecture his Inspector, remembering how bad things have got, but is interrupted.

"Alright, Sergeant," Abley pulls back the door, and they enter a much more attractive proposition to his home. It is warm, and the smells of lunch shoot up their nostrils. "Hello, a pint of bitter and?" Abley looks to Lemon.

"Just an orange juice, I'm driving. Aren't you?"

The bartender already recognises Inspector Abley and is about to launch into some friendly banter when Abley shakes his head subtly at him and introduces his guest.

"This is my Sergeant. Lemon," Abley says, ignoring Lemon's question.

The pub landlord smiles a hello, then nods when Abley points at the food menu on a chalkboard above the bar.

"Would you like lunch?" The landlord asks.

"The pasta thing sounds good," Abley replies.

"Two," Lemon adds.

Abley takes his pint, hands the juice to Lemon, and they walk over to a table by the fire.

"Have you heard from Godric? Is she coming?"

"It might be too early," Abley says, "I wish Leedham would get a move on. Maybe the poor lad's heart just gave out."

"You don't think that though, do you? I think you need your favourite police consultant. And, we've already learned poison is involved. Surely, time for Professor Elizabeth Green," Lemon replies.

"I'm not paid to speculate about Mr Hugo Grader. We'll know soon. Until then, we wait for Leedham. I'm sorry you had to get up so early."

"I haven't been to bed yet. This is breakfast. It's like the hours I was doing in Oxford. So many night shifts on overtime. Rosie seems to be frustrated. She's followed me back but never sees me."

"It's my fault," Abley feels guilty for Lemon running off to Oxford to escape his own bad policing. "For all the upheaval."

"No, it's really not," Lemon looks at the fire knowing how Abley's words are partly true. He looks back at Abley, wanting to forgive him and move on. "You should stop treading on eggshells, you know. This is better than Oxford. I've come home. It's good."

Abley clinks Lemon's glass and looks out the window.

"I'm back too, you know. You have nothing to worry about. I'm just having the one." Abley looks at Lemon, trying to reiterate the point.

"What I don't understand," says Lemon, "is even if Hugo Grader died of natural causes, is how all his friends can just carry on like nothing's happened? The play. Two of them were larking about on the radio just now. Heard it in the car on the way over," Lemon is desperate to change the subject. The less he remembers about his Inspector going AWOL that time and leaving him to do everything, the better. Time to move on. He knows his friend was heartbroken. That's what love does, Lemon thinks. And if that is what it does, he's not sure he wants to get any deeper into it himself.

"I know what you mean. People do go into shock when someone dies. Don't always act how they should," Abley replies.

"I suppose. We don't know if the carrot poisoning was an accident or deliberate, do we?" Lemon asks his Inspector.

"No, an odd choice to poison everyone at this time of year, don't you think," Abley mulls.

"What?"

"Valentine's Day tomorrow. Shouldn't it have been

poison by heart shaped chocolates, not carrots?" Abley sighs.

"Oh yes, how can we forget that it is Valentine's Day?" Lemon looks around the local pub, which has a few red hearts on the bar, and the food menu on the chalkboard has 'Valentine's Specials' written in red chalk.

"Right. Are you doing anything nice for Valentine's?" Abley asks.

"Dinner. To be honest, what with it being a leap year, I'm a little concerned."

"Eh?" Abley draws a blank.

'When girlfriends can propose, isn't it? Rosie, she's quite the modern woman," Lemon explains.

"We're not still in the fifties, Lemon. She can propose any time she likes. And, you're punching above your weight there."

"Alright. I was never in the fifties. I preferred you when you were treading on eggshells." Lemon looks at Abley, then at a member of staff carrying two dishes of penne and vegetables covered in tomato sauce. "She's been dropping hints. I'm just not sure I'm the marrying kind. I must be a commitment-phobe. I just can't see it working out forever. That's a long time. Isn't it?"

"Leap year, eh? How exciting."

"Here am I, talking about my life," Lemon replies, feeling bad for his Inspector.

"Oh, it's okay. It is what it is," Abley smiles weakly.

"Have you heard from her?"

"Maureen's lawyers. Found the divorce papers on the doormat. Her moving in present. Or, at least the envelope looked sinister enough. Can't bring myself to open it, as it happens."

"Right." Lemon doesn't know what to say, so starts stabbing at his food.

"It's okay, honestly. I've just got to get on with it. I am getting on with it."

"I like your place," Lemon replies brightly.

"Thanks."

"I do. Nice to have food right by here." Lemon watches Inspector Bob Abley pick up some pasta and shove it in. "Who stuffs a poem in someone's mouth?" Lemon adds, trying to change the subject so his Inspector doesn't dwell on his failed marriage. And definitely not telling his Inspector that it is a factor in him not wanting to marry Rosie himself. The pain he can see him in is all too real. "Could it maybe be a suicide and that was his note? Godric thought it possible."

"Leedham will tell us when he finally pulls his finger out. When have we ever found a suicide who has taped their own eyes shut? With daffodils?" Abley stabs at some more pasta. "I'll have Raynott on my back soon. You know how he sucks up to the bigwigs in their ivory towers."

Lemon smirks. The pub manager brings over some crusty bread, spread and cheese to grate on the pasta but can see that they have both already made some headway into their food. He starts to grate over the Inspector's plate first, after the Inspector nods.

"Thank you," Abley says to the manager, lifting his pint as he swallows another mouthful of pasta. "I bet it's good to be back in Cambridge. Just love this place. Being back with me, eh?"

"I'm just thinking about how murder seems to follow you around. You come over to Oxford, and before we know it we have a multiple murderer on our hands. I'm back for two seconds and–"

"Shh. Don't even think it. And, if I remember rightly, murders were happening before I arrived in Oxford. I could as easily say that they follow you around."

"You're both coppers? Isn't that part of the job?" The pub manager asks confused, then looks at the police car outside.

"Not for me. I'm having a vegan week." Lemon tells the pub manager as he is about to grate some cheese on

Lemon's pasta.

"Not you, and all," Abley rolls his eyes.

"It's healthy. I'm on a fitness drive," Lemon pulls up his sleeve and tightens the muscles in his arm, showing them off to Abley, before laughing. "Feel those bad boys."

"You'll put me off my food," Abley replies, then smiles.

"What? My guns?"

"No, it's not that. It's this. This again. You. Here," Abley gives Lemon a grin. Lemon is happy, but returns a much more cautious smile, hoping things will stay on an even keel this time.

30
VALENTINE'S LOVE FESTIVAL

The Valentine's Festival of Love is well underway on King's Parade. From St Mary's to Bene't Street, stalls are set out in pretty pastel colours. Chalked hearts drawn on the road, pink and cream bunting stretched out between lampposts and a mariachi band playing on the wall of Bene't's College grounds. All these things frame the city centre in a glow of love. Cooing couples mill around stopping at stalls with rings, while young girls pore over necklaces, and a vinyl record stand plays crooning love songs. Godric and Nisha wander through the crowds, observing happiness in the air, but themselves both feeling decidedly on edge.

Godric has chosen to keep busy this morning. If the play is going ahead with his name on, then he'd better not let things slide. Phoning home every half an hour – his nanna still ignoring him – he tells himself he'll pop back soon but give her time to calm down, which she clearly wants. So, he and Nisha have given themselves the task to hand out flyers for the play. Godric has also brought some more laminated posters to clip to the railings to put with the ones already there.

They pass what looks like a Punch & Judy tent but in fact, is a post-modern 'Compliments Booth'. Inside the little tent, behind a stripy curtain and only revealing his head and shoulders, a rather large man is charging fifty pence to pay passersby a compliment. Nisha pulls Godric over, and hands the man a fifty pence and points to Godric. The man nods, then starts to speak.

"You're clearly a good lover, and have made this young woman very happy," then the compliments booth man smiles and takes a bow, as Godric laughs, then puts fifty pence on the tent shelf.

"Her turn."

"For the young lady. Of course." The compliments booth man turns to look Nisha directly in the eye. "Mademoiselle, your good looks are a given. But your bravery will know no bounds in the future." The man finishes, takes the money, then puts up a sign 'back in five minutes', and with a swish of the curtain, he disappears.

"Well, he nailed me. Spot on," Godric says wryly, walking away.

"Such a good lover," Nisha pushes Godric jokingly, then takes more leaflets and turns to start handing them out. "What did he mean about my bravery? Weird."

"I have no idea what anything means right now. I'm trying to ignore celestial messages." Godric turns and watches a street busker tune his violin, wearing a cupid outfit.

"But, brave?"

"Maybe he thought you were brave being seen with me. Ha!" Below the busker, Godric sees a cap with coins and chocolate for his last song. He places a pound in the hat, and the busker smiles. Then, out of nowhere, Alex taps Godric on the shoulder.

"Watcha," Alex says.

"Where did you spring from?" Godric is actually

pleased to see this man with dimples, as a welcome distraction, even if he is wearing the brightest red jacket.

"Is all this making you feel romantic?" Alex looks around at the festival of love and the stalls selling Valentine's chocolates, Valentine's roses, red dresses, chocolate fountains and other love themes gifts

"You know, no. It really isn't." Godric looks at Alex, wondering how he hasn't spoken to him before.

"I have my eye on a Valentine's dream catcher," Alex nods at a stall nearby, "And, how are you doing?" Alex flutters his eyelashes.

"I just want to get the play over the line. And, are you always this coy?" Godric replies.

"Can I help you with the play? An odd job man?" Alex suggests chirpily, offering his services, "And, I didn't think I was being coy, I thought I was being obvious," he grins again.

"That would be great," Godric finally smiles at Alex handing him some flyers, "You're right. You're transparent."

"I think we should do this and then go and get a drink," Alex suggests, watching Nisha hand out flyers.

"I cannot believe I'm saying this, but I'm too ill to drink. I need oxygen, then water. Nish?" Godric asks. Nisha has gone a little quiet and just nods.

"The Tent it is then," Alex replies.

Godric looks at Nisha, wondering what is the matter, but she gives nothing away.

*

After Godric, Alex and Nisha have popped into Tent, the only oxygen bar in Cambridge, they head on their way to get something plain to eat. Godric insists it cannot be more than toast, and Alex ribs him for being so adventurous. They bump into Darcy, Lance and Miles heading from Christina's, after swinging by to pick up

Lance after their radio interview.

"How did the promo radio interview go?" Godric asks.

"Alright," Miles replies, rubbing his hands together in the cold.

"We've sold more tickets online, and some here too," Nisha says. Darcy looks around and scowls at the same street busker, his red bow tie now lit up and flashing.

"Back to mine?" Lance offers.

"See you later," Alex smiles at Godric and walks off towards Trinity Street, mouthing back "Essay."

Godric feels uneasy again. What is it about Alex that makes him feel so good on such a bad day? As he watches Alex disappear into the crowd, he realises he already feels more at ease with him than he does with his new companions. In the corner of his eye, Godric is sure he spots his nanna crossing by the Cambridge University Press bookshop. She stops when she sees him. It must be her. But then, she is gone. Godric is about to chase after her when Lance interrupts.

"Come on. I have food that won't make us sick. Not a carrot in sight." Lance puts his arm around Nisha and leads the way.

*

Lance Fernard lives in a flat almost opposite Bene't's College, on King's Parade, above an art gallery. They pop down a narrow alley, near The Green Magician, and enter through a small back door. Once they've climbed a staircase inside, Lance unlocks, and they stumble into his home. Godric hasn't been inside Lance's flat before and is surprised by the space. It is more like a city warehouse apartment than the outside would suggest. He starts to phone home as the others pile in.

"Help yourself to anything you can find," Lance shouts for all to hear as he enters and walks over to the window. Miles heads over to a glass coffee table and sees a packet of cocaine. He empties a little and starts to make tiny lines using a metal utensil on the table. Godric hangs up, no reply, then looks at Nisha's worried face, as Darcy goes over to join Miles. Godric quietly whispers to Nisha.

"Let's look inside this enormous fridge to see what we can find? Then I have to go. I need to find my Nanna and put these on the railings." Godric puts down the laminated posters. But when Godric opens it, they both look at each other as the smell of food seeps out and they both realise they are still feeling fragile. Godric shuts the fridge and fills up the kettle, "Better idea. Tea with sugar." Then Godric turns to the others, "Is everyone else okay in your College now?"

"Yes, apparently only a handful are still in hospital. We're a tough bunch," Darcy replies.

Nisha kneels to stroke a big ginger cat who says hello. Nisha looks for cat food.

"Aw, you're such a good helper," Darcy says sarcastically, then snorts a line of coke.

"Leave Nish alone. Nish's feeding Fred while I'm away. It's going to be a while when we're on tour," Lance says.

"So we're still going?" Miles asks, looking relieved, having not known how to bring up the issue what with Hugo gone. Lance nods and shrugs a 'yes'.

"How can you think of going now Hugo is—" Darcy starts but is interrupted by Nisha.

"I don't mind," Nisha puts down a bowl of food.

"Is he stuck inside?" Godric asks about Fred. "No cat flap?"

"He's an indoor cat," Lance replies, "Too posh for the streets outside."

"I want to work with animals," Nisha says to Godric.

"Brilliant, doing what?" Godric asks.

"Maybe building structures to protect habitats."

"Boring," Miles interrupts, "come on Miss Acharya-Gorpade. Get wasted."

"No, thank you," Nisha says quietly.

"I'm good," Godric adds. Miles won't take no for an answer and walks over and picks up Nisha, then carries her to the sofa.

"Hey!" Darcy says, "What are you doing?"

"Making you jealous," Miles smiles, "I'm king of the world!"

"Very bad idea, chum," Lance interrupts, then pulls Nisha out of Miles' grip.

"I'm not feeling well. I think I might go back to College," Nisha says, staring at Godric, willing him to rescue her as she stands back up from the sofa.

"I'll walk you back," Godric offers, not wanting to cause any awkwardness, adding "nice place, Lance. Really swish."

"Nonsense. We should have a party! A party for Hugo. A celebration of his life. Play some music, take some happy pills!" Miles shouts.

"Pills? Really? You got anything confiscated?" Lance asks.

"Lance." Miles stops himself in his tracks and looks at Lance's smile. "Only happy pills. Nothing else," Miles replies.

Darcy, Miles and Lance lay back, feeling the cocaine enter their body.

"Our friend died," Miles inhales deeply on a spliff Darcy has just made. "He was so well. He really was king of the world. The king is dead, long live the king," Miles grimaces as he exhales, pointing at himself.

"I feel like he's here with us now," Lance says as the drugs take over his power of reason. "He's here, and he's saying find out what happened."

"Okay, I'll see you at rehearsal," Nisha heads for the door with Godric. They both leave, and the others hardly acknowledge their departure.

"What do you mean?" Darcy looks around, nervously, "I can't see him?"

"Oh, Hugo's here. He's looking at us to find justice," Lance replies.

"D'you think he didn't die from carrot poisoning?" Darcy asks.

"We've been through this. Of course, he didn't. The police don't think so either. And, we're not ill. He didn't even eat in College. None of us did," Miles answers, leaning further back into the sofa and blowing smoke circles.

"Poor Nisha. You've driven her away," Lance tells Miles. "And, you know, you've got the most to win from Hugo's death. You're the lead in our play."

"Hey! You think I want to lose my friend, just to be the lead in everything? Some kind of band now, now there's just the two of us."

"You want to end it? The band?" Lance asks.

'No!" Miles sits up quickly. "I'm just saying. He was my brother. I loved him. Deffo doing the band though." Miles grabs Lance's hand for a fist bump.

"Well, he's gone, and we can't do anything about that," Darcy says.

"My heart is breaking, have you got anything strong?" Miles asks Lance.

"Speed, ketamine," Lance replies.

"Give me some of that." Miles looks at Lance eagerly.

"And I thought you were supposed to be watching me," Lance stands up to fetch the drugs from a sideboard. He opens a cupboard and pulls out what looks like a child's bucket.

"You're okay, aren't you?" Miles grimaces again, "Still creative as hell."

"Just because you're in a band, it doesn't mean you can be A class junkies," Darcy replies, "Unless I'm included."

"Try some?" Lance comes back with a bucket of drugs, "They're on me. I've no need."

"Give me some of that." Darcy pulls some drugs out of the bucket.

"I'm supposed to meet Barclay," Miles remembers.

"He can go to hell and back," Lance replies.

31
BROKEN PROMISE

Professor Barclay has been waiting a while. In fact, Barclay would not wait so long for anybody else. At first, he stood at the site of the new proposed Christina College theatre, staring at daffodils. Then, after thirty minutes, he decided to check the dining hall, in case there had been a miscommunication. Coming away alone, he checked back at the proposed theatre site again. The only difference being that the sun had gone in and the temperature had dropped a little. But no one was there. Professor Barclay was giving this particular student more than the benefit of the doubt. Doubt had come and gone, along with hope. This was now down to pure faith that the young man who goes by the name 'Miles Bonneville' would eventually turn up.

Professor Barclay decides to go back to his College study and wait there. At least he can work, or attempt to. However, the whole issue is far too distracting. Some might say it is reaching levels of obsession. So, when Miles eventually arrives but chooses not to knock on his door or wait for permission to enter, it is a surprise to both parties when, as the young man wanders in, that Professor Barclay hurls a book at him.

"Late!"

"Hey!" Miles's first reaction is to laugh. Ordinarily, he would have been cross and probably would have turned around. But Miles is filled with a concoction of illegal substances elevating his mood to extraordinary levels.

"What do you have to say for yourself?!"

"I quit, angry man. Haven't you heard? I'm going to be stratospherically successful."

"Are you drunk?" Barclay asks.

"I'm high, and it feels great. No more essays. Ha!" Miles leans on the back of the sofa.

"But you agreed. You said you were going to perform for my high donors. We have the Edinburgh show. You have to do both. You gave your word."

"Like you gave to Lance Fernard when you said he could do a PhD, then you rescinded the offer weeks later? Your word meant bollocks. But I don't care anymore. I'm zen."

"But we need you to read some of Shakespeare's Sonnets."

"I came to tell you that you can sing for it and to stop leaving notes for me everywhere. What is it? You have a crush on me or something, old man?" Miles laughs again.

Professor Barclay gets up from behind his desk and walks over to Miles, getting up into his face.

"You could be such a bright star. I made you. When you met me, you were just a frightened fresher. It was me who encouraged you to join the drama group. I gave you your first lead in a play, your confidence, taught you everything."

"I'm a star. I don't care about your silly plays," Miles scoffs, then frowns, "Just leave me alone. Stop being pathetic. I don't even know why you care about it so much? It's just a theatre, just some shows of plays people have seen oh so many times before. Ugh."

"You don't understand. You don't understand at all. This is the theatre. The highest form of art. The expression of truth, meaning. It is everything," Barclay says, feeling emotional. Miles walks out of Professor Barclay's study. Moments after, Barclay grabs a cushion from the sofa and punches it.

"Christ!"

32
MISSING

After walking Nisha back to her rooms, Godric trudges home to Foxes' Haven. He has had quite enough excitement for one morning and could do with a lie down. But he needs to talk to his nanna. When he opens the door, however, he finds an empty home, with dogs shut in the kitchen, which he knows his Bunny never does. They jump up and race around him when he lets them out. Then he pulls out his phone and dials Emily.

"Is she with you?" Godric waits for an answer as he looks around and spots his nanna's slippers. They look old and worn, pulling her vulnerability into sharp focus. "Because she's not here." Godric listens, as Emily explains how Elizabeth walked off this morning and left the dogs with her. And can Godric refill their water bowls? "Yes, I'm looking at the flowers. Yes, from Grandpa." Godric pauses. "Wait. What?" Godric listens to Emily, looking at the flowers still in their delivery boxes, sitting on the side in the kitchen. He frowns. "What do you mean from

Grandpa?" Godric looks about the surface and sees that there is a card. Two little cards. He reads them. "Oh my god?" He says, closing his eyes. "I thought she'd bought these for the house. I didn't know what I thought. Mother is always buying flowers." Godric listens to Emily explain. "Who doesn't buy roses?"

Godric then nods, adding, "Why, do you think we should look for her? She might just be shopping?" Godric listens. "What do you mean she left the dogs with you? She'd never do that?" Godric grows more concerned. "Where was she going in that dress?" Godric listens to Emily and starts to frown. "Can you look for Nanna too? I can walk up to Fen Ditton if you maybe check Granta and the department?" He listens again. "Of course not. Don't blame yourself. I'm just trying to work out what the bloody hell is going on." Godric starts to walk to the garage. "No, it's not out the front." He opens the internal garage door. "It's gone," he replies, looking at the empty space where the Talbot Lago usually sits. Godric thinks about what he has to do next before he can rush out of the house as he continues to listen to Emily. "Yes, it is awful. I didn't know him well." Godric listens to Emily asking about the death and about the poisoning. "On the news? Yes, I feel wretched. But better than I was." He runs upstairs to check she has really gone and when there is no one he gives the dogs water, then puts them on their leads.

*

"Right." Emily stands in her kitchen, Pepper in her bed asleep. Emily's briefcase is on the counter as she was about to go into her own department to work, "I'll go and see if I can find her at Granta." Emily opens a jar on the side and pops a dog biscuit by Pepper's bed. She locks the patio doors and looks around her kitchen for her keys. Just like Godric, she is worried about her friend. She didn't want to worry Godric about Elizabeth's earlier state and omitted to tell him what Elizabeth said when she told Emily earlier, 'What's the point? Nothing feels worth it anymore'. Those words still ringing in Emily's ears.

33
WEST ROAD

English undergrads sit in Professor Barclay's Faculty Room in a circle. The room is lined, floor to ceiling, with books, and has a smell of academia, stationery and stress. The undergrads all remain silent – a couple looking a bit pasty having succumbed to the carrots in College. Barclay, having left his College rooms in a hurry to make it here in time, is still reeling from Miles's refusal to help him. Barclay writes something on white paper stretched across an impossibly old easel – his pen squeaking and scratching. He turns to face the undergraduates, some of whom are finishing the Valentine's biscuits Dr Trotsham was munching on earlier. He looks at the crumbs she left on the carpet and frowns.

"Can anyone explain the premise of Man and Superman?" The room is silent. "Come on. Someone." A quiet voice pipes up, this class are all terrified of the Professor, knowing he holds their grades in his hands.

"It is a philosophical debate between Don Juan and the Devil," the student suggests.

"Missing entirely the point Shaw was making about men really being in the hands of women," Barclay slams the student back into a muted state.

Dr Guinevere Trotsham knocks and walks straight in, then backs out a little.

"Oh, have you got a minute?" She asks.

"Making Shaw's point. You see?" Professor Barclay says to his students, then following Guinevere out the door and into the corridor.

"The police phoned the Faculty. They'd like all of Hugo Grader's books and access to his logins. They are sending a Sergeant Lime or something. I didn't want you to be surprised if they interrupt you."

"So, you decided to interrupt me to warn me about a possible interruption? Dr Trotsham, what has got you spooked? They're just doing their job. We've already had the pleasure of giving them statements after meeting that delightful Inspector."

"But what if it wasn't natural causes? That's what people think in College. Many were speculating at lunch. What will that do for the department?"

"Department and College are entirely separate." Professor Barclay goes as white as a sheet.

"What about your theatre?"

"The two are completely unrelated. Stop trying to find things in common."

"But he was quitting the English. That looks strange," Dr Trotsham stares as Professor Barclay, hoping for answers.

34
OLD HAUNTS

Emily is on her bicycle, knowing she has a lot of ground to cover. She starts in Granta College and walks up to Elizabeth's grand rooms which overlook Mill Pond. She is fortunate to arrive just as the cleaner is running a vacuum over and emptying a waste paper basket. But on enquiring if Professor Green has made an appearance today, the cleaner shakes her head.

Next, Emily shoots along Silver Street, heading for Downing Street to pop into the Faculty of Plant Sciences. But, when she arrives, Mrs Howcroft, the department's secretary – who has her nose in everything – explains that she hasn't seen Professor Elizabeth Green and is there a number she can call if she spots her later? Emily backs out before becoming embroiled in gossip. Next, she visits Brown's restaurant nearby to see if Elizabeth is hiding in the corner. She bumps into the maître d'.

"Hello, how are you? I don't suppose you've seen Professor Green today?"

"Ah, the lovely Professor. How is she? We do love

her honest feedback about our menu. She keeps us on our toes."

"Have you seen her?" Emily presses.

"No, Professor Masters. But would you like us to let you know if we do?"

"Yes please, that would be super." And Emily hands the maître d' her card.

"No need. We have you on speed dial," he gives it back.

Emily walks her bicycle a few hundred yards and pokes her head into Fitzbillies café. No luck there either.

When Emily makes it to the river, she tries one more place they recently ate in for breakfast, Snobs. Though Emily knows Elizabeth wasn't that enamoured – too much meat on the menu – so holds out little hope. Still wearing her bicycle helmet and holding a pair of gloves, Emily walks right up to the back of the restaurant. But all she notices are some rather loud hoorahs sitting in the window seat, so she leaves, heading to check in the University Arms Hotel bar, in case she has more luck there.

*

In the window seat of Snobs, Miles Bonneville, Darcy Nighy and Lance Fernard are winding down from their over-imbibing at Lance's earlier. Miles has been ripping Professor Barclay to shreds for being a weirdo. They sip cocktails and eat caviar with little passion, trying to dull the pain of Hugo's death.

"I've had a missed call from the police. They want me to come in to talk to their Sergeant again," Miles says.

"Me too," Lance replies.

"I think we've all had one. Time to sober up," Miles suggests.

"That's no fun," Darcy groans. "We've already given them statements?"

"You never liked Hugo," Miles looks at Darcy.

157

"Why?"

"Rubbish, I'm as shocked as you. We all show grief in different ways," Darcy replies.

"His parents are coming up to see the Master. I said I'd go and say hello. Before rehearsals," Lance explains, sipping his cocktail.

"Well, I'm not. They're vile. He hated them," Miles replies.

"They're grieving. They're hardly likely to be vile now." Lance takes a cracker and puts a dollop of caviar on it.

"Probably, just pleased they can use his trust fund for a new boat or something," Miles scoffs.

"What do the police want to know?" Darcy asks.

"I've no idea," Lance finishes spreading the caviar and pops it in, "But, I can tell you one thing, whatever it is they're looking for, they won't stop until they find it."

Miles gets a text, looks irked, then announces "I have to go."

"What?" Darcy asks.

"See you later," Miles replies, giving no explanation.

*

Godric arrives in the heart of Fen Ditton Village, the churchyard walls lined with lichen and winter jasmine. He hears a pigeon coo-cooing. It reminds him of his Bunny, who always tells him it is her favourite bird song. He vividly remembers numerous summer walks to The Plough, to have a drink and eat crisps before going back to Foxes' Haven for a late supper.

But this time there is no Elizabeth. How could he have been so stupid? Valentine's Day. He tries to comprehend how the flowers could have arrived, given his Grandpa is no longer here. Godric has a sense of foreboding. His nanna just doesn't act like this. They need to find her. It is cold, and she is wearing that dress. He wishes she had a mobile, was easily contactable. She could be anywhere.

As he makes his way back down to the river, the only souls he sees are a few rowers, other dog walkers and the local heron. He's glad for the company of Hector, Monty and Clive, as it feels very lonely without knowing where his nanna is. He notices a family of swans by the riverbank and pulls out some bird food. His Bunny is always telling him to carry some in the winter, always putting it in his pockets. He once ate some by accident when he was drunk and hungry. He looks at it twice now. It could just be a flapjack? No, Godric. Give it to the birds. If he avoided food like this, perhaps he would not be so ill. He throws the food on the bank.

With time for his mind to wander, he remembers when he first moved up to Cambridge. Silly really, but it wasn't his friends and College, although they were so much fun. No, it was Bunny. His own mother had failed so miserably at mothering. Whereas, with his Bunny, it wasn't anything big, not the grand gestures. It was the slow drip of love she infused into every part of his life. Warming his slippers by the fire, marking with a yellow highlighter classic films she thought he should watch in the Radio Times. How she liked to bake him things. Even though they were awful, he could see that she had tried. And how she listened. Not many people in his life listen. And, what had he done for her? What did he ever do for her? She was his rock, his person, his go to. But, who did she have? As Godric turned for home, he promised himself that when he found his nanna, he would listen to her more. As he really doesn't know what he would do without her.

35
GREAT ST MARY'S

Miles looks behind him before he enters Great Saint Mary's Church. He then makes his way to the shop to buy a ticket before starting to climb the steps, up past the bells, and out onto the roof, where Dr Guinevere Trotsham is waiting. Once on the roof, Miles can see the Colleges surrounding the Church, and out across as far as The Backs. Directly below is Market Square, with all the stripey awnings covering individual stalls. He looks down at the tiny people milling around the shops below.

"Hello." Guinevere smiles and strokes her hair. "How are you feeling. Has the terrible news been too awful to bear?"

"Hugo is dead. Just stop talking about it. Move on," Miles huffs, adding, "What is this anyway?" Miles frowns, still feeling a buzz from all the drugs he has taken to dull the pain of what happened to Hugo.

"I wanted to see if you were okay?" Dr Guinevere Trotsham asks.

"You have to stop contacting me. You have to hear

me when I say nothing can happen. It was a mistake." Miles looks down again and feels queasy, the edge seems quite low and far too near.

"We weren't nothing," she pleads, "It was pretty special."

"You're, well, you're all grown up. I'm just starting out. I'm a mess," he replies.

"You're not." Guinevere grabs Miles's arm and pulls him towards her and leans in for a kiss.

"I have a girlfriend," Miles says, allowing Guinevere Trotsham to get close up into his face, then pulling away from her.

"Yes, and isn't she a piece of work." Guinevere looks down across Bene't's Chapel, disappointed by the failed embrace.

"That isn't for you to say. You should stay away." Miles rubs his shoulder where her grip was strong.

"What we had–"

"Look. We had fun. You're a good woman. I like you, really, I do. But I don't want to give you any false hope."

"We're good together," she turns, looking lovingly at him.

"Oh, for crying out loud. I've tried to be kind. When is it going to sink in?"

"We can be friends. Friends with benefits?" Guinevere sighs, looking back into Miles' eyes.

"Good friends would know when someone needs space."

"Why did you come then? You clearly can't keep away," Guinevere gives Miles a flirty look.

"To tell you you've lost the plot. You can't send me these," Miles pulls out a pair of knickers in an envelope. "If Darcy'd found them she'd skin you alive, and slowly."

"You still love me though? I can tell. I can help you heal after losing your friend."

Guinevere lunges towards Miles for another attempt at a kiss. Miles frustration explodes.

"For chrissake! I don't need your help. I'm fine about Hugo! And I never loved you. You're a lonely desperate old woman who threw herself at me when I was pissed and too drunk to say no. In this light you look older than my mother. I want nothing to do with you. Leave me alone! Don't follow me!" Miles throws the envelope at her feet and walks off, back down the steps, pushing roughly past some sightseers.

36
HOLKHAM BOUND

"Yes. Yes. I'll let you know if we find her." Emily cuts the phone to Godric.

Inspector Bob Abley is in the driving seat of his car on the A106 heading towards Holkham. He likes driving, often frustrated by the traffic in central Cambridge. But here he can see the big skies and feel joy at the empty roads – either side of which are cabbages, or freshly ploughed soil ready for spring planting.

It could be picture postcard if he didn't have a rather snooty passenger in the form of Elizabeth's friend, Emily Masters, sitting beside him. He knows women like her don't like him. And she makes the hairs on the back of his neck stand up too. For, despite being highly attractive and immaculately dressed, all that comes out of her mouth are words of disappointment.

"Thank you for driving us, but do you have to go so fast?" Emily says, leaning as far back as she could in her seat.

"I have a clean licence, no speeding points. You can

relax." Bob Abley squeezes the wheel a little harder.

"That's good to know. Though, it must come in handy, being a police officer, if you do have speeding issues?" Emily puts her hand in a side pocket of the door to hold on, but feels something and pulls out a golf ball. She looks at the Inspector.

"Won a trophy with that ball. It's lucky," he tries to make conversation about golf. "Makes the car safe."

"Looking at the road ahead when you're driving tends to create more luck and make the car safer." Emily nods at the road. "Why do you play so much golf? Cuthbert said your handicap grew over the past couple of months?"

"It's been an unusual time recently. I don't play anywhere near enough. I'd live on a course if I could," Inspector Bob Abley replies, annoyed that she has pointed to his average increasing over eighteen holes.

"Why don't you find a job in golf?" Emily asks, plopping the ball back in the door pocket.

"Ha! You'd have me quit? Just when we're on a missing person mission?" Abley replies, falling silent for a while. Then he asks as warmly as possible, but clearly revealing he's festering over her previous comment, "Don't you have any hobbies?"

"I'm an academic. You think I have time for hobbies?" Emily replies.

"What is it you do again?" Abley remembers why he hadn't warmed to Emily the first time he met her. Bloody academics.

"Classics."

"Right, you find that useful then, in the real world?" Abley tries to tease gently. But it falls on deaf ears.

"Man has a habit of repeating the same mistakes in the so-called real world," Emily replies, now pulling out more golf balls from under her seat.

"Only man? I seem to remember Maureen always locking the garage door keys in the garage."

"Deus in adiutorium meum intende," Emily sighs.

"Don't these explode under extreme pressure? Not really safe if there is an impact?"

"Let's just find Elizabeth and bring her home," Abley replies, having no clue what to talk about with this woman. Emily looks out the window for a while, then finally speaks again.

"I've never seen her like she was this morning."

'We'll find her," Abley replies, looking across at Emily reassuringly.

"She didn't correct anyone on the Common's Heart of Dogs event. There were so many indiscretions in her animal welfare code. She just stood there. Nothing came out of her lips. Even when she saw this woman had dressed her dog in a pink tutu. Like she'd given up."

"That doesn't sound like the Elizabeth I know. But everyone has their off days."

"She wasn't present, Bob." Emily says, softening towards this man who is helping her find her best friend. They both know that Elizabeth is often easy to find, despite not having a mobile phone, as she works hard and loves her animals so much. So, she is either in her College, department, or home. With her car gone, it felt the obvious place to try first.

"Well, it is sensible to look here," Abley replies.

"We both know it is her favourite place, outside Cambridge." Emily thinks how Elizabeth scattered Gerald's ashes on Holkham Beach. She was there with her. The wind took him far along the beach and out to sea.

"I used to bring the family many moons ago."

"It was odd, all those students falling ill like that?" Emily attempts to change the subject.

"Carrots. So not that odd," Abley replies.

"What about the death?" Emily presses, curious.

"Ah, that. I can't talk about that."

"But it wasn't carrots? Do you know what the cause was?"

"Not yet, but we will," he replies.

Emily opens the glove compartment and sees a packet of buns inside.

"How long have they been there?"

"Eccles cakes. I love an Eccle."

"So hygienic," Emily replies, back to her old self.

"And your car doesn't smell of dog?"

Touché, Emily thinks.

"D'you think we are going to find her?" Emily asks, more seriously.

"I don't know. It strikes me that if she doesn't want to be found, it is not going to be easy," Abley replies, thinking about his friend and where she might be.

37
ON STAGE

It is late afternoon, and everyone has reassembled at The Swan Theatre. The production rehearsals have commenced again today – after the stop start affair with the police turning up earlier. Godric cuts a call he has just made to Emily, who phoned him from the Inspector's car on their way to Holkham. He tries not to worry but finds it hard, given they think it is serious enough to drive all that way. He sighs and vows to keep calling home every half hour.

On stage at the Swan Theatre, in costume and lit by the tech desk, Mercutio and Tybalt begin their argument in Act Three of Romeo and Juliet. Lance acting the part of Tybalt, and Godric is reading in as Romeo, as they both stare at Miles. Miles walks through the lines of Mercutio for the actor who will shortly be taking his place, freeing up Miles to play Romeo. All this, as they wave their swords about.

"Okay, everyone. This is good. Thank you for coming back. I think it was really worth it, as this is the last dress rehearsal before the first performance tomorrow on Valentine's Day. Quick break everybody. Ten minutes!" Godric shouts, then more quietly as he walks over to Darcy who is watching from the stalls in the front row. "Can I have a word?" Darcy nods as Godric jumps down.

Miles, meanwhile, walks behind the curtain to pick up some water for his throat, then grabs Lance's arm.

"You didn't mean that," Miles says forcefully.

"He phoned. The PhD is there if I want it. I must admit, I'm as shocked as you. Barclay turned me down twice already. Thought you should know," Lance replies. "I can't help it. I've got to admit, I'm a bit torn." Lance then shrugs and pulls an 'I'm sorry' face at Miles.

"But, the band. We're in contract to the music label anyway. You have to do it."

"I think Hugo's death might have changed that. And, anyway, we'd have to audition for a lead singer, realistically."

"I'm the lead singer," Miles replies, aghast. At first, Lance says nothing.

"Alright." Lance smiles at Miles, but it doesn't quite reach his eyes.

"If we don't leave now, we'll never be free. Don't take this the wrong way, but I think Barclay is trying to wreck our band. He wants me to stay. It might explain his change of heart about you and the doctorate."

"That's a bit insulting. But I don't care. I like it here. Apart from what happened to Hugo. You have Darcy." Lance looks at his friend, unsure what else to say.

*

"How are you feeling? It's a difficult time." Godric puts his hands through his hair, looking at Darcy in the eye.

"I'm fine. Spit it out," Darcy says, "What is the note?"

"It's hard to focus on the nuances of the performance, given what's happened over the past twenty-four hours."

"Tell me about it."

"But you did ask." Godric pauses. "Your performance is too confident at the moment, a little stony. One note, perhaps. There is no vulnerability, fragility."

"That's called feminism. Deal with it. Woke."

"I hear you. I just wonder if you're playing a far too pushy Juliet. I mean, would the Juliet you're playing even like Romeo?"

"Maybe she would. Maybe she wouldn't. I'm making her authentic."

"You're feeling blood pump around your veins, and that's the performance you're giving. I suggest if you want to impress your would-be-agent on opening night, you lose the cocaine."

38
HOLKHAM DUNES

Emily strides along the boardwalk between tall pine trees, heading towards Holkham beach. She has walked this curvy path over the sands often, usually with Elizabeth and the dogs. This time, Inspector Bob Abley follows a few steps behind, having parked up and grabbed a coffee from the retro refreshment van.

Despite the wind whipping through the huge pines, which emit their strong scent, Emily can already feel the salty, iodine rich sea air on her face. It is an intoxicating fix for the senses and, ordinarily, she would be looking forward to seeing the sea. Many have tried to describe this place's otherworldliness. But none can quite recount just how vast and alien it really feels. Elizabeth describes it as heavenly, and Emily cannot disagree.

But today, Emily is anxious. What if Elizabeth has done something stupid? Elizabeth's last words echo in her head. Inspector Abley reminds Emily that the Talbot Lago is nowhere to be seen. So, they walk, somewhat guessing it will be futile. But with each step, a sense of dread builds.

When Emily and Inspector Bob Abley reach the edge of the trees, a massive expanse of beach stretches out ahead and both sides for miles. The colours, pale blues, greys and yellows, blend into one. Time begins to seem meaningless. Seagulls glide above and cry.

As they head down onto the sand, it soon becomes evident that Abley hasn't thought ahead. While Emily is wearing an expensive looking pair of wellington boots, the Inspector's brogues are not quite the match for Holkham.

"You'll ruin your shoes. Why don't you take them off?"

"It's February! I'll be alright. Don't fuss," Abley replies. But the water begins tipping over the top and seeping into his socks. It isn't long before his feet are sodden.

The wind whips along from the North Sea, biting at their ears on this bitter February day. They start to head towards the dunes, able to see that no one is near the water's edge today. After a while, in the distance, Emily can just make out some thirty or so military horses being exercised and heading straight for them. It is hard to estimate how long it will take before they are close, but judging from the growing thuds from their hooves, it won't be long.

"Let's run for the dunes!" Emily shouts as the equine silhouettes grow closer. The horses come galloping along the sand, and before they both have a chance to make it up onto the bank, the stallions charge right past, just in front of Abley. The noise is deafening, and the horses bear down and almost turn the sky black as they thunder by. Then, as quickly as they came, they begin to grow smaller, kicking sand up behind them like an afterthought of sheer power.

"She's not here, is she." Emily looks across the dunes, which are deathly quiet. They sit in silence for a while, until Emily continues, "Something just made me think. Because it's always been such a special place, to be close to

Gerald."

Inspector Abley pats Emily on the back, and they both look out to sea. Then Abley looks back at the horses, still galloping away in the distance.

"Well, if she is, she's been trampled by a stampede of stallions!" Abley shouts, still a little in shock at how close the horses came.

They look up and down the empty beach. The only other person they can see for miles, and far away on the other side of a tributary, is a man and his Jack Russell who is digging a hole – though it is too far away to know what they hope to unearth. Bob Abley and Emily sit in the dunes for a while, united in their aim to find Elizabeth, but also a little out of breath. After a while, Inspector Abley breaks the silence.

"What this beach could do with, is an ice cream van."

"Aside from it being the middle of winter, that's exactly what this beach does not need. Thank god it's devoid of all the trappings of modern day life. A true oasis of calm. No sugar hits, no noise pollution, none of the kiss-me-quick, penny arcade, crab fishing paraphernalia which destroys the soothing quality of this coast."

"I just like a ninety-nine when I'm at the seaside." Abley takes off his shoes and squeezes out his socks. Emily tries not to look at Abley's now almost blue feet.

"Let's keep searching," she says, standing up.

"She's not here, and there's no car. Where does she drink her peppermint tea?" Inspector Abley hurriedly puts his shoes back on, now holding his socks, and has to run to catch up with Emily, who has already shot back down the dunes onto the beach.

*

Emily and Inspector Abley arrive in Wells-Next-The-Sea, a mile down the coast. A small town, much of which survives through tourism and fishing. As Abley's car drives slowly along the front, Emily scans the cars parked for a Talbot. Nothing. They head up to Buttlands, a square a few hundred yards back from the sea, where grand Georgian homes and a couple of hotels enclose a green lined with lime trees.

"She likes this square," Emily tells Abley as she walks inside The Crown. Abley follows. "She could be parked in their car park out back."

As they enter, the warmth from a roaring fire hits them as well as laughter from a few happy customers standing at the bar.

"I think it would be rude not to make a quick pit stop. I'll ask if they've seen her. Go and perch by the heat. G&T?" Abley looks at a tired and worried Emily, who nods.

"Just one, then back to Cambridge."

Inspector Abley takes off his shoes and puts them by the fire to dry along with his socks. No one in the bar bats an eyelid, used to this kind of thing what with it being by the sea. Emily, on the other hand, moves seat to be further away from them. An action not missed by Abley.

"We are not going to find her, are we?" Emily asks, knowing the answer.

"It makes no sense," Abley replies. "I can always find Elizabeth."

"What if she's done something stupid?"

39
OFF SCRIPT

"Here's to my love." Miles drinks liquid from a vial of poison and starts to fall down next to his Juliet.

"No, no, no!" Darcy sits up from her pretence of being dead – but sleeping – Juliet. "I can't even feel your tears drop on my face. Your performance is wooden," she screams.

"Stop!" Godric walks over and quietly pulls Darcy aside again as Miles leans back and falls to the floor, sighing. Out of earshot of the others, Godric says, "Darcy, we have no room for selfish acting. You're not helping the other actors. Give them a chance, and leave the notes to me. Let's do it one last time, but we have to get other scenes in today before we do the whole thing for real tomorrow, so no more stops." Then he walks back to the stalls and shouts to everyone else. "Okay! Let's go again!"

Miles then gives a fantastic death speech and swallows the poison vial again. Professor Barclay, who has been watching in the back, stands up and applauds loudly.

"Bravo! Everyone else needs to up their game,"

Barclay says to those on stage.

"We are all jolly well trying in the circumstances," Godric replies. Is this Professor for real? "It doesn't help to get that kind of comment at this late hour," Godric adds.

"And can't somebody do something about the light?" Barclay adds, ignoring Godric.

"Thank you. I've been saying that all week," Darcy replies.

"You would do well to find something honest in your performance and make it less eggy," Barclay lectures Darcy.

"Let's turn to Act 3, Scene 1, which is next on our schedule. If everyone in the wings is ready please. Stand by. We're running late, and we have a lot to do. Once with Miles as Mercutio, then as Romeo, please!" Godric shouts then turns to the Professor. "If you could please remain quiet through this and just give me any notes you have after, I would be most grateful."

"Lower the lights a little then," Darcy replies running off stage and carrying some props with her. Godric mouths 'sorry' to Nisha, who then lowers the lights some more. The atmosphere builds. Professor Barclay takes his seat, and Godric shouts, "Action!"

The Capulets and Montagues crash onto the stage, and the crowd of men jeer at Mercutio and Tybalt as they start to argue. Godric is now up on stage to temporarily read Romeo while Miles is this time around playing Mercutio to again show the actor who will soon replace him how to fight the sword fight as Mercutio. Godric looks away up at Nisha in the technical box, pointing to get more of a spotlight on Lance, playing Tybalt. They pull out their swords in preparation to fight. Their words spat at each other.

"I am for you!" Lance shouts – playing Tybalt – at Miles who is temporarily playing Mercutio.

"Come, Sir. Let's begin," Miles shouts back, showing

the stand-in actor how he is holding the sword. The sword fight between Tybalt and Mercutio begins, with much clashing of blades. The actor, Peter, who will replace Miles as Mercutio, watching closely from stage left. Godric shouts out his lines as Romeo to try to stop the fight, as it reaches its crescendo, the stakes high, the sheer energy of a sword fight building to the last blade.

"And cut! Great! I could really feel the tension. Great performances all round. So, let's reset ready to go again, this time with Miles as Romeo and Peter, please take your place as Mercutio." Godric jumps down to the stalls, ready to direct this time. But when he turns, he notices that while others start to walk off, Lance hasn't moved from the spot, nor has Miles from the floor. Lance opens his mouth and lets out a blood curdling scream.

"No, no, no, no, no!" Lance cries. He watches the blood dripping from his sword and then drops it. It clangs down onto the stage floor, making everyone turn and look. As they do, Lance stands over Miles, now motionless on the stage floor, unmoving. Lance grabs him, shakes him. "Miles, Miles. C'mon, Miles." Lance looks at Miles's chest and can see blood oozing. "Doctor, we need a doctor. No, no, no," Lance falls down next to Miles, near weeping. Godric can see Lance collapsed on the stage floor leaning over Miles, as Lance cries, "Someone! Call an ambulance!" Lance shakes Miles again.

"Stop! Don't move him!" Godric shouts. Godric quickly removes his jumper and puts it over the wound in Miles's chest to try to stem the blood loss. In the mayhem of screams and terror, Lance shouts again, "Get a doctor!"

"He's not breathing," Godric replies calmly. Blood has soaked Miles's costume and Godric's jumper already and is beginning to pool around his body on stage. Professor Barclay has climbed up on stage and is about to pick up the sword. "Don't touch it!" Godric turns to Barclay and shouts instinctively, from years of listening to his nanna. "Evidence." The reality of the word hits both

Barclay and Lance. Godric sits down next to the body and pulls out his phone and dials 'Bob Golfie'. It goes to answerphone, so he calls 'Lemon Coppa' and it rings, and a voice at the other end picks up. "You need to get to the Swan Theatre. Miles is dead," Godric says, then lowers his head.

Darcy, having previously gone back to the dressing room to touch up her make-up comes back out on stage, sees the commotion and screams. Nisha, who has run down from the gallery onto the stage, grabs Darcy and gives her a big hug. It isn't long before Godric starts to hear sirens. All then falls quiet on stage, as if they are acting out a scene which has a disastrous end.

"I never bought you a present, Miles. I'm so sorry," Godric whispers to Miles's body, remembering Miles at the night of the Banquet pestering him about it. "I'm so sorry."

40
BY THE SWORD

Godric's troupe of actors and crew are all sitting in the bar, slumped in chairs and still in costume. Alex is bringing them water and a couple have their heads between their legs, looking pale. They are all in shock and have been detained to give statements. SOCOs have cordoned off the stage, seating in the stalls and backstage, including the dressing room. Sergeant Lemon is standing in a corner with Lance Fernard and Constable Petticoat, a little way away from the other actors and crew; although some are close enough to hear.

"So, what you're saying is that you didn't know it was a real sword?" Lemon asks Lance. Constable Petticoat is taking notes. "And we will need you to come down to the station with us. So, I should caution you that although you are not being immediately arrested, you do have the right to use a solicitor."

"Of course not. We use props. I thought I was using a prop. Christ man, my best friend is dead! Why are you here and not looking for whoever did this?"

"I beg your pardon, Sir?" Lemon asked, clearly perplexed.

"Who swapped the prop for a real sword?" Lance says, forcefully.

"So you're confirming again that you didn't know you had a real sword?"

"Like I said when you first arrived, we have props. Props are used which are safe. They retract. We have them in the dressing room. Have you checked yet?" Lance asks. "I told you."

"I don't understand how you thought you were holding a prop that wasn't a sword?" Lemon asks again. "Surely, you can tell?"

"We use very realistic props," Godric pipes up, trying to help explain things to Sergeant Lemon.

"That's right, not a real one. Just one that looks like a sword," Lance replies, sweating profusely.

"I don't know, Sir. If, indeed that did happen. Who do you think might have done it?" Sergeant Lemon asks Lance.

"If I had any idea, d'you think I would have used it?" Lance looks at his hands, they are trembling. He can see blood on his tabard. "I need to get out of these clothes." He looks at his costume.

"Actually, we will take those as evidence. You need to come to the station as you are," Lemon says. "We will have to formally question you. Like I said, you have the right to a solicitor. My Constable will read you your rights."

"I didn't do it. I didn't kill him?" Lance looks confused and looks at Darcy. "I didn't do it."

"Yes, you did," Darcy says firmly from her chair, her face covered in tears, "we all saw it."

"Darcy. Please. Just let the police do their job!" Godric shouts, losing his temper. "We're all very stressed. Me included. Just put a cork in it!"

"It was an accident! You were in the dressing room

anyway. So you can shut up!" Lance shouts back at Darcy.

"Who's responsible for the props?" Sergeant Lemon asks the group. Lance says nothing, Godric is still trying to gain his composure. Meanwhile, a few in the room turn to look at Nisha, who is sitting in the far corner, her hoodie up.

"I am," Nisha replies, pulling down her hood.

"Do you know anything about the sword?"

"There's a basket, in the dressing room, by the door," Nisha whispers.

"You'll have to speak up," Sergeant Lemon says, irritated by this young woman.

"It's like an umbrella stand. We have so many swords. They're interchangeable, anyone can take one," Godric replies, finding his voice again.

"What do you mean?"

"I mean there are sword fights in the play, numerous scenes where swords are carried, with more than one character owning a sword."

"So, you could have taken any sword. Was this random?" Lemon asks Lance.

"I have no idea. I actually put my sword on my dressing room table. I don't use the basket. So, whoever swapped them must have known it was mine. They must have," Lance says.

"Do you not take more care of weapons?" Lemon asks the group more widely.

"We are an amateur group, Sergeant," Godric replies, remaining formal with Lemon in front of the others.

"We are no troupe at all. Miles is dead," Darcy says darkly. "We're a cursed troupe. Hugo's dead."

"It was an accident. Someone is out to get us," Lance looks suspiciously at the cast and crew sitting around in the bar. "I bet I'm next. It's someone trying to stop our band. I'm next." Lance trembles.

"If you can go with the Constable to get your clothes and then the station, Sir." Constable Petticoat puts away his notebook and stands by Lance, waiting for him to leave with him quietly and cooperatively.

"I will go. But, you have to promise you'll find Miles's killer."

"We have numerous witnesses who saw you kill this young man, Sir," Sergeant Lemon replies.

"You can't pin this on me. No, no, no, I don't need lazy policing now. Not when I've done nothing wrong. Can't you see, I'm being framed? Why would I kill my best friend I was about to go on tour with?" Lance storms out, with Constable Petticoat following. Sergeant Lemon takes out his mobile.

"Inspector. Are you on your way?"

*

Inspector Bob Abley and Emily Masters have finished their drinks, which turned into a small snack and a comfort break in Wells-Next-The-Sea. Bob Abley has put the heater on in his car, and is pointing out to Emily how his individual heated seats work, when his phone rings. He pins it to the hands-free contraption, which connects the call to the car's speakers.

"Hello?" Bob Abley says.

"Sir?"

"Yes, what is it?"

"Are you on your way?" Lemon asks.

"Come again?"

"Where are you?"

"In the car, Wells. Just leaving," Abley replies.

"Wells?"

Abley takes his phone off speaker and holds it against his ear and chin.

"I'm with Elizabeth's friend. We came out here in case we could find Elizabeth." Inspector Abley listens, and can hear the concern in Lemon's voice. "Yes, well, apparently, she's missing." Abley listens again. "Calm down. I'll be there shortly. Don't let anyone leave. Get the Constable's—" Abley is interrupted. "I know, I know," Abley listens again, "No we didn't find her." Abley looks at Emily. "Yes, I know it would be good." Abley cuts the call. The silence hangs in the air until Emily speaks.

"You can't keep relying on Elizabeth. She's clearly not as strong as we both think. And you just broke the law."

"Oh, I was hands free. There has been another death."

There is a pause in conversation, until Emily can hold her thought in no longer.

"Don't you have a team who can research poisons? That's what I pay my taxes for. And that was not hands free."

"Yes, we do. This wasn't a poisoning."

"Well. So you can leave Elizabeth out of this, this time," Emily replies.

"Yes, if she will let me. A boy has been stabbed in a play."

"Like I say, completely out of Elizabeth's area of expertise."

"Her grandson's play."

41
PROP

After the police finish taking everyone's statements and the rest of the cast and crew disperse, Godric, Nisha and Alex hang back in the theatre bar for a while. Nisha has been in tears, blaming herself for what has happened. Godric has his arm around her. Alex brings Nisha a glass of cola.

"I know this sounds unlikely right now, but everything is going to be okay." Godric squeezes Nisha. Alex pulls out a tissue.

"I can't believe it," Alex says, stunned "did you all actually–"

"Don't," Godric stops Alex from asking about the gory details.

"What's important to remember is that there would have been no prolonged suffering. I can't believe I just said that. I don't know what I'm saying," Alex says, wandering across to the bar to fetch Godric and himself a cola.

"Why didn't I check the swords before they

started. What will they do?" Nisha asks.

"Who?" Godric asks.

"The police."

"I don't know," Godric replies, now a bit lost in the past twenty four hours and trying to keep it together, for Nisha's sake.

From the corner of the bar, the three of them notice a SOCO passing through from the stalls entrance in the theatre. He is carrying a sword in an evidence bag. They only get a quick glimpse, but can clearly see it is covered in Miles's blood. In the SOCO's other hand, they notice a second bag with another sword, this time clean.

"Perhaps that's it. Perhaps they found the prop sword?" Alex suggests, adding, "Maybe Lance was telling the truth, and someone swapped the real and fake swords."

"But who would have reason to frame Lance?" Nisha asks.

"And, who could have gained access without being noticed?" Godric adds.

"You're saying it was someone we all know?" Alex frowns at them, then sips his cola.

"I've no idea. I wish I could ask my Nanna what she thinks," Godric replies. "I don't think you should be alone, Nish. It doesn't feel safe around here anymore, does it?"

42
AUDITION TALK

After the police allow people to leave the Swan Theatre, Darcy Nighy heads for the English Faculty. Still in shock, but she can't miss her opportunity to audition for Professor Barclay's Rep Company today, especially now Godric's play is almost certainly dead in the water. As she heads across the city centre, she realises Professor Barclay is only twenty feet ahead and so runs to catch up.

"I don't know how you can think of coming to the auditions after what's just happened," Barclay says, dismissively, trying to lose her.

"I'll do anything to get a part. Now Hugo and Miles... I have nothing. I need this," she pleads.

"You need to stop. Go home, Miss Nighy. Talk to your loved ones. Don't come into the Faculty today."

"No. Please. Please listen to me. I need this!" Darcy tugs at Barclay's jacket and looks as if she might faint. He reluctantly stops, as she is making a scene. Darcy continues, "What choice do I have?" Then she changes from pleas to persuasion, "I can channel my emotions into my performance." But Professor Barclay just looks away. Darcy's voice falters, "The alternative is doing nothing and having a nervous breakdown." But she can see that nothing is getting through to him. Darcy looks at Professor Barclay's face. "You seem calm? After what just happened."

"Decades of practice. Besides, I have a department to run. If you're coming, just come now." Professor Barclay is mildly irritated that Miss Darcy Nighy looks like she has run out of steam and is holding him up.

"Right," Darcy is excited but then looks down and can see Miles's blood on her jumper. She leans against the wall on the corner of Sussex Street and the local music shop.

"Are you coming or not? I haven't got time for this," Barclay says impatiently. Darcy says nothing.

"Wait here!" Barclay shouts. He walks off into a nearby café and comes storming out seconds later with a glass of water for Darcy, who has already slid down the wall by an old disused post box. "Drink."

"Thank you." Darcy takes the glass and puts it to her lips, gulping down the water like a thirsty gazelle.

"I'll hold an audition over for you if you come and see me in the next twenty-four hours. Tomorrow. I'm not a monster. But I'm not promising anything. You have some bad habits. Get a grip of your performance. The world is cruel. I need fighters in my troupe."

"Of course, thank you. Thank you." Darcy replies, then puts the glass to her forehead.

And, with that, Barclay leaves, glad to be rid of the nuisance student, but mildly impressed by her hunger for the role in light of the fact that her boyfriend had just been killed.

*

When Professor Barclay arrives at the Faculty of

English on West Road, he stumbles across Dr Guinevere Trotsham in an empty staff room.

"How did rehearsals go?" She asks.

"I can kiss goodbye to my beloved theatre. Who will sponsor me now?" Barclay replies leafing through his post and slamming it back in his pigeon hole.

"They'll get better before tomorrow's opening night," Dr Trotsham tries to reassure him.

"Bonneville is dead. Lance bloody killed him!"

"What?" Guinevere staggers a little, leaning into Professor Barclay to regain her balance.

"What is it about the fairer sex? I'm supposed to treat you equally and yet you're all wilting around me?"

"Miles Bonneville is dead? What are you talking about?" Dr Trotsham says the words slowly.

"And you're deaf too?" Barclay replies, sarcastically.

"Why do you have to be such a complete bastard?" She frowns at him

"I am trying to create a beautiful new theatre. I'm not the guilty party here. I haven't fucked anyone who is now no longer with us."

Dr Guinevere Trotsham finds an armchair and sits, closing her eyes.

"You're going to sit there all day now?" Professor Barclay pulls a face.

"You didn't do this, did you?" Guinevere Trotsham opens her eyes and looks directly at Professor Barclay accusingly.

"I beg your pardon?" Barclay says, his eyes wild and rolling.

"Well, he said no to you. He wouldn't be in your bloody troupe, and now he's dead!"

"He was your lover. Did you do it?" Professor Barclay scoffs.

"I thought you said Lance Fernard did it?" Dr Trotsham replies.

43
POLICE STATION

Inspector Abley walks into Cambridge Police Station on Parker's Piece where Sergeant Lemon is waiting for him in reception.

"Sir," Lemon hands him a file.

"Tell me what you know," Abley opens it, looking at the images of Miles Bonneville.

"We have the young student in an interview room. We have nine witnesses of the stabbing. We have the sword," Lemon replies, heading off for the room.

"Should be a quick interview," Abley follows.

"But his prop sword has turned up." Lemon stops walking, causing Abley to stop too. "It was in the bin in the alley, behind backstage. It had been seemingly disposed of there. So, there could have been a switch. That's the story he's claiming."

"Great! C'mon." Abley starts off again along the station corridor, keen to get this interview done, then, "Hang on. D'you have any change?" Abley asks, stopping again near a vending machine. Lemon rifles about in his pockets, then hands Abley some coins, allowing Abley to grab a coffee from the machine before they enter.

"Thanks for lunch," Sergeant Lemon says, while they wait for the froth on top of the coffee to squirt.

"You getting the jitters about tomorrow?" Abley then sings, "Here comes the bride, all dressed in white."

"Hell, yeah. I'm hoping to pull a double shift on this. Be all tied up," Lemon replies, letting out a deep sigh.

"Ah, this'll be wrapped up by tomorrow by the sounds of it."

"Not without Professor Green, it won't. I checked with Leedham, and he still has no clue what caused the first student's death, at Christina's. We are no further forward on Hugo Grader."

"That man would come third in a race with a sloth and a snail," Abley replies. "All those pens and he was planning when to plant his vegetables on our police computer."

"You didn't find Professor Green. Is that worrying?" Lemon enquires, choosing some sweets from the vending machine.

"I'm going to get that bloody woman a mobile when she turns up."

"She wouldn't use it," Lemon smirks then checks himself, realising it is most unlike Elizabeth Green to pass up on helping with a case. "Leedham did say that Hugo Grader was healthy and he is also pretty sure he didn't die of natural causes or suicide."

"Great! So, we have two possible murders on our hands. Why didn't you tell me before?"

"I'm telling you now. You've not been here," Lemon stares at his Inspector, then pops in a mint.

"Fair enough, I'm happy to take the lead in this interview. Chip in whenever." Abley then looks at Lemon's mints. "Are they vegan?"

Lemon looks down at the packet labelling and follows his Inspector in. The two men walk in to see Lance, sitting at the table, with his head in his hands.

✦

"For the tape, Inspector Abley and Sergeant Lemon have entered the room. And the interviewee has waived his right to a solicitor." Abley leans across the table, "Why did you kill your friend, Mr Fernard? Weren't you going to be the next big thing?"

"I've made my statement. The prop was changed," Lance says quietly.

"We have found your prop sword," Abley replies.

"Oh, thank god," Lance leans back in his chair, visibly relieved. "Thank god. This is a nightmare. Poor Miles. But, to be accused of it."

"No one is accusing you. You haven't been arrested. Yet," Lemon says, leaning forward.

"Because I didn't do anything!" Lance shouts then waves his arms about. "I'm a victim here too. I mean, I know I'm alive, but someone is trying to frame me. Clearly, someone who didn't want us to be successful. The 'Three Charming Men', I mean."

"I should caution you that you are likely to be charged, so would recommend you organise a solicitor," Inspector Abley stares at Lance.

"But, I'm innocent. You said you found the prop sword. Have you checked for fingerprints?"

'We are not going to discuss that with you," Sergeant Lemon replies. "You need to tell us exactly what happened."

"Someone has framed me for this. Miles was my friend. I don't know who, but someone has set me up. And my friend is dead. This is insane. If you're not going to look, then let me out, for chrissake. So I can find out who did this."

"Can you tell us if you'd had a fight with Mr Bonneville?" Lemon asks.

"We never fought. Miles and Hugo were always bickering, but they loved each other. We all did."

"Yes, well. Both are now dead. One by your hand. At the very least you're probably looking at manslaughter," Lemon suggests firmly.

"Miles was a good bloke." Finally, Lance breaks down, and tears run down his cheek. "We were just together before the play. We even managed to relax, despite what had happened to Hugo. We were still in shock from that. I'm still in shock. How can Hugo be dead?" Lance shuts his eyes for a while and hangs his head, then adds, "Have you found out what happened to Hugo?"

"What do you mean?" Inspector Abley asks.

"Well, if someone has framed me for this, don't you think you should be looking at the cause of death of Hugo?" Lance opens his eyes, and looks directly at Inspector Abley.

"Sir, we are not the ones being questioned here," Lemon replies. "I understand, from speaking to the cast that you frequently like to use recreational drugs? We shall be obtaining a search warrant for your home, so I urge you to consider your answer carefully."

"Yes, I do like a small amount of coke every now and then. But you can buy it like sherbet these days. I'm far from alone."

"Expensive habit," Abley says.

"Not that I'd noticed," Lance says, then picks at his hair.

"So, it was possible that you were in fact under the influence of an illegal substance at the time you thrust your sword into your friend?" Abley suggests.

"It wasn't my sword, and no, I wasn't," Lance replies, knowing that he probably was under the influence, but not so much he had lost his senses.

"You won't mind if we do a blood test?" Sergeant Lemon says, not really asking.

"Test away. Test the prop sword for fingerprints

while you're at it, and Hugo's body. You could talk to that bastard, Barclay," Lance suggests. "What was he even doing there? He doesn't come to rehearsals. What did he say?"

"Professor Barclay?" Inspector Abley asks, curious.

"He had a row with Miles. Was trying to blackmail him into being in his new 'troupe'. What a farce. No one likes him. No one wants to join."

"A row?" Abley pushes for more.

"Threatened he had to join or else. But, we were leaving to go on tour."

"Or else?"

"I don't know. Miles was pretty mad when he came back from seeing him, yes," Lance replies, adding, "Then, Barclay offered me a PhD. Miles said it was because Barclay would do anything to make us stay. I'd been trying for ages, and he'd declined twice before. But, today, he just suggested it?" Lance gets out his phone and shows them Barclay's emailed offer. "Miles warned me, and I told him I was insulted. But, it all makes sense now?"

"And you? You have no band now?" Abley asks.

"Are you not listening to me? I'm not going anywhere with the 'Three Charming Men' now."

"So the band is dead?" Abley presses.

"D'you know that your eyebrows are like caterpillars?" Lance stares at Inspector Abley's face. Then he turns to Sergeant Lemon and watches him scratch at his arms, but decides to look back at Abley's eyebrows. "They should be in the Zoological Museum."

"Are you high?" Inspector Abley looks at Lance Fernard's slightly dilated pupils.

"No, though that might have enhanced the whole eyebrow experience," Lance continues to stare at Abley's eyebrows.

"I'd suggest you refrain from flippancy during a police investigation," Abley says.

"Can you get some more up-to-date equipment then,

if I'm to take this seriously? I mean, where did you get this from? A '70s TV prop sale?" Lance looks at the recording machine in the room. "I need to get far away from this. Maybe India. Visit the ashram in Rishikesh. If it's good enough for John Lennon?"

"Isn't that a bit before your time?" Sergeant Lemon replies.

"Everything is a bit before my time. Haven't you noticed my age?" Lance scoffs.

"Well, you're not going anywhere yet. We've definitely not finished with you," Abley gets up from his chair and goes to leave the room. Lemon stands up to follow, registering for the tape that the interview is suspended, then nodding at the Constable in the corner as they go.

Lance looks at the door as they leave. Is he going to be charged with murder?

44
DROWNING SORROWS

Tea time, and while others rush home under a darkening sky, Godric, Alex and Nisha shuffle from the bar at the Swan Theatre to one on St Andrew's Street. Godric certainly isn't going to let Nisha back to her room alone. And as for Alex, although Godric is not entirely sure why he has tagged along, he is grateful for Alex's sunny disposition, despite present circumstances. And Alex is most definitely easy on the eye, which is hard to ignore right now.

It is a random choice – after they have wandered aimlessly together, chatting, trying to process things – to find themselves enticed in by the age-old offer of a 'Happy Hour' bar from the selection down this way. Anything to sit and find a warm place to be away from the university for a while, away from anyone who knows them, who might want to talk about what has happened, want to ask questions.

Godric is still feeling ill, and in no way thinks he can drink, but lets Alex order him a whisky, "so long as I have a water on the side", he says. In truth, Godric wants the place to swallow him up. To let him sleep. To find some way other than booze in his current state to drown his feelings, numb the pain of what has just happened. He tries to call home for the umpteenth time. But just gets the answerphone, again. Emily has called him and is still looking, but found nothing. At least she is keeping him posted.

"I can't stay long. I have to go home," Godric says, completely preoccupied and torn between looking after his friend and finding his nanna. For now, he needs to sit, to rest, to take stock.

"I'm just so scared," Nisha replies, looking at him.

"Don't be scared. You're not alone. This will get sorted," Godric says, only half believing it himself.

It isn't long before, through the power of constant messages, Darcy finds them. They all now sit, stunned in silence, surrounded by lovers and groups of people celebrating Valentine's Day a day early.

"I've never felt less loved up," Darcy says, swigging the whisky Alex bought Godric, then giving it back.

"I'm sorry for your loss," Alex replies, "had you been dating Miles for a long time?"

Godric pushes the drink back to Darcy, then signals to the barman to bring him some more water and one for Nisha.

"I wasn't dating him. I was the love of his life," Darcy replies, "Who are you?"

"My friend. Leave him alone," Godric says acerbically.

"Waify, did you swap the props?" Darcy scowls at Nisha.

"C'mon!" Godric shouts, "Stop! You were accusing Lance earlier. Are you intent on picking us all off one by one until you've created utter misery?" Godric spits at Darcy, cross at her attitude.

"What? I'm only saying what everyone is thinking,"

Darcy says.

"I wasn't thinking that," Alex says, "I was thinking that I could do with something to eat. I'm Hank Marvin," then turning to Godric, who shakes his head.

"Just avoid carrots, and whatever killed Hugo. Waify?" Darcy continues to pester Nisha as she takes another gulp of Godric's whisky.

"I didn't swap the props, and I don't know why Hugo died," Nisha says quietly.

"Can you just calm down, Darcy! We're all in a bad way. Not just you. We all liked Miles and Hugo. I didn't know them as well as you. But they seemed very decent. It's devastating. We're all in shock." Godric has had enough of Darcy.

"Perhaps we should go somewhere quieter?" Alex suggests to Godric.

"We have to wait for Lance. He's coming. They've just released him. I texted him. He's beside himself. It's clear this is a stitch up," Nisha says, looking at her phone.

"Haven't they charged him?" Darcy asks, surprised.

"Thought you said I was the guilty one?" Nisha replies quietly.

"You are. But he has a lot to answer for. He stuck the blade in. He murdered Miles."

"It's only murder if he intended it," Godric corrects Darcy.

"I think we should all stick together. I'm sure he'll be happy to see you, Darcy. You're his friend. He's your boyfriend's friend," Nisha says quietly.

After a short while, the doors to the bar open and in walks Lance. He looks sweaty, and he's wearing a red jumper under a large black puffer jacket.

"They took the costume and the shirt off my back too. How can there be lost property in a police station?" Lance shakes the coat from lost property. "Nobody sniff me."

"Why did they take your clothes?" Darcy asks.

"I have no idea. DNA or some such. I know I need to get pissed! Could be my last," Lance plonks himself down between Nisha and Darcy. He turns to look at Darcy. "You still think I'm a murderer?"

"No," Darcy says quietly. "I'm sorry," Darcy shakes her head. "Miles is my boyfriend, the love of my life," she replies, her voice breaking.

"They were my family too, my brothers. Darce, I'm shit scared. Someone is playing with me. Am I next?" Lance looks at them all for answers, putting his arm around both Nisha and Darcy. "They've killed Miles by swapping the props and Hugo must have been murdered too. He was strong, stronger than all of us."

"If someone hated Miles enough to murder him, then I could be next." Darcy glares at Nisha, then clings to Lance, hitting him in the chest, "You killed him, you killed him!" She cries. "Anyway, what d'you mean your last?"

"They're building a case against me. Or, that's what it feels like. Don't think they believe the props were swapped. They are going to charge me with manslaughter at the very least. The only reason I'm out is that they are not sure whether to charge me with murder. Building that case."

"They found your prop," Godric replies.

Lance snatches Godric's whisky from Darcy then signals to the barman to bring the bottle.

"Yes, they said. Like I say, I'm released pending charge of criminal manslaughter, criminal negligence or murder. They've taken my passport. Likely charge me in days. I'm innocent." Lance knocks back the last of Godric's drink. "Ironic now that Barclay has just offered me a PhD."

"Congratulations," Nisha says, smiling.

"Yeah, as if I can do it now," Lance says, adding, "Are you okay, Nish?" Lance notices Nisha is trembling.

"I will be. Godric has been looking after me," Nisha leans into Godric's shoulder. Darcy cannot stand the

197

cosiness now that she has lost Miles.

"What about me?" Darcy asks the room, staring at empty glasses and hoping someone gets in another round of drinks.

After a while the bar fills up, and the karaoke machine is switched on, with the first happy drinker belting out a ballad. Someone at the next table pulls party poppers and a champagne cork pops, causing the group to jump a little. Lance has drunk a good many whiskies, as has Darcy after Lance bought a bottle. After a while, Darcy gets up.

"See you tomorrow. I have to sleep so I can enact my revenge on the killer. I will dream of ways to make them suffer."

"I'll come back with you that way," Lance replies. "I have to get out of this convict garb, and you're welcome to come back to mine for some happiness in a bucket," Lance looks at Darcy jogging her memory about his bucket of drugs, then turns to Nisha. "Can I walk you back, Nish?" Lance asks.

"Godric has said he will, so it's okay."

"Good, so long as you're not alone," Lance smiles at the group then turns to follow Darcy, who is already out the door.

Nisha sips her soft drink.

"Well, that felt more than a little uncomfortable. She more or less accused him of killing Miles, and now they're best pals?" Godric says of Darcy leaving with Lance. Then turning to Nisha, "You feeling okay?" Godric asks Nisha.

"A bit. I still feel weak. You?" Nisha says.

"Same. C'mon, let's go. Let's get you to your bed."

"I checked my coat earlier. Will catch you up outside," Alex adds turning to the back of the room to the coat check.

"Thank you, Goddy. For everything," Nisha replies.

"Don't be daft. I've hardly done a thing."

"You've been a good friend, and I'm really grateful,"

Nisha replies.

"Alright, well. Don't sound so dramatic. I'm not going anywhere," Godric smiles at a worried looking Nisha.

45
OLD FOLKS

Professor Elizabeth Green sits at the piano in the 'old folks' care home on Carlyle Road, still wearing the dress with little daisies that Gerald bought her a few years ago. It is dark outside, but the curtains remain open so that residents can look out onto Alexandra Gardens and enjoy the floodlit trees and dog walkers weaving across the lawns.

Elizabeth sits next to John, a silver haired gentleman who lost his wife, Agnes, a few years back. Elizabeth has been coming to play duets with John for six months now, after they met in the Co-op and struck up a conversation about the unnecessary plastic packaging around bunches of bananas. John has mild dementia, but shared with Elizabeth early on in their friendship that when he plays music, he can remember his beloved again. So, how can she refuse his offer of a regular cup of tea and evening with Debussy?

Whenever John and Elizabeth play the piano, the 'Happy Days Residential Care Home' common room fills up with residents, arriving for the free concert. Staff have decorated the room with roses, ready for Valentine's Day tomorrow. Red and cream paper chains have been lovingly made by residents, and red paper hearts cut out and stuck on the windows. For the first time this week, Elizabeth feels safe. Feels known. Her pain is not unique here. A resident called Morris comes up to the piano.

"Can you play 'Cheek to Cheek', Edna?"

"Edna?" Elizabeth asks John quietly.

"His wife, who's left us."

"Morris, what a good choice," Elizabeth replies.

John and Elizabeth start playing Irving Berlin, and there is an audible warm sigh in the room. A man in an overlong maroon cardigan slowly lifts himself from his chair and asks a nurse to dance. Before long, a number of octogenarians are up on their feet and merrily shuffling.

Elizabeth looks around and feels like she is with her people, but very soon after is hit by a pang of utter loneliness and desperation. An image of Gerald dancing with her at that open-air Portofino concert a few years ago then pops into her head. The sun already having kissed his face with honey colours, as the sunset bounced off the beautiful homes surrounding the harbour. Heavenly. She plays the notes and shuts her eyes. She can smell his shirt, his arms, her jumper catching on his watch and him telling her she's 'stuck on him'. Him twirling, dipping her in dance then pulling her up in an embrace. Elizabeth is intoxicated by the memory and carried away to a happier place. She can feel her heart turn over.

A resident knows the words and starts to sing from her chair, which brings Elizabeth back into the room. At that moment, in the care home common room, Elizabeth sees souls transported to a happier place, their independent memories intertwining as they smile and sway. Eventually, the music comes to an end and Elizabeth waits for the next request.

"'Blue skies', please," Morris shouts. Elizabeth holds

back any more tears, as she starts to play a few notes, waiting for John to join in on the lower keys.

"This was Agnes's favourite," John says quietly.

Before too long, joyous dancing lifts further the atmosphere in the room, and residents begin to sing along. The room is full of wonderful memories. Elizabeth looks at the smiles, behind which lurk thoughts of better days. The forties, fifties, for some the sixties. Is this all that is left? She'll take it if it means she can remember Gerald. It is better than forgetting, as with John and Morris's forgetfulness. Elizabeth worries one day she will forget Gerald. Everything is fading. Life is fading. Her dreams are faded. A chill runs down the back of her spine, as the room sings, "Nothing but blue skies from now on."

"D'you know any Elton John?" someone shouts, and laughter ripples.

"Neil Diamond!" Another shouts to more laughter.

Elizabeth wishes young people would come and visit these souls more often. You are never old until you're dead.

46
CARS GO FAST

Godric follows Nisha out onto St Andrew's Street.

"I'll walk you home. You'll be safe in your room. Porters are mad fierce in Christina's. You'd have to be a ninja warrior with superpowers to get past them," Godric says, trying to make Nisha smile, waving his hands about like a ninja.

"Okay, thank you," Nisha replies.

When the cold air hits Nisha out on the pavement, she stumbles a little, still feeling weak from her earlier carrot poisoning. Godric grabs her to stop her from falling. Nisha drops her glove and they bend down to pick it up. It is dark, and the street has quietened down. A person in a hoodie rushes up and stands right in front of them. As they look up, the stranger blows powder in their face, which puffs out around them like a white cloud and they inhale and are immediately blinded by it. Nisha starts to shake her head from side to side, but she can't focus properly. She sees a stranger, hidden behind a bandana, and feels them grab her hands and start to lead her away.

Godric has Nisha's keys in his hand and tries to reach for the stranger to stop them from taking Nisha.

"Hey," Godric tries to shout, but only a tiny voice comes out. The stranger says nothing.

Godric can see the stranger leading Nisha and now pulling him too towards the road. Godric can feel what is happening to him but cannot understand why he seems powerless to resist? Before he can do anything to stop the stranger's actions, he finds himself being pulled down to lay on the road. After no struggle, his head on the tarmac and Godric watches from the middle of the road as the stranger leads Nisha away. After a while, he sees in the far distance Nisha standing by a wall with the stranger. But a car zooms past Godric's head, not having spotted him lying in the road, missing him by inches.

Godric looks up at the stars unable to move. He feels remarkably calm. A second car whooshes by from the opposite direction, probably a taxi Godric thinks, as this is a zone which is off limits to most cars. He looks back at the pavement to see if he can see Nisha, but all he notices is a very anxious looking Alex running towards him. Another car passes. He hears Alex scream, then from behind, Godric thinks he spots the stranger again. Godric feels cold, and watches Alex jump in front of a car. He wonders why Alex is doing something so dangerous and tries to warn him to stop, but his voice is so quiet. He hears brakes screech and feels Alex's hands behind his back, willing him to stand up.

"Godric! C'mon! Stop being an idiot," Alex is now screaming at Godric, but Godric still can't move. "Get up!" It isn't long before Godric whispers that he is having trouble, so Alex pulls him up, and half carries him to the pavement. Alex becomes worried when Godric lays down again and is unresponsive. Alex hails a taxi and asks it to take them to A&E. As Godric lays in the back of the taxi, he wonders what has happened to Nisha.

47
TEA FOR TWO

As Emily steps out of the front door of Foxes' Haven, the neighbour, Mrs Cloud, is putting out the rubbish.

"This is about the fourth time I've seen you today. Have you moved in with Mrs Green?" Mrs Cloud shouts across to Emily as Elizabeth's security light snaps on to illuminate outside.

"Oh, no. Hello. No, actually," Emily pauses, having gone back to check to see if Elizabeth was at home, but unnervingly found nothing, ushering the dogs in behind her.

"What Dear?" Mrs Cloud stands, staring and waiting for Emily to explain.

"I'm not sure where Elizabeth is? I was supposed to be taking tutorials this morning, but have found myself looking for her for most of today. She seems to have disappeared? Though I see her car is back." Emily looks at the Talbot in the drive.

"Oh, Elizabeth never disappears. She just hides. She's particularly good at not answering the front door. She not there?"

"No,"

"I'm sure she'll turn up," Mrs Cloud replies.

"No, really. I've tried her department, College, all her local haunts, the Commons. Even her favourite beach," Emily clearly looks worried.

"Not all the way to Holkham?" Mrs Cloud is surprised.

"Sand in my socks to prove it."

"Well, I'm er, not sure why you need to see her, but she likes her privacy. Maybe I can take a message?"

"I'm Emily, Emily Masters. A friend. She wasn't herself when I saw her last. Honestly, I'd just feel better if I found her. To know she's okay."

"Mrs Cloud, Irene. Elizabeth has spoken about you before. You're her stylish friend. She says you're so glamorous. What is that, Chanel?" Mrs Cloud examines Emily's clothes.

Emily hasn't got time for this and looks back frantically at Mrs Cloud. After a long pause, and seeing the worry that Emily is not going away, Mrs Cloud reluctantly suggests another location that Emily might like to check.

"Have you tried 'Happy Days'? She's been spending quite a bit of time there recently. My Mother lives there now, and says Elizabeth is very good on piano," Mrs Cloud replies, a little uncomfortable about sharing this private information on Elizabeth's whereabouts, knowing her neighbour likes to keep herself to herself. Emily looks confused, so Mrs Cloud continues. "Up on Alexandra Gardens. Across the road."

"Only across the road?" Emily asks.

"Want me to draw you a map?"

"No, no. You're good. I'll find it."

*

Elizabeth spots Emily walking towards the 'Happy

Day's Residential Care Home'. She sees her cross Alexandra Gardens outside in the ever-darkening night. Elizabeth sighs. She has been rumbled. It isn't long before Emily pops her head into the common room door. When the two lock eyes, Elizabeth can see the concern and feels guilty for worrying Emily and so mouths "I'm sorry." But Emily doesn't have time for niceties and walks through the dancers to Elizabeth.

"It's Godric."

48
A NANNA'S LOVE

Elizabeth, still in her clothes from yesterday, carries a tray into Godric's bedroom. She places it at the end of the bed and opens the curtains a chink to let in some sunshine. She sits in a chair in the corner of the room, and for a while, watches Godric asleep. It isn't this action that wakes Godric, rather all three dogs bounding in and jumping up on the bed. Elizabeth leaps up to save the breakfast tray.

"Off! Get off! Hector! Monty!" Elizabeth shouts. "Who said you could come up here? Clive! This is the premium lounge. Get back into the economy. Cats only. Out!" And, she points at the stairs. The dogs, who know better than to challenge, jump off and run back down the stairs. "And stay!" Elizabeth watches from the door as the dogs look back from the bottom of the stairs, disappointed. She hears a laugh from Godric, who then pulls a face from his headache.

"You're back then," Godric beams. Then tears spike in his eyes. "I was so worried."

"Seems I have to be more worried about you?"

Elizabeth raises her eyebrows.

"I'm okay." Godric tries to sit up.

"Just take it easy." Elizabeth fusses over Godric's pillows to make him comfortable. Godric notices Alex's jacket from last night on a chair in the corner. Elizabeth explains, "Your new 'friend' didn't move from your bedside. He stayed here last night in the small hours when I had to go to test the sample to see what caused this. Completely besotted. I sent him home for some sleep when I got back."

"He stayed?" Godric purses his lips in a half smile, happy to have met someone nice in this awful time. Elizabeth nods.

"What worries me most in all this is that he said he had to pick you up out of the middle of the road. Miss Acharya-Gorpade was being robbed, and you were being left to—"

"Die?" Godric finishes her thought.

"Don't. Don't." Elizabeth cannot think of such an outcome.

"All the deaths have been young men so far," Godric says what his nanna is thinking.

"I think you had better fill me in, for all our sakes."

"Oh, Bunny. It's been positively awful. I don't think I'm cut out for all—"

"I'm back. I'm here. You're not alone." Elizabeth looks at Godric's huge eyes reassuringly.

"But, why was Nisha targeted? Is she okay?" Godric asks.

"Perhaps she just got in the way, wrong place, wrong time. The important point is that you're okay."

"Nisha? Is she okay?" Godric repeats.

"Yes. You need to rest and stop thinking about other people now. Your body has gone through it," Elizabeth says, holding Godric's hand, adding, "Poisoned twice in two days.

"But, still here. With your kind nursing back to health."

"You have to thank Alex. He saved you when I wasn't there," Elizabeth looks down and stops talking.

"You're always there. You're here, when it counts," Godric smiles at his nanna as she looks back at him. "You just said you've been testing things, haven't you?"

"I ignored the warning signs. Too wrapped up–"

"Don't." Godric stops his nanna from beating herself up.

"I spoke to the consultant. Ms Acharya-Gorpade was able to describe being drugged. I think you inhaled more of it. You were poisoned with 'Devil's breath'."

"What? What's that? It doesn't sound very appetising."

"A shrub from Colombia, Borrachero. Clever plant actually."

"I don't understand. Obviously more clever than I–"

"You were both drugged using it," Elizabeth interrupts. "It comes as a fine white powder. Ground up seeds, I suspect. Blown in the face. Renders victims harmless and helpless, but persuadable. Still conscious. It's used sometimes as a date drug. This time, apparently, a thief used it, or that's what Nisha described. Said she was led to the cashpoint and using her mobile they made her empty her bank account. Is she wealthy?" Elizabeth asks.

"Very."

"Anyway, it disappears really quickly from the bloodstream. I was just lucky Emily had driven me to the hospital to see you. You were on the same ward as Ms Acharya-Gorpade, and I heard her talking about a powder being blown in your faces, etc... The consultant was also quick and took the sample to test."

"Are you sure she's okay?"

"Yes, they have kept her in. You both have exhaustion. I wanted you home. Had to put up a stink to get you out. I always think people get better quicker in their own bed."

"Thank you. I'm glad to be here," Godric smiles

weakly. "You know how I detest hospitals." Then he thinks, adding, "Those gowns with the open backs though. They could take off in the clubs."

"You're recovered then," Elizabeth puts jam on some toast.

"Crumbs, Bunny. Someone did all this just to rob Nisha?"

"Perhaps you got in the way when the powder was blown. I'm afraid I don't know. But it sounds odd."

"D'you think it is related to the deaths?" Godric asks.

"I think you need to fill me in on exactly what's been going on."

"I'm just so glad you're here." Godric smiles, so relieved that his nanna is talking again. "You know, I don't think I can function without you looking after me?" Godric picks up his cup of hot chocolate.

"Oh, you just like my hot chocolate. You can make it yourself, you know."

"No. It's not that. It's home. This is home. You're home to me." Godric looks at his nanna seriously.

"Oh." Godric's words floor Elizabeth. Is she really home? Is this what life is now?

"I don't think I say it enough, but you mean the world to me," he continues.

"Alright, don't get all gushy. It's the poison." Elizabeth cannot cope with this. Not this week. What would she have done if something had happened to Godric? Elizabeth tries her hardest to hold back the tears. But, try as she might, her eyes fill up, and one escapes.

"Bunny," Godric reads Elizabeth's mind. "I'm not going anywhere. Even devil's breath, or whatever it's called, can't do me in. Or carrots!"

"Well, get on with filling me in? Whoever is doing this is getting far too close for my liking."

"Did you hear anything I said to you when I stayed up all night and slept outside your door?"

"You can't stay up and sleep at the same time,

Goddy."

"Miles is dead. Lance killed him but swears he did it by accident, and they did find swords switched, so it looks like he was telling the truth, but still might be charged," Godric takes a sip of his hot chocolate, stirs it some more with a dainty spoon, then continues, "Hugo is dead. He died first. And we think he's been murdered. Now Miles is dead. Miles thought someone was trying to kill off the band. Before he was killed."

"Who is left in the band?"

"Lance Fernard."

"What does he look like?" Elizabeth asks, taking a bite of the toast Godric hasn't touched.

"I suppose he looks a little like me. Tall, blonde. Though his hair is longer. A bit more mousey. But it was dark? Hang on, do you think they were trying to kill Lance and got me instead?"

"Perhaps there was a case of mistaken identity? Where was Mr Fernard when you were poisoned last night?"

"He'd been with us in the bar. He'd just come from the police station and was drinking heavily, as he thinks he's going to be framed for Miles and Hugo's deaths. He was going off with Darcy to get drunker."

"So, you came out of a bar, at night, in the dark. And, it's not inconceivable that this Miles Bonneville was right. Do they have enemies? This Hugo Grader died at the Banquet?" Elizabeth picks up a strawberry from the breakfast tray and pops it in her mouth.

"Ah, so you were listening. And sounds like you've already been checking up on them."

"I couldn't help it. You were talking very loudly outside my bedroom door all night. And I spoke to a Constable Petticoat who turned up at the hospital following reports of a man lying in the road. You." Elizabeth pauses, still feeling anxious about Godric lying in the road. She forces herself to think about the case, "It was serendipitous for Hugo Grader's murderer, if he was murdered which indeed looks likely, that you all got organophosphate poisoning. It masked their actions. I'm going to have to see Leedham."

"Is that allowed? If you're not on the case?" Godric asks.

"Eat," Elizabeth shrugs and passes a piece of toast to Godric.

Godric sits up and wonders if his stomach will let him eat again.

"I saw the flowers," Godric says quietly, taking a small bite. "Why didn't you say?" Godric asks, but his nanna remains silent, so he continues, "Sometimes, life throws a curved ball, and the mind can't lock it away quick enough. The heart bears the brunt."

"When did you get all philosophical?" Elizabeth plops a strawberry on Godric's toast. "And, not if you don't get better. Eat." Elizabeth pours Godric an orange juice from a silver jug and puts it on his bedside table. As she does, the doorbell rings. Elizabeth shoots downstairs to find Alex outside with a small bunch of daffodils.

"Well, it's officially Valentine's Day," Alex says, "And I forgot my jacket."

"So it is. Do come in. He'll be pleased to see you. I'll get a vase for his room."

"No, they're for you," Alex hands the daffodils to Elizabeth. "I know you must have been worried like me. Well, more than me, I've only met him this term, and I've been going out of my head. I promise not to tire him too much."

"I'll brew some more tea." Elizabeth takes the bunch of flowers and watches Alex run up the stairs, two by two. She knows that his kind gesture is supposed to make her feel happy, touched. She doesn't feel anything. It is like someone has flicked a switch, and all she can feel is pain. The telephone distracts her from her thoughts.

"It's for you! It's the Inspector!" Godric shouts down.

He just texted me."

"Why didn't he just phone me?" Elizabeth shouts back up to Godric, then quietly to herself, "texting you first. What's the world coming to?" Elizabeth, unimpressed by modern technology, walks over to the telephone table as the phone continues to trill.

"Because you weren't here! They went to Holkham!" Godric shouts back down.

"What?" Elizabeth starts to shout back. Godric starts to cough, so Elizabeth picks up the phone.

"Hello Inspector, what's this I hear about Holkham?"

"Your friend Emily leaves something to be desired. Too cold, too hot, I was driving too fast, too slow. I wasn't looking where I was going. Turn right, not left. Proper bossy boots. Hated my car sweets, nosed in all my pockets. Then her gin and tonic didn't have enough ice!"

"You were on a date? I supposed Cuthbert is abroad," Elizabeth replies.

"Very droll."

"Well, I'm here now. Don't know what all the fuss is about," she replies.

"It would appear. I had intel from Constable Petticoat," Abley says.

"I need to see Leedham, find out what killed this young man in College? Hugo Grader."

"Hang on. I was going to ask you if you could help him. Let me actually get a word out, so I can at least pretend it was my idea," Abley replies.

"Meet you at the station," Elizabeth orders Inspector Abley. Before Bob Abley can say another word, Elizabeth has hung up. She strokes the dogs by her feet and then walks back up to see Godric. When she pokes her head in, she notices Alex lying beside Godric on top of the covers, reading poetry, his head in Godric's lap. Alex sits up immediately.

"Don't move, calm down. Hugs are good. Hanky panky no. He needs rest," Elizabeth says, standing in the doorway.

"Bunny!" Godric pulls a face.

"He'd have to brush his teeth first," Alex chuckles.

"May I leave you to let the dogs out? I took them earlier," she asks them both.

"Of course," Godric replies.

"I can help," Alex offers.

Elizabeth nods. Anyone who saves her grandson she trusts with the dogs.

"When you were on the street, and Godric was on the road, did you see Nisha Acharya-Gorpade?" She asks Alex.

"No."

"But, the cashpoint was just a few feet away, near the Arts Cinema," she presses.

"I was coming out of the bar and just saw Godric. I suppose I wasn't looking that way? I don't know."

"Weren't you curious as to where she'd gone?" Elizabeth asks.

"Not really. Too much alcohol," Alex admits.

"And yet, you work in a bar Godric tells me."

"Bunny, enough of the questions," Godric says, his eyes conveying for her not to ruin things.

"I'm just trying to picture everything," she replies.

"No, it's fine. Honestly. If I remembered more, I'd say. I just ran to Godric."

"My knight in a shining red box jacket," Godric smiles, looking at Alex's coat.

Elizabeth wishes she knew more about this man bringing daffodils.

49
ON THE CASE

"Well, well, well. Professor Green. I wondered how long it would be before you turned up. You know I'm perfectly capable–"

"Mr Leedham, let's not swing our egos about. I've come to collaborate, that's all," Elizabeth attempts to walk into Parkside Police Station's pathology lab, and bumps into the station's chief pathologist.

"How refreshing of you. Of course, I have to follow procedure. Has the Inspector given you permission?" Leedham asks, standing in front of the doorway, blocking her entrance into the pathology rooms.

"Yes." This time, Elizabeth closes her eyes. "Are you going to invite me in?"

"Would you mind showing me your slip?" Leedham remains in the doorway.

"He's on his way. Look, I don't have time for this," Elizabeth replies.

"No doubt. Somewhere. But I've heard no sound of him today? Perhaps he's on the golf course. Best to wait and–"

At that moment, Inspector Abley walks along the

corridor, having heard the golf course reference.

"You hung up on me?" Abley says to Elizabeth, interrupting Leedham.

"Mr Leedham wants to see my slip, or some such. Do you want my help or not? I mean, I can find this killer without the police. I don't have time for this. Someone attacked my grandson!"

"Okay, everybody calm down. Leedham, she's on the case. So please let's cooperate. Professor Green, we would much appreciate your help. Thank you," Inspector Abley nods and so Leedham turns and walks in and over to a desk and opens the file on Mr Hugo Grader. He begrudgingly starts to pass it to Elizabeth, sighing as he knows this will mean him stepping back into the shadows.

"I've checked his heart, lungs," Leedham says, fiddling with a pen in his mouth. "I haven't identified anything to suggest it wasn't natural causes. But I've been running more tests on his liver, kidneys, just to be on the safe side."

"I'll take a copy of this over to my lab," Elizabeth says, looking at Abley who nods. Leedham rolls his eyes, as she snatches the file.

"Should I just stop then?" Leedham asks the room.

"Whatever for?" Elizabeth replies, "You carry on. You might turn up something. You never know." Without waiting for Leedham's response, Elizabeth walks out of the room, then pokes her head back in. "Are you coming?" She asks the Inspector.

"Where are we going?" Inspector Abley replies, confused. They both disappear, leaving Leedham utterly demoralised.

"There you go, run away. Chop chop, and do as matron says. And take everything!" Leedham adds, realising Elizabeth has taken the only copy of the file. Leedham raises his arms, only to drop them dramatically against his sides. Now he will have to start from scratch on the kidneys and liver.

*

"Hello back at you," Inspector Bob Abley laughs, pleased to be driving Professor Elizabeth Green to Christina College, mainly because it is good to be with a familiar face today of all days. "Statements in there," Abley nods towards the car's glove box and the file sticking out.

"I said hello already," Elizabeth replies, defensively, looking at the inside of his new car. "This is different."

"No, you actually didn't," Abley corrects Elizabeth. "We haven't seen each other since Christmas."

"Well that's a good thing, isn't it? No crime for me to help you with? Sounds like you have your hands full now."

"I just thought you'd be more pleased to see me?" Abley teases her.

"If I'm not much mistaken, I bought you a present, and I haven't had a thank you yet?"

"I've been busy. I was going to thank you. Course I was. Elizabeth, c'mon," Bob Abley laughs at Elizabeth's brusque manner. "Are you going to help me with this case?"

"I thought it was perfectly clear that's what I am doing," Elizabeth pulls a silly face at Inspector Abley, but drops it quickly. Inspector Abley can't ignore that Elizabeth is much more crotchety than usual, but is grateful for the slight defrosting of her tone and jumps on it.

"Well, glad to have you on board. Your pass obviously still works to get into the station, so that's good to know. Let me know if there is anything else you need. Leedham is taking too long to figure it out."

"Superintendent Raynott has given me a permanent post," Elizabeth replies.

"I know, I know. But, I was just checking that had filtered down to your pass. You'd be surprised."

"I wouldn't. Thank you for checking."

"You're working for me not him though, right?" Abley asks.

"Correct, Bob. I haven't spoken to him and have no intention."

"Good. Good. Just checking."

"Is he being any nicer?"

"No, not really. It's not his job. Well, we need to find whoever did this and quickly," Abley replies.

"That's why I've asked you to take me to Mr Grader's rooms," Elizabeth says.

"I don't know. We searched them thoroughly."

"I need to see for myself," she replies.

As they pass through the part of town that allows cars, Inspector Bob Abley can't help but notice couples in love, hearts and flowers in shop windows. He places his flashing light on the top of the car and drives through the barrier that stops all other cars from entering King's Parade. They drive past Senate House, and for some reason, a hologram is being projected up the forty feet building, of a bouquet of flowers for this most romantic of days.

"What the hell?" Abley remarks. That wasn't there yesterday?

"It's to raise money for charity," Elizabeth replies matter of factly, looking out the window.

"It's all got so out of hand," Abley replies.

"People need to be told they're loved. We're very needy creatures," Elizabeth stares out the window at the colossal hologram which is now turning into a red heart, and she watches as an arrow shoots across the building, heading for the heart.

"I'd ban it. It's commercial twaddle. What about all those people not in love?" Abley asks.

"I wonder what that is like?" Elizabeth wonders what it must be like to be happy and not feel the pain that is pervasive inside the front of Inspector Abley's car.

"Me too. Poor buggers." Abley realises both are still in unrequited love of sorts.

"Have you heard from Maureen?" Elizabeth asks, warming a little to her friend as they drive down Trinity Lane.

"No. Penny says she's happily ensconced in her new home with the traitor. But I'm doing some cognitive behavioural therapy to push through the pain."

"Oh, what does that involve?" Elizabeth asks, turning, interested.

"A couple of pints in the pub only a hop and a step from my new home, then a bottle or two with Sid – my new neighbour and best friend – in our gardens."

"Ugh," Elizabeth replies. What has really changed with the Inspector since before Christmas? She supposes at least he's dressed and seeming to be aware of the case.

"By the way, did you deliberately name your dog Clive after my son?"

"He came ready named, Bob. What can I do? Always in the wrong. Never in the right."

"Clive is not a dog's name," he replies.

"Tell that to Clive. And, there is a perfectly good tea orchard in Grantchester. You don't have to spend every waking hour in the pub."

They pull up in the car outside Christina College, and before Bob Abley has had a chance to unclick his seat belt, Elizabeth is out and walking towards the Porters' Lodge. By the time he catches up with her, she is already being led by a Porter to Hugo Grader's rooms. Inspector Abley flashes his badge to the Porter.

"We're police," he explains.

"That's alright, Sir. We all know Professor Green here," then the Porter turns his back on Bob Abley and continues nattering with Elizabeth. "I still have those black Hellebores you gave me a few years ago. They're coming up a real treat in the garden."

"Oh, good, good," Elizabeth replies. Inspector Bob Abley behind notes her tone is much warmer to the Porter than to him!

"Spread quite a bit, and mixed with some pink ones we subsequently bought. They're not as nice as the black ones," the Porter continues.

"They will hybridise," Elizabeth replies in a soft voice. "Lift out some of the black ones if you'd like to keep them pure, and move them to another place in the garden."

"While I've got you, I've been covering an olive tree I've got with a resistant frost cover. I got olives one year, but not another?" The Porter asks as they cross Bramble Court.

"You need a couple of months below ten degrees, but they also often need pollinating with a different cultivar, or if self-pollinating need some wind to pollinate. So, make sure they're not in a wind free spot."

"Oh, that could be it. The tree is in the corner of a courtyard. Not exposed," The Porter says, wandering past an arch catching a glimpse of the fountain in Whisper Court before it is gone again.

"What is the variety? Sometimes, it takes years before they produce fruit. Sometimes, it's quick."

"What is this, Gardeners' Question Time?" Inspector Abley asks.

"Speak later about it," Elizabeth raises her eyebrows, "Have there been any unusual visitors to the College?"

"Not that I've noticed. It's been quiet," the Porter looks at Elizabeth.

The three of them walk up the steps in the corner of Bramble Court and through the police tape still stretched across Hugo Grader's door. Elizabeth has already heard from Godric about this young man's wealth, so she is not surprised by the uncharacteristic opulence of a student's rooms.

"I imagine there was a lot of coming and going?" She says, continuing to speak to the Porter.

"Nice gentleman. Especially at Christmas. Hamper at the Lodge. All sorts of thank you presents." The Porter nods.

"Popular?"

"I'd say so," the Porter replies.

"Gardener?" Elizabeth looks out of the window down at the daffodils.

"Oh no, I believe a rock star, Professor," and the Porter leaves them to it.

"So, you have the pathology, the statements to read," Inspector Abley says, recapping to Elizabeth what she might need.

"I shall get to them," Elizabeth is a little more clipped with Abley. She leans out of the window and looks down at the garden. She glances about then pulls her attention back into the room. She picks up a book of poems by Wordsworth from his bedside table and flicks through.

"English undergrad," she says almost to herself.

"He had a page from that stuffed in his mouth," Abley replies. We didn't tell Godric that. So, you may not know.

"Daffodils."

"Yes, how do you know?" Abley asks.

"Well, it is the most known of Wordsworth. And Seasonal. Early ones look, outside." Abley walks to the window and sees the daffodils below Hugo Grader's window in the College flowerbed that he hadn't noticed before.

"Not really into poetry, I must confess," Abley remarks. "What does it mean?"

"Ah, there has been so much interpretation about the poem. I'm a scientist, not a poet, as well you know," she puts it back down.

"Have you read it?" Abley asks.

"Yes, of course. It's well known."

"And?"

"Scientist," Elizabeth responds, looking around the room at the mess. Bottles, food packets. She notices more poetry on a bookshelf. Brushes, hair grips, lip balm. Some aftershave.

"And?" Abley presses.

"It's about loneliness, not being lonely in nature, I think? I don't know. He gives the daffodils human like qualities, 'fluttering', 'dancing'." Elizabeth feels tired. "I think I need some air."

"Is that it?" Abley asks.

"I'm trying to imagine the young man's last moments," Elizabeth replies, a little defensively. "You gave me the statements. I'll come back to the car with you and get them. Then, I think I'll walk to my lab. No need to drive me."

"Right." Abley wonders what that was all about?

*

Elizabeth leaves the Inspector, walks down King's Parade, past the Valentine's Festival of Love, and is now on Trumpington Street. Many students are milling this Valentine's Day, either heading out for takeaway, to a lecture or just taking a walk with their lovers. As Elizabeth gets further away from the centre, the city opens up to residential homes, some of the most expensive in the city in the likes of Panton Street –Tardis type homes and not far from the Botanic Garden.

Elizabeth enters the Garden and breathes in the fresh air. She is deliberately choosing to use the Botanic laboratory today, rather than the Plant Sciences Department, to work undisturbed. But she also has something she needs to check, which only the seed archive will have. Once inside the Garden's research buildings, Elizabeth peruses the seed and bulb stacks in storage. The facility manager is surprised by her removal request.

"But you can buy these anywhere?" He asks.

"That's the point," Elizabeth replies. And, with a small brown paper bag, Elizabeth makes her way to the work station and laboratory equipment.

She puts down the paper bag on the bench, then looks out of the window. Early daffodils fill a bed against a sunny wall in the gardens of the café below. They shimmer, the bright yellow tips gleam like beacons of sunshine on earth. They raise Elizabeth's spirits, which she has so far paid no attention to since she heard Godric was unwell. Elizabeth has a sudden urge to speak to him and picks up the phone receiver on the wall. But then replaces it. Let him sleep, she tells herself. Solve the case for him to keep him safe. That is all there is now. He's all that is left.

50
CASTING COUCH

In a Faculty of English lecture hall, Professor Barclay and Dr Guinevere Trotsham sit behind a table in the middle of the room. On stage is an undergraduate who has just finished his audition to fight for a place to be in their new Christina Theatre troupe, which hopes to kick off their first production this summer at the Edinburgh Fringe. Or, at least that is what Professor Barclay is telling all the new young hopefuls. Beads of sweat run down the young auditionee's forehead, his mouth as dry as a packet of sherbet.

"Thank you. Next!" Shouts Professor Barclay. The young man walks off, not confident about anything.

Next, Darcy Nighy walks out on stage. She is wearing all black and glides on as if already possessed with a mood most sombre to reflect the part she is about to perform. It all hides the biggest hangover.

"When you're ready!" Dr Trotsham shouts over. As Darcy starts her monologue, Professor Barclay stops listening.

"I don't want her. She's so affected. I almost feel sorry for her. And that's saying something for me. But she's extremely irritating and should not be on the stage," Barclay whispers to Dr Guinevere Trotsham sitting beside him.

"Hmm. She's determined, and I'm not sure many people say no to her," Dr Trotsham replies.

"Including Miles Bonneville. Was that hard for you?" Barclay asks.

"I'm ignoring that, Barclay," Dr Trotsham replies while studying Darcy carefully. "Ultimately, casting's your choice. But I agree with you. Darcy Nighy cannot act," Guinevere Trotsham taps her pen on the desk.

"Okay, thank you!" Professor Barclay shouts at Darcy to stop.

"But I haven't finished?" Darcy places her hands on her hips.

"It's okay. We've seen enough, thank you, Miss Nighy!" Barclay shouts back.

"I can do a different monologue?" Darcy offers.

"Thank you. We'll be in touch. Next!" Dr Trotsham shouts, lending her support and sealing the last nail in the coffin.

*

Darcy storms out of the lecture hall, pushing past other auditionees.

"There's no point. It's a stitch-up," she remarks to those who will listen. The other students look wary. Surely, she can't be right.

Darcy steps out onto West Road and starts walking away from the Faculty. She takes out her phone from the bottom of her bag, ready to call Lance, someone who will understand. She hasn't seen him this morning, having got very drunk with him last night. Him thinking it might be his last evening of freedom, her to bury the pain from

Miles's death. She presses her phone to call but gets no reply. Instead, she hovers over a voicemail from Miles, wondering if she can bring herself to listen again to the message he left her yesterday.

She hits play: "Where are you?" He starts, "You said you'd be here. I'm in the dressing room already. Where did you go after Snobs? We said we'd meet here, right? Well, wherever. Be careful. I don't think Hugo died from natural causes. I think he was bloody murdered. I'll talk to you after rehearsals, but I have my suspicions. It didn't make sense, and now I know why. Watch out for Nisha." The message from Miles ends. What did he mean, she thinks? What did he know? Watch out for Nisha? She has been playing the message repeatedly since she first heard it, but she still doesn't know what to do with it. One thing for sure. She was right about Nisha. Nisha is trouble.

Darcy continues over to The Backs and walks through the daffodils. She arrives at Silver Street and stands on the bridge. She scrolls through her contacts, dials and holds the phone to her ear. It rings, then jumps to voicemail. "I know what you did," she spits. Then cuts the call. Darcy leans over the bridge and watches a punt start to disappear underneath the arch below. The passengers are laughing at something the chauffeur has said. One of the men in the punt looks up and spots Darcy. He smiles. She stares back coldly before checking her bank balance on her phone. Oh god, it is so badly overdrawn.

What is she going to do? Moving off towards the Swan Theatre, Darcy spots a swan passing under the bridge, hissing at the punters. Perhaps she should hiss more herself, she thinks. The sun is shining, but there is a bitter easterly wind whipping through even the thickest tourist coat. She needs to get some money and quick.

51
FEELING FLAT

Nisha Acharya-Gorpade ducks down an alley off King's Parade towards The Green Magician then turns a key in the lock of a somewhat hidden door to take her up to Lance Fernard's flat. She climbs the inner stairs reaching a tiny landing, and as she puts a different key in an internal door it opens from the inside, making her jump.

"Oh," Nisha staggers a little, almost falling back down the narrow stairs.

"Careful!" Lance grabs Nisha. "Nice surprise. I was just coming to find you while I'm still a free man. You okay?" Lance smiles, looking exhausted and hungover.

"How are you doing, you know, about everything? Losing Miles," Nisha asks, observing Lance's hair stuck up at the back, and that he is still wearing the same clothes he had on yesterday from the police station's lost property.

"Thanks for asking. No one seems to care that I'm distressed about it too, positively wretched," Lance looks at Nisha straight in the eye, adding, "I think I'm too in shock to feel anything other than horror?" Lance then wanders back into his large open-plan flat and picks up a packet of cigarettes from the coffee table. "My days are numbered. Half of me wants them to arrest me just so I can feel safe. But you hear about people being knocked off in prison. Nowhere's safe, is it. I don't know why someone is trying to kill us all?" Lance pulls at his hair. "I've wracked my brains, but our music is hardly controversial. It's mainstream. Who'd object to it? Someone with a vendetta, that's for sure."

"Are the police going to charge you?" Nisha steps through the doorway and loiters by the open plan kitchen area, the light streaming through the large windows.

"I've no idea. I'm surprised I'm out, to be honest. Maybe you are too. You didn't think I'd be here, I bet," Lance lights a cigarette.

"I believe you didn't mean it. And, I'm sorry I didn't take more care of the props. It's my fault," Nisha replies, looking around for Fred, the ginger cat. She spots him jumping up on a kitchen surface.

"Don't be ridiculous. You're the tech support. You can't be backstage watching what's going on with the props. It's Godric's fault for giving you both jobs," Lance replies, then inhales.

"I offered. He couldn't find anyone."

"That's the kinda girl you are," Lance walks over to Nisha, then kisses the top of her head and gives her a big hug. "Don't worry about it. Really."

"You don't think you will go down, do you?" Nisha asks, sounding worried.

"Who else is a suspect? I stabbed him, for chrissake," Lance lets go of Nisha, then walks across and throws himself on the sofa and covers his face with his arm. "Oh, my god. I really stabbed him." There is a momentary silence that hangs in the room. Then Lance uncovers his eyes and stares at Nisha. She wants to hug him, but cannot find the energy. They both watch Fred, licking his paws, sitting on a kitchen surface by a saucer of half-eaten pilchards.

"I was just returning your key," Nisha doesn't know what else to say. She feels for Lance but is not sure anything she says can help. "I didn't think you'd need me to feed Fred now you're not going on tour."

"Quite." Lance looks at her and smiles weakly. "Keep them. I'm still likely to go away. Maybe for a long time. Be good to count on you."

"Okay, yes. Of course," Nisha replies.

Lance looks at Nisha and sees that she's not okay.

"What's up? I mean, apart from the obvious."

"Nothing. I don't know," Nisha shakes her head.

"Come on," Lance places his bare feet on his very messy coffee table and pats the cushion beside him, "Tell me. Something's clearly bothering you. What can I do?"

"Oh, we have to go to rehearsal." Nisha looks at her phone and sees a missed message.

"Come on. There's no play now. I murdered Miles, didn't I."

"Yes. Oh, sorry, I don't mean yes. I should – Are you okay after your time at the police station?" Nisha stands beside the sofa, looking down on Lance.

"You mean after the police arrested me and think I did it intentionally and are systematically working to prove it?" Lance takes another long drag from his cigarette.

"I might go home," Nisha drops her bombshell.

"What? No. You can't abandon me? I absolutely forbid it," he blows out smoke.

"My course, it's so many hours. I'm falling so far behind."

"I can help you catch up?" Lance offers.

"You can help me with electrical circuit theory and code?" Nisha raises her eyebrows, temporarily amused by Lance's offer.

"No. You're on your own on that," Lance smiles, then looks worried again, "But don't leave me." He pats the sofa again, so Nisha sits down. Lance looks at her, continuing, "You must be feeling poorly from the carrots. I've just woken up myself. Feeling fragile. Quite the night with Darce. She brought back all kinds of booze Miles had left in her room." Then Lance has a thought. "We could go and get some food?"

"It's okay. I'm not that hungry," Nisha pauses. "Actually, I've just come from the hospital."

"What?" Lance says, sitting forward, his eyes wide open.

"Someone blew some stuff in my face last night. It's odd, though. I'm feeling fine now? Apparently, it's used as a date rape drug. So, I guess it could have been worse. They were just thieves," Nisha leans against Lance, feeling a little weak about it.

"What?? You were robbed? When? How much did they get? Surely, most of your stuff is in a trust fund?" Lance asks.

"Well, I told the police that the person who drugged me took me to the cashpoint and made me take out money for them. But when I just looked at my account, it's all there? I remember them doing it. I wasn't dreaming. But who's going to believe me?"

"I believe you," Lance replies. "If you were mugged and you remember, you were mugged. You should have told me straight away. If I can get my hands on whoever did it!"

"You'll kill them," Nisha looks at Lance.

"Yup. Though in the circumstances, it might be better just to rough them up."

"You're in enough deep water without getting involved at all."

"You must remember something. Their hands? A smell?"

"I felt like a zombie. I couldn't–" Nisha shakes her head and tears start to stream.

"Hey! It's going to be alright. We'll get through this. They'll catch whoever is doing this."

"You think it's all linked?" Nisha asks.

"How the hell would I know. I've been framed. You've been robbed. Hugo's dead. Miles's dead. All in two days."

"And Godric. Godric was with me. He had the powder blown in his face too."

"Blimey," Lance replies, leaning back.

Nisha sits down and nestles into Lance's chest, and the two sit in the middle of Lance's couch, not moving. In front of them on the coffee table is Lance's script for the play. Next to that are some lines of coke, left over from when Miles was in Lance's flat.

Fred walks over and rubs his legs against Nisha.

Outside, on King's Parade, a group of students walk past below the windows, laughing and joking without a care in the world.

"Why did you come, Nish?" Lance sits up, suddenly wondering.

"What do you mean?"

"Why are you here, now? Surely, you must feel terrible? Why aren't you in hospital? Or, in your room?" Lance asks.

"I was dropping off your keys," she replies. But Lance stares at her.

"I'm glad," Lance says. "It's good to see you. We're safer together," Lance kisses the top of Nisha's head again, then leans back down on the sofa. His face now with just the slightest frown showing over Nisha's shoulder.

52
JESUS GREEN

Professor Elizabeth Green walks back from the Botanic Gardens towards home, to check up on Godric's health. But when she reaches Park Street, she can already see Hector, Monty and Clive chasing about on Jesus Green. She heads a little bit further out onto the grass to call her dogs and wonders why they are loose. In front of her are empty tennis courts and children kicking footballs on their lunch break from the primary school nearby. One or two Professors and post-docs are also scurrying to their respective departments. Behind all this activity, Elizabeth spots Godric sitting in his white coat on a bench in the winter sun by the river, surrounded by daffodils. He looks pensive. Instead of interrupting his thoughts, Elizabeth walks towards him until he can finally hear her footsteps on the path.

"Hello," he looks up and smiles, pleased to see his nanna.

"How are you feeling? It's a bit cold to be out here, isn't it?" Elizabeth notices Godric has a hip flask.

"I'm fine. Feeling much better, actually. Myself again in body if not in spirit. Think the one poison must have cancelled out the other, or something." Godric offers his nanna some whisky, seeing she's spotted his vice.

"Well, getting some fresh air is very sensible if you're sitting and taking it slow. Bit early for the other." Elizabeth thinks Godric still looks pale. She sits down next to him.

"It is a bit early for everything really," Godric replies, resting the hip flask on his knee, "but when loved ones make such delicious toast and strawberries, a spring in one's step formed, and here I am."

For a while, they watch the dogs sniffing and exploring nearby. The sun is moving just above Victoria College, and every so often, when the wind changes direction, they can hear students playing rugby behind the trees in College fields. Godric takes his nanna's hand and gives her the flask. "Time to turn over a new leaf. Well, today, at least."

"Good idea," She says, pocketing the flask, more than a little surprised. This is not the Godric she knows, who would ordinarily have to have alcohol prised from his hands using bribery or considerable force? Elizabeth can see he is most definitely in shock. Two dead, him having almost been the third, and still not sure if his near-miss was a case of mistaken identity or intentional.

"Did you catch up with Mr Leedham? Are we any less clueless about this whole debacle? I'm so glad you're on the case," Godric sighs, feeling hopeful that there is now light at the end of the tunnel.

"I did indeed. Most illuminating. Though the little man does take on a rather unhelpful tone out of earshot from the Inspector. Anyone would think he wasn't grateful for my efforts."

"What, Mr Leedham was illuminating this time?"

"Gracious, no. The samples I had to prise out of his fingers and subsequently retested at the Botanics."

"Spill the beans," Godric watches his nanna's face.

"I'm glad you're sitting down, as it's not good news."

Elizabeth squeezes her grandson's hand. "In fact, I would describe it as grim." Elizabeth looks at the buds on the trees just beginning to sprout.

"Hugo was murdered," Godric shuts his eyes.

"You're getting good at this," Elizabeth says affectionately, sad that Godric has to be involved at all. "I have discovered he was murdered in a very sophisticated way. Which leads me to think we are dealing with no ordinary killer. I can't quite put two and two together."

"Nisha is going to be very upset," Godric says, desperate for a drink, but trying his best to change for his nanna.

"What is it about this Nisha person? She is always upset. I'm more worried about you." Elizabeth frowns, "I suspect you're going to need your wits about you today."

"Oh, damn it," Godric's phone beeps, and he looks at a reminder. "I'm supposed to be at the theatre, to go on as Romeo to save the show." Godric stands up, letting go of his nanna's hand. Then he slumps back on the bench, realising he has not thought this through properly. "How ridiculous. We don't have a show anymore. How can we? What am I thinking?"

"Well, if you do, I'm checking all the swords before every performance," Elizabeth replies.

"I suppose I have to be there in case anyone turns up?" Godric looks to his nanna, almost to help him make his decision. "Just to talk about what we do about tickets. I need this like a hole in the head," Godric pulls his coat tighter around him.

"If you think it necessary to go, would you mind using your mobile and calling Bob and asking him to be there," telling, rather than asking Godric. Godric dials, and hands the phone to Elizabeth. Elizabeth takes it, adding, "You'll be okay. But, I'm coming. I want to meet this motley crew," she says as the phone rings.

"Find the killer, Bunny, then perhaps I'll start to be. I don't think I can cope with this alone anymore. I just can't be alone."

"We're all alone, Goddy. Born alone, die alone. I'm here for you for as long as I'm spared. You know that. But, if I've learnt one thing this week, it's that although it is inordinately hard, it makes sense to get used to it." Elizabeth looks at Godric. "Keep your wits about you. The murderer hasn't finished." Elizabeth hears Inspector Bob Abley's voice and starts to speak to him down the phone. "It was definitely murder." Elizabeth gets up, moving away from Godric, to give him just a few moments longer to be in the dark. She is going to have to tell him if only to keep him safe. This murderer feels far too close to her grandson. Far too close.

53
DAFFODILS

Godric holds the door open for his nanna, as she joins him at the Swan Theatre, for his emergency meeting. He hands her a letter and a programme.

"I'm dreading having to be Romeo," he says.

"That's not going to happen," Elizabeth replies, looking in the programme at her grandson's photograph above the word 'Director'. Amid all the chaos and tragedy, she cannot help but feel proud.

In the foyer, waiting for them are Inspector Abley and Sergeant Lemon.

"Professor Green," Inspector Abley says, "Thanks for the tip-off of the reassembling."

"Professor Green," Lemon beams at Elizabeth, pleased to see her on the case.

"Sergeant Lemon. Cambridge is better than Oxford, no matter how big the challenge one is facing," Elizabeth smiles.

"Oh yes, leaps and bounds better. I missed everything," Lemon beams at Elizabeth.

"Aww," Abley replies.

"I said everything, not everyone," Lemon says, opening his eyes wide at his Inspector, then smiling just a little.

"The narcissus bulb, eh?" Inspector Abley asks Elizabeth, choosing not to rise to Lemon's teasing.

"What?" Godric asks.

"Hugo was poisoned, Godric, with daffodils," Elizabeth sighs, realising it is time Godric knows, and that she cannot keep him in the dark about it any longer.

"Do you have to say everything in front of your grandson?" Inspector Abley asks, shaking his head. "Given the connection."

"Oh, for goodness sake. Yes. Godric is my assistant. Consultants need assistants. Hugo was poisoned with daffodils, and now Godric knows," Elizabeth replies, "And I'm sure he will say nothing to the others," Elizabeth then glares at her grandson.

"No, of course not," Godric says. "Cross my heart, and hope not to die from daffodils."

"He cannot be your assistant, Elizabeth. He is involved in the case. Please do not share details of the investigation with him again," Abley says.

"Okay, but he knows this now. So, might as well hear the rest. Daffodils are not of themselves deadly, although in small children they might make some ill, and possibly the frail or elderly." Elizabeth looks around the foyer to check they are still alone before continuing, "It's the lycorine that makes you unwell, which is highly concentrated in the bulbs," Elizabeth says, now looking back at Inspector Abley. She then switches her attention to Sergeant Lemon, pleased to see him back and wanting him to be sure she thinks he's just as important. "Hugo Grader had high concentrations which would have lowered his blood pressure and damaged his liver. It was his blood pressure that the killer focused on. I found opioids too, probably pure opium. It would have just stopped the heart beating.

He died from a slow pulse, essentially. The two combined," Elizabeth explains.

"One way to go, I suppose. To shuffle off high as a kite."

"Yes, quite. However, the bulbs also contain needle-like oxalates, which would have caused burning to his lips, tongue, mouth and throat. So, combined with the poem stuffed in his mouth, he would have suffered localised pain," Elizabeth explains.

"Why didn't Leedham find this earlier?" Inspector Abley asks.

"It wasn't obvious. He wouldn't have known to have looked for it even if he'd had more time," Elizabeth says, "But, combined with the opium in high concentration, what I find fascinating is why anyone would go to such lengths and use daffodils? Why not use a more obvious poison? Whoever murdered Hugo Grader wanted to send a message, perhaps just for their own amusement? They most definitely wanted to give him a dramatic send-off?"

"Daffodils?" Godric looks around him.

"To no one," Abley glares at Godric, who nods.

"Yup. Must have ground up the bulbs. Would have had to be ingested in a large enough dose. I also found traces of snowdrops? A veritable spring poisoning," Elizabeth adds, almost talking to herself now.

"I don't understand. Why poison him?" Inspector Abley asks, "As this other chap was just stabbed."

"You know that most killers poison because it doesn't require being present at the death. And there is the physical strength required to kill if one uses one's hands don't forget, or the noise if one uses a gun. Even a weapon can be turned against the attacker," Elizabeth replies, adding, "Hugo Grader was a strong young man I'm led to believe. No, poison is often used by the fearful or the coward. But, in this instance, I think it was the killer wanting to send a message. Perhaps there are even two killers."

"Killers, who have a thing about daffodils?" Lemon

asks, confused.

"Hugo Grader had a book of poems by Wordsworth on his bedside table. Daffodils on his eyes and in his mouth. Of course, it was the first thing I checked," Elizabeth shrugs.

"On his eyes? When all at once I saw a crowd," Godric says quietly.

"Exactly. But why poetry? Did the killer hate Hugo's love of literature?" Elizabeth ponders.

"He was headed for a third, from our notes. So, hardly much love there," Lemon replies.

"Hmm. Loving something and being good at it are two different things," Elizabeth remarks.

*

Professor Elizabeth Green starts to walk up the stairs to get to the theatre's stalls, holding the letter Godric gave her while looking at all the actors' photographs and biographies in the rest of the programme. When she opens the door, she notices the cast and crew sprawled out across the seats, waiting for their director. Most hope this show will end, as they are none too keen on becoming the next victims. All, that is, apart from Darcy – who is willing to risk it all on the chance of an agent and the hopes and dreams for significant future roles.

As Godric follows behind with Inspector Abley and Sergeant Lemon, the mood noticeably changes.

"What's happened now?" Darcy asks.

Godric spots Professor Barclay and Dr Guinevere Trotsham sitting at the back.

"Thank you all for coming," Godric says, his voice much weaker than before, sitting down in a stall chair and hoping his nanna will take charge.

"Are you going to play Romeo? You have to," Darcy replies, oblivious to his clear state of unwellness.

"It's time to cancel the play before anyone else gets

hurt," Lance suggests, leaning forward and emerging from behind Nisha in the seats.

"What? And, that is a bit rich coming from you," Darcy shakes her head.

"It was an accident. I've not been charged. We've argued about this 'til the cows came home last night. You forgave me."

"Don't plan any exotic holidays," Inspector Abley says under his breath to Lance.

"He didn't do it on purpose," Nisha quietly defends her friend.

Professor Elizabeth Green jumps up on stage. The room goes quiet, most not knowing this is Godric's nanna. She pauses for effect for a while before speaking.

"Godric tells me some of you are keen to continue with the play, how 'the show must go on'," Elizabeth says. "I'm a scientist, so I have never properly understood the theatre. But I find this saying very strange. Must go on? Aren't you at all concerned another of you will be murdered?" Elizabeth asks, cocking her head to one side and waiting for a response.

"I didn't murder Miles. He was my friend. It was an accident," Lance protests, speaking up first.

"I asked if any of you were scared. You sound very defensive. Did you not stick a sword into his chest? If you prick me, do I not bleed? Different play, but–"

"By accident. What is this?" Lance interrupts Elizabeth, looking around, wondering who this strange lady is.

"You couldn't tell the difference between a prop sword and a real one?" Elizabeth continues, "Oh Edgar... Might I but live to see thee in my touch, I'd say I had eyes again." Just as Gloucester did when speaking in King Lear after being blinded, Elizabeth holds her hands in front of her eyes. The reference passes straight over most of the heads in the room. Elizabeth opens her eyes and then stares at Lance, waiting for a response.

"I couldn't see the difference. One sword collapses the other didn't. That was the only difference," he says. "But why would I think to check. It was fine through previous rehearsals. Who are you? And why are we even listening to you?" Lance asks.

"Where are my manners? Professor Elizabeth Green is an academic here at the university." Inspector Abley says, walking up some side steps and onto the stage to join her.

"Oh, well that's alright then," Lance replies.

"She is also a consultant for the Cambridge Police Constabulary, due to her expertise in poisons."

"What?" Darcy asks, "What has that got to do with anything?"

"Are you ready to listen now? Or, shall I see if that trolley freezer has any vegan ice cream?" Elizabeth asks, adding, "I'm beginning to get my appetite back?" Elizabeth looks at Godric, who smiles a little. Alex stands up and creeps to the trolley, handing Elizabeth an ice cream, before returning to sit back next to Godric with two ice cream pots for them too.

"It's like watching a real live pantomime. Nice white coat by the way, not sure I've seen that one. I guess your other needs a clean from all that road dirt. We're very on point aren't we? Me in red, you in white. Very Valentine," Alex whispers to Godric, trying to cheer him up. But Godric just stares ahead.

"Ooh, lovely. Strawberry." Elizabeth opens the lid and removes the little wooden spatula. She looks at Inspector Abley, who nods for her to continue. "The police will be making an announcement shortly to the media that the young man in College was murdered with poison. There is no doubt about that," Elizabeth says, popping some ice cream into her mouth. "So, here we are, with a flamboyant collection of individuals, used to a bit of high drama. And, Professor Barclay. Pleased to see you here too at the back." Professor Barclay nods. Elizabeth continues, "We want to see if any of you have any comment on the murder, now you know we know."

"Sergeant Lemon will be taking fresh statements with his Constable," Inspector Abley chips in. Sergeant Lemon nods. The room is silent, aside from gasps and whispers about Hugo Grader. Poisoned? "This show, or play, or whatever you call it, is cancelled or at least postponed while our investigations are active," Inspector Abley adds. There is shock and some groans from the seats, and Godric and a few more breathe a sigh of relief.

"What poison?" Darcy asks.

"Nisha and I were poisoned last night as well," Godric replies weakly.

For the first time, Elizabeth properly looks around the building and notices all the Valentine's Day decorations which have been put up over the past day to dress the theatre ready for opening. Each seat in the stalls has a red bow on the back, there are crepe paper red and white hearts on the walls, and the stage is lit red. For a moment, it is all too overwhelming. Elizabeth focuses again on the face sitting in front of her. Godric. Home. She pops more ice cream into her mouth. Sugar. She needs sugar. But it is making her feel sick.

The back rows are full of crew and cast with minor roles, their faces almost in shadows. Inspector Bob Abley walks to the edge of the stage and speaks to Lemon who is standing in the front row. Lance and Darcy are now quiet and still looking at Elizabeth. Alex is busily eating ice cream beside Godric. Elizabeth looks at the tub in her hands but somehow can't eat any more. Alex signals he'll have it, so she throws it down to him. In that action, Elizabeth catches a glimpse of Nisha, who is fidgeting in her seat, and looking remarkably sweaty next to Godric.

"So that is two members of the band gone," Elizabeth says, pacing the stage.

"Did you like the music, Ms Acharya-Gorpade?" Elizabeth turns and glares at Nisha.

243

"Yes, er, yes. I listen to it a lot. I don't quite know it backwards," Nisha replies frowning.

"Nobody knows it backwards," Lance sighs. "Nor will they ever now, probably." Lance hangs his head.

"Ms Acharya-Gorpade, may we have a word?" Professor Elizabeth Green asks, moving to the front of the stage.

"I knew she did it!" Darcy shouts. Everyone looks at Darcy, who shrugs, then at Nisha.

"Have you found them?" Nisha asks Elizabeth. Inspector Abley leaves the stage and heads up the aisle towards the bar.

"You mean the person who drugged you? I think we should speak privately about it," Elizabeth replies, heading to the stage steps which drop to the stalls. Nisha stands, leaving a concerned-looking Godric with Alex, who is still eating ice cream.

Inspector Bob Abley ushers Nisha into the bar, followed by Sergeant Lemon and Professor Elizabeth Green. When they are firmly all in the bar's foyer, Sergeant Lemon locks the door so that no one can overhear.

"Thank you for coming out," Inspector Abley says, pulling back a chair for Nisha to sit.

"What is it?" Nisha asks, worried.

"Professor Elizabeth Green here thought we should speak to you privately," Inspector Abley replies.

"Please, what about?" Nisha looks at Inspector Abley, Sergeant Lemon and Professor Elizabeth Green, waiting for an explanation.

"Perhaps you were not drugged at all." Elizabeth stares at Nisha. "Perhaps you got someone to drug Godric," Elizabeth suggests. "Perhaps you were trying to murder Godric. You got someone to administer what you thought might be a lethal dose of 'Devil's Breath' to Godric given he would not be able to get out of the road. You could have made it look like you were also poisoned but with a much smaller dose. Did you hold your breath when the powder was blown?" Elizabeth asks as she joins Nisha in sitting, and without taking pause continues, "Did Godric say something to you about your props? He did tell me that you had responsibility for the props, so you could have caused Miles Bonneville's death." Elizabeth observes Nisha, who says nothing and just sinks further into her chair. "Did you do it?" Elizabeth presses.

"No. I was poisoned. I didn't do anything to Godric. Why would you think that?"

"I'm thinking everything, Ms Acharya-Gorpade. I got you out here to talk to you about what you gave to Godric outside, just before we came into the theatre today."

"Oh, what are you going to do? He'll kill me," Nisha replies.

"Stay here." Elizabeth stands then turns and marches up the stairs again to the theatre door, opens it and disappears back into the stalls. Nisha's eyes follow her, concerned. Inspector Bob Abley and Sergeant Lemon stand silent, waiting. Neither sure why Elizabeth asked Nisha these questions.

Elizabeth Green pops her head around the door and spots Professor Barclay.

"Professor Barclay, may I have a word?" Elizabeth calls to Professor Barclay, who slowly stands and stretches, before saying something to Dr Trotsham, then squeezing past her legs along the aisle, making his way to Elizabeth at the exit.

"Professor Green. How the devil are you? I see Cambridge Police need you again? Your Inspector asked us to come. I must say, I don't have time for this. It feels remarkably like an abuse of power."

"These are your students," Elizabeth replies, uninterested in Barclay's concerns, as they walk back to the bar together.

"They're university students. I merely impart my knowledge and wisdom to them for as long as they care to listen while here for a mere seventy-two weeks. Thankfully, most of those weeks, they choose to play rugby, row or throw a frisbee to avoid my lectures and tutorials, which makes our contact almost tolerable."

"And yet, you want to build a theatre, a College theatre, which will no doubt be full of younglings you seek to distance yourself from," Elizabeth replies, not looking directly at Barclay, as they walk back down the stairs towards the bar.

"Ah, one of life's bitter ironies. The love of words, the stage, a yearning for that wondrous moment, the elixir of seeing the Bard's words come to life. I mourn young Bonneville's death, as he was the only one in this rabble who could put up a halfway decent performance. To have died by the sword, on stage no less, was somewhat prophetic for a young man of his talents."

"I heard he turned down a place in your troupe. You had a shouting match with him about it. You were overheard. It was reported to the police after his death. It's in the statements," Elizabeth says, stopping at the door to the bar.

"He was a headstrong boy," Professor Barclay says, unphased by Elizabeth's question.

"The report said you threw something at him."

"He was belligerent. I grew frustrated with his inability to see sense. It is not an uncommon action on my part. I'm sure you could find dozens of students with blackboard rubber indents in their foreheads. Never did them any harm."

"He didn't want to act for you. He was going to leave on tour with his band. But your theatre. It is so important to you. Enough to seek your revenge?" Elizabeth asks.

"Don't be ridiculous. It's just a theatre?" Professor Barclay begins to feel irritated, moving into the bar.

"It isn't, though, is it. Your own research grants are tied into the theatre's success," Elizabeth presses.

"I think you need to calm down, Professor Green. You said it yourself. The theatre isn't your forte. One visit today and your imagination is running riot." Professor

Barclay looks around the bar and sees the Inspector and Sergeant and wonders what is happening.

"Hmm, a man pointing out that I need to come to my senses, who is himself being reported as violent, shouting. And one who thinks he's above the law? Above reproach? It doesn't take much imagination to be curious about you, does it, Mr Barclay," Elizabeth now follows Professor Barclay towards the others.

"What is this?" Professor Barclay stops by Nisha.

"Ms Acharya-Gorpade, would you mind repeating what you told Godric yesterday over drinks. You know, when he phoned you this morning to ask you how you were doing?"

Nisha looks very awkward but knows exactly what Elizabeth is referring to. She shuts her eyes.

"I said Professor Barclay had written to me to ask me to persuade Miles to stay in Cambridge. Not to leave so he could act in Cambridge."

"Do you read English?" Elizabeth asks, knowing the answer.

"Sciences," Nisha replies.

"So why did he send the letter to you, d'you think?" Elizabeth asks Nisha, then looks at Professor Barclay, who is frowning.

"I don't know," Nisha replies.

Elizabeth pulls out the letter from inside her programme.

"Is this it? The letter you gave Godric, just now in the theatre when he asked to see it."

"Yes," Nisha replies.

"So, you were so keen for Miles Bonneville to stay in Cambridge that you were writing to his friends?" Elizabeth turns and looks directly at Professor Barclay, who is stumped and then glares at Nisha.

"He talked about her. Said she had a powerful draw. I thought she might talk sense into him. Help him see that running away to be in a wretched band was lunacy,"

Barclay replies.

"Seems quite an extreme thing to do? Were you that disappointed when he said he was going anyway that you'd do anything to stop him?"

"Don't be ridiculous. Utter conjecture," Barclay says, turning away.

Elizabeth shakes her head to Inspector Abley. She is done questioning.

"You may go," Inspector Abley allows Nisha to rejoin the others. Once she has left, Professor Barclay continues to protest.

"I'm very busy. If you are quite finished with your charade, I shall take my leave as I have a lecture to give!" Professor Barclay says, then storms out the front of the bar towards the street. They watch him go.

"Keep a close eye on Ms Acharya-Gorpade. I think she's not telling us everything. Far too quiet," Elizabeth says to Inspector Abley and Sergeant Lemon.

*

Nisha walks back into the stalls from the bar, looking for a friendly face. Abley and Lemon follow behind. Darcy can sense Nisha's panic. Darcy leaves Lance and moves closer to Nisha.

"Hey, Waify, you need to get a grip."

"The police think I did it," Nisha replies.

"They have every reason to believe it."

"Lay off, Darce. Not now," Lance shouts across the chairs, having heard Darcy's bitter words.
Dr Trotsham walks over to join them.

"Oh, that's all we need," Darcy says quietly to Nisha, then changes her tone, "Dr Trotsham, how are you?"

"I have some bad news. There never seems to be a good time at the moment. It's all truly awful. I'm sorry to compound anything," Dr Trotsham replies.

"I didn't make the cut," Darcy says, already knowing

the answer.

"We just felt that those we chose for the troupe were better suited to work together," Dr Trotsham smiles a cold smile, "though of course, we think you show tremendous promise. You can always audition next year."

"I'm a final year. This was my last opportunity. You're my tutor. You know that."

"Ah, so you are. Well, I'm sure we will see you in professional productions of one thing or another in the future."

"You had a hand in the decision?"

"The panel made the decision."

"Nothing to do with the fact of who I was dating, and you were jealous?" Darcy scoffs.

"I beg your pardon?" Dr Trotsham frowns, surprised by Darcy's gall.

"Oh, come on, you always wanted Miles to love you. He just screwed you when he was off his head one night, and regretted it ever after. He told me he thought you were a dried-up old prune," Darcy glares right at Dr Trotsham.

"You have an anger in you that is not becoming. I'll thank you to hold your tongue," Trotsham replies.

"It doesn't matter. He's dead. Maybe someone murdered him because they couldn't have him. You hear about cases like that all the time, don't you?" Darcy suggests, looking at Nisha.

"I think you should stop, Darcy," Nisha says.

"Why? I wouldn't put it past her," Darcy scowls at Dr Trotsham.

"Listen to your friend, if you know what's good for you," Dr Trotsham warns Darcy.

"Is that a threat? Are you going to do me in too?" Darcy asks.

Dr Trotsham walks off. Standing behind her is Professor Elizabeth Green, who has heard everything.

54
LIVE AND DIE A ROCK STAR

Professor Elizabeth Green says her goodbyes at the Swan Theatre, and after Godric swears he is heading straight home to recuperate, she decides to go for a stroll in the hope it might help untangle her thoughts. Cambridge is sunny but cold. She heads up towards Trinity Street, and it isn't long before she is in the bustle of milling tourists and undergraduates, rushing to and from shops, Colleges and departments.

Elizabeth is finding this case much harder to untangle than usual. Her concern for Godric is making her more than a little jittery. Whoever is murdering these young men seems calculating, evil in their method. Elizabeth knows full well that some murders are committed in the heat of a moment, but daffodil bulbs and sword swaps? She fears what the future might bring if she doesn't have a lucky break soon. As she mulls all the facts, she looks up at the clouds passing across the historic buildings either side of the street. The high College walls and the gargoyles are guarding occupants inside against evil. Elizabeth wishes she could give her grandson the same protection. Her feet lead her back to Christina College in the hope to find answers.

*

Soon, Elizabeth is turning into Trinity Lane, where the numbers of people reduce significantly, and she can hear her own footsteps. Two students walk past, their lacrosse kits over their shoulders off for a game, their high spirits and good health bouncing off the walls. She notices the chalk mark on the corner of the College building, which reads 'To the River'. It has been there for decades. It always reassures her to know that some things don't change. She pushes on towards Christina College.

When Elizabeth enters the College Porters' Lodge for a key to Miles Bonneville's room, Head Porter, Alf, doesn't even question her right to take a peek. Within the Porter Community, Professor Elizabeth Green is a hero for solving the terrible Porter murder case at All Saints. They often still send her treats for Soot, and ask her how the pussy-cat is doing. Alf leads the way as they start to walk towards Miles's rooms.

"What was this poor boy really like?" Elizabeth asks Alf.

"Young Miles Bonneville? He was a goodun. Such a happy chap. I know some complained about the racket he made with guitars, but I just took out my hearing aids. At night, it helps to be able to hear only half the stuff that goes on around here, you know," Alf chuckles.

"Did he have many friends?"

"Bit of a ladies' man. Had the looks," Alf sticks his chest out. "Before I married my Rita, some said I was quite the dish in my youth."

"I have no doubt," Elizabeth tries her hardest to make small talk, but is keen to get to the facts. "I hear he was going to be a rock star?"

"We were always taking down their posters, the

'Three Charming Men'. No self-promotion allowed. Only outside the Banquet Hall. Not all over the place. Making a mess. They were quite famous in the city."

"Famous?"

"Oh, packed it was when they held their concerts in the bar. Nightmare at the Lodge, trying to keep out townies."

"I don't think you're supposed to call them–"

"Locals," Alf interrupts, correcting himself. He leads Elizabeth under an arch and through Front Court and Bramble, towards Whisper Court, with its tidy green lawns and pretty fountain. Elizabeth spots a beautiful fig tree in a sunny corner.

"That's grown a lot, hasn't it?" Elizabeth looks at a giant fig tree.

"We had figs last year."

"Can I try one if they come again this year?" Elizabeth asks.

"I'll save you a punnet. I took some home to the wife. She made figgy pudding," Alf replies, pointing, "Right up this staircase, Professor Green."

"I'm right behind you."

Alf opens the door.

"There you are. The police came and went. His parents are abroad and were supposed to have flown in. Still not come yet. A bit jet-set, I reckon."

"Thank you." Elizabeth stares as Alf jingles his keys and leaves.

Elizabeth is momentarily overwhelmed by the objects in this young man's room. To die before his life has properly begun. The room is in a normal level of mess for a young student. There are empty biscuit packets and beer bottles discarded on shelves containing books thrown at odd angles, rather than all neatly lined up. She spots a Valentine's Day card on the floor, with a picture of a heart on the outside, and a 'will you be mine' and 'true love' above and below. Elizabeth picks it up and reads the note inside. 'Happy Valentine's Day, Always here, your Darce x'. Elizabeth puts it on the table. On the same table, she notices some tablets in a bottle with the label removed. She recognises these, having first-hand experience of someone who was addicted. Elizabeth opens the bottle and removes a pill. She takes out a packet of tissues and wraps the pill inside the tissue then pockets it.

Elizabeth rifles through papers on the table but finds nothing. She sees a dirty laundry sack on the floor and tips it out. Another Valentine's card falls out, caught up in a towel. This one has a photograph of Guinevere Trotsham posing almost naked. Elizabeth screws up her face and drops the photograph. "Eww." Guinevere Trotsham's eyes stare back at her from the carpet, so she covers the image in dirty laundry.

Elizabeth feels a little queasy, so sits on Miles Bonneville's bed, surveying all the guitars and amps, until finally lying back on Miles's pillow. She stares at the ceiling and sees that Miles, or someone, has put a dozen or so luminous stars up there. Elizabeth stretches her arms up towards them and then back over her head. Her hands come down to rest on the headboard. Her fingers feel a crumpled piece of paper squashed behind. Clearly discarded, and perhaps missed by the police as this room was not a crime scene, she uncrumples the paper and reads the typed note.

'Steer clear of Nisha, unless you want trouble at your door. Nothing good can come of it.' And that was it. No signature. Nothing more. Elizabeth pockets the note and sits up. She sifts through Miles's vinyl beside his bed, grabs an album and leaves with more questions than answers. Why is every road leading back to Nisha? Why steer clear of Nisha?

55
PUNTING CAFE

On her way back from Christina's College, Elizabeth decides to pop home to make Godric some food. She is relieved she has no lectures today but knows she must also prepare for some tutorials next week, and thinks how she'd prefer to be at home in Gerald's study to prep for them rather than in her department right now.

As she walks up Bridge Street, Elizabeth spots her sharply dressed friend popping into The Punting Café – a little café built right on the bow of the bridge, allowing customers a bird's eye view of the river. Elizabeth thinks about going in, but she doesn't quite know what to say, feeling a little more than guilty. She tries to walk past unnoticed but fails miserably, hears her name being called and the café window tapped. Elizabeth looks back, and Emily is beckoning her in.

Elizabeth pushes open the café door and is immediately hit with smells of cinnamon buns, carrot cake and tea. Emily beams and waves her over to join. The two women embrace, and Elizabeth sighs with relief as she removes her duffel coat and green mittens.

"Thought I'd sneak a piece of chocolate cake before I go back to College to mark a series of second year essays on Nero. A Valentine's Day treat to me," Emily says, starting the conversation and papering over the cracks of yesterday.

"Happy Valentine's Day. The papers on Nero, or the cake? Which is the treat?" Elizabeth says, then looks away, knowing Emily went all the way to the beach to find her. A waitress comes over just as Elizabeth was going to say something, anything, to apologise. But instead, Emily turns her attention to ordering.

"She'd like the vegan chocolate cake and a peppermint tea, please. Same for me but with a Latte. Thank you," Emily smiles, and waits for the waitress to leave before saying, "Happy Valentine's Day, Elizabeth."

Elizabeth sits down opposite Emily, and the two women pause from speaking. The room is noisy, full of couples mainly, laughing and cooing at one another. Finally, Emily strikes up conversation.

"The horses were spectacular. I think your Inspector thought for a moment I'd taken him there to meet his fate. They charged only metres from us. Quite the thrill is Holkham."

"I like horses," is all that Elizabeth can muster.

"Yes, quite impressive." Emily stares into Elizabeth's eyes, reminding Elizabeth that she cannot shut out her friend. "That grandson of yours is quite the softy. Who knew? He was in direct contact with me from the moment you left the dogs. I normally can't get two words from him?"

"Oh," Elizabeth looks at the menu.

"It doesn't matter one jot." Emily takes Elizabeth's hand across the table, "What matters is that you're okay."

"At least you and Bob had some quality time together," Elizabeth looks up and smirks for the first time.

"Oh, stop. Did we hell! He played some god-awful radio all the way there, with pop music and a presenter talking to us like we were five years old. My bottom was cooking from the heated seats," Emily laughs.

"His new pride and joy, I think," Elizabeth replies quietly.

"I told Cuthbert to disconnect the ones in his car. Heated seats. Feels like I'm wetting myself. Most disturbing. And then, he drives like a maniac along the B-roads. I had to remove my nails from the dashboard when I got out. And the constant chatter about golf, Liz. He can't stop talking about it. Cuthy has recently had a few rounds with the man. Well, he talked me through each one, hole by wretched hole, until I had to beg him to stop."

"Bob likes you," Elizabeth sighs, wishing the two friends would get along.

"He bought me the posh peanuts in the pub." Emily looks at the face of her friend. "You know I'm here for you anytime."

"I know. I thought I was on top of things –"

"Maybe you could think about going on holiday? Easter's coming up." Emily suggests lightly.

"That feels like a long way away," Elizabeth hasn't got time to think of holidays. "What would I do with the dogs?" She replies dismissively.

"Take them."

"Cats?"

"I'd look after the cats. And, you have Mrs Cloud. You deserve a break." Emily squeezes Elizabeth's hand again. The waitress brings over a tray with cakes and hot drinks. "There's always sugar," Emily says.

"I'm sorry to worry you like that." Elizabeth sighs, finally admitting that she has not been herself.

"Today is a new day. Sometimes, today has to be enough." Emily shrugs her shoulders. Changing the subject, Emily looks at Elizabeth, down at the delicious looking cakes, then back at Elizabeth. She grabs a fork and smashes it into her slice of cake, then shoves in far too much and her cheeks have to puff out to accommodate. She looks at Elizabeth and laughs, trying her best to hold in the cake. Elizabeth takes a stab at her cake and copies Emily. Both friends with full cheeks, laughing, trying not to spit out cake. After some time munching in silence, Emily asks her friend.

"Where are you going now?"

"Home. I need to know Godric is safe. I was on my way to cook him a meal. I don't know the last time he ate," Elizabeth replies, putting her head in her hands. "He was nearly killed, Em."

"But he wasn't. He's okay," Emily replies, doing her best to reassure her friend. "And, he really does love you, doesn't he," Emily says. Emily looks out the window, down at the punts going by on the river. They are full of Valentine's Day decorations, with red blankets, heart shaped bunting draped around the edges, and chauffeurs wearing red jackets.

"Isn't that Godric?" Emily taps on the window.

"What? What's he doing?" Elizabeth asks shocked, looking down to see Godric in a punt, and beside Nisha. "Can I borrow your telephone?"

"That's what I'm here for," Emily passes Elizabeth her mobile. Elizabeth looks at the phone and the flat screen in frustration and hands it back to Emily.

"Can you phone Godric?" Elizabeth asks. Emily hits a couple of buttons and hands it back to Elizabeth. The phone rings and Godric picks up.

"Where are you going?" Elizabeth listens for a while and then hands the phone back to Emily. "He says he can't speak. Something about looking after Nisha. Look, look. He's putting his arm around her."

"Is he still poorly? Is that what you're worried about?" Emily asks.

"I'm worried for his life," Elizabeth gets up and

rushes out of the café. Emily throws down some money and runs after her.

56
VALENTINE'S DAY PUNT

The Backs, one of the most romantic places in Cambridge, is teeming with punts on one of the most organised days of the year for lovers. With reason, this place is often called 'another country', and today it is on its best display for all the dreamers. Couples have come from far and wide to profess their love. They huddle, cosy, under blankets while punt chauffeurs glide the love birds slowly as if in a dream past drippingly beautiful lawns, flowerbeds of early spring colour and majestic College buildings.

When Lance suggests a punt trip to Darcy and Nisha as something to take their minds off the dreadful series of events, they don't need much persuading. Doing something that requires no effort appeals to Darcy, given her own string of bad news of not making the cut for Barclay's drama troupe. Nisha confesses her nerves are frayed and says she just wants to relax, so long as Godric comes too.

It is not long before their punt drifts away from Castle

Hill and towards the Colleges which back onto the river. The three of them are by far failing any incognito test. Godric sits in his white winter coat next to Nisha, who is tucked under a blanket in a bright green velvet jacket. While Lance, only wearing a flimsy shirt, sits next to Darcy, who is sporting the largest wide-brimmed black hat she pulled out of the costume box. Punt poles clunk on the bottom of the river bed, laughter trickles from lovers' mouths on passing crafts. But the four remain silent, however, trying to process the past forty-eight hours. None of it makes sense.

Darcy drops her fingers into the water, but it is icy cold, so pulls them out quickly, sinking further under a red blanket. Not wanting the affair to be too glum, Lance pops open a bottle of bubbly and pulls snacks out of his pockets. Having paid the chauffeur to "be quiet and just punt", the peaceful rhythm takes over, and they start to drift away in their own thoughts along The Backs.

"Well, a man has to eat, has to drink. And quite frankly, who knows when the police will come knocking," Lance says, taking a large glug of champagne then passing the bottle to Nisha. Darcy snatches it away.

"My Miles. He was the love of my life," Darcy swigs from the bottle.

"It's such a terrible tragedy. But, one day, I'm sure you'll love again," Nisha replies.

"What's that supposed to mean? Way too early, Waify," Darcy says, frowning.

"She's just trying to make you feel better," Godric declines the bottle offered to him from Darcy, trying to be good for once for his nanna.

"Do you all even care?" Darcy asks, taking another swig.

"Of course," Lance takes the bottle.

"Do you even love anyone?" Darcy looks at Nisha.

"I have loved and lost," Nisha replies.

"Not like this. My boyfriend has been murdered. You

were in charge of props," Darcy pulls the bottle back off Lance and takes a long swig of champagne.

"Now, now. We all love each other. Look at the romance around us. It just might save us." Lance offers Nisha some peanuts, but she shakes her head. Lance then takes the champagne back from Darcy. Impatient, Darcy looks in Lance's bag and opens a new bottle.

"I loved Miles," Nisha replies.

"Sure you did," Lance pats her on the knee.

"No, I did. I loved him," Nisha says, pausing. Then looks at Darcy. "We loved each other. We were lovers."

"Are you insane?" Darcy stares at Nisha in complete surprise. "Don't tell such lies. What a terrible thing to say. When he's not cold in the ground," Darcy says. Lance chucks Godric a bag of peanuts.

"You were seeing Miles?" Godric asks, surprised, having been a little quiet up until now and wondering if the madness between these so called friends will ever end.

"She's talking rubbish!" Darcy says angrily, but also confused.

"I'm sorry, Darcy. We didn't mean to hurt you. Miles said he was going to tell you. I think he was trying to find the right moment." Nisha looks at Darcy, apologetically. Lance and Godric glance at each other and then back at the women. Did they hear right? Can this be true?

"Shut up, you silly bitch!" Darcy shouts.

"I don't know what to say. I'm really sorry. Miles wanted me to go with the band because we were seeing each other. You heard him invite me the other night, but not you," Nisha looks at Darcy, then at Lance and Godric.

"Miles?" Lance asks, mouthing 'What the–'

"You bitch! Shut up!" Darcy interrupts, throwing a bottle of champagne at Nisha's head. But, Godric manages to intercept it just in time.

"Pull over to the bank, now!" Darcy shouts at the chauffeur, who although used to arguments, is relieved to allow this unpleasant woman off onto All Saint's lawns.

Darcy jumps out of the punt. "You're dead!" Darcy shouts back at Nisha before she storms off.

*

"Well, isn't this just the most romantic time?" Lance says after the three remaining friends have travelled a while in silence, digesting what has just happened. The chauffeur asks if he should start up with his verbal tour only to have a frown from Lance with a firm head shake. Finally, Nisha speaks.

"D'you think I should have gone after Darcy, to see if she's okay?"

"Definitely no," Lance replies, "Tempers are high. Let her calm down. I'm sure you're aware, darling Nish, but Miles did play the field somewhat and tell his conquests he loved them all."

"He told me he loved me. That he's stopped all that. He was going to speak with Darcy. He invited me on tour," Nisha replies firmly, "You heard him."

"What about feeding Fred?" Lance looks at Nisha, slightly irked she had offered to feed his cat.

"I was trying to find a replacement. I thought maybe Godric?"

"Nish, how could you?" Lance looks disappointed.

"I know how to feed cats, you know," Godric says, picking up Darcy's blanket and covering his feet.

"But you're not going now. So, it doesn't matter," Nisha tries to persuade Lance not to make a big deal about the cat.

"But you gave your word," Lance takes another long drink. "I'm quite surprised. I thought you were my friend."

"Can we all just get some perspective? I'm getting a little sick of everyone sweating the small stuff. Hugo and Miles are dead!?" Godric butts in, feeling his irritation growing. A pair of swans swim past the punt as it kisses a willow tree. Godric pulls Nisha's blanket over them both.

"Can we all stop arguing, please?"

"Perspective?" Lance takes a large swig of his champagne and indicates to the chauffeur to move on. "I need to know Fred will be okay if anything happens to me, that's all."

*

Elizabeth and Emily have been in negotiation with the punt office to have a punt of their own with a chauffeur, with Elizabeth demanding they call their company owner, who she knows well. After something resembling a Mexican stand-off, Elizabeth finally gets what she wants, and they are on their way. Two women. One punt and a dashing young man in a boater hat and jacket standing on the deck with a long pole trailing behind.

"Can you go any faster? We need to catch a punt!" Elizabeth shouts back at him.

"Ooh, like an old-fashioned cop chase," the chauffeur smiles and takes the central line down the river and speeds up, overtaking many more of the leisurely punts.

"We're looking for a punt, one of yours, with two men and two women. A man in a white coat, and a woman in a green jacket," Elizabeth explains.

"What will we say when we catch them?" Emily asks Elizabeth.

"You two in love then?" the chauffeur tries to make chatter, as Emily pulls a blanket over Elizabeth's knees, "You look cute together."

"I love this woman with all my heart," Emily laughs then gives Elizabeth a big hug. Elizabeth stares ahead, ignoring the banter. As the chauffeur speeds up under the Bridge of Sighs towards St James's Bridge, heading towards All Saints', Elizabeth spots Dr Guinevere Trotsham acting most suspiciously.

"Pull up over there!" Elizabeth shouts, pointing at Dr Trotsham.

"What about the chase?" The chauffeur asks, mildly disappointed.

"We need to follow that woman! I have a feeling she'll know what's going on," Elizabeth says, mainly to Emily.

"I know her. That's Guinevere Trotsham? She studies classical texts. Our paths cross. She's English, isn't she?" Emily asks.

"She also slept with one of the young men who is now dead. And, I can see she's dragging a suitcase. What is she doing? I bet she doesn't have classical texts in that."

"How do you know she was seeing one of the victims?" Emily asks.

"She sent Miles Bonneville a Valentine's Day card with a very suggestive photograph of herself in it. I found it in his room. He'd hidden it in the dirty laundry. I presume the police didn't find it there."

"What a strange place to hide something, and if I might say, what a strange place to look," Emily replies.

"What I find stranger is why would Mr Bonneville keep it at all? Was he blackmailing her, or her him? He had a girlfriend, by all accounts. Why care about this, unless she meant something to him. Which I suspect is the case. So, we need to follow that suitcase."

The chauffeur lets them out of the punt and onto Christina College's lawn, on the Queen's Road side.

"Here's twenty pounds. Keep looking for that punt and phone my friend here when you find them. It has precious cargo on it," Elizabeth leans back over to hand the chauffeur the money. Emily gives him her card. The chauffeur nods, liking the idea, leaving Elizabeth and Emily to run towards an avenue of trees and after a very suspicious looking Dr Guinevere Trotsham.

*

Darcy has run out all her anger. She finds herself

standing at Mill Pond, near Granta College. She walks into a bar and orders a pint and takes it out by the river, crossing onto Laundress Green. An empty bench beckons. A few tourists braving the chilly February day wander along the river path towards Grantchester.

Darcy can't escape the couples milling hand in hand, seemingly carefree. She notices on a hotel lawn on the opposite side of the river, couples sit under outdoor heaters on tightly mown lawns in expensive wicker chairs and share hot chocolates within its grounds. Darcy shuts her eyes and shakes her head. She is broke. Her boyfriend is dead. And now she hears he cheated with Nisha of all people? It is the final straw. In that moment, she is glad he is dead.

She wonders what her next move can be. No place in the show, or Christina College troupe. She gets out her phone and find's Lance's number and texts: "I need you to get me out of here." Then pockets her phone and drinks her beer.

57
BONFIRE IN THE HEART

Professor Elizabeth Green and Emily Masters find themselves hiding behind trees as they creep up the avenue towards Christina College's back fields near the Queen's Road, pausing as Dr Guinevere Trotsham stops to tie her shoelace. Elizabeth momentarily fondly remembers the outdoor summer Shakespeare performances where she has sat in years gone by with Gerald and watched Henry V, Othello and more. She reminds herself to think again about those memories when she gets home. Happy days. Right now, she has to think of finding the killer so Godric can stay safe. She signals to Emily that Dr Trotsham is crossing the road and disappearing up a muddy path.

Now on the same path, Elizabeth and Emily hear twigs snap under the suitcase wheels not far up ahead. They tiptoe around the corner then jolt back, as not twenty feet in front of them, behind what looks like a gardeners' hut with wheelbarrows outside and garden forks and hoes propped up against the wall, Dr Trotsham now stands with the suitcase. They watch as she takes out a match and lights a fire in a brazier, wondering what on earth she is doing. As the fire starts to rage, full of dry leaves, Elizabeth and Emily watch Dr Trotsham unzip the suitcase, pull out clothes then throw them on the fire. Elizabeth waits to let her repeat the action just once, before leaping out of the bushes to confront her, with a less sure Emily following behind.

"What on earth are you doing?" Professor Elizabeth Green asks, emerging from the bush with leaves now stuck in her hair.

"Are you following me?" Dr Trotsham is taken aback.

"You've hot footed it up here after our Swan Theatre meeting? Feels a little odd, wouldn't you say?"

"Hello, Guinevere," Emily says, also now slowly emerging from the same bush and pulling out leaves from her hair.

"I'm burning old costumes, that's all." Dr Trotsham continues picking up clothes from the case, a little shocked by their abrupt appearance. "I didn't want anyone to use them again as the whole play seemed jinxed."

"These are not costumes. They're a young man's clothes? Stop this at once!" Elizabeth lunges at the pile of clothes in Dr Trotsham's hands which she is about to throw on the fire. "This is evidence." Dr Trotsham raises her arm above Elizabeth's head and is about to strike her. Quick as a flash, Emily jumps forward and catches hold of Dr Trotsham. Elizabeth grabs the clothes and the suitcase, while Emily holds Dr Trotsham back. "Miles? This belongs to Miles Bonneville!" Elizabeth shouts as she sees a name label in a lapel of a sports top, confirming her suspicions.

"He asked me to keep some of his clothes in the Faculty. So he could change quickly! Alright? It's none of your business," Dr Trotsham replies.

"What?" Elizabeth helps Emily by grabbing hold of Dr Trotsham's other arm to restrain her. "You said you were burning costumes a moment ago. Which is it?"

"This is none of your business!" Guinevere Trotsham breaks free and steps back from Emily and Elizabeth.

"Oh, come off it. A murdered man. You, burning his clothes?" Elizabeth shakes her head. Emily examines her hand, a little bruised from having to hold onto Dr Trotsham like that.

"Look, if they bother you that much, take them." Dr Trotsham takes a few more steps away from the fire. Emily now warms her hands in the heat, so Elizabeth pulls the suitcase over to her and asks her to keep hold.

"Burning them in secret?" Emily chips in.

"Why did you send Miles Bonneville a Valentine's Day card with a photograph that left nothing to the imagination?" Elizabeth asks, giving Dr Guinevere Trotsham a hard stare.

"How dare you. That was private!" Dr Trotsham starts to walk away.

"Did you murder him for rejecting you? He wasn't seeing you, was he? He was dating Darcy Nighy."

"I'm not doing this now. You've no idea what you're talking about!" Dr Trotsham shouts, just before she turns and runs away.

"What was that?" Emily turns to look at Elizabeth.

"A spurned lover. That's what that was." Elizabeth replies. "You never can tell what crazy things they'll do. Come on. I need to get back to Godric, and quick."

58
RED SIRENS

Police sirens echo across the water as Godric, Lance and Nisha's punt glides under the Scientific Bridge.

"It seems my time is now up," Lance says looking at the sky as they emerge on the other side. He takes another long gulp of champagne, realising he was always only just playing a waiting game. Two police cars and a Tesla stop on Silver Street Bridge, confirming his fears. Three police officers appear and lean over the wall, watching as the punt disappears under Silver Street Bridge only to reappear again in Mill Pond. Godric spots Inspector Bob Abley looking directly at him.

"Pull over!" the Inspector shouts, as the police hurriedly walk to stand by the punt dock.

Godric can see all the milling tourists' eyes focused on their punt, so he decides to wave at them like the Queen. Finding himself in the storm of a murder investigation does not suit Godric's disposition. He much prefers being his nanna's assistant on such cases. She would know what to do in this situation. Godric, on the other hand, feels frozen. He wonders where she is, and thinks he should have taken her advice to go home. He is also a little concerned too that the Inspector just said he couldn't be Bunny's assistant anyway because he was too close to the case. What did that mean?

"Everything will be alright," he says as he feels Nisha trembling under the blanket. "At least the police won't kill us. We will be safe if they're around, I suppose" Godric says, then glances at Lance who gives him a 'they've come for me' look. Lance stands up to help the chauffeur guide the punt towards the bank.

"Miss Nisha Acharya-Gorpade, we need you to accompany us to the station," Inspector Abley shouts across the water.

"What?" Godric is shocked, then immediately guilty for having only just a moment ago reassured her things would be okay. "They must be mistaken?" He says to Nisha.

"What for?" Lance shouts across to the Inspector, equally perplexed.

"Miss Acharya-Gorpade, we have reason to believe you have important information about this case that you are withholding. You need to come with us now," Inspector Abley continues, still focused on Nisha.

"Why the drama?" Lance asks, frowning.

"If you can stay out of it, Sir," Lemon replies.

"Can I come with her?" Godric checks with Inspector Abley.

"Actually, we'd like to question you as well," Inspector Abley looks mildly uncomfortable when turning to look in Godric's direction.

"No problem," Godric replies, unsure what else to say. Godric gets to his feet and helps Nisha out of the punt, trying not to show that his heart is pounding and adrenalin rushing through his veins.

Further away from the moorings, across the bank, Darcy watches everything.

"You murdered Miles, didn't you! You little bitch!" She shouts at Nisha.

Sergeant Lemon takes hold of Nisha's hand to help her out of the punt and guides her into a police car. Lemon nods hello to Godric and points him to get into the other car. Godric looks at Constable Petticoat holding open the door to the back seat. Godric shrugs then begins to climb in, Petticoat pushing Godric's head into the car as he sits. Why do they do that, Godric thinks, annoyed at being manhandled. When Nisha and Godric are both safely shut inside on back seats, Sergeant Lemon turns quietly to Inspector Abley.

"Professor Green is going to kill you."

Inspector Abley looks at Lemon, and pulls a face.

"Call ahead to reception and make sure she doesn't get past it for an hour or two. Will you?"

Sergeant Lemon pulls out his mobile and makes the call. Not far behind, another punt chauffeur gets out his phone and a piece of paper and makes a call.

"Is that Emily? You asked me to call when I caught up with them?" The chauffeur asks as he watches the punt passengers disembarking and some being taken away.

Inspector Abley walks over to his car. He looks for a moment at the scene in front of him. He is used to the chaos caused by sirens. But something about today being Valentine's Day. He can almost smell the testosterone and oestrogen in the air. Seeing all the happy faces in shock, hands being held tighter, arms over shoulders and around waists clinging. The packed punts full of couples celebrating with champagne and roses aghast at the seeming police arrests. The whole thing makes him feel more alone than ever. And now he has to take his friend's son to the police station for questioning?

59
LAUNDRESS GREEN

Elizabeth and Emily both have hold of Dr Guinevere Trotsham's suitcase and are pulling it along the Queen's Road when they hear sirens.

"That's Bob's car," Elizabeth listens.

"You know his siren from the others?" Emily is impressed.

"There's a jump in it. Hear it?" Elizabeth replies.

Emily nods, listening to the irregular whirr.

"Like a wheeze. Maybe there's a real emergency? He's run out of golf balls," Emily quips, a little tired from all this walking in heels up muddy tracks and dragging heavy objects. Then Emily's phone rings. She hits accept and listens for a bit. After a brief moment, she says "Thank you" then cuts the call.

"Who was that?" Elizabeth asks, stopping for a moment.

"Our chauffeur. When he got to Mill Pond. Says he didn't see four, but there were three people and two looking a lot like those we described on a punt pulling in.

Two were being arrested."

"I need to get to Godric," Elizabeth replies, now starting to walk more quickly. "Find out what happened. Stupid of me to follow the suitcase. Stupid."

"Not stupid at all. Don't you think Guinevere is a guilty as hell? Burning a dead man's clothes?"

"It's very suspicious," Elizabeth replies.

Both Elizabeth and Emily break into a run, the suitcase now bumping along behind them.

*

Lance grabs himself and Darcy more drinks then the two of them walk out onto the island opposite Granta College and Mill Pond. Punt poles clang, laughter strikes up again, and life has gone back to normal around them as the two stand looking at the river in the winter sun. Lance throws a stone in the river below his feet, watching the concentric circles widen. Finally, he speaks.

"You know, if anyone had done this, I'd've put money on it being you," Lance says, glancing sideways at Darcy.

"You stabbed my boyfriend. How you're still on the outside, I'll never know," Darcy replies flatly, adding, "I'm thirsty."

"Touché," Lance replies. "This was just a quick one, to steady my nerves. I need to see if they're alright. If they need bail."

"Nisha can afford her own bail," Darcy says dismissively. "What about looking after this friend."

"You know it doesn't work like that," Lance replies.

"I'll be getting smashed then," Darcy then feels in her pockets. "But I'm broke."

"My treat." Lance hands her a few twenties. "Have one for me. I've probably had my last."

"You keep saying that," Darcy replies, pocketing the money before Lance can take it back.

"Because it's true. If the cops don't get me, the killer will." As Lance tips back his head and gulps down the last of the cold beer in his glass, he doesn't see Professor Elizabeth Green approaching. By the time he's finished his long glug, she is standing right under their noses, with Emily following in her high heels, carrying one of Miles's coats and still pulling the suitcase.

"Tell me what happened here. The sirens. I want to know. You were in a punt with my grandson," Elizabeth glares at Lance.

"Your grandson has been taken in for questioning, with Nisha," Darcy replies, wishing this woman would leave them alone.

"When was this?" Elizabeth glares at Darcy.

"Didn't you hear the sirens?" Lance asks.

"Hey! What are you doing with Miles's clothes?" Darcy spots them in Emily's arms as she approaches. "And that's his suitcase?"

"Did you know your boyfriend was seeing other people, Ms Nighy?" Elizabeth asks.

"I don't think anyone could have guessed he was seeing so many people," Lance replies.

"I'm talking about Dr Guinevere Trotsham," Elizabeth shares the news.

"Ugh. How many people are going to drag that up?" Darcy scowls, "It was a mistake, a one off. He was embarrassed about it. She's ancient," Darcy puts down her glass and takes Miles's coat from Emily to smell.

"I'm not sure she saw it that way. Are you sure it was over?" Elizabeth asks Darcy.

"Excuse me, but what has this got to do with you? I don't see anyone else asking me such personal questions. Come on, Lance," Darcy says about to put on Miles's coat, then turns to Elizabeth again, "I'm telling the police you have Miles's clothes."

"I think she works for the police, Darce," Lance puts his pint glass on the floor next to Darcy's. "Actually, I think I'll head to the police station to see if Nisha needs any legal. Don't get too pissed. I'll call you."

Darcy nods and walks towards The Mill for another pint, now wearing Miles's coat.

"Are you not mad at Ms Acharya-Gorpade?" Elizabeth asks Lance who buttons his shirt, still hardly dressed for the weather. "She was in charge of props and was so bad at it that you killed your best friend?"

"Nisha is many things, but I don't think she's a killer." Lance looks at Elizabeth.

"I didn't say she was?" Elizabeth stares back.

"Why have the police arrested her?" Lance asks Elizabeth. "You're part of them."

"I'm sure you'll find out in due course. So, you don't blame her?" Elizabeth presses.

"It's the last thing on my mind," Lance takes out a cigarette. "My friends are dead, and I'm responsible for one of them. Even though it was an accident, I killed him. How d'you think I'm sleeping? Top it all, the killer, if indeed that's who we are looking for, likes tall white men in their twenties." Lance inhales deeply.

"You seem more worried about Miss Acharya-Gorpade than staying with your friend, Miss Nighy?" Elizabeth presses.

"She'll make some new friends at the bar. Not shy is our Darce. Nish, she's a different kettle of fish entirely. Likely to confess to something she didn't even do. Just to keep people happy. If you'll excuse me. I have to get walking."

Elizabeth and Emily watch Lance Fernard head off to the police station.

"Er, are you going to pick these up?!" Elizabeth shouts at him for leaving their glasses on the grass. He ignores her. "Oh, for goodness sake. No wonder things are going to the dogs." Elizabeth picks up the pint glasses.

"You're not thinking of walking to Parker's Piece, with this are you?" Emily looks down at the suitcase and her muddy heels. "We should have asked him to carry it, if he's going," Emily replies.

"Let's take it to Granta. I can go and get the car."

"I'll have to love you and leave you once we get there. I need to do some marking and find a way how to break it to Cuthbert that I'm not on the flight he thinks I'm on."

"You're not going to Russia?" Elizabeth asks.

"No. I thought it would be too cold on the feet," Emily replies, looking down at her wet shoes.

Elizabeth takes hold of the suitcase and drags it quickly over the grass, as Emily totters behind her. Elizabeth feels like the blood has started to pump back around her veins. She has to help Godric and fast.

60
BACK AT THE STATION

Outside this afternoon, on Valentine's Day, the sun is still shining down on people enjoying the daffodil display on Parker's Piece. Inside Cambridge Police Station, the air is tense as Inspector Abley and Sergeant Lemon sit opposite Nisha Acharya-Gorpade at a table in a grey windowless room. The room is somewhere within the labyrinth of corridors at the station. Nisha looks close to tears.

"Miss Acharya-Gorpade, you have waived your right to a solicitor," Inspector Abley reminds Nisha, continuing, "You see, what you told us in your statement isn't adding up with our information." Inspector Abley pushes over a piece of paper with some figures on it, then continues. "In your testimony, you state you were drugged and taken, against your will, to a cash machine and then robbed."

"Yes, that's right," Nisha replies, looking confused at the figures.

"Yet there is no money missing from your account. We have looked at the records. Nothing appears to have moved out of your account as you say it did."

"I just saw that today myself. I really don't understand what happened? I promise you. I was taken to the wall to extract money, then they grabbed my phone. You have to believe me," Nisha replies, looking worriedly at the paper and the figures.

"Why didn't you tell us? You could have told us at the theatre this morning?"

"I would have. I was trying to figure it out myself. I'm sorry," Nisha replies. "I know it's not an excuse, but I was scared."

"Is there anything else you have omitted to tell us?" Sergeant Lemon joins in the interrogation.

"What do you mean?" Nisha looks up, her saucer-sized eyes like rabbits in the headlights. "No, I don't think so?" Nisha rubs her hands nervously on the cuffs of her green velvet jacket.

"That we should know," Lemon adds, "That isn't in your statement?"

"No?" Nisha shrinks back into her chair.

"It has come to our attention that there was a withdrawal of money from St Andrew's Street at the time you mention you were there. At the same time, Mr Godric Cartright-Green was lying on the road. But the money was withdrawn from an account belonging to the young man who was stabbed. Mr Miles Bonneville. His account, not yours," Lemon explains.

"Miles's? I don't understand."

"Yes. Not only was his money taken on that night," Inspector Abley adds, "but, the account was checked and, since Mr Bonneville's death, we saw that a number of additional separate payments have been made from his account into your account. Quite a significant amount."

"I talked to my bank about unexpected payments recently. I didn't know they were from Miles? I swear," Nisha pleads. "They just had a bank sort code and account number. Not a name. The bank wouldn't tell me any more than that."

"Again, why didn't you tell us?" Inspector Abley presses. "This is highly relevant information to the case."

"I didn't think the two were linked?" Nisha's eyes are now wide open. "I didn't think it suspicious. Why would I? How is a banking error related to my friends being dead?"

"Didn't think large sums were suspicious?" Sergeant Lemon asks.

Nisha pauses, choosing her words carefully.

"I'm not poor, Sergeant. Those large sums you call them, they're a drop in the ocean," Nisha sighs.

"We can see that," Inspector Abley acknowledges. "We will be corroborating your story. We will need to get a new statement from you. But it doesn't look good, and we don't think you have answered our questions," Inspector Abley stands up. "Perhaps you can think about it before you commit your statement to the record again. We want the truth." Inspector Abley then leans into the microphone on the table recording the interview. "This interview is temporarily suspended at fourteen thirty-four, fourteenth of February." Inspector Abley and Sergeant Lemon stand up and walk out.

"I'd like to have her money," Lemon says, once outside the room.

"Me too," Abley turns out his empty pockets as they walk towards the coffee machine.

Have you got any change?"

"Nothing changes does it," Lemon huffs, as he hands over some coins from his pocket.

"Yes. Yes, it does." Inspector Abley replies, putting Lemon's money into the coffee machine, buying himself a coffee. Then over dramatically putting the small amount of change in the confectionary machine to buy Lemon a bar of Fry's Peppermint Cream. "I give gifts now." Bob Abley picks out the chocolate bar from the window then gives it to Lemon.

"D'you think she's guilty?" Lemon asks, papering

over Abley's bad habit by changing the subject.

"No. But I don't know why she has Miles Bonneville's money?"

"It's like these kids are being framed. She's loaded. Did you see all those zeros? Not like she needed any more," Lemon suggests.

"These kids?" Abley smirks, "You one of us oldies now?"

"I've been a grown-up for some time, you know," Lemon raises his eyebrows. "Nisha doesn't look like a murderer."

"It's always the quiet ones," Abley replies.

"Godric next?"

"Yes, let's go," Abley sighs.

"You think he's guilty or knows something?" Lemon asks.

"I'm just doing my job. He was there when Nisha stole the money. If that is what happened at all."

*

Godric sits across a table in a slightly nicer room with a window. A Constable has brought him a coffee, no police officer is standing in the corner, nor is there a recording machine on the table. Godric seems a little more relaxed for someone in a police station. Inspector Abley beams at him as he walks in, to put him at ease.

"Would you like another coffee?" Inspector Abley looks into Godric's empty cup. Godric shakes his head, pulling a face to indicate he did not like the first one.

"Do you have any hot choccy?" Godric asks, his eyelids heavy. "Something soothing?"

Abley pulls Lemon's bar of Fry's chocolate cream out of Lemon's hand and gives it to Godric.

"Have some sugar," Abley says.

"Ooh, thanks. I haven't had one of these in ages.

Bunny likes them. They're vegan." Sergeant Lemon pulls a face as he watches his chocolate bar being demolished. Inspector Abley and Sergeant Lemon sit down opposite Godric.

"Am I under arrest? Does Bunny know? She'll be so worried. She'll kill you. Is Nisha okay? What's this all about?" Godric asks, sucking on the chocolate.

"Whoah. Too many questions. We ask you the questions." Abley breaks a piece of the chocolate off himself and pops it in. "Hmm, nice. But seeing as it's you. I hope Elizabeth doesn't know, and yes, she will kill me. But no, you're not under arrest. Do emphasise that point when you see her."

"You brought me in with sirens," Godric says, the chocolate calming him a little, "It was like a movie."

"No. It's real. We brought you in because we thought it might give your friend in the other room a pang of conscience. Cause her to squeak. If she thinks you are in trouble. But nothing."

"Squeak?" Godric asks.

"We wondered if she's said anything to you about large sums of money from Miles Bonneville going into her account?"

"No?" Godric looks puzzled. "Nisha is loaded. What would Miles be giving her money for?"

"As your Nanna earlier wondered, we are now not sure if she was actually even drugged. You didn't see her get robbed, did you?" Sergeant Lemon asks, seeing the last square of his bar of chocolate disappear into Godric's mouth.

"These need to be bigger." Godric looks at the wrapper and then back up to Lemon "I'm not sure. I think so. But I was out of it. I saw someone blow powder into my face."

"Could it have been Miss Acharya-Gorpade who blew the powder?" Inspector Abley asks.

"I don't think so, no. Oh, I'm not sure. I heard Nish

scream," Godric replies, swallowing.

"Is it inconceivable that it looked to you like she was a victim, when in fact Nisha and an accomplice had you drugged?"

Godric pauses to think. Could Nisha have poisoned him? It never even crossed his mind.

"Why go to all that trouble? And weren't there traces of the drug in her system?" Godric asks.

"This particular drug doesn't stay in the system for long. So, she could have administered a little to herself after taking the money. Just so it looked like she had been more badly drugged."

"I just don't get it. And, who could be her accomplice?" Godric pauses, not entirely wanting to say the next thing, for fear of being a little mean. "She doesn't have many friends. I don't think she's made any female friends? She wants to go home," Godric feels sorry for Nisha.

"The question is, Godric, what was she doing with all of Miles's money?"

*

Pulling up directly outside Cambridge Police Station is Professor Elizabeth Green in the Talbot Lago. As always, the car is getting far more attention than Elizabeth would like. The Desk Sergeant on duty, having spotted Elizabeth, leaves his post and comes out to greet her.

"What a beauty your car is. It never fails to make me smile. Does it still run on petrol?"

"Electric now," she replies, uninterested in making small talk.

"What? How?"

"Converted. I've come for my grandson."

"Before you say anymore, he's not here," the Desk Sergeant replies.

"Your eyebrows always dance when you're lying,

Simon." Elizabeth walks past the Sergeant. "I hope you covered the vine. You didn't put it on a South wall."

"Professor, you're not allowed through. Yes, it's a bit of a wind tunnel around the back. It died."

"Died?" Elizabeth asks.

"Stop! Please," Simon shouts for Elizabeth to stop heading for the police entrance, immediately regretting shouting at Professor Green.

"Are you going to manhandle me?" Elizabeth tries to duck around him, but he is too quick and takes a step sideways. "This is ridiculous. Why am I not allowed in?"

"I'm sorry, but those are my orders. And I'm going to have to ask you to move your beautiful car."

"Give me a ticket." Elizabeth looks back at the Talbot which is up on the kerb, not ten feet from the Police Station entrance. "And, unless you let me in, I shall sound my horn every minute. If the vine isn't completely black, lift it now and put it in a greenhouse. It might be salvageable. You need to put it on a south facing wall round there in the summer."

"There isn't a south facing wall," replies the Desk Sergeant, who returns into the reception, temporarily locking the reception doors to prevent Elizabeth's entry. True to her word, Elizabeth starts to beep her car horn. It is much louder than Simon anticipated for a classic car. She will ruddy well get to see her grandson, and no Desk Sergeant is going to stop her.

*

"What is that god awful racket?" Abley asks Sergeant Lemon as they sit with Godric in the same interview room.

"That's Bunny, coming to rescue me." Godric smirks, "She won't stop. She's like a tiger, defending her young."

"More like a T-Rex. Wait here," Abley tells Godric. Abley then nods to Lemon to leave the room. Outside, in the corridor, they have a conflab.

"We could release Miss Acharya-Gorpade, see what she does next? We don't have enough to charge her, do we?" Lemon asks.

"Make sure we keep Miss Gorpade's passport and tell her not to leave Cambridge. We need to find some kind of evidence linking her to Hugo Grader's death. Anything. If we can do that, together with her link to the Swan Theatre props it might be enough to charge her. Get someone on her tail," Abley says. Lemon nods and leaves in a flash.

*

The desk Sergeant has come back outside and is trying to stop Elizabeth from repeatedly pressing her horn. But she has successfully locked her doors and is sitting inside the car. He is pleasantly surprised when, mid beeping of her horn, she stops, opens the car door and gets out.

"Finally, reason prevails," he says to anyone who will listen.

"Over here!" Elizabeth shouts over his shoulder as she spots Nisha coming out of the police station. Nisha stops, recognising Elizabeth from the Swan Theatre, and Godric explaining she is his nanna.

"Hello," Nisha says, looking more than a little exhausted.

"Can I offer you a lift, Ms Acharya-Gorpade? Where are you going?"

"College, I suppose," Nisha replies.

"Jump in." Elizabeth guides Nisha to the passenger door. She looks back at the Sergeant, "Tell the Inspector to send Godric home straight away, and if he doesn't, that I will come back and haunt him with my beeping!"

Before long, Elizabeth is driving Nisha along the side of Parker's Piece, past the University Arms Hotel, heading for Christina College. Nisha's nose twitches as the car still smells of burnt clothes, though she doesn't say anything.

"You know, I wouldn't care what you got up to, only

you've involved my grandson. And for that, I'm angry with you."

"He's my friend. Have they released him?" Nisha looks at Elizabeth, whose eyes are on the road, and now wonders what she has let herself in for having accepted this lift.

"And, do you think he's in danger?" Elizabeth asks.

"I don't know. I don't know what's happening."

"Were you really drugged, Nisha?" Elizabeth looks across at Nisha.

"Yes. And, I don't know how or why Miles's money has gone into my bank account. I don't know why they wanted to talk to Godric. I'm sorry. It's all my fault. I told them that Godric is kind." Nisha looks down at her dress, rubs her hands together, and then pulls out a lip balm from her green jacket pocket.

"Were you having an affair with Hugo Grader?"

"No," Nisha replies, glancing sideways at Elizabeth.

"I saw your hair grips and lip balm on Mr Grader's shelf," Elizabeth looks at the same style of grip now in Nisha's hair, covered in green flowers, and the lip balm in her hands, putting two and two together. "Saw some next to his brush?"

"I was his friend, sure. We spent time together. But I wasn't having an affair," Nisha replies a little too defensively.

"You expect me to believe there was nothing between you? We can go back through his things with a fine toothcomb. Perhaps even find something which proves you killed him."

"The police have already asked me all this." Nisha shakes her head and looks out of the window at the people on the pavements.

"You have to help me catch the murderer before they strike again."

Elizabeth turns into Downing Street. Elizabeth feels the silence hang in the air and realises if she pushes this young woman too far, Nisha might clam up completely.

"You know, Godric hasn't always lived with me," Elizabeth says, trying a different tack. "He used to board at school. He told me he hated it. Something about being too different. And then, he was home schooled for a while, by a hired teacher. His mother, my daughter, well, let's just say she wasn't cut out to bring up children. Godric has a sister, Ottilie. Did he tell you?"

"Yes, he says he rarely sees her," Nisha replies.

"She's going through the same thing he did. A boarder. I hear she's coping better, thank goodness."

"Good," Nisha looks at Elizabeth, pleased for the change in subject.

"When Godric came to stay with me in Cambridge, he didn't go out at first. Just to his lectures. Hard to believe now. He seems to either live at the theatre, the bar or the boathouse. A proper gadabout. But it took time," Elizabeth pauses, wondering whether this is getting through to this young woman. She continues, clicking on her indicator as she crosses over to Silver Street to reach Queen's Road and the entrance to Nisha's College. "I think he had to feel safe first. Like someone had his back. Oh, I know he likes to frequent the clubs, an emotional crutch perhaps. But, to see him happy. It's well. There are no words. So, you can see this Nanna's love runs deep. I would do anything to protect him."

"Okay," Nisha replies, seeing where Professor Elizabeth Green is going with this.

"So, I need to find out who murdered Hugo and Miles and quickly. As I think Godric is in danger. Young men are being murdered. Do you understand?"

"Yes," Nisha looks in front of her, at the daffodils up ahead on the grass.

"If it helps me find who the murderer is, I need to know the whole truth. You don't want Godric to come to harm?"

"No. Definitely not," Nisha says with concern in her

voice. Then she pauses for the longest time, before replying, "I did have a very short relationship with Hugo. But it was months ago, very short. Not an affair. No one knew. We kept it a secret. He made me feel so happy. Well, until he broke it off. He was out of my league. I moped about for weeks. It floored me, to be honest."

"You told no one? Why?"

"Hugo didn't want anyone to know," Nisha shrugs. "Said people would talk. And, it really wasn't for long enough to talk about? I think he was embarrassed by me, as it happens."

"Why haven't you told the police?"

"It was such a long time ago," Nisha replies, then looks at Elizabeth. "I thought you were the police?" Nisha pauses again, then adds as she looks out the window at couples with happy faces in love walking along the pavement. "I suppose I thought the police would wrongly think I was guilty of hurting him, especially when Miles was murdered by a swapped prop, which was my responsibility." Nisha fiddles with the cuffs of her jacket, her hand still holding her lip balm.

"You lied to the police."

"They didn't ask me. I didn't lie. I just didn't tell them. I really didn't want Hugo to suffer. I'm not a bitter woman," Nisha replies. But Elizabeth Green gives her a look to make it clear they both know that she withheld evidence.

61
THE TALBOT RETURNS

After dropping Nisha Acharya-Gorpade back at Christina College's gates and watching her enter, Professor Elizabeth Green turns the Talbot around and heads back to the Police Station. The Desk Sergeant's heart sinks when through the reception window, he catches sight of the car heading back along Park Terrace. As Elizabeth pulls up on the kerb right outside the door, he has to go out and have strong words. Though he already knows they will be futile.

"Your grandson was released fifteen minutes ago. He left you this." the Desk Sergeant hands Elizabeth a short scribbled note, which reads: 'Bunny, all is well. They just took me in for show. Gave me a chocolate bar. I'm heading home. I'm buying you a mobile phone. Goddy x.'

"Right, thank you, Simon."

"So, you don't need to come in right now," the Desk Sergeant says, following his orders. Elizabeth steps back across the road onto the grass. The Sergeant wonders what she is doing. She looks up and spots Inspector Abley behind his office window, swinging an imaginary golf club, with Sergeant Lemon by his side. Sergeant Lemon notices

Elizabeth and waves, causing Abley to turn and see her too. She then shakes her head and points at the entrance. She walks towards the car and pulls out the suitcase. The Sergeant's phone trills at the front desk.

"Wait here," the Sergeant pleads, but she barges through.

Moments later, Elizabeth walks out of the lift on Inspector Abley's office corridor, then arrives at his open door. Inspector Abley and Sergeant Lemon are not surprised to see her but are impressed by her speed of arrival.

"Was it worth it? Arresting my grandson? Nisha told me about Miles's money and her account." Elizabeth plonks the suitcase down. "And, I thought I was working for you. Blocking me from entering the station? Bit of a contradiction?"

"What is that stink?" Inspector Bob Abley tries to dodge her questions and looks down at the suitcase Elizabeth has dragged in. "Jumble?"

"Hardly. Designer. Emily and I found Dr Trotsham behind the gardener's shed at Christina's lighting a bonfire and trying to burn these, if you please."

"Of course she was?" Abley shakes his head, not knowing what Elizabeth is talking about. He clicks open the suitcase and picks up a shirt, observing the label. "Miles Bonneville?"

"I presume you know that they were also at it?" Elizabeth asks.

"Is there anyone not 'at it' on this case?" Inspector Abley opens his eyes wide.

"It is Valentine's Day, Sir," Lemon smirks, reminding him of the coincidence.

"What I don't understand, is why Dr Trotsham would want to burn all this. Surely, if she's innocent, she would come forward?"

"We took her statement in College a couple of days ago, and at the theatre earlier. Not a dickie bird about clothes," Lemon replies.

"Sergeant. Can you follow Dr Trotsham and see what you can find?" Inspector Abley asks.

"Yes, Sir." Lemon makes to leave.

"And do a sweep of her rooms?" Abley shouts after Lemon.

"Right ho. What about Nisha Acharya-Gorpade?" Lemon asks.

"Let's keep the tail on too. Can I leave that with you?" Inspector Abley asks. Lemon nods then leaves, closing the door and smirking slightly at the earful he knows his Inspector will get from Professor Elizabeth Green.

"Right, we need words," Elizabeth says quietly, pacing around the Inspector.

62
VEGAN PASTRIES

It is growing dark on this eventful Valentine's Day, and after words were had with Bob, Elizabeth cannot be more pleased to be driving home. She parks the Talbot and looks down at the snowdrops in a few pots by the front door. She loves the metal fox door knocker Gerald bought her all those years ago when they first moved in.

"Hello! Goddy?" Elizabeth shouts, being welcomed by three wagging tails. She runs her hand through the dog's hair.

"Bunny!" Godric approaches from the kitchen wearing an apron. "I've just boiled the kettle. Tea?" He disappears back into the kitchen after he gives Elizabeth a gentle peck on the cheek."

"Is your friend a murderer?" Elizabeth asks, following him in.

"Nice to see you too. Nisha? She couldn't harm a fly."

"Hmm, strong instincts." Elizabeth watches, not quite believing her eyes. Godric has brought back some pastries boxed up from The Vegan Kid Café, and is pouring hot water into a teapot.

"She's a friend. They don't really think she's responsible?"

"Evidence is mounting," Elizabeth replies.

"If anyone's guilty, it's that Professor Barclay. He was fuming when he heard about the band, incandescent when Hugo and Miles wanted to be in my play but not his."

"But, a murderer? Over a play?" Elizabeth watches as Godric stirs a peppermint tea bag into a teapot and a breakfast bag into his own mug. He opens a cupboard and pulls out two plates.

"I bought these on the way home. Thought it might fill a hole? Now you're feeling a little better?"

"This is a nice surprise." Elizabeth opens her eyes wide at the lovely delicate pastry, not quite remembering the last time Godric made a fuss like this. "How are you feeling now?"

"I just wanted to treat you. You know. Show you that–" Godric hugs his nanna then looks at her straight in the eye. "Well, you mean–"

"Alright, alright. Don't fuss." Elizabeth interrupts and breaks free from his grip, not sure now is the time for sentimentality. "Just be careful, okay?"

"How many? Two each?" Godric takes a fork to lift out the pastries.

"Just one for me. Thank you." Elizabeth worries her response was a little too frosty and looks at Godric. "Thank you for the food. It's lovely. Go on then. I'll have two. I'm glad you're okay."

"Better, now the play is postponed. Can't believe I'm saying that. I mean, I'm disappointed. But I can't think, with everything that's happened." Godric then looks at the flowers on the side. "They're beautiful."

"I never really cared for the day," Elizabeth says, glancing at Godric then back at the flowers. "My father used to say it was a day made up by the gift card industry.

It stuck with me," Elizabeth brushes some petals. "Ever the romantics, our household when I was a young girl. It was just the flowers. Made me, made it–"

"I get it." Godric wraps Elizabeth in his arms again and gives her the biggest hug, and she closes her eyes.

"And now this. I'm worried about you," She holds onto Godric.

"What are you worried about? I'm sure you're getting close," Godric starts to sway his nanna in his arms.

"I don't feel it this time. I don't feel it at all. It's fuzzy. Maybe all the hearts and roses have thrown me off the scent."

"Want to know what I think?" Godric asks.

"Always."

"You can never have too many flowers. We should put them in some of your lovely vases." Godric lets go and starts to root around in cupboards for vases, "And, place some in every room. Then, you can see flowers that Grandpa sent you everywhere. They really are lovely." They both stare at the flowers.

"What do you know about Dr Trotsham?" Elizabeth asks, going over to the sink to wash her hands.

"Nothing. She's an English Don. That Professor Barclay's lackey? A bit desperate?"

"Goddy."

"Well, she's inappropriately dressed for a woman of her age."

"It's not up to society what attire a person may wish to adorn," Elizabeth replies.

"Fine, I'll dig out some bright green speedos and wear them under a garish yellow rain mac next time I go out," Godric continues to open cupboards looking for vases.

"I thought that's what you wore to the bars anyway. Have you come across her while out drinking?" Elizabeth asks, rubbing her hands together in soapy bubbles.

"Yes, she does seem to hang with her students come

to think of it. I think I've seen her in Bene't's bar."

"What else can you tell me about Hugo Grader?" Elizabeth asks, rinsing her hands.

"I've told you everything I know. He was a bit of a show off. Like most front men in bands."

"Did he ever have any contact with Dr Trotsham?"

"No idea. Darcy is fuming. I think she's convinced Nisha did it. I should probably go and see if Nisha's alright," Godric replies.

"What about the flowers?" Elizabeth smiles. Godric starts to fill the vase. "Nisha told me she had a fling with Hugo. I just gave her a lift to College, when I was looking for you. You'd obviously come home already."

"She just told us on the punt she was about to run away with Miles?" Godric lifts some flowers out of the display. "Now Hugo? Go, girl!"

"It's okay. I'll do it." Elizabeth wipes her hands, then walks over to Godric to take the vase. "And, now both are dead." The two stand in the kitchen in silence for a moment. "Can you please just sit with me in the drawing room for a while?"

"That's why I bought the pastries. I'm starting to get my appetite back."

Godric lifts the plates as Elizabeth carries the cups and they both disappear into the drawing room to sit where Godric has already lit a fire. The animals gather, hoping for crumbs.

"You know, being friends with Ms Acharya-Gorpade might be the most dangerous thing in the world right now," Elizabeth replies, concerned.

63
CAT FIGHT

Nisha Acharya-Gorpade's eyes are closed as she dozes on her bed in her room at Christina College. She lies underneath a decorative net, a blanket draped over her legs. The College doesn't scrimp on heating, and the room is toasty. Nisha can no longer hear the crunching of gravel on the court path outside her window, as people now shelter from the cold inside their rooms. A groundsman's radio tuned to BBC Radio 3 – the only station permitted inside College grounds – is now switched off as it is too dark to garden.

In the quiet, Nisha hears footsteps on her corridor landing. Before she can sit up, her door flies open and Darcy bursts in, hurling herself at Nisha. She lands on top of Nisha, grabbing her throat before Nisha has a chance to escape – the net falling over Nisha's head, trapping her in this frenzied attack.

"You bitch! I knew it. You're dead." Darcy squeezes Nisha's throat. Nisha's eyes are full of fear, her face growing redder, as she flails, trying to wrestle Darcy's hands from her neck. Nisha manages to get one arm from out of the netting, as Darcy screams in her face, "He was mine. He loved me, not you! You skank! You think he would have looked twice at you if you hadn't thrown yourself at him?" Darcy screams louder. "You need to give me some money. I know what you did!"

"What?" Nisha croaks.

"Twenty thousand should do it. To keep quiet. A bit of blackmail between friends, eh?" Darcy tightens her grip on Nisha's neck.

"I didn't do anything," Nisha chokes. "And you won't get a penny if you strangle me," Nisha's voice is strained. Nisha grabs a glass from her desk by her bed and smashes it on Darcy's head, covering the bed in shards of glass.

"Argh! My eye! My eye!" Darcy falls back, putting her hand to her eyes. "You bitch, my eye!"

"Sorry, sorry." Nisha sits up and wriggles out from under Darcy and the net, already regretting smashing the glass. "You were choking me. I'm sorry."

"What have you done? Argh, my eye!" Darcy runs towards Nisha's door, clutching her eye. She kicks open the door to the bathroom, pulling her hand away from her eye to look in the mirror. She screams as she sees a shard of glass lodged in her eyelid. "You've blinded me!" Darcy panics and runs out of Nisha's bedroom and back down the stairs, screaming, "Someone get me an ambulance!" Nisha chases after her. Darcy makes it to the Porters' Lodge. "Help me, please. I've glass in my eye. I need an ambulance!"

"Darcy. Let me call one," Nisha says, reaching for her phone and dialling 999.

"She did this, keep her away from me. She's a murderer!" Darcy screams to anyone who will listen. She reaches the Porters' Lodge and slows down to go inside.

"Alright, Miss Nighy. Try to keep calm. Sit here, and we'll take a look." Hearing the screams, a Porter comes out to meet Darcy. He guides her into the Lodge. Taking one look at Darcy's eye, he thinks he's seen much worse before. He hears Nisha nearby talking to 999. "It's okay, your friend here is on the phone now for an ambulance."

At that moment, Lance walks through into the Lodge and sees Nisha on the phone.

"There you are! I've just been to the station looking for you. They made me wait ages before telling me you'd been released!" He heads towards Nisha. Nisha puts her finger to her lips to stop Lance talking.

"Ten minutes? Thank you," Nisha says into her phone.

"What happened to you?" Lance asks Darcy who is sitting on a chair, drinking a glass of water fetched by the Porter.

"She threw a glass at me!" Darcy shouts, pointing at Nisha with her good eye.

"Because you were strangling me," Nisha points at her neck, which still has two hand marks around it, "Is it red?"

"Hell yeah! Darce, what were you thinking?" Lance takes a photograph of Nisha's neck and Darcy's eye.

"I'm going blind here," Darcy cries.

"Perhaps you should take Miss Nisha to wait outside, and I'll wait with this young lady here until the ambulance comes," the Porter suggests to Lance.

"Okay," Lance replies.

"Do you need to see a paramedic about your throat, Miss Nisha?" The Porter shouts across to Nisha.

"No, I'm okay," Nisha smiles at the Porter. Lance grabs a water from the cooler in the Lodge, puts his arm around Nisha and guides her away from Darcy.

"Get her out of here!" Darcy screams again.

"That's what I'm doing." Lance winks at the Porter indicating that he'll help ensure there is no repeat of the cat fight. "I leave you both for ten minutes and look what you do. Let's go and sit for a bit."

They walk over to the fountain in Whisper Court and sit on the edge. Lance hands Nisha the water. "Are you okay? Why on earth did she do that?"

"D'you know where Godric is? I need to see him," Nisha replies, ignoring Lance's question. "He was taken to the station with me. I have to check if he's alright."

"Godric always lands on his feet," Lance pulls out a tissue and offers it to Nisha.

"He's been good to me. I'll just message him." Nisha messages Godric if he's okay and what just happened. "Maybe I should phone him?"

"Just breathe. You're in shock. Does it hurt?" Lance strokes Nisha's neck. "Ouch."

"I can't feel my neck? She was really mad about Miles. Miles said he was going to tell her about him and me," Nisha looks at Lance, searching his eyes for understanding. "I feel bad. What have I done?"

"You need your heads banging together." Then Lance adds, "Honestly, Miles? I had no idea you liked him." Lance looks back at the water in the fountain. Then adds, "I can't believe he's gone. You know, I have this ominous feeling," Lance looks around Whisper Court, "What if someone hates the band so much that they want to kill us all? What if my days are really numbered?" Lance looks at Nisha straight in the eye.

"Don't say that," Nisha replies.

"It makes sense. It's what we have in common."

"And acting," she suggests.

"Just keep watching my back. Maybe I need you as a bodyguard, with action like that." Lance nods back at the Lodge and Darcy.

"Is everything going to be okay?" Nisha asks Lance.

"Course it is," Lance says hugging her. But he is not so sure.

64
MY OLD RECORD PLAYER

Elizabeth has left Godric in the drawing room with pastries and a second cup of tea. He is under a blanket, enjoying another romantic Valentine's Day movie. At last, Elizabeth can relax that he is home while she turns her attention to solving this case. She watches him from the drawing room doorway. He glances back and smiles. She thinks how tired and pale he looks. How stupid she has been, moping about, while he was being attacked. Elizabeth cannot let herself imagine how he could have been killed. It just makes her more determined than ever. She picks up her bag on the telephone table and retrieves a vinyl album she took from Miles Bonneville's room earlier.

Retreating into Gerald's study, Elizabeth shuts the door behind her so as not to disturb Godric. In the corner, behind a large Kentia palm, is Gerald's old record player he bought in the 1980s. It is sitting on a shelving unit, with all his albums, which she remembers dusting just last week, but looks like it could do with another clean. The varnished wooden player makes Elizabeth smile. Gerald lovingly cared for it, and there isn't a scratch on it. An album by Nat King Cole still rests on the deck, the last one he played. One that she sometimes plays to herself when she comes in to sit and feel his presence. She gently lifts the vinyl off, placing it in its sleeve. Elizabeth then replaces it with the one she wants to listen to, or at least for the purposes of this case. She pulls up a chair, flicks the switch and a glowing red light beams out from the wood to show that the player is ready. Lifting the needle, Elizabeth holds her breath. There must be something in the music.

The first track is a love song, which she finds irritating. She lifts the needle and places it down carefully onto the next track, which appears to be about a bottle of whisky. Godric would probably love that one, but it is also so repetitive. Perhaps not. She lifts the needle through the tracks, about California, trains, doves, and then gets to one called 'My Amigos'. The song starts with Spanish guitar and then Hugo's voice. Elizabeth lifts the needle. She has heard enough.

She watches birds on the multiple feeders outside the study window as thoughts swirl around her head. Elizabeth sighs, then drops the needle one last time, letting the album play. She starts to fiddle with the knobs on the side of the record player. She remembers Nisha telling Lance she loved the songs but didn't quite know them backwards. Not much of a fan really, then? It felt like Nisha was lying, but why lie? They were a new band, weren't they? Lance did reply at the time that no one knew it backwards and they probably won't now. Not now Hugo Grader and Miles Bonneville are gone.

Elizabeth remembers Gerald buying the record player as it had all these different settings. Elizabeth messes with the knobs some more. She turns the album onto a different speed, and the voices all start to sound like Pinky and Perky. Then she sees the button to play it backwards. She lifts the needle, then flicks the backwards switch, then puts the needle down on the album again at the start. The backwards button also makes the singer's voice higher than before, so it is difficult to hear the words to begin with. She can make out lyrics like 'flower power', 'loving you forever', 'one true love' and 'you're mine'. She sighs, thinking of the flowers Gerald gave her. What is she doing?

After a while of watching the birds and listening to 'Three Charming Men', she walks through to the drawing room, still carrying the album cover to have a conversation with Godric. But Godric has gone? Only three dogs asleep on her sofa, almost on top of each other. Elizabeth calls up the stairs, but there is no reply. Then, she walks into the kitchen where she spots a note: 'Sorry, Bunny. Nisha messaged me. There's been a fight. I have to go. I know you'd have stopped me. Please forgive me. I'll be safe. Don't worry. I will call you when I'm coming home. Gx.'

Elizabeth sighs. How is she going to protect him now?

65
DR TROTSHAM

Sergeant Lemon has looked everywhere for Dr Guinevere Trotsham, from searching the Faculty of English, Christina College, back to the Swan Theatre and more. Lemon thinks that it is always the last place he looks that he finds people, as he pulls up his car along The Backs and spots Dr Trotsham walking with Professor Barclay among the floodlit daffodils.

Sergeant Lemon turns off his headlights and slowly tails them. Perhaps they are just going for a walk, he thinks. Professor Barclay starts to shout, but Lemon cannot hear what about, so he opens his window. But, still no joy. Lemon decides to park the car, gets out and sneaks behind a tree. But he still cannot hear them. He then sees Dr Trotsham slap Professor Barclay and run off towards College. Lemon doesn't know who to follow, but decides to stick to instructions to keep a tail on her, and walks down the avenue of trees leading from The Backs towards Christina College, a hundred feet or so behind Guinevere Trotsham.

When they arrive in College, he sees her disappear into the Porters' Lodge. She is in there for some time before exiting and heading up a staircase to her rooms. When the coast is clear, he pops his head into the Lodge and flashes his badge.

"Can you tell me what that Don wanted?" Lemon asks a Porter, who is doing the crossword on the front desk.

"Dr Trotsham? She wanted to know if there had been any post for Miles–"

"Is there post?" Lemon asks.

"Yes, but it's not hers to take. Mr Bonneville's parents have been delayed but are coming later from abroad. I can give it to them when they arrive."

Sergeant Lemon puts on his evidence gloves and holds out his hands to take the post. The Porter nods and passes it across the desk. Sergeant Lemon opens the first envelope and stares at it. Godric sneaks up behind, having come in to see Nisha but spotted Lemon through the window.

"What's this?" Godric asks, then peering at the Porter's crossword. "Verisimilar" Godric taps the paper. "Depicting realism?" The Porter nods a thank you. Then Godric looks back at the card.

"A Valentine's Day card?" Lemon wonders who sent it.

"Sent on the day of his death." Godric looks at the envelope and at the postmark.

"Look at that? 'Roses are red, violets are blue, now you're dead' That's a mean message?" Sergeant Lemon says. The two look at each other. "I'm going to sit outside Trotsham's rooms, in case she does anything else suspicious. But I didn't tell you that, because you're too close to the case," Lemon says quietly to Godric.

*

After the Porter asks Godric what three down is in his crossword, "eight letters and having a presence of a divinity?" and Godric picking up the pen and writing 'numinous', Godric makes his way to the staircase and Nisha's rooms. He taps gently on the door before opening.

"Hello," Godric whispers into the darkness. Nisha has pulled at her bedding to remove all the glass and is lying on a bare mattress. On hearing Godric, she throws open her arms.

"Let me see," Godric pulls back the curtains and cannot miss the angry red marks around Nisha's neck. He sits on the edge of the bed.

"She has glass in her eye."

"Does she, and did she try to strangle you first?" Godric reassures Nisha but is also a little shocked by Nisha's actions.

"I think Darcy was high," Nisha replies, hugging Godric and not letting him go.

"How does she afford the coke? She doesn't seem—"

"Rich? I suspect it came from Miles. He was always sorting them for uppers or downers."

"Could be why she launched at you? She's probably run out. Wired. I think it is best you stay here, okay? I can come back later, and we can talk," Godric suggests.

"Please don't leave me," Nisha replies, almost digging her fingers into Godric's arms.

"Why don't we go for a quick walk then? Fresh air is probably good for the both of us," Godric says, seeing Nisha does not want to be left but heeding his nanna's warning to keep his wits about him.

"That would be nice," Nisha smiles, putting her hand through Godric's then adding "Thanks for being such a good friend."

66
CRUMPETS WITH ALEX

Godric has made it home after what turned out to be a longer than planned walk with Nisha. He opens the front door to be greeted by a worried Elizabeth and Emily, both wearing their coats and still standing in the hallway, with three bounding dogs excited to see him. They have only just beaten him back to the house.

"Where've you been?" Elizabeth asks, worried.

"You two are quite the Houdinis," Emily quips, glad to see Godric and pleased that her friend's face now has relief right across it instead of fear.

"I'm here now, don't worry," Godric steps in the door and his nanna gives him a big hug.

"Emily has been to Bene't's, Christina's, the theatre. I went to the department, other College bars. It's not safe to be roaming about," Elizabeth says, worried.

"I was in Nisha's room. Then we went for a walk. If you had a mobile you could have texted me," Godric replies, trying to be helpful.

"Oh, yes? They're such useful contraptions" Elizabeth

pulls back from the hug and takes out his mobile phone from her pocket. "You left it in the drawing room."

"Ah." He sighs. "Here, you never guess what. Dr Trotsham was trying to sneak Miles Bonneville's post from the Porter's Lodge. Darcy attacked Nisha, nearly strangled her to death. There are two suspects, right there."

"Even more reason to stay home," Elizabeth removes Godric's coat and points at his shoes.

"Ah. I said I'd take Nisha to the Valentine's Speed Date event in Christina's bar tonight. I tried to convince her to stay in her room, but she's having none of it. I can't leave her on her own can I, Bunny? We won't go far. I'm sure all the action will take place on a few tables with people staring haplessly at each other. I thought it might be fun to watch? Be glued to the interactions, no doubt."

"We'll just have to get Inspector Abley to give you a bodyguard," Elizabeth replies.

"I'm perfectly safe," Godric says, not quite believing it himself, but trying to reassure his nanna as he slips off his final shoe.

"This murderer has already tried to have you killed on the road. I'm not taking any chances, even if you are," Elizabeth picks up the shoes and putting them in the cupboard under the stairs.

"Try not to worry your Nanna, Goddy," Emily says, walking into the drawing room behind Elizabeth and Godric. The three of them sit, glad to be back. The house is warm, the dogs fed, the cats sit by the fire.

"I've been listening to the 'Three Charming Men's' music," Elizabeth says to Godric. "It's very forgettable, isn't it. Extremely hard to concentrate on."

"I knew they had a band but hadn't gone to see their shows myself. I don't know really. Hugo was the lead singer, Lance the genius behind the writing and production and Miles. Miles apparently wanted to be the lead. So a bit jealous?" Godric replies, looking at the album cover Elizabeth has left on the coffee table.

"Did Nisha have a favourite?" Elizabeth asks.

'Nish? What, in the band? I've no idea. I think they saw her as a bit of a groupie, or at least that's the impression I got," Godric strokes Soot, who has just jumped up on the arm of the settee.

"What do you mean, groupie?" Emily asks.

"I don't know, like a mascot or something. Lucky charm."

"And how did she feel about that?" Elizabeth asks.

"As it happens, I think Nish is close to cracking up. I'm not sure she's enjoying Cambridge. She declined to go on tour with them, just the other day too." Godric puts the album cover down. "I wonder what Lance will do now. He was okay on the punt, but a bit jittery, worried about his own safety, I think."

"You seem very loyal to this friend of yours, Nisha," Elizabeth replies. "Are you sure she's not–" The doorbell interrupts their conversation. Elizabeth jumps up and opens it, seeing Alex on the step.

"Hello. I brought crumpets?" Alex holds a bag with food in. Elizabeth invites him in. Emily and Godric jump up to join them, then they all walk into the kitchen.

"Did I hear food?" Emily asks. "Perfect timing! I'd love a crumpet, what a jolly good idea. I'll toast." Emily takes the bag off Alex and starts to unwrap the crumpets.

"Last time you came, you mentioned you're studying languages," Elizabeth asks, lifting the kettle.

"Yes," Alex replies. Godric mouths thank you for the crumpets and looks for the spread and plates.

"Ooh, how many languages?" Emily interrupts, always keen to meet a smart student.

"A few," Alex smiles.

"Stop underselling yourself," Godric replies. "Show off a bit."

"Esplêndido, pragtfuld, fantastisch, superbe, guapísim, krásny, prekrasan, upea, ursnygg, blah, blah, blah"

"What is your take on these murders?" Elizabeth stares at Alex, leading him to sit at the table in the kitchen.

"What murders?" Alex asks, sitting down and staring blankly at each of them. There is silence in the room as his words reverberate. Then he finally says, "I'm teasing." There is a collective sigh in the room. Alex continues, "I'm glad I'm not in that band the 'Three Charming Men'. Bit cursed, isn't it?"

"You think the deaths are related to the band?" Elizabeth asks. "I was wondering the same."

"What else?" Alex asks.

"It all sounds very tragic," Emily says as she opens the cupboard and lifts down the Marmite. "Thank goodness for tea."

"Did you know them well?" Elizabeth persists with Alex.

"'Fraid not. I'm more of a show tune type of guy, me, God," Alex looks at Godric and beams.

"I like a power ballad," Godric smirks, catching the crumpets that have popped up from the toaster and placing them on plates for Emily to transfer to the table, along with the spread and Marmite.

"Don't call him God. He already has a superiority complex." Elizabeth tells Alex, then indicating for Alex to go first with the crumpets.

"I do not," Godric fakes affronted, passing Alex the Marmite.

"And what about Darcy Nighy and Nisha Acharya-Gorpade? How well do you know them?" Elizabeth asks Alex.

"That Darcy seems a bit of a bitch," Alex says.

Emily opens her eyes wide at his candid talk.

"Why?" Elizabeth does not blink, waiting for Alex's response.

"Godric messaged me what she did to Nisha. It's not the first time. I've seen her scrap in College. Once over a last bottle of beer behind the bar. Quite the madam."

"Pour Alex a cup of tea," Elizabeth tells Godric.

"Yeah, come to think of it, she's quite the violent missy. Even saw Lance holding her back in Christina's student bar when she was having a go at that Nisha. She was about to punch her. Right pissed off, she was. Proper drunk. Proper missy," Alex adds.

"You say you study languages," Elizabeth asks.

"Ci."

67
VALENTINE'S CHARITY SPEED DATE

Love is the theme in Christina College's Student Bar. However, most students are drinking less than usual, still recovering from the carrot poisoning. Plus, the bar specials – a tomato cocktail resembling blood, and pints of lager with red dye in them – are a little too much for most tonight. As it is common knowledge that Hugo Grader died and that the police suspect murder.

Christina's bar is long and wide and full of old comfy chairs and sofas filled with pale recovering faces. A large space has been made down the middle of the room for old trestle tables and benches, ready for the 'Valentine's Day Charity Speed Date', the main event about to start. Some are subdued, despite the love songs playing loud enough to shake the windows. But more than several stalwart students are standing or leaning on furniture, determined not to spend any more hours in their rooms, and hoping – like mad fools – to find love tonight. The room has been decorated with a large banner, which advertises the evening and reads, 'Only a fiver to find true love!!'. Immediately underneath there is some sort of tombola affair, with what looks like bottles of alcohol and condoms.

As Godric walks in with his nanna and Alex, there are a few cheers for Alex. Being a barman, he knows most of the occupants and has shared a few free drinks in his time, so is quite the popular man.

"I do the odd shift here," he explains it away to Godric and his nanna. A man walks up to Alex, half cut, and drags him over to watch someone else drink a yard of ale. Alex excuses himself by saying he'll be back soon, as Godric spots Nisha and smiles at his nanna to take his leave.

"I'll be careful. You'll have me in line of sight," Godric says, as he walks away. This leaves Elizabeth in the room on her own, still unsure who is responsible for the deaths. She spots Darcy Nighy and Lance Fernard at the bar. Miss Nighy has a patch over her eye. Elizabeth also sees Professor Barclay talking with Dr Trotsham, sitting in a couple of comfortable chairs in an alcove window. Lemon is standing not far away in the corner. He is pleased to see Elizabeth and walks over to say hello.

"The Inspector will be here shortly. He had me tail Dr Trotsham, but she's not been anywhere for the past few hours. I even managed to get a bit of dinner from the hall. Ate at the Porters' Lodge. Hard to find anything vegan on the menu, though. Ended up with potato and leek soup and kale crisps? How do you do it?"

"You're joining the fray? Come to Granta next time. We have a healthy vegan menu," Elizabeth says, pleased.

"Yeah, wanted to feel less stressed, and also do something for the planet and animals. You know, something," Lemon makes the kind of small talk Elizabeth likes.

"I do," Elizabeth replies, knowing most are still sleepwalking into oblivion. "Thanks for the call earlier. It was useful to know what happened. If she hit Professor Barclay earlier, strange they are now socialising, isn't it?" Elizabeth watches Dr Trotsham laugh.

"Lover's tiff?" Lemon replies, wondering where Inspector Abley is, adding, "I think she's a bit pissed. Have you seen the Inspector?"

"You think they're an item?" Elizabeth asks.

"He's married. Could be an affair?" Lemon replies, his eyes scanning the room.

An announcement comes over the room's speaker system, "Take your places. Speed dating is about to begin! Once the bell dings, you each have three minutes. Then when it dings again, those on the far side move one space to your left to the next person."

Elizabeth and Lemon are surprised when they see Dr Trotsham join the student Speed Date.

"What is she doing?" Elizabeth asks as many students start to sit down, ready for the dating to begin. Elizabeth looks over at Godric and Nisha, Lance and Darcy, who are all standing this one out. The bell sounds. Much giggling and an eruption of conversation and laughter echoes around the room. At this point, Inspector Abley walks in and spots Lemon with Elizabeth.

"Here he is," Elizabeth says. Lemon is pleased that Inspector Abley has been reliable tonight, and hopes he has turned a corner.

"No new movement on the case," Inspector Abley says, coming to a standstill by a bunch of red heart shaped balloons beside Lemon and Elizabeth.

"Whoever is responsible could be playing the long game," Lemon offers.

"I wouldn't be so sure," Elizabeth replies.

"We have back up ready, including an ambulance," Abley says, unconvinced, "If you really think we need it. You think the killer will strike?"

"I do," Elizabeth replies. "It's Valentine's Night. I'd expect the killer who poisons with daffodils from a romantic poem and has someone die by the sword in Romeo and Juliet to strike on Valentine's."

"Alright, the ambulance is here. Like I said." Abley knows he should trust Elizabeth, and so has a sinking feeling about the evening, especially as he still feels completely unsure about the case.

"My money's on Nisha Acharya-Gorpade," Lemon says.

"Let's not speculate," Abley replies, "Perhaps Professor Green has more information she can share?"

"I've been at home this afternoon. It just doesn't make sense. If Ms Acharya-Gorpade was the killer, why would she be in clear view? She is such an enigma. Are you staying here?" Elizabeth asks Lemon. Lemon nods. Elizabeth checks that Godric is still sitting with Nisha, close enough to watch the speed dating shenanigans. "Keep an eye on Godric, will you? Call me if he leaves the room?" Elizabeth waits for Lemon to nod and then leads Inspector Abley out of the bar.

*

Elizabeth heads towards the Porters' Lodge with Inspector Abley to pick up some keys. They climb the staircase to Hugo Grader's rooms and open the door.

"Why are we back here again?" Inspector Abley asks, commenting, "We've combed this from top to bottom."

"The clue has to be here somewhere. There's something not quite right about this. The two men. They have Nisha in common. They both ended relationships with her. Did you see she was wearing a daffodil necklace tonight?"

"Is she doing that on purpose?" Inspector Abley asks. "Does she know about the daffodil poisoning?"

"Godric promised not to tell. Did you not mention it when you brought her in?"

"No. So you think she's taunting us?" Abley adds.

"Is she? There's more to this." Elizabeth shakes her head. "I'm so slow this time. I can't think." She steadies herself on the back of a chair in Mr Grader's room. "My mind is not my own." She shuts her eyes for a long time and then opens them and starts to rifle through books, pulling them down and placing them on the desk.

"It's Valentine's Day." Inspector Abley touches Elizabeth's arm, his tone warmer, taking a couple of books from her hands and placing them on the table. "I can't wait for this bloody day to be over."

"I can't think. It's impossible to see clearly," Elizabeth replies, walking around the room, looking for a clue but cannot see anything. "Take me to Miles Bonneville's." Elizabeth won't give up.

As they walk out of Hugo Grader's and across the Bramble Court, Inspector Abley thinks about what he'd rather be doing on Valentine's night and considers that this is preferable to sitting at home alone. He's never figured out how Elizabeth's mind works, but he's pinning a lot on her deductions on this case. Before there is another murder. They walk under an arch and cross Whisper Court, crunching over gravel past the fountain, and start to climb a different staircase.

"It's good to be back," Abley tries to find kind words to console Elizabeth.

"What?" Elizabeth carries on walking, not looking up.

"Lemon, you, me."

"There is nothing remotely good about this," Elizabeth replies matter of factly. Inspector Abley sighs. He knows his friend well. Knows she is stressed. They open the door and Elizabeth picks up both the card and the note.

"Why didn't you tell me about this before?" Inspector Abley asks, looking at the Valentine's Day card from Dr Guinevere Trotsham, and the separate note warning Miles off Nisha.

"I told you about the card," Elizabeth replies.

"Not the note," Abley corrects Elizabeth.

"Must have slipped my mind. See? Not on form," Elizabeth looks at Bob Abley. "Dr Trotsham is a little obsessed with Miles Bonneville. Did you catch up with her after the clothes burning? Lemon said he has been tailing her, but have you questioned her?"

"Not yet." Abley then looks more carefully at the printed note in Miles's room, warning Miles off Nisha. "Who sent this note I wonder?" Inspector Abley turns it over between his finger and thumb, then pulls out an evidence bag. "Godric is with Nisha Acharya-Gorpade now?"

"Lemon is watching them," Elizabeth replies.

"Lemon?" Inspector Abley calls his Sergeant. "Can you still see Godric? Nisha?" Abley listens. "Call if they disappear." Abley cuts his call.

"Thank you," Elizabeth replies, grateful. She sees the pill bottles on the desk and picks one up again, having checked their contents before. They have torn off labels on the front.

"Miles Bonneville didn't have that in his bloodstream. His doctor didn't issue a prescription for these," Abley explains.

"Yes, I tested them too," Elizabeth replies. She opens a bottle, trying to wonder what else could be a clue in the room. She peers in at the tablets, and her fingernail gets stuck on something in the lid. She looks at the lid more carefully and starts to peel back the little white circle. As she does, she sees what Inspector Abley sees. Underneath is a tiny label – the prescription note.

"That's because they are not Miles Bonneville's. That's Lance's surname?" Elizabeth examines the tiny prescription note she has unwrapped.

"What is Miles Bonneville doing with Lance Fernard's pills?" Inspector Abley asks.

The two stand in the room, not sure how they both missed the hidden label. Inspector Abley's phone rings. It is Sergeant Lemon.

*

A large number of students have spilt into the courtyard outside the bar. A winter flowering jasmine creeps over a long archway, while open crypt pillars on one side lit up with fairy lights provide further shelter to the now chilly students. Godric and Nisha have said a brief hello to Lance, standing under the arches. Lance is doing his best to keep Darcy away from Nisha.

"Darcy hates me," Nisha says to Godric.

"She is being rather aggressive, that's true. Still, she only has one functioning eye to catch you with. I think you're safe with me here," Godric says, and he and Nisha sit on the edge of the fountain. "You look like a princess tonight, Nish. Fancy necklace too. Is that a daffodil?"

"Yes," Nisha replies.

"Huh," Godric wonders.

"Why do you say huh?"

"You know how Hugo died?" Godric asks.

"He was killed, but no. The police haven't released any details to the media, have they? I've not seen anything."

"I didn't know if they told you at the station. I'm not supposed to say. But, given we've both been taken in for questioning," Godric pauses. "He was poisoned with daffodils," Godric looks at her straight in the eye.

"What?" Nisha looks at Godric, shocked.

"Did you not know that?" He asks.

"No. I told you. How do you know?" Nisha looks around, now not quite herself.

"What's the matter?" Godric stares at the necklace and glances at some writing but cannot quite make it out.

"Oh, nothing." Nisha turns over her necklace. "Cheers," Nisha says as she picks up her beer balanced on the fountain and takes a swig. Alex spots them and walks over, having finally left the bar. He sits down next to

316

Godric.

"Valentine's Day, and here you are. We lost you at the bar. Thanks for the drinks and the tricks," Godric says.

"Where else would I be? Had to come and find you, though." Alex leans in for a kiss from Godric, and after Godric has playfully dodged it for a while, they lock lips. They don't notice Nisha start to wilt. It isn't until she falls backwards into the fountain and doesn't get up that Godric says something.

"Yes, I know it's mushy, but it's my Valentine's kiss," Godric smiles at Alex after hearing the splash. Godric finally looks to his side and sees Nisha in the fountain but still not moving. "C'mon. I get it. We should get a room." Godric laughs, but when she doesn't move, he shouts, "Nisha. Nisha? Nisha?!" Godric pulls Nisha up, but her body is limp. "Help me!" He calls to Alex. They lift her over to the grass. Godric is about to give Nisha mouth to mouth when, coming down from Miles's room, Elizabeth steps out into Whisper Court and spots him.

"Stop! Don't touch her lips!! Godric. Don't touch her lips!!" Elizabeth rushes over, closely followed by Inspector Abley.

"She'll die!" Godric screams.

"Get the ambulance out front!" Elizabeth shouts back to Abley, who is already pulling out his phone. A crowd of students start to become aware of the commotion and move closer to watch.

"Get back, everyone!" Sergeant Lemon shouts, having come out earlier to monitor Nisha and Godric. "Dr Trotsham left from the other exit. You asked me to tail them both. Thought this was more important," Lemon hurriedly screams over to Inspector Abley and Elizabeth. Abley nods back.

"Don't touch her lips or her glass," Elizabeth is firm, now close to Nisha and her grandson. Alex has jumped back, in shock at what is happening around him. Then, he starts to take off his jacket and covers Nisha to keep her warm.

"What can I do?" Godric asks his nanna, frantically.

"Be the pump for her heart. Keep doing short bursts of pressure on her chest. But don't touch her mouth. She's likely been poisoned with something nasty to take effect so quickly." Elizabeth bends down and puts her fingers on Nisha's neck to check for a pulse. She notices the daffodil pendant around Nisha's neck and turns it over to see inscribed the words: 'You'll always be my daffodil. Lx'. She looks up and around the crowd and spots Lance and Darcy. She can see a slight smirk on Darcy's face.

"What are you doing?" Darcy asks.

"There's no pulse." Elizabeth looks up at Inspector Abley and Lemon, then across to Godric, "but keep going, Goddy, until the paramedics arrive." Elizabeth watches Lance move along the line of pillars heading towards the Chapel.

68
TOWER OF LOVE

Leaving Godric still pumping frantically on Nisha's heart, Elizabeth stands, her eyes now fixed on Lance disappearing into the crowd.

"He's getting away. My legs aren't fast enough!" She shouts back to Inspector Abley, aware the young man can outrun her.

"Right behind you," Abley replies, reassuring her as he catches up. "Who are we chasing?"

"Him!" They both see Lance Fernard disappear into the Chapel.

"What do you know?" Inspector Abley shouts as they run across the gravel.

"I just saw her necklace. Nisha's. He gave Ms Acharya-Gorpade a daffodil necklace. It all makes sense now," Elizabeth puffs, trying not to lose sight of the Chapel door in case Lance sneaks back out. "It says, 'You'll always be my daffodil. L' and there was a kiss. I think he killed his friends," Elizabeth looks across at Abley.

"All that from an inscription on a necklace?" Abley asks.

"We have to catch him. He loved her. It was all about her."

"Who?"

"Nisha. Yes. He loved Nisha Acharya-Gorpade!" Elizabeth reaches the Chapel door and grabs hold of the brass handle. "Gerald's record player," she says.

"What?" Abley asks, confused, now right behind her. "You'll have to give me more of a clue."

"Vinyl. Old records. Nisha said she loved the band's music but didn't know it backwards. He looked so sad when she said it. I don't know. It must have stayed with me. Lance said no one knew it backwards, and now they never would."

"I don't understand," Abley says.

"I listened to it backwards," she glances at Abley.

"What, one of their albums?" Abley grabs the door handle for Elizabeth and pulls the heavy door back, opening up the Chapel for her to enter.

"Come on." Elizabeth steps inside and then stops midway up the nave. She can see the beautiful vaulted ceiling, the stained-glass windows. But the Chapel looks empty. She starts to creep along the pews, in case Lance is hiding, and whispers to Inspector Abley, "If you play the 'Three Charming Men' album of the same name backwards, you can hear a message of sorts. The person singing is confessing undying love. I listened at first but could only hear words like 'flowers' and 'love'. I had to fetch a cup of tea and concentrate on it intently. My mind isn't—"

"I'm still not understanding," Abley interrupts.

"You see, the voice didn't sound like the one played forward," Elizabeth explains, her eyes still scanning the Chapel. "It didn't sound like Hugo Grader's. It was Lance Fernard's voice. I don't know how he did it. Modern technology. But it was from Lance to Nisha."

"A message? What kind of message?" Abley asks quietly looking along the pews, still unsure what Elizabeth is explaining.

"A love song. Unrequited, as it turns out. Godric mentioned Nisha had been seeing Miles. And Nisha admitted to me she'd been seeing Hugo. But not Lance Fernard."

"A message of love? She was seeing Hugo? Miles?"

"She only just told me not long ago about Hugo. As it happens, she just confessed too about Miles to Godric," Elizabeth replies, adding "You have to play it at seventy eight and backwards. You couldn't hear the words unless you changed speeds too," Elizabeth says, stopping and holding up her finger for Abley to be quiet, thinking she heard something. But they both listen for a while and all is quiet, so she continues to whisper, walking along more pews, scanning everything. "They used to do similar things in the sixties and seventies. Gerald told me some musicians would send little hidden messages at different speeds on vinyl. Godric told me that Lance had edited the record. Hugo Grader had called Lance a genius the night he died, Godric said."

"I wasn't born yesterday! I've listened to hidden tracks. Our team have listened to those songs?" Inspector Abley raises his eyebrows. "But backwards?" He shakes his head, speaking to himself. "How the hell?"

"I wouldn't beat yourself up about it. I'm sure his own bandmates didn't even know about the message," Elizabeth replies, now having looked along all the rows of pews, and arriving at the pulpit. She climbs up the steps to get a better view of the Chapel to see if she can see Lance.

"Be careful," Inspector Abley says.

"It's eight steps," Elizabeth replies.

"Alright," Abley acknowledges the irony of him telling Elizabeth to be careful about climbing a few steps up to a pulpit when they are likely chasing a murderer. "But what has this case got to do with a love message?"

"He stabbed Miles Bonneville dead because of jealousy," Elizabeth explains. "The whole prop swap was nonsense. He poisoned Hugo Grader with daffodils and opium too."

"What evidence have we got of this?" Abley asks.

"I'm sure you'll find traces of daffodils on something in his flat. You have him stabbing Miles. He poisoned Nisha by accident outside just now. It was meant for—" Elizabeth cannot say Godric. "He was after—" Elizabeth says, then shakes her head. "Nisha Acharya-Gorpade drank the poison by accident. He was going to try to kill—" Elizabeth pauses again. Then she looks at a stained-glass window and exhales. A renewed determination passes across her eyes. "Come on." Elizabeth starts to wander down the steps into the Chapel crypt. "We have to stop this man and his twisted actions."

"Godric is okay. He's going to be okay." Abley says, trying to reassure Elizabeth.

"Not until we catch Lance, he's not." Elizabeth walks around the crypt and through the arches. The air is cold, the shadows dark. For a while, both Elizabeth and Bob Abley tip-toe around, the hairs standing up on the back of their necks, waiting for something to happen. But nothing. Finally, they walk back up into the Chapel nave.

"But why murder your bandmates when you're about to go on tour?" Abley whispers. They start to look around the Chapel again and hear a door creak. Inspector Abley points and leads the way.

"Jealousy, unrequited love," Elizabeth replies. "I think he wanted to stay. Actually, Lance has just been offered a PhD, hasn't he?"

"The roof," Abley puts his fingers to his mouth, pointing towards a door in the corner which is gently swinging closed.

Elizabeth and Abley start to climb the stone steps up to the roof. They hear Lance Fernard's footsteps further up.

"He was jealous of his bandmates?" Abley whispers as

they climb the stairs.

"They both dated Nisha, didn't they? Miles Bonneville wanted her to be with the band on tour. Maybe Lance loves her. But, for whatever reason, she hasn't been his girlfriend. So, he killed them. Revenge."

"Who in their sane mind would do that?" Inspector Abley says, creeping up the steps.

"Ah, but he isn't taking his meds, is he? Miles Bonneville had them," Elizabeth explains. "And, I hear from Godric, Lance likes to take his own recreational."

"Why?" Abley asks.

"I don't know," Elizabeth whispers as they near the top of the steps to the roof.

"We need back up," Abley speaks quietly into his phone to Sergeant Lemon, "Now. Chapel. Yes, still in Christina's. We're climbing to the roof."

*

Both Elizabeth and Inspector Abley creep out into the cold night onto the exposed rooftop turret which opens out further to slanted brickwork and gargoyles. Immediately, they see Lance standing on a gutter wall.

"Get down!" Abley shouts.

"Come any closer, and I'll jump!" Lance shouts back.

"Just get down, and we can talk," Abley replies, "Nobody's jumping today.'

"We know you murdered your friends for using the woman you loved." Professor Elizabeth Green cannot hide her anger towards this man who tried to kill her grandson twice.

"They're not my friends!" Lance shouts, balancing on the wall in the cold night air, and looking down at the gathering crowd and sparkly red lights in Whisper Court.

"But you were in a band together? They cared about you?" Elizabeth persists.

"They were just too thick to write songs or lyrics,"

Lance sneers. "Wanted to be famous. Booze and drugs. That's all they cared about."

"I found your note, your note to Miles warning him off Nisha. He'd hidden it behind his bed. You wrote that, didn't you? At first, I thought it was a warning to be careful of a dangerous Nisha. But I realise now it was you warning him to stay away from her as she was yours. Did Miles cotton on that you killed Hugo? Did he have a clue? Is that why you killed him too?"

"Miles didn't care about Nisha. He was using her. Like he used all women," Lance spits.

"He didn't buy her necklaces with daffodils on. Neither did Hugo, did he? So you poisoned Hugo with daffodils. A fitting ending," Elizabeth says, willing Lance to admit it.

"Don't talk to me about Hugo. He told her he cared and then dumped her but wouldn't let her be free. Kept taunting her. Always reading her love poems, romantic poems. When he didn't even want her. Tossed her aside like an old crisp bag." Lance screws up his face. "He was cruel. He deserved an ending equally fitting."

"So you bought her a daffodil necklace?" Elizabeth says, leading Lance to admit more.

"Just to cleanse her of him. She's my daffodil. I would treat her right."

"You cared about more, about love," Elizabeth replies.

"Yes!!"

"I understand the power of love," Elizabeth says. "I listened backwards to your album, to your love song." In the distance, they hear the ambulance siren leaving with Nisha. Lance's feet wobble on the edge. Abley inches towards Lance, then quietly calls Lemon again.

"We need the suicide squad. Yes, the roof."

"That was for Nisha! A secret song for her!" Lance shouts to the sky. "She meant everything, and I've killed her. There is nothing left for me now," Lance breaks down.

"What did you give her? Perhaps we can save her?" Professor Green asks.

"She'd be okay if it wasn't for your wretched grandson. Always flouncing about, always flirting with the ladies." Lance scowls.

"My grandson likes Nisha, but not in that way. What did you give her? What poison?" Elizabeth presses.

"And now she's going to die," Lance cries.

"The ambulance. They can try to save Nisha. But they need to know what you used. You must tell us now," Elizabeth demands, still angry at Lance.

"Oh, it's no use. Tetrodotoxin. It's too late," Lance says. "Fish."

"Pufferfish poison?" For Inspector Abley's benefit, Elizabeth checks to make it clear to him without spooking Lance so Abley can phone the ambulance to let them know. "That it is a deadly toxin," Elizabeth continues, speaking slowly and staring at Inspector Abley, "found in the pufferfish's skin, eyes, liver and reproductive organs. One fish could kill twenty people. Tetrodotoxin is a neurotoxin. Attacks your nervous system by interfering with signals from your nerves to your muscles. You stay fully conscious but can't breathe. You die from asphyxiation. She needs to get to a hospital very quickly." Elizabeth eyes Abley to make sure he heard everything so he can call in the poison. Abley nods and quietly picks back up his call with Lemon, which he has left open on speaker and starts to speak quietly away from Lance.

"I didn't mean to harm her," tears breaking free on Lance's cheeks.

"You were trying to murder my grandson," Elizabeth says. "Well, you failed."

"He was getting too close to her. She's mine," Lance whines like a child.

"He loves Nisha as a friend. Nothing more," Elizabeth says.

"Godric was coming between us. Always there, always providing a shoulder to cry on, to speak to. He was always dropping everything for her," Lance's voice turns almost to a whisper, "She was more interested in him than me. Why?" Lance looks madly at the moon.

"So, you tried to kill my grandson with Devil's Breath. Lay him down in the road to make it look like it was an accident." Elizabeth waits for Lance to admit it, but he says nothing, so she continues. "Godric said you were going back with Darcy to drink. But you left Darcy to get some supplies and to meet you at your flat. You just had time to swing back and capture Godric coming out. Only, you didn't think Nisha would still be there. It made you angry. Perhaps you wanted to drug her too?"

"No! It was not meant to get into her face. Poor Nisha. I felt so bad," Lance's voice breaks.

"So, you took her to the cashpoint and gave her Miles's money to try to make up for it?"

"He left his card on my coffee table. For the coke. It was the least I could do. Pay her for her services to him. He treated her like his servant. You can never have enough money. He owed her," he sneers.

"You nearly killed my grandson!" Elizabeth shouts.

"He appears to be indestructible," Lance sighs.

"But you really did stab Miles. Your friend. You threw your prop sword just far enough away that it would look like it had been discarded by someone else, but close enough to be found by the police. Another planned killing."

"It seemed like the right play for a coward!" Lance shouts, carried away with his own sense of justice.

"When did you stop taking your medication?" Elizabeth asks quietly.

Lance is thrown that Elizabeth knows. His mood changes from fragile to angry.

"It's none of your business!" He shouts, his feet wobbling a little.

"It can drive dark thoughts," Elizabeth acknowledges.

"Shut up!" He replies.

"We found them in Miles Bonneville's room. Why did he have them?" Elizabeth presses, watching Lance's feet get closer to the edge.

"Shut up!" He shouts.

"D'you know what I think? I think he took them from you, as they were affecting your creative process. You wrote better music when you didn't take them." Lance looks straight at Elizabeth, surprised she is so astute.

"They dull your senses until you feel nothing. I asked Miles to keep them away from me. It was the least he could do, knowing that I was creating everything for all of us."

"They kept you sane," Elizabeth replies.

"Oh, I'm sane. You're the interfering old bat. You're lucky your grandson didn't have that drink. But, you're not clever enough to have stopped it. I know that much," Lance scoffs.

Lance's comments hit home. Elizabeth is all too aware that this time she failed to protect Godric. All of a sudden, her legs give way, and she falls back against the sloping roof. A tile becomes dislodged, and it slides down and over the edge, smashing to the ground. Elizabeth starts to fall down the roof, her feet failing to find safe footing. Very quickly, she nears the edge. Abley sees and dives for Elizabeth, holding on to her to stop her from sliding, but he can't prevent them both from slipping further. They both tumble over the edge and hang precariously onto the gargoyles on a ridge.

Screams can be heard from below as they watch the Inspector and Professor Green clinging on by their hands. Lance looks down and chuckles at their predicament. As he does, he loses his footing falling backwards off the roof over their heads. As he slips, he screams, and a few seconds later, Abley and Elizabeth hear the thud underneath them.

Moments after, police backup arrives on the roof. Godric grabs Elizabeth, pulling her up safely. Meanwhile, Sergeant Lemon holds out a hand for his Inspector. Abley grabs Lemon's hand, but then it causes him to further swing out from the roof, only to hear the gasps below. Finally, Lemon pulls Bob Abley up to safety.

"Cutting it a bit close?" Abley looks up to Lemon who is out of breath and in shock that he nearly lost his friend.

"I think you have my guns to thank for that," Lemon replies, squeezing one of the muscles in the top of his arm. Abley sighs, relieved they are both safe. Lemon has saved him again, and he doesn't know how to start to say how grateful he is.

Elizabeth looks down at the crowd and can't see Godric. She panics, as she thinks she sees the paramedics helping a man to the ambulance along with Nisha. Then she feels arms around her and can smell that familiar smell of her grandson.

"My Bunny," Godric squeezes his nanna gently. Elizabeth opens her eyes and realises the arms that pulled her to safety are Godric's.

"I couldn't save you. It was meant for you. The poison Nisha took. It must have been in your drink."

"We were both drinking lager. The barman turned them red for Valentine's Day. Everyone was drinking it," Godric explains.

"Lance Fernard wanted to poison you. And, I wasn't fast enough to work that out. You could have died," Elizabeth repeats, almost half to herself, clinging to Godric. Godric takes a moment to digest what his nanna has just said.

"Shh, it's okay. I'm here. It's all good. They found a pulse on Nisha. They can help her fight it," Godric says, hopefully.

"It could have been you."

"Why?"

"He was in love with Nisha. He was jealous."

"I'm here. I'm here." Godric looks into Elizabeth's eyes.

*

Now covered in a police blanket, Elizabeth steps out into the lit courtyard along with Godric. They see a new ambulance parked up on the lawn across the river, and paramedics attending Lance Fernard's body on the gravel nearby. It is evident to the medics that Lance is dead and there is no opportunity to resuscitate. Police are cordoning off the area and ushering students to leave the courtyard, though many faces behind dorm windows look out at the ghoulish goings-on.

"How's Nisha? Elizabeth asks Lemon who walks over to join her after he came down off the roof a few minutes earlier and has been speaking with the paramedics."

"The hospital has informed us that she's on a respirator in intensive care."

"I want to go and see her," Godric replies.

"No visitors. They will update us tomorrow," Sergeant Lemon explains.

"So, home." Elizabeth stares at Godric, who hasn't let go of her since the incident above. "Like you say, she was caught within the hour, so has a chance," she adds, trying to give Godric hope.

After witnessing Lance's death, Darcy has been sitting by the fountain in shock. On seeing Godric emerge from the Chapel, she heads over.

"Are you okay? Is Nisha going to be okay?" Darcy asks, angst all over her face.

"We don't know, Darce, as it happens," Godric replies.

"Miles. He left me a message, 'watch out for Nisha' he said before he died. I thought he was warning me against her," Darcy says, confused.

"No. Miles may well have had suspicions about what Lance could do, as it turns out," Elizabeth explains.

"Nisha is completely innocent," Godric looks blankly at Darcy. "And you left her that message saying you knew what she did, didn't you? You've been beastly to her."

"I can't believe it?" Darcy replies. Godric sighs, realising Darcy has lost her boyfriend in all this, and all her friends. "She just annoyed me. She was so bloody rich. They all were. They don't know what it's like to be a normal student with no money, always broke. Rubbing my nose in it."

"Right," Godric replies, thinking Darcy looks so frail. He sees her clothes as if for the first time. Her coat does look tattier than he noticed before. He gives her a quick hug, then watches as Darcy walks away, dumbfounded and feeling terrible for making Nisha feel so bad.

"Poor Nisha. The Compliments Booth man. Said she'd have to be brave." Godric says quietly to himself, watching Darcy get a hug off another College student.

"They've trampled my plot!" Professor Barclay walks past, his hands on his head, cross that his new theatre plot has been used by the police and ambulance crew to park.

"A man has just fallen from the roof?" Sergeant Lemon replies, astonished at Barclay's lack of compassion.

"Students often choose to end it. Suicide?" Barclay asks.

"Accident," Lemon replies.

"Tragic. Still, better for the College that way," Barclay nods and walks on.

"Bloody academics," Abley says, having now come to join the group after a paramedic bandaged his wrist.

Godric and Elizabeth spot Alex, waiting for Godric behind the police cordon.

"Can Alex come back to ours?" Godric checks with his nanna.

"Definitely," Elizabeth is happy to hear Godric wants to go home. "A night in."

"Sure. A night in. But I have to check on Nisha." Godric walks over to Alex by the police tape, pulling Elizabeth with him.

"You know, Alex was doing his signature trick with our glasses at the bar," Godric remembers, explaining to his nanna. Then turns to Alex, "I think it might have been you who switched our glasses, throwing them in the air? Poor Nisha," Godric says.

"You saved my grandson twice." Elizabeth looks at Alex. "I don't know how to thank you?"

"I'm starving," Alex replies.

"Done," Elizabeth says, we have food at home. "Can I just have a minute?" Elizabeth walks across Whisper Court towards the fountain, sits down and puts her head in her hands. Godric joins her. She shuts her eyes, and the two sit in silence.

69
OLD FRIENDS

Back home at Foxes' Haven, and Elizabeth checks her watch as she prepares to put on her duffel coat. The front door opens and in walks Godric with Alex. Godric has something wriggling inside his white coat. A big ginger tail pops up from above his collar.

"I take it the rest of that bump is a cat, or you really are ill?"

"This was the only place," Godric replies.

"Who do we have here?" Elizabeth beams with joy, looking at the big fat face that has now escaped between coat buttons and is staring back at her, nonplussed.

"This is Fred. Lance Fernard's cat," Godric stares knowingly at his nanna.

"Okay. You look well fed, loved. Come and stay with us for a while and see if you like it," Elizabeth replies guessing why Godric has walked in with him, stroking Fred without batting an eyelid.

"I remembered him. We persuaded the Constable to let us have him. One less for the pound, he said. I don't think anyone cares about this little thing?"

"We do, and can foster him until Mr Fernard's parents have been contacted," Elizabeth looks up at her grandson, moved by his actions for rescuing this little creature. There is hope for Godric somewhere under all that whisky and gambling, she thinks.

"He's never been outside," Godric tells Elizabeth, pulling a sad face.

"Let's keep him in for a week, then help him explore the real world to his heart's content. Spring is just around the corner," she looks at Fred and strokes his chin. "Put him in my bedroom for now with some water and sardines. I'll be back in a few hours."

Godric nods and takes Fred upstairs, with Alex running into the kitchen to get supplies.

"I'll see you later!" She shouts to Godric and Alex.

"See you later! Godric shouts back. "We intend on draping ourselves across a sofa to watch more romantic films and are going nowhere."

"Good," she replies.

*

Elizabeth starts the Talbot. It isn't long before she finds herself on Grantchester Road, and crossing onto Broadway. She parks up outside the Blue Ball Inn, a loaf of bread and a bag of sugar on her passenger seat. She picks up the gifts and rings the doorbell to hear her friend shouting, "Coming!"

"I can't stop," Elizabeth says as Inspector Bob Abley opens the door.

"Hello. Come in. Come in!" Bob Abley replies, beckoning.

'No, I won't tonight. I'm late. But I wanted to give you these. Good luck, apparently."

"Oh, well, I won't say no to that." Inspector Abley takes the bread and sugar. "Wait, the loaf's rock hard?"

"No, it isn't. I made it. It's crusty," she replies.

"Well, then I'll enjoy it all the more." Bob Abley holds the bread, which feels like a

lead weight. He taps it lightly on the wall. It sounds like concrete hitting brick, but he just says, "This is so kind. Thank you." Then he changes the subject, "So the carrots were just a coincidence, according to Leedham?"

"Yes, they blurred the truth for a while there, didn't they? Obscuring the first murder." Elizabeth looks around at the dead and dying plants in Inspector Bob Abley's front garden and winces.

"Don't worry, I'll see to them," Abley says, wanting her to stop judging him and his garden borders.

"You've just moved in. It's not your fault. But how someone can do that to a box hedge, I'll never know? Do you know how long it takes to grow?" Elizabeth looks at the bedraggled and spindly specimen and strokes it. Abley sighs.

"Come on, come in. Just for a minute." Abley opens the door wider. "Stop fussing about my garden. You're making me nervous." He is pleased to see Elizabeth, if just for a while on Valentine's night. Not to be alone.

"Just for a minute then."

"Can I get you a drink? Wine? Something soft? I have juice."

"Just a water." Elizabeth walks through the house and to the back door. She puts her head to the window, trying to peek outside.

"Not a bad length. Hundred foot?" Bob Abley says, looking at the dark windows which make it hard to see out now. He flicks a switch to a light outside, illuminating the patio and ten feet or so of the overgrown lawn.

"You always get more outside of the city. Looks like you've got your work cut out there too," Elizabeth tuts.

"The young man's clothes. We didn't find anything. We won't be arresting Dr Trotsham." Abley changes the subject back to the case. Anything to forget he has his hands full with this house. Perhaps he'll hire a gardener.

Fat chance, with what's left of his money after bills, he thinks.

"Right." Elizabeth looks at Inspector Abley. "Bit odd, isn't it? Saving a lover's clothes. She was obviously burning them so we didn't find them and draw conclusions. Godric said she was trying to steal his post."

"I can see how she looked guilty. We found another Valentine's card she sent him. It came today. She was, let's just say, in clothes more appropriate for summer."

"You're not supposed to have affairs with students. A sackable offence, she is guilty," Elizabeth says, crossly.

"Right. Here you go." Inspector Bob Abley hands Elizabeth a glass of water. "Lemon saw Dr Trotsham and Professor Barclay rowing. Apparently, Barclay had wanted an affair with Trotsham behind his wife's back, Lemon discovered. But Dr Trotsham was having none of it. He was jealous that she couldn't keep her mitts off her students."

"Thank you." Elizabeth looks at the jam jar Inspector Abley has delivered her water in. "Ugh. Nothing good comes of cheating, does it?" Elizabeth replies, but then realises what she's said. Abley smiles, indicating it is okay. Elizabeth tries to change the subject. "Will you find evidence to prove Lance Fernard killed Miles Bonneville and Hugo Grader?"

"We're fingerprinting, running DNA in his flat. It's likely. All things considered. Lemon is looking at all the shops that sell swords like the one we have, and we found opium in Lance Fernard's flat already. So if it is a match, or has any daffodil traces." Abley then walks over to the sofa. "Here, let me move those." He picks up some golf balls which have fallen into a sunken bit of the sofa, to make space for Elizabeth to sit down.

"Ah, okay. This is hard to sip from," Elizabeth says, lifting the jar as she sits, moving a jacket onto the back of the sofa.

"They're all the rage in the trendy bars." Abley smiles,

then explains the jam jar. "No glasses yet."

At first, Elizabeth tries to ignore the golf on the TV, but it is right in front of her. She stands up and turns it off then sits back down. Inspector Abley looks at what she's done but bites his tongue. His security blanket cut off.

"So, the young lad with a Wordsworth poem stuffed in his gob who was poisoned with daffodils, well, turns out he had done a piece of coursework on the poet when he first arrived at the uni. He was quite vocal about it, apparently from the statements we collected, he 'wouldn't stop going on about daffodils' and kept reciting the poems to anyone who would listen. He was seeing Nisha at the time. But I know you know that she told you and you didn't tell us straight away. You should always keep us informed, Elizabeth."

"I will, if you don't lock me out of the police station and arrest my grandson." Elizabeth raises her eyebrows, then sips her water before continuing. "Yes, the daffodil necklace linked everything, didn't it? And, this makes it hard to drink from." Elizabeth holds up the jam jar.

"We had to confiscate that, as evidence. The young woman—"

"Ms Acharya-Gorpade."

"I know her name," Abley pauses before explaining. "Anyway, she said she hadn't worn it for ages. That she didn't think. But, apparently, when Lance saw her wear it, he told her to take it off, but she refused. She told him she wanted to show that he was innocent. It was a lucky charm. The young woman's statement from hospital said how ironic it was. She had no idea."

"Poor girl. Is she going to be okay?" Elizabeth asks.

"She's very ill. But the consultant hopes—" Inspector Abley trails off, wondering about the terrible case. "To have killed his best friends? Who does that? We found that Lance Fernard did have the credit card of Miles Bonneville in his wallet, as he admitted."

"Mr Fernard was trying to kill my grandson."

"I think he was. As you say, jealous of anyone who got too close to Miss Nisha Acharya-Gorpade," Abley pauses. "As you say, jealousy does terrible things." Abley pauses again. Elizabeth knows why. "And we didn't arrest Godric, so don't think that we did."

Elizabeth raises her eyebrows, then decides to forgive.

"This is a nice place," she says, looking around at the house that is clearly in need of more than a lick of paint.

"It's mine. There's a roof which doesn't leak."

"It's cosy."

"Small you mean. Room enough for one."

"Well, and golf clubs." Elizabeth acknowledges the club bag at the other end of the sofa. Abley moves it and perches on the arm.

"But there are all these holes," Abley adds.

"Holes? Where?" Elizabeth looks around the living room.

"I found one in the backdoor, but on posts, a table too." Bob Abley walks over and opens the backdoor. "Look, even here?" They both look at the perfectly round hole bored into the wood about an inch thick on the table outside.

"Well, you're not alone. You have a Woody." Elizabeth laughs.

"What?"

"Not what, who. Woody, the woodpecker."

Stepping outside, Inspector Bob Abley puts his finger in the hole.

"Looks like he's found his home too. Best you start feeding him," Elizabeth adds.

"Well I never," Inspector Abley smiles, then looks serious, shutting the backdoor and walking over to the sofa.

"You want to check the pecker isn't looking for wood-eating insects. The items he's making holes in really aren't big enough for a home," Elizabeth suggests.

"Oh, great," Bob Abley sighs. "I heard about the

flowers," he adds, looking at Elizabeth.

"Unexpected," Elizabeth replies, then pauses for a while before picking up a golf ball and transferring it between hands. "It was just a moment. I'm okay now."

"A lovely gesture."

"I am aware that I might have been a little crotchety today."

"Really? I hadn't noticed," Abley replies, lying.

The two pause, in silence, without awkwardness.

"How was Holkham?"

"Cold. Wet. Beautiful. Thank you," Abley replies.

"I should be thanking you. For caring," Elizabeth says.

"No, for the case," Abley explains.

"I don't like that it got too close this time. He got too close." Elizabeth frowns.

"It's Valentine's Night. It's bound to throw us off a little," Abley smiles knowingly. "Oh, and thank you for the mirror. But I didn't know what you gave me that for?"

"For your beard."

"I'm not trimming it."

"I know." Elizabeth stands. "I'd best be off. I'll be late."

"The day will be over. It's just one day," Abley catches Elizabeth's eye. "It will get easier, you know. Time is a great healer."

"I don't want to be healed." Elizabeth turns and looks straight at Bob Abley. "I can't forget him. He's my life. Who I am. He knew me."

"Well, give Emily a kiss from me," Abley nods, knowing how true Elizabeth's words are.

*

The Talbot takes Elizabeth to Emily's home, up on Cranmer Road. As she shuts the Talbot's door on the gravel drive, she looks back at Gerald's expensive toy and

the memories flood over her. One from a trip to Old
Hunstanton in the car. She closes her eyes and tries to
remember the seagulls, Gerald's sunburnt nose. She holds
the memory, the rustle of the dune grass, sand in Gerald's
flip flops. Elizabeth doesn't want to open her eyes, but a
security light flicks on, and Emily is at the door, wearing
her ushanka. Elizabeth walks into the home past Emily
and shuts the door.

THE END

Thank you very much for reading *Valentine's Day*, Book 5
of the series The Cambridge Murder Mysteries.

<u>Titles available in The Cambridge Murder Mystery
Series:</u>

Book 1: Poison

Book 2: Cursed

Book 3: Blood Moon

Book 4: A Christmas Mystery

Book 5: Valentine's Day – Kiss of Death

<u>Short Stories and Novellas in the Cambridge Murder
Mystery Series:</u>

Christmas Eve in Grantchester

Green *(available by subscribing to my newsletter)*

<u>Other titles by Charlot King:</u>

Animal Tales. Woof

Animal Tales: Pup

For more information on the other books in the series please do visit www.charlotking.com where you can also subscribe to Charlot King's VIP Club. If you'd like to follow what Charlot King is up to you can find her on Twitter: @queencharlot and other social media. And, if you enjoyed this book, Charlot would be so very grateful for a review on Amazon and Goodreads as well as telling all your friends. Much appreciated! Thanks again, and very happy reading.

Made in the USA
Monee, IL
10 March 2021